"OM AYUSE SAMHARAKESVARE HUM PHAT!"

Trembling on the rooftop, Bill paled at the words.

The Master stepped closer, out of the swirling snowstorm, and pointed directly at the girl in Bill's arms.

"OM AYUSE SAMHARAKESVARE HUM PHAT!!"

Bill retreated, until snow slipped off the near edge of the roof. The Master hesitated.

"I am Master Sri Parutha," he whispered rapidly. "Give me the girl!"

"No," Bill protested, shaking his head, afraid of the Master. "I won't! She's mine!"

Bill's left foot was already slipping on the ice at the edge of the roof.

"GIVE HER TO ME!" the Master shouted.

Janice screamed from where she stood at the ventilator, and Borman climbed over the ledge, revolver drawn . . .

Novels by Frank DeFelitta

Audrey Rose
The Entity
For Love of Audrey Rose

Published by
WARNER BOOKS

FOR Love of Audrey Rose

Frank DeFelitta

WARNER BOOKS

A Warner Communications Company

WARNER BOOKS EDITION

Cover design by Gene Light

Cover art by Charles Moll

Warner Books, Inc., 75 Rockefeller Plaza, New York, N.Y. 10019

 A Warner Communications Company

Printed in the United States of America

First Printing: July, 1982

10 9 8 7 6 5 4 3 2 1

For Buddy

FOR
Love of
Audrey
Rose

PROLOGUE

Article from THE AMERICAN INQUIRER, reprinted in its entirety, dated February 3, 1976.

WHERE ARE THEY NOW?
        by Shawn Tyneham

Exactly one year ago today, the trial concluded which shocked New York and sent ripples of horror and dismay throughout the nation. On December 5, 1974, Judge Harmon T. Langley, presiding over The People of New York versus Elliot Suggins Hoover, opened session for the first time in the Criminal Courts Building, Part Seven, in downtown Manhattan. The charge: kidnapping. The victim: 10-year-old Ivy Templeton, daughter of a rising young executive in the advertising world. But in less than two months, Ivy was dead. Not from her ordeal at the hands of the suspect, Elliot Hoover, but as a result of the bizarre and inexorable machinations of Judge Langley's own court.

Where are they now? What happened to the defendant, Elliot Hoover, to the aggrieved parents, William and Janice Templeton, since that tragic day that Ivy strangled to death in front of a horrified jury? What happened to old Judge Langley, or to the prosecutor, Scott Velie, or the defense counsel, Brice Mack?

Readers of this column will remember the trial, the crowds that made entrance and exit impossible at the doors of the Criminal Courts building. For days New York was treated to the spectacle of orange-robed Hindus wrestling with blue coated cops, impassioned and unorthodox oratory from attorney Brice Mack, and the celebrities who marched in and out of Judge Langley's court to testify for Elliot Hoover. But many weeks of arduous research and investigation have unearthed the bizarre circumstances that led to the trial and to Ivy's tragic death.

It began early in October, 1974, when Elliot Hoover appeared outside the Ethical Culture School. He was forty-six years old, recently returned from seven years in India, and he was waiting. Waiting for Ivy Templeton.

During the next weeks, he shadowed William Templeton, a junior partner of the Pel Simmons Advertising Agency. He sent obscene notes, gifts to Ivy, gifts to Janice Templeton, and began telephoning. He insisted on seeing them. And day after day, like a shadow that would not fade, he waited for Ivy outside the school.

Finally the Templetons agreed to see him. The following account is based on trial records and recollections of the staff of the bar and restaurant at the Hotel Des Artistes, where the meeting took place.

● DEMANDS DAUGHTER

The meeting began in an atmosphere of hostility and tension. Hoover appeared very nervous, fumbling with his tea cup, swallowing his words, unable to control his trembling fingers. At length, his incredible and uncanny story began to emerge.

He had been, he claimed, a successful Pittsburgh steel executive until, on August 4, 1964, his wife and daughter were killed in an automobile accident south of Pittsburgh. The daughter's name was Audrey Rose. Then, according to Marie Kronstadt, waitress at the restaurant, Hoover launched into a long and incoherent account of his travels through India. When Bill Templeton angrily demanded he come to the point, a strange and seductive expression came to Hoover's face. Audrey Rose, he said quietly, had been reincarnated and her name now was Ivy Templeton. To prove it, he continued, Ivy was born within minutes of Audrey Rose's death.

● THE NIGHTMARE

Unable to procure police protection, the Templetons sought legal advice. Their attorney advised a second meeting to determine precisely whether Hoover's demands were financial or sexual in nature. Accordingly, Hoover came to the Templeton apartment.

Trial records indicate a tranquil and surprisingly affable meeting. Hoover rambled at length about certain experiences in India. In particular, he displayed an extensive technical knowledge of the doctrines of reincarnation. And once again, he demanded certain rights over Ivy.

Before the Templetons could clarify Hoover's needs, however, the telephone rang with astounding news.

Ivy had been sleeping downstairs with a neighbor, Carole Federico, in order to leave the Templeton apartment clear for the meeting with Hoover. Shortly after Hoover arrived at the apartment, however, Ivy began to display symptoms of frenzied anxiety, delirium, and generalized fear. The Templetons entered her room to find the girl sleepwalking, her arms flailing, knocking over the furniture and painfully oblivious of chairs, desk, and dresser in her way.

She called "Mommydaddy mommydaddymommydaddy hothothot!!" in a voice Mrs. Federico described as "unearthly and like a prayer caused by unbearable pain."

But the worst was yet to come.

Unable to subdue the savage nightmare of his daughter, Bill Templeton turned to see Elliot Hoover standing in the doorway. A look of "inexpressible sadness" mixed with love appeared on the intruder's face. Then, slowly, with confidence and authority, Hoover stepped toward the girl and called to her. And gradually, she grew quiet and fell asleep in his arms.

He had called her Audrey Rose.

● ESCALATION

Hoover continued to bombard the Templetons with gifts, mostly books on the subject of reincarnation. He demanded to speak with them again. He telephoned Bill Templeton at work. All to no avail.

Within the week, Ivy was subjected to a second nightmare, worse than the first.

Possessed with alarming strength, she seemed unstoppable, smashing through her bedroom, crying in pain, calling over and over for her "daddy," yet completely unresponsive to Bill Templeton's frantic efforts to calm her. By now it was evident that the child was in serious danger of harming herself.

In fact, that night she suffered first and second degree burns over her hands, mostly along the palms. During the trial, Bill Templeton related that she had grasped the hot radiator during her frenzy and could not let go. Mrs. Templeton, however, contradicted that testimony. Ivy's hands had been burned, she said, when they beat against the ice-cold windows of the bedroom.

As the trial wore on, it became clear that Audrey Rose had died slowly and painfully, trapped within the overturned automobile beating her hands in vain against the glass of the burning wreck.

- THE THIRD NIGHTMARE

The third, and most intense, convulsive nightmare occurred when Bill Templeton was overseas on business.

This time there seemed no doubt that the child was in desperate straits, in a state of panic, and insane with suffocation and fear. She broke free of her bedroom where Mrs. Templeton had tried to sequester her, and ran into the living room, beating at the cold, dark windows, crying "HOTHOT HOTHOTHOTHOT!!"

Unable to get her family physician on the telephone, Janice Templeton allowed Elliot Hoover to enter her apartment. Her reasons, according to the trial testimony, were unambiguous: to secure the immediate safety of the child and to end the danger of grievous self-inflicted injury.

For the second time, Hoover calmed her, and the exhausted girl fell asleep against his chest, her hands bloody and her face bruised from her hour-long fight with unimaginable terrors.

And for the second time, Hoover had soothed her by calling her Audrey Rose.

What followed then is difficult to make out, yet it was the critical point in the entire sequence of events. According to the doorman, desk clerk, and elevator operator, all of whom had by now taken note of the strange, intense man frequenting the lobby of the building and demanding access to the Templeton apartment, Elliot Hoover did not leave the residence for nearly an hour, and when he did, his steps were "jaunty, like he'd just done something terrific."

Mrs. Templeton denied that anything improper had transpired between her and Elliot Hoover. Rather, he had spent the time trying to persuade her more forcibly of the truth of his philosophy. Whatever happened, dawn found Janice Templeton and Ivy fleeing New York by special limousine for the isolation and security of a cabin resort in Westport, Connecticut.

CALM BEFORE THE STORM

Over a month had passed since Elliot Hoover had intruded into their lives. The strain was beginning to tell, not only on Janice Templeton, but on Ivy as well. Though she had no memory of what happened during the on-slaughts, she knew that the night brought on dangers that the waking self did not know. Exhausted, her hands still painfully bandaged, Ivy began to muse aloud on the shores of Westport, vaguely aware that things had altered forever in her young life. Her relationship with her mother remained warm, yet an intolerable tension seemed to follow them wherever they went.

It was also clear that the Templeton marriage was beginning to crack and crumble under the stress.

On November 13, 1974, Janice and Ivy returned to New York.

THE KIDNAP

Almost before Ivy was asleep, the most violent nightmare of all seized her. Bill Templeton, returned from overseas, called the doctor. But the seizure exceeded his wildest expectations. She bit, kicked, and screamed and, sweating freely, he was barely able to subdue her by tying her to the bed. The doorbell rang and, thinking it was the doctor, Bill ran down to admit him.

It was Hoover.

He lived in Des Artistes now, he explained. He had just moved in. Now he wanted to help Ivy. Bill and Elliot Hoover struggled violently at the door, but Hoover was able to force his entry into the apartment. Janice, fearing for Bill's life, came to his aid in the corridor. Hoover locked them out of their own apartment.

In the violence that followed, the stories from the score of onlookers are remarkably consistent. Bill Templeton, in a fury of rage, tried to break down the door.

A house key was produced just as two police officers appeared in the corridor. Shouting, cursing, Bill led the officers back into the apartment and into Ivy's room.

Both Hoover and the girl were gone.

They had gone down the rear exit and were ensconced, behind locked doors, in Hoover's new apartment. There under threat of drawn revolvers, Hoover reluctantly and silently opened his door. He was immediately seized and wrestled into handcuffs.

Not far away was Ivy, calm and breathing easily, and only a bit sleepy for all her ordeal.

Subsequent medical examination revealed the girl had not been molested. Elliott Hoover was arraigned on a single count of first degree kidnapping, bail denied.

● THE GREAT CIRCUS

Which brings the case to December 5, 1974.

Jury selection proceeded slowly. Only the Enquirer covered any of the trial opening, and that with a single reporter. The prosecutor, Scott Velie, was a tough, battle-scarred veteran of almost three decades of legal jousting, and it was widely assumed that he would wrap up the case within a few weeks.

Elliot Hoover's attorney was Brice Mack, a public defender without notable prior experience.

It was not until the opening remarks that Brice Mack revealed the strategy of defense.

Not guilty by proven reincarnation.

Judge Langley immediately suspended proceedings and conferred over two hours in his chamber with both attorneys. Whatever arguments Mack produced, they were effective, for a subdued Judge Langley overruled the prosecution and the trial proper began.

As the days dragged on, the seats in Part Seven of the Criminal Court Building began filling up. First with news reporters, then with spectators, and finally with orange-robed supporters of Hoover's, who chanted and swayed when the major bulwark of Hoover's case, the venerable Gupta Pradesh of India, took the stand to explain the mechanics of reincarnation to a bewildered, skeptical and often amused jury.

Whatever dignity the court may have salvaged from the opening remarks was clearly destroyed when a small riot broke out between courtroom guards and the Hindus.

By now the trial was international news. Mystics and psychics paraded into Courtroom Two, testified for Hoover, and the atmosphere of the court took on the flavor of a county fair viewed through delirium tremens.

The delirium escalated into hallucination when Janice Templeton testified for the defense.

● "YES, I BELIEVE HIM!"

The reasons behind Janice Templeton's surprising and dramatic testimony are now clear, though in the superheated atmosphere of the courtroom it came like an electronic spark into a chamber of volatile gases.

Ivy had been removed to a girls' parochial school in the countryside not far from Darien, Connecticut. There she participated in a winter pageant, traditional to the school, of the burning of a large and decorated snowman, to herald the coming spring.

Hypnotized by the flames, she had broken from the chorus of girls and slowly, irresistibly, had entered the roaring mass of logs and straw, flame, and smoke. Ivy suffered minor burns to her face and scalp, singed hair, and some effects from smoke inhalation. The Templetons interrupted their vigil at the trial and raced to the hospital in Darien.

It was there, apparently, that the great transformation in Janice Templeton's thinking solidified. She recalled Hoover's words, spoken so fiercely to her once before. That not only was Ivy the reincarnation of Audrey Rose, but that the struggle of a soul in torment would lead Ivy back to danger, back into the fire and smoke from which she had come.

Fearing for Ivy's life, and believing that Hoover possessed the key to safeguarding the child's future, Janice testified in Hoover's behalf. It was the final break between the Templetons.

● THE DEATH OF IVY
  TEMPLETON

It was at this point that the prosecution inaugurated the test which led so tragically to the death of Ivy Templeton. Incensed at the antics of the defense, and the malleability of Judge Langley, Scott Velie proposed to put to rest once and for all the question of reincarnation.

Since the child was alleged to be recalling states of mind prior to her birth, it was incumbent upon the court to regress Ivy, hypnotically, and try to show whether that was in fact the case, or whether Hoover had been able to put his own convenient interpretation on a simple case of delirium.

Judge Langley, having agreed to much more for the defense, reluctantly ordered the test.

In a small laboratory at the Darien Hospital, the jury, Judge Langely, Hoover, Bill Templeton, and the officers of the court were sequestered behind a mirrorized window stretching the width of the room. Behind the mirror, visible to the court but able to see nothing of them, was Dr. Steven Lipscomb, doctor of psychiatry. Ivy, pale and still weak from the ordeal by fire, entered the room, the lights were lowered, and she was easily and swiftly placed under hypnosis.
Janice Templeton did not attend the court, but watched through television monitors installed in an adjacent hall for the benefit of visiting newsmen and spectators.

At first the hypnosis went smoothly. Ivy was brought backwards in time to her eighth birthday, then to her fourth, then to her third. The girl not only remembered in exact detail all the events of the birthday parties, but her voice underwent a dramatic change, growing younger and younger, more and more like an infant's.

Finally, nervously, Dr. Lipscomb instructed Ivy to go back to a time before she was born.

Ivy curled into the prenatal position.

Then, as Dr. Lipscomb's voice droned on, urging her backward, ever backward in time, she suddenly bolted upright, eyes open.

She seemed to look happily ahead, but then her face clouded over. Her eyes widened and her mouth opened in a terrible scream. Unable to bring her out of the trance, Dr. Lipscomb tried to comfort the girl, who rocked pitiably on her couch.

Suddenly, Ivy threw herself—or seemed to be catapulted—onto the floor. Screaming in pain, she ran the length and width of the room, her lip bleeding from the fall.

The litany, which the Templetons had heard all too often, now poured out of the twisted mouth of their daughter: "Mommydaddy mommydaddyhothothothotll"

Dr. Lipscomb wrestled vainly with Ivy, unable to stop the frenzied delirium.

Then, as she had repeatedly done in the Templetons' apartment, she threw herself at the long glass in front of her. Her face reddened to an alarming degree, her nostrils flared, as though she were suffocating. She began writhing in convulsions that signified a disintegrating nervous coordination.

Hoover rose against the opposite side of the great mirror and tried to shout to her, but the hypnosis chamber was soundproofed. In the melee of screaming and fainting jurors, it was Hoover who had the presence of mind to hurl a chair through the glass, and the officers of the court tumbled into the chamber just as doctors rushed in through a side door to relieve the panic-stricken Dr. Lipscomb.

Despite the administration of oxygen and injections of adrenalin, Ivy's respiratory system had failed for too long. The brain had gone almost five minutes without oxygen. At 10:43 A.M. she was declared dead by physician R.F. Shad. Cause of death; laryngospasm, or convulsive closing of the larynx, obstructing the intake of air into the trachea.

● WHERE ARE THEY NOW?

The tragedy at Darien Hospital will not be quickly forgotten, even for those who only knew of the events through the news media.

But for those who were there, the Templetons, the attorneys, Judge Langley, what thoughts must have gone through their minds since that day? And what has happened to each of them? It has taken months to piece together the whole picture, and finally the denouement for the major participants can be revealed:

Elliot Hoover: Acquitted of the charge of first degree kidnapping. Spent two weeks in New York City, praying at the Hompa Hongwanji Buddhist Temple at Christopher Place. Known to have purchased a one-way ticket to India. Presumed to have retreated to a temple in the central plains. Precise destination unknown.

Judge Harmon T. Langly: Under attack from all quarters of the legal profession, Judge Langley retired early. He lives with his sister in Booklyn Heights and refuses to see reporters. Suffered a mild stroke in early June, 1975.

Scott Velie, prosecutor: Successfully fought to retain his license to practice in the State of New York. He is known, however, to have lost the more difficult battle against alcoholism. He has not appeared in court since The People of New York versus Elliot Suggins Hoover.

Brice Mack, public defender: Now president of well-known firm of Mack, Lowenstein, and Fischbein. Author of moderately successful book on the trial of Elliot Hoover.

William Templeton: Collapsed after being forcibly restrained during the final moments of the fatal test. Was treated for symptoms of dislocation, severe paranoia, and a morbid, guilt-ridden depression. Released, he returned to his apartment at the Hotel Des Artistes. He has subsequently been institutionalized and at this writing is confined to a sanitarium in Ossining.

Janice Templeton: Supervised the cremation of Ivy Templeton. Known to have sent the ashes to India for dispersal. Now works as assistant designer for Christine Daler, Ltd., firm that specializes in women's sport and casual wear. According to those who know her at Des Artistes, she no longer accepts the beliefs which she once, under the influence of Elliot Hoover, publicly embraced.

No other event presented in this column has been so obliterated by time. Even Brice Mack has grown wary of public comment and no longer will speak about the trial. Nor have any of the participants, including the staff of the Darien Hospital, been willing to discuss what happened. Perhaps it can never be known, exactly what Janice Templeton believed when she testified. What did her husband believe before he collapsed and reason fled?

What has life been like, the apartment empty, with not even an echo of the smiling blonde child who once shared their lives, and not a trace of the intruder who waited so calmly, so omnisciently, outside of Ivy's school? All unresolved, unsolved, waiting for time to work its slow but certain cure, to transform the violence and pain to a tender acceptance.

But perhaps the list of actors in this tragedy is not complete. Perhaps, in memory of the quiet girl whose courage could not in the end save her, we must add:

Audrey Rose: Born September 5, 1959. Died August 4, 1964, thirty seconds before the birth of Ivy Templeton. Death due to smoke inhalation.

Ivy Templeton: Born August 4, 1964. Died February 3, 1975, 10:43 A.M. Death due to convulsive closure of the larynx.

Did Audrey Rose return August 4, 1964? And, if so, **who died February 3, 1975, 10:43 A.M.?**

BOOK I

BILL

"I become the fire of life which is in all things that breathe,
In union with the breath that flows in and flows out I burn."

The Words of Krishna

Chapter One

It was dark. Bill tasted salt on his lips. Suddenly he became violently nauseous. Terrible images pulled at the back of his brain, grinning monsters who violated Ivy in sparkling space. There was a feeling of black pressure, of perpetually drowning.

Bill heard a deep gurgling, like water choked in a filled drain.

"Are you awake, Mr. Templeton?" said a soft voice.

The gurgle had been his own voice, disembodied, with a torpor thick as tar.

A pretty face moved into his field of vision. Soft brown eyes and short brunette hair swept up under a white cap. She smiled.

"Can you hear me, Mr. Templeton?"

A gentle hand and sponge wiped at his mouth and chest.

27

Bill's head was turned to the side and the breathing came more easily.

A small light went on, a soft amber that glowed against cold green walls. The sheets were stained from Bill's nausea. He became conscious of the rhythmic breathing of his own chest, drawing, expelling, drawing, expelling.

"Janice," he mumbled weakly.

"Your wife waited six hours," the nurse said. "Then she was taken to a hotel. She'll come back in the morning."

Bill turned his head around. Now he knew where he was. The hospital ward had four beds in it, but his was the only one occupied. The others were freshly made and the screens pulled out of the way. It was abnormally quiet. Outside there seemed to be a black screen over the windows. Then he saw her watch. It was nearly midnight.

"Janice," Bill repeated.

"Your wife is at the Darien Central Hotel."

Bill groaned. His lips were so parched, they had cracked. The nurse dipped her finger in a glass of water and spread it across his lips, then helped him drink. The sensation of cold water going down into his body revived him.

Suddenly his eyes darted around the room. He stared at the nurse.

"Where's Ivy?" Bill whispered.

The nurse hesitated. "There's been an autopsy."

Bill's face slowly transformed into a dolorous mask, the kind that is sold hanging on sticks for Chinese New Year, a human face distended into curved lines of grief.

"I'm sorry," the nurse said quietly.

Bill tried to move his limbs but all that happened was that his chest rose and his back arched away from the bed. The nurse mopped his forehead with a soft cloth.

Bill stared into the soft brown eyes. He had the wild, distraught face of a madman.

"I didn't mean to," he hissed. "The test was supposed to—to— Oh, God—" Bill fell back and began to weep.

28

The nurse discreetly pressed a small plastic button by the bed. After several minutes, a physician walked into the room. His eyes were red and he needed a shave. He had a barrel chest and short, beefy arms with white hair and a thick gold wrist watch.

The physician put a comforting hand on the nurse's shoulder. She made room for him, and he sat down next to Bill.

"Listen to me, Mr. Templeton. Your wife waited here almost seven hours before we insisted that she get some rest. She was in a state of near-collapse."

Bill's mumbling ceased. Then his eyes narrowed. He faced the wall as though angry or afraid of the physician.

"Where's Hoover?" Bill asked.

"Who?"

"Hoover, God damn it!"

The physician leaned forward and gently eased Bill back to face him.

"It was all my fault. *My fault*—!"

There was an awkward silence. Both the physician and the nurse felt a tremendous need to find something to say, not to let the accusatory silence mount up over the patient like an imprisoning wall. Bill's eyes darted from one to the other guiltily. But neither could think of anything, though their minds raced, and suddenly the music became audible from the corridors, a ballad about love burning in one's heart.

"Shut that damn thing off," growled the physician.

The nurse left.

"Look, Mr. Templeton," the physician said, licking his lips, "the court—er, ordered the test, legally. There is a mechanism of law that works through the judge and jury and the court officers. The hospital only acted as a tool of that legal apparatus."

Bill realized the doctor was trying to exonerate the hospital.

"It was my idea," he moaned. "I fed it to Velie. I helped him come up with it. Oh, my God . . ."

The nurse came back. Now the silence was complete. She

had closed the doors and the air was still, smelling faintly of clean linens and antiseptic.

"I don't like the way he's responding," she whispered.

"Some clown gave him fifteen cc's. His system's all junked up."

"Is there somebody he could talk to?"

"Just the psychologist. Lipscomb. I sure wouldn't bring him in here."

Bill heard their words, discussing him as though he were not there. The words did not reach down into his brain. Nothing reached down. Several sheets of steel separated his brain from his body, or at least it felt that way. There were no connections anymore. The body parts had retreated as though to survive on their own as best they could. Brain in one place. Feelings in another. Eyesight registering. And grief. Grief and guilt, like a whole universe, radiated through him, flowed like electricity along every nerve fiber, obliterating each and every memory, each and every hope.

"I . . . meant . . . to save . . . to save . . . her. . . ."

"You did everything you could, Mr. Templeton," the physician said, squeezing Bill's shoulder.

The physician conferred with the nurse, and then was gone. After a few minutes, the nurse left for other patients. Bill staggered to the closet, found his clothes, and dressed. Wobbly, he peered out into the corridor. When the desk nurse answered an emergency light, he walked, reeling, down the receding floor to the elevator, then heard steps, turned, and ran stumbling down the stairway.

Tears flowing from his eyes, he ran across the icy parking lot, clutching his thin coat around his chest. Overhead a dim break showed pale gray between the night clouds.

Suddenly he came upon the Darien Central Hotel. He recoiled. Had he escaped from the hospital to be with Janice? Or had he escaped to avoid seeing her later? Bill ducked into an alley. His shoes filled with icy slush, his socks were soaked, and he wandered among the garbage cans and parked buses of the Greyhound Bus depot.

Inside, people milled about the terminal, staring at him. Surely they knew that he had killed his own daughter. He was a figure of ridicule, pathetic and morbid, a creature of the hospital, morally deformed, who had concocted a wild scheme.

In the distance, the tall, dark silhouette of the hospital loomed. A few lurid yellow lights gleamed in long rows at the top floor. Bill wondered if that was where they stored the bodies.

His reflection in the dirty window looked abnormal. He looked like a murderer.

Behind his reflection, he saw a small, humpbacked clerk turn on a light. On the wall were arrival and departure schedules. Bill whirled around, saw two elderly women staring at him, and then he went quickly inside.

The two elderly women still looked at him through the window. They were certainly discussing him.

"May I help you?" said the clerk.

Startled, Bill turned. The clerk was a round-faced woman, her eyes squinty, with freckles over a tiny nose.

"You want to buy a ticket?"

"Yes—a ticket."

"Where to?"

"What's the next bus?"

"Southbound," the clerk said. "Interstate to Baltimore."

"When?"

"Should leave in an hour and thirty-five minutes. Depending on the roads."

"I'll take it."

"One way?"

"Yes."

"Twenty-five fifty, please."

"Will you take a check?"

"Sorry. Not allowed to."

"Credit card?"

"What kind?"

Bill showed her. The clerk frowned but retrieved a banged-up roller from under the shelf and filled out the credit card slips. Bill signed.

"No baggage?"

Bill shook his head. "I'll wait outside by the buses."

"It's your frostbite."

Outside, several giant buses stood in the blue shadows under a corrugated roof. Beyond the alleys and telephone poles, the west wing of the hospital rose high, cream colored, its windows reflecting the pale blankness of the snow.

Bill watched several cars pull up to the hospital parking lot by the wide revolving doors. A van without a rear window drove around to the back. A choking gasp coughed out of his lungs.

A bus driver looked up from a clipboard at Bill. "You okay, mister?"

"Which is the bus to Baltimore?"

"You're leaning against it."

"Mind if I get in?"

"No, go ahead. But we don't leave till three."

Bill stepped up into the cold bus, walked to the rear seat, and huddled for warmth. He saw the humpbacked clerk making conversation with the driver. Another light went on inside the station. Bill shivered and could not stop shivering. All he knew was that he had to get away from Darien.

At 2:59 the driver stepped in, turned on the engine, and then the passengers, dressed in heavy overcoats, got in. The baggage compartment slammed shut like a coffin lid and the bus drove away. Darien slid by on both sides, wet roads and dirty stores, cars smeared with heavy, muddy slush underneath, a general air of downtown poverty. The only modern edifice was the hospital.

Bill started to cry. When he stopped, they were rolling onto the broad Interstate, past flat white fields, in a thick, gentle snowstorm.

Six seats in front, a mother bounced a small blond girl on her knee, drew pictures on the frosted windows, and sang softly.

"This is the way to Grandmother's house, Grandmother's house," the mother sang. "This is the way to Grandmother's house, so early in the morning."

It was a melody Bill had sung to Ivy. Ivy had loved the snow. Her blond hair and fair complexion had been a throwback to Scandinavian ancestors Bill had never known. She had learned to ice skate almost before she could walk. She was happiest when the fat white snowflakes came down like a blanket, obscuring everything but the trees.

"This is the way to Grandfather's house, Grandfather's house. This is the way to Grandfather's house, so early in the evening."

Bill covered his ears with his hands.

"Please stop!" he whispered hoarsely.

Then it was silent. The road hummed gruffly under the wheels. Bill realized that the passengers were staring at him.

"Why did that man say stop?" said a little girl's voice.

"Shhhhhhh," her mother cautioned.

The bus detoured into a small town, with the familiar series of dismal streets, an occasional pedestrian wrapped in a winter coat. But here the streets were slick with ice, and icicles hung down from garages and telephone wires.

Bill stared at his hands. They were shaking like leaves in a storm. There was no feeling in them.

I am a murderer, he thought.

Deep down, he knew why he had supported the idea of the test. It had nothing to do with Ivy's well-being. He wanted to crush Hoover. Torn to pieces by the strain of the trial, Bill had wanted to make sure that Hoover was destroyed. That was the real purpose of the test.

Bill's hands rubbed, gouged at his eyes as though to

eradicate the images of Ivy beating at the mirrored glass. He moaned. This time the bus driver turned around.

"You feel okay, back there?"

Bill did not answer.

"We don't allow drinking on here."

Two hours passed. Bill dozed. Awoke. Dozed again. He had a dream. In the dream he was sitting on the witness stand, explaining to Janice why he had left the hospital. Suddenly, Gupta Pradesh rose, dressed in fiery red swirling cloth, and held in his arms the body of dead Ivy. Gupta Pradesh reached down, touched her leg, and then contemptuously threw gray ash into Bill's face.

"Ahhh—" Bill jerked awake.

As soon as he opened his eyes, the dream vanished. All that was left was a sensation of having wanted to explain things to Janice. His mind violently obliterated the dream.

Outside, the snow was streaked and dotted with patches of dark gray ice. Bare trees hugged the hills and hollows. Farms spread out, cold and isolated. Then there were electric transformers, auto garages, and a series of brick warehouses. The density of cars and people increased. After two stops, Bill recognized the Hudson River, troubled and turbulent, deep gray and rolling swiftly under the brown and white hills.

"We'll be in New York in about fifteen minutes," the bus driver called through a static-ridden microphone. "Stopover for breakfast, thirty-five minutes."

Bill watched the tall buildings, the forbidding gray canyons, slush, taxi cabs, early morning pedestrians, the violent rhythm of the great city awakening around him. He became frightened, vulnerable.

At the bus terminal, twenty more passengers tried to get on but were told to wait for thirty-five minutes. The driver checked the passengers coming off, making sure they still had their tickets. Bill followed them out, stepped on an escalator, found a grill in the main hall, ate quickly without tasting, then wandered out through the main doors.

A smell of vomit reached him, mingled with roasted chestnuts and salt pretzels heated on a grill. Hundreds of people strolled in through the wide doors. New York always had a stony, murderous quality, and this time it had almost a physical taste.

Bill was lost. After walking several blocks, oblivious of the taxis which missed him by inches, the drivers hurling epithets, he found himself in Hell's Kitchen. Even in the cold, there were crates of fruit slanted by the doors to attract buyers. Cold eyes watched him go by, suspicious eyes sizing him up.

Motion was the only cure for what Bill felt. He walked a mile uptown, a second mile backtracking, and lost any sense of direction. It was approaching the noon hour. Suddenly, he had an abnormal, almost infinite desire for alcohol.

Inside a pink, smoky bar full of laborers and Hispanics, Bill peeled off the last of his five-dollar bills. All that was left were four singles. Dark eyes scrutinized him, the expensive suit gone dirty with mud and slush, the handsome face now drawn in to resemble some kind of fleshy death's-head. Bill plastered down his hair with a shaking hand.

"Double whiskey," he said.

Bill sat at the wet, stained bar. The bartender brought him a bottle of whiskey and a glass. Bill watched the liquid pour into the glass. He lifted the glass to his lips. I wish to die, was his thought as the burning liquid traveled quickly down to his stomach, etching its way into his body, promising deliverance.

He ordered a second drink.

His hands stopped trembling. Dream images of snow-driven landscapes occurred to him. In his reverie, he looked out of a dirty bus window and saw distant farms wheeling past in great perspectival arcs. Then he also saw, on the horizon, the clearly visible, long, dark-roofed shape of the hospital in Darien. He drank.

Then he saw Ivy behind the window glass, beating her fists at the mirror, frightened.

Bill lowered his head onto his arms and wept.

No one paid him any attention.

After half an hour, he walked out into the cold, bitter wind howling up from the Battery. His legs were numb, though whether it was from the whiskey or the cold, he no longer knew. New York roared around him in an angry maelstrom of murderous voices, dark accusations.

In horror, he saw Des Artistes loom in front of him.

By some innate homing instinct, he had walked back through Central Park, past the lakes, and had drifted over to Sixty-seventh Street.

Before he could retreat, Mario, the doorman, spotted him.

"Mr. Templeton . . . Wait . . ."

Bill ran back through the park, sweating, then cut south and east and finally ended up at the derelict warehouses among the concrete piers of the East River. Somehow the day had passed and it was night again. Several bums sat in the shadows of a bridge, cooking beans, and he wandered into their circle to keep out of the cold wind.

In that darkness, the smell of beans and grease filled the space that also glistened with tar leaking down from the bridge. Trucks rumbled overhead, gears switching, carrying tonnage out to the west or bringing foodstuffs into the city markets.

"Warmer by the fire than it is over there," said a thin, coughing man with a greasy gray coat and an ascot stained with tar.

Bill approached the low fire, rubbing his hands. He declined sweet amber wine. They left him alone. As he looked into the fire, he felt a deathly chill spread out within his body, a chill that no fire could reach.

Outside in the night, the lights of midtown gleamed; the Empire State Building rose high into the lighted clouds like a mirage of happier times.

One by one, the men drifted away. Bill watched them shuffle into the darkness on the roads. They were a kind of subterranean living species he had never talked with before. Now they were gone and he had no company but his thoughts.

Ivy bolted from the blue couch. She threw herself violently to the floor. Then she was running, running and screaming, down the length of the glass.

"Huh?" Bill said, startled.

A noise died in the darkness of distant stone, then there was a stealthy rustle.

"Who's there?"

Bill quickly shoveled a burning ember onto a piece of cardboard and threw it into the darkness. There was a scamper. Then it was quiet as before. Rats, Bill thought. City rats. He listened. No sound.

"... *daddydaddydaddydaddydaddydaddy*—"

Suddenly Bill's heart pounded. He covered his ears with his hands. I'm going mad, he thought. I've got to think. To reason.

But the fatigue made it difficult to think. Only images came, and the images were distorted. Snowy landscapes. The Greyhound station in Darien. The cold, long hospital. And Hoover, standing, shouting through the glass. Bill rubbed his eyes until red sparks danced.

Something became horribly clear: when it counted most, Hoover had had the presence of mind to smash the glass. Bill remembered only paralysis.

"Ivy," he wept over and over.

Shivering, he dozed off, jerked awake, and went to the bridge support to urinate. While there, he saw the long lights of investigating policemen. Two men in uniform finally appeared at the rusted can, kicked the embers apart, dousing the coals, and left. Bill waited, then walked out onto the street.

Pools of water rippled under the brisk wind, throwing freezing spray over the broken pavements.

Far away, a truck pulled up at a deserted newsstand and a man tossed down a heavy bundle of papers.

When the truck roared away into the predawn darkness, Bill walked up and pulled out the top copy. It was a morning tabloid, and under a two-inch headline was Hoover's picture.

REINCARNATION MAN PROVES CASE, the headline read. In smaller type, it read: SHOCKING DEATH OF DAUGHTER IN HOSPITAL CONVINCES JURY. Bill ripped open the newspaper to the continuation on page thirteen. The jury had not even been sent into deliberation, he read. Hoover was free. Bill started to crumple the newspaper in his fists when a final paragraph caught his attention.

A memorial service would be held at ten o'clock for Audrey Rose at Hompa Hongwanji Buddhist Temple, 14 Christopher Place, New York.

Bill's eyes bulged in rage. For *Audrey Rose?*

Angrily, he tossed the newspaper into the gutter and stormed on into the heart of the still-dark city.

Number 14 Christopher Place was a small brick building that had served as an alternative school, a radical arts center, a vegetarian health information society, and now had been converted into an esoteric Buddhist place of worship. Bill peeked into the windows. One adolescent, wearing an orange robe, swept the worn wooden floor. Another in a blue shirt and white skirt set flowers at the front, where an altar of sorts had been constructed from doors and benches. On the wall were photographs of Gupta Pradesh.

Bill recoiled. He walked across the street and pretended to browse at leather crafts displayed on iron hooks in a boutique

38

window. Time after time, as though drawn magnetically, he turned to stare at the self-styled temple.

Something was being sprinkled on the floor. Maybe holy water, Bill thought. Maybe sweeping compound. Rage filled his body, and he knew he was capable of murder.

An hour later, several more adolescents in orange robes walked up to the door, bowed, and entered. Through the window Bill saw incense lighted. At 9:45, Judge Langley walked to the door, checked the address, and hesitantly entered. Bill dashed for cover into a small supermarket. Over the avocados he saw Scott Velie drive up in a black Mercedes. Next came Hoover's lawyer and Dr. Lipscomb. Then a taxi drove up, and Russ and Carole Federico, wan and red-eyed, stepped out. Uncertainly, they waited, then saw Scott Velie motioning them in from the window, and they went, arm in arm, into the temple. Janice would be next.

Bill ran up the alley, circled several blocks and found himself cutting back toward Washington Square. He changed direction, walked on and on, for two hours, and did not stop until he sat on a bench in Central Park.

By now Bill knew that he could run no more. His brain was whirling. His nervous system was on fire. He felt like an animal with one paw in the steel trap. By instinct, he got up, walked on through the park, past lanky teenagers throwing Frisbees, past couples necking on the cold grass, and crossed to Des Artistes, the one place he knew Janice would not be.

Mario stared at him, his eyes filled with sadness.

"My keys— I lost my keys, Mario—"

"Sure, Mr. Templeton. I'll have Ernie take you up."

Mario led him to Ernie, who opened the Templetons' apartment with a passkey. Ernie brushed against Bill as the apartment door opened, and he felt the icy cold of the man's hands.

"You going to be all right?" Ernie asked softly. "You want I should call a doctor?"

Bill croaked out a negative reply. Ernie stood, watched Bill collapse on a chair by the window, head slumped down, shivering. The radiator hissed, which meant he would be warm there, Ernie thought, and closed the door.

In the apartment, Bill sat alone, dimly conscious of the cold leaving his bones, but otherwise conscious only of sinking, waiting, and trying not to think.

"... *daddydaddydaddydaddydaddy*—"

"Ahhhhhh!"

Bill slammed his fist against the wall.

When it was late in the day, almost twilight, he heard the elevator door open in the distance. Janice's footsteps came slowly over the carpeted hallway. Bill wanted to turn, to face her, to defend himself in a physical way, but his body no longer responded. He sat, slumped, his arms heavy as cast iron, and only the hair at the back of his neck stirred, prickling, when he heard the door slowly unlock:

Chapter Two

Janice closed the door softly. Though Mario had told her that Bill was in the apartment, she was still surprised to see him, a silhouette against the stained-glass windows. It had been so long since she had seen him. Even his silhouette looked different. It belonged to a weary, broken man.

Janice took off her coat, then her hat.

Bill's shadow, a bulk of darkness, followed her as she moved in the room.

"Is it over?" he whispered hoarsely.

"Yes."

Overhead, the paintings on the ceiling were now lost in gloom, the dancers and dressed monkeys stilled, erased in twilight's shade ahead.

"She will be . . . cremated."

Bill bent over, crumpled, as though to avoid her. Janice now saw the shirt, once so white and freshly pressed, filthy, wrinkled, with streaks at the sides and shoulders.

"I didn't mean to, Janice . . . it was an accident. . . ."

Bill rose, raised his fist as though to strike it against the wall, but instead his hand opened up and he simply leaned, exhausted, against the wallpaper, head down, in the growing darkness.

"I didn't mean to," he repeated. "It was . . . an accident. . . ."

Janice stepped farther into the room. Alone, she had had to bear the responsibility of dealing with the hospital, the court, and the representatives of the Mount Canaan Mausoleum in Valhalla, New York. She alone had signed the official papers. She alone had been at the autopsy. If it had not been for the support of the young Buddhists, and Scott Velie, and the Federicos, she would have collapsed.

With pained scrutiny, she examined the husband who was a stranger to her. His hair was wet, disheveled. The trousers had stains of slush and tar and were torn at the knees. The broad, athletic shoulders twitched from nervousness and lack of sleep.

"Janice!" he sobbed. "Is it possible?"

Janice wanted to go to him, to comfort him, but the words of comfort that she knew would have sent him into a frenzy. Their minds had become incompatible. Their beings had separated. Janice looked away from Bill, as though to avoid the sight of a destroyed relationship.

"I asked you a question," he said coldly. Bill had turned. His eyes had an odd, burning quality, a shining feverish quality that frightened her. "Tell me, Janice," he said.

"You saw with your own eyes," she said simply.

"He bewitched her. Didn't he? He bewitched all of us."

"No, he did not bewitch her."

Bill sighed wearily.

"I went to the temple, Janice . . . but I couldn't go in. I wanted to, but I couldn't. . . ." His voice trailed away into a sibilant, meaningless whisper.

Janice wiped her eyes at the kitchen door. She found the

light switch. The glow filled the dining area. Light sparkled from the china in the cabinet, off the Mexican vases. Bill stood immobile, in the center of the room.

"Please, Janice, forgive me," he pleaded.

"Nobody's blamed you, Bill."

"Janice, I'm begging you."

"In time. You'll forgive me in time, too. But we need time."

Janice turned, more to escape the sight of Bill's manic, sleep-deprived stare. When she turned on the kitchen light, the sudden glare shocked her. The physical reality of stainless-steel sinks, water faucets, calendar on the wall, and plates and cups, restored a sense of gravity.

Janice found remnants of an old roast, and cold potato salad. They ate in silence. She saw Bill's hands tremble; the tears fell down from his face as he shoveled the food into his mouth.

He took a deep breath, washed his face at the faucet. The harsh light bounced off the yellow kitchen walls as though to bleach them both of each and every facade, to reveal each of them utterly naked to the other, all softness and illusion destroyed in a terrible finality.

Bill could not turn to face Janice. He tried, but a kind of magnetic pull prevented it. He wiped his face in a dirty kitchen towel. When he finally spoke, the silence broke under the cruel, cold voice.

"It was because I approved the test," Bill croaked. "It was all my fault."

Time passed like a dark tide, scraping them, tossing them about in inchoate currents of bitter regrets and self-accusations. Janice remembered key words from the temple service, from Hoover's crudely articulated philosophies, and they brought a kind of balm. A diffused substitute for serenity that outdid Dr. Kaplan's Valium at any rate. Bill had nothing. He lay on the couch, eyes wide at the ceiling. From time to time, his arm jerked from nervous exhaustion.

Janice brought some scotch and water to him, but he ignored it.

In the morning, Janice dressed in a soft beige suit and a dark hat. Bill huddled in his dirty clothes on the couch.

"I can't go," he whispered hoarsely, breaking a night-long silence.

"No one will be there," Janice said. "Only us. The Federicos."

"I can't—I can't go—"

"Do you think it's wise to stay home alone?"

"I won't go and have them accuse me!"

Janice knew it was useless to argue. The cremation took place without him.

Flames roared from gas jets arranged in a semicircle around the entire wooden casket. It was so hot that the interior walls, cast iron, flaked off in large patches. Ivy, who had fled in panic from the fire, was consumed in an obliterating flame.

Only a few ounces of pebbly ash were left of the human body.

Steel instruments gathered the ashes into a brass urn. The urn was placed in a small varnished mahogany chest. A thin man with sober eyes lifted the chest into a compartment in a marble wall.

On the marble wall was a brass plate: IVY TEMPLETON —1964–1975 No. 5693452. There was nothing else left.

Janice stood in the marbled hall. Ivy, she silently prayed, forgive us. Forgive and understand us. She prayed for the liberty of her child's soul. Then she added a Catholic prayer that she remembered from her own youth. When she was through, a great silence filled the chamber.

She walked away on the arm of Russ Federico. Outside, the sun glinted on patches of snow on the small lawn. Running water glistened in the roads. It was Ivy's kind of spring—a quick transition, full of clean snow, warmth, and icicles melting with musical drops into the muddy ground below. The crisp air breathed hope.

At the door of Des Artistes, Carole and Russ took their leave.

"Sure we can't come up and sit with you?" Carole asked.

"Thank you, but Bill wants to be alone."

Russ shook his head. "My father always said that grief is something you can't work out on your own."

"I know, Russ," Janice answered, "but I think it's better if we wait until tomorrow."

"As you think best."

Stepping alone onto the ninth floor was an eerie sensation. It seemed denuded, all the life sucked out of it by death. Janice plucked up her courage and stepped into the apartment. Bill had not moved from where she had left him that morning.

He moaned softly as she closed the door.

She tried to get him to eat but he refused. She brought fresh clothes from the bedroom and he slowly dressed. Throughout the day, she answered the telephone, calls from family and relatives, the parents of Ivy's friends. A small delegation of Ernie, Dominick, Mario, and several members of the restaurant staff came to pay their respects.

Later that night, a massive bouquet of flowers arrived from the Hompa Hongwanji Buddhist Temple, with poems that expressed how the flower reincarnated the soul of the plant.

Bill began to bite his knuckles until they grew raw and bleeding. Janice slipped a crumbled Valium into his dinner but it had no effect. He paced through the apartment, restless as a caged panther, saying nothing.

Suddenly the wind blew and the pressure slammed the door of Ivy's room.

Bill stopped, frightened, and stared up at the landing, at Ivy's door. He put his hands over his ears as though to block out inaudible screams, the scurry of twisting, pattering feet.

At 10:30, two reporters came with questions, but Janice excused herself and closed the door. She instructed Dominick not to send up any reporters. Dominick apologized, saying they had passed themselves off as members of the family.

By 11:30, Bill fell asleep on the couch. Exhaustion showed plainly on his face. Janice worried about him. Even in his sleep his face twitched, grimaced. Janice took two Valium and slept alone. Beyond the wall was Ivy's room, and a dark silence, as though waiting.

Five days after the cremation, Janice went to Ivy's room and cleared away most of the clothes. These and the toys, she sent to a relief agency in India. Many of the small mementos she kept: the aquarium with its fantailed Mexican shells, the picture albums, the panda bear, pages of her artwork, and the crude vase she had fashioned in a summer's course of pottery in Central Park, things that were still alive with her creative spirit. The rest she hoped would find their use among children who also had but a brief time on the earth for happiness before the responsibilities of adulthood or poverty or death claimed them.

With the removal of each box of Ivy's possessions, Bill sank deeper into guilt-ridden gloom, until he could no longer speak, but hung about the living room like a scarecrow, devoid of soul.

One afternoon, the young Buddhists appeared at Des Artistes but Janice asked them not to come up. Instead, she went down and they talked in the lobby. They told her that Hoover, after being acquitted, had stopped by to offer his prayers. They had a letter for her.

Janice opened a small yellow note and read the even, small handwriting that filled the page to the margins.

> Dear Janice—My thoughts are with you and Bill now as they have been ever since the trial began. I

pray that understanding has come, and with it the serenity to accept and bless what the divine universe has created. For destruction is but the beginning of further creation, as the falling seed is but the preparation for the growth of the milk pod. Please accept my prayers for you and for Ivy. I think I speak for Ivy in saying that the great struggle is at last over, and that her soul is now free to continue on its long, never-ending journey to perfection. Janice, may you find favor in life, and wisdom in your search for happiness, for love has spread its canopy over you and will bless you with profound peace, if you but let it.

I shall be returning to India, where I have friends, and where I can pray, and work, and find the solitude necessary to my meditations. But know that even in India I shall continue to pray for you and Ivy, and that my thoughts are ever with you. Yours in eternal prayer, Elliot Hoover.

Janice wiped away a tear, went back to the apartment and drafted a letter to the mausoleum. Ivy's ashes would be sent to India, scattered there, and serenity would fill the emptiness the way that sunlight fills a rose garden, lending color to everything, filling the warm air with subtle perfume.

Several requests from magazines and newspapers came in the mail for articles and information. Janice threw them all away.

The steady flow of people into the apartment gradually diminished. Pel Simmons, the founder of the advertising agency in which Bill worked, made a discreet call. When he saw Bill seated, hollow-eyed, on the couch, he asked Janice if Bill needed medical attention.

"He needs a few more weeks, Mr. Simmons."

"Of course, Janice. It's not that. It's just that he looks like death over there."

"I'll speak to Dr. Kaplan."

Dr. Kaplan prescribed antidepressants, stronger than Valium. Janice slipped it into his lunch. She also hid the alcohol, even though Bill was not drinking. Just in case, because it would mix into a lethal combination with the drugs.

With the antidepressants, Bill became numbed, his limbs relaxed, and he grew rubbery, dazed, and incoherent. But he could not override the paralysis of grief and guilt.

"If I hadn't left for Hawaii," he mumbled. "That was the moment. When he came up here. Why did I go to Hawaii? I don't remember anymore. . . ."

By the second week, Bill had still not shaven. Janice changed his clothes, shaved him as best she could, combed his hair. But when Don Goetz, Bill's assistant, called from Simmons Advertising, she had to plead for another few days. No hurry, Goetz replied. They were just expressing their support.

In the third week, Jack Belaver, senior partner to Simmons Advertising, came to visit. Shocked at the sight of Bill, he maintained his composure.

"Look, Bill," he said softly, "I know what it's like. When I lost Marianne, I thought the world had ended. Well, nobody's blaming you. Nothing can ever change what's happened, but—"

"Who's blaming me?" Bill shot at him.

"Nobody. Bill, listen to me. You've got to march ahead. The grief will pass away, but it needs something to supplant it. It needs life, work, joy. You can't cut yourself off from society."

"You said somebody was blaming me."

"I mean for staying inside, Bill. Look, it's natural to want to be alone. Anyone would. But it's time to come out of the cocoon. We'll help you, Bill. We're all pulling for you. Don Goetz has arranged the files and even set up two meetings for Monday. I'll be there if it gets difficult. You've got to reenter, Bill."

But Bill had retracted behind his wall of silent brooding. Belaver sighed. "All right, Bill. Have it your way."

At the door, he suggested to Janice that Bill see a psychiatrist.

"I've tried, Jack, but he won't listen to me anymore. I can't break through the barrier."

Belaver nodded sympathetically.

"Simmons can wait a few more weeks," he said. "Six weeks, eight. But sooner or later—we're all very fond of Bill, but— It's so damn competitive out there."

"I understand, Jack."

"That's unofficial, Janice."

"Yes. Thank you. I'll try to get him to a psychiatrist."

"Oh, by the way, is money a problem?"

"Not yet," Janice said cautiously.

"Well, not to worry. Between Bill's stock options and pension fund there'll be plenty for a good long time."

Dr. Manny Gleicher had read about the Templeton case. It had sparked his interest and now he was surprised to find the affair walking into his office. Mrs. Templeton was much younger and better educated than he had guessed from the newspapers.

It was a small, cluttered office, and Dr. Gleicher was a thin, nervous man in his early fifties, balding, with rapid, awkward gestures. He studied her quickly as she sat down.

"How long has it been, Mrs. Templeton?" he asked.

"Two months."

"And in all that time, he has not left the apartment?"

"No."

"Does he have friends over, speak on the telephone?"

"No."

"Does he talk to you?"

"Rarely. Not at all in the last four days."

"What kind of things did he say?"

"It's always about Ivy. He blames himself for arranging the test. Nothing can shake it from him."

49

Dr. Gleicher stroked his mustache and looked at Janice. She waited for his response, at his mercy.

"It would be natural for Bill to feel responsible," Dr. Gleicher said. "But after a point, he should realize that the court was also responsible. The court and the hospital."

There was a silence. Dr. Gleicher understood from Janice's expression that logic and argument had ceased to penetrate Bill's grief. He took out a small cigar, asked if Janice minded, then lit it, exhaling luxuriously over his head.

"I read," he said slowly, "that there was a kind of meditation service. Did Bill go?"

"No."

"Did he attend the cremation?"

"No."

Dr. Gleicher's eyes narrowed.

"Do you mind if I ask you about your relationship with this other man, this Mr. Hoover?"

"There was no relationship."

"Yes, but according to the papers, you testified—"

"Dr. Gleicher, I felt, and still feel, that he was the only one who could have saved her. That was why I testified."

"Your acceptance of Mr. Hoover's, er, ideas, must have seemed a bitter betrayal to your husband."

Janice looked down at her hands, folded in her lap.

"I'm sure he thought of it in that way," she said softly. "I only meant to save Ivy. There was nothing between Mr. Hoover and myself."

"Did Bill think there was?"

"I don't know. I don't think he would have put it so—so directly. He just felt that I had deserted him by testifying. By not trusting in him."

"Perfectly natural."

Dr. Gleicher paused, thought for a moment, then relit his cigar. All the while, his eyes scanned Janice's face and body for hidden gestures, nonverbal clues to her emotions behind the words.

"Do you think Bill is still angry at you?"

"Yes."

"Do you think he's withdrawing as a way to punish you? To force you to attend to him?"

"No. I think he blames himself for Ivy's death. I don't think he knows I even exist anymore."

Dr. Gleicher nodded sympathetically and then, satisfied with Janice's answers, stubbed out his cigar and sat on a leather chair next to Janice.

"I don't suppose you could convince your husband to come and see me?"

"No, Doctor."

Dr. Gleicher sighed and simply smiled, a professional but warm smile.

"All right, I'll go to him then."

Dr. Gleicher stepped out of the elevator. Ernie watched him walk softly down the corridor and ring the Templetons' bell.

Janice opened the door, smiled wanly, and Dr. Gleicher entered the apartment.

"Good evening, Mrs. Templeton. Hello, Bill."

Bill looked up from where he sat opposite the couch. The way his collar was askew suggested that he had not dressed himself. The dark, hopeless eyes followed Dr. Gleicher into the room, and Bill looked frightened and withdrew into the chair.

Dr. Gleicher sat on the couch, affecting geniality, but in reality studying Bill's every move.

"What a lovely apartment," Dr. Gleicher said. "This place is rather famous, isn't it?"

"Yes," Janice agreed. "Some well-known artists have lived here. They built it around huge studios and when the artists left, most of the suites were converted to duplex apartments."

"Those ceilings. Italian, aren't they?"

"Ersatz Fragonard."

On the coffee table was a pewter pitcher of lemonade. Janice offered a little rum to mix with it, but Dr. Gleicher shook his head. He sipped for a while, relishing the cool air in the room, then sucked on the slice of lime perched on the edge of his glass.

"Bill," he said gently, "do you know who I am?"

Bill said nothing, but his eyes showed that he appraised the stranger with apprehension.

"My name is Manny Gleicher. I am a practicing psychiatrist at the John C. Schreyer Clinic. Perhaps you've heard of it? On Thirty-fourth Street."

Bill shook his head, an almost imperceptible gesture. A kind of deep weariness showed on his face, as though there were something intolerably oppressive about Dr. Gleicher, Janice, and every other intrusion into his solitude.

"Your wife has discussed with me your last two months here. Has she told you that?"

Bill's eyes narrowed in suspicious hostility. He darted a glance at Janice.

"I explained everything," Janice said softly.

"Well, in any case, I should like to speak privately with Bill."

"Yes. Of course."

Janice removed herself upstairs to the bedroom, closing the door. She tried to listen but could hear nothing. She opened the door a crack and saw Gleicher lean forward and touch Bill on the knee to get his attention. Bill started, as though awakened from a light sleep.

"Bill," Dr. Gleicher asked. "Can you tell me who I am?"

Bill's arm twitched, but he did not speak.

"I just told you my name and profession. Do you remember?"

"Haul ass."

"Excuse me?"

"Get out."

"Now, Bill, one does not play games—"

Suddenly, Bill lurched forward, grabbed the pewter pitcher, and threw the contents into Dr. Gleicher's face. The pitcher bounced off the surprised man's chin with a loud and painful crack.

"I said, get out!"

"Please listen to me, Bill. I am a doctor of psychiatry."

Bill rose unsteadily to his feet. The effort of heaving the heavy pitcher—or rage—seemed to have exhausted him. His arms trembled, but his eyes narrowed in hatred.

"You can't come here," Bill stammered.

Dr. Gleicher instinctively rose to face Bill. He loosened his collar and gently daubed at the sticky lemonade running down his shirt.

"I can. Your wife invited me."

Bill turned slowly to face the upstairs bedroom door. A cruel, ironic smile twisted his lips.

"It's not the first time, Hoover!" he roared.

"Bill," persisted Dr. Gleicher, "it is very important that we talk—"

"*Wasn't once enough?*"

Janice, shaking, came from the bedroom and stood gazing down over the top of the banister.

"Bill," she whispered, "I beg you. Listen to Dr. Gleicher."

Bill tried to laugh crudely, but it came out a choked, hoarse crying sound. He stared upward at Janice as though trying to see through a pouring rain. He angrily wiped the sweat from his face.

"*Get out!*" he yelled, turning to Dr. Gleicher.

Dr. Gleicher stepped backward, feeling his way from the couch into the main part of the living room.

"No, Bill. I am going to talk to you."

"*Both of you! Get out!*"

"Calm down, Bill!" Janice begged. "For God's sake!"

Bill stared at Dr. Gleicher, who positioned himself at the end table like a French statuette, chest out and legs firm. Bill

53

reached down and took up a heavy stone mask from Africa in the shape of a double monkey, with sharp ears coming to a point. Dr. Gleicher paled but did not retreat.

"I'm warning you," Bill hissed.

"There's no need for gestures, Bill."

Bill advanced a step, saw no reaction, then raised the stone mask higher over his shoulder. Tears rolled from his eyes and he furiously brushed them away.

Janice came halfway down the stairs. She hardly recognized him now. Even the shape of his face had altered. His eyes rolled and the pupils were abnormally tiny.

Bill took another step, knocking over a lamp. Suddenly harsh shadows crossed over Dr. Gleicher. Janice gasped and came down into the living room.

"She was fine until you came here," Bill whispered.

"Who was fine?" Dr. Gleicher shot in.

"Ivy, you bastard!"

"Who do you think I am, Bill?"

"I should have killed you," Bill said softly. "That first night I saw you!"

"Put down that mask, Bill."

Bill's eyes suddenly bulged. The veins in his neck strained, and he threw himself forward with all his might. Dr. Gleicher gaped, fell, and ran toward the door. He opened it and threw himself into the corridor. Behind him, the stone mask smashed into the doorjamb, showering painted splinters in an arc over him.

"YOU BASTARD! YOU KILLED HER!"

Janice grabbed her purse and, in that instant, saw all the shadows reverse. Bill had caught his foot on a second lamp and had sent it crashing ahead of him. She fled, slamming the door behind her.

"YOU AND YOUR CASTRATED GOONS! YOU KILLED HER!"

Janice locked the door from the outside. There were violent sounds inside as Bill went into a frenzy, smashing ceramics, hurling ashtrays through the stained-glass windows, and heaving the desk off its legs, into the front door.

"IVY!!!"

Bill's cry came in a long, drawn-out bellow. It was a cry of deep and obliterating pain, loneliness, and confusion. It became silent. Dr. Gleicher and Janice stepped nervously to the door and put their ears against the wood.

Inside, Janice heard a hoarse, labored breathing. It sounded drugged, coarse, unnatural. At the top of each breath, there was a tiny extra intake, as though Bill gasped for breath.

"Open the door," Dr. Gleicher whispered to Janice.

Janice stared at him, took courage from his pointed gesture at the lock, and turned the key. Dr. Gleicher eased his way inside. It was nearly dark. Only the light from the landing fell onto the living room, a broad spotlight on the shambles below.

Glass and ceramic shards covered the floor and the fabrics. A wooden leg from the desk had lodged its way into the china cabinet. Warm, sultry night air came in through jagged holes in the long windows.

Against the couch, his right leg twisted up under him as he lay partially on the floor, his head on the couch itself, Bill knelt as though in a mockery of prayer. Dr. Gleicher gently eased his leg straight and moved Bill onto his back so he could breathe more easily. His forehead, furrowed in doubt and rage, glistened from sweat.

"He's going to be very depressed when he wakes up," Dr. Gleicher whispered. "The violence will turn inward."

"You mean—"

"That's what suicide is. Rage that turns inward."

Janice knelt down at Bill's side. She touched his forehead with a wet napkin. At her touch, his forehead trembled, and he moaned, as though fire roared through his nerves.

"Mrs. Templeton, you know that your husband needs intensive help."

"Yes."

"He needs to be removed from this apartment. From you."
She turned, startled. "He needs to go away, where he can recover at a guided pace."

"I—I won't allow it."

"You have no choice, Mrs. Templeton. You're not professionally trained."

"No—"

"Mrs. Templeton," Dr. Gleicher repeated, patiently, crouching down with her over Bill's tormented face, "there's a good clinic at Ossining. It's up the Hudson, a bit east. A very good clinic."

"No. I won't do it. I can't."

"What's best for Bill, Mrs. Templeton? To be left here where Ivy grew up? To be accused night and day by everything he sees, by everything he hears, by a thousand memories of her? You must see that you have no choice at all."

Bill's head turned away, against the pillows on the couch. He seemed to be trying to talk in his sleep. Janice leaned her ear close to his lips. She heard his thick, husky voice, sounding now like a death rattle.

"...Ivy...the glass...Ivy...the glass..."

In the morning, Dr. Gleicher telephoned the Eilenberg Clinic in Ossining and prepared Bill's admission. Janice packed a small valise. At noon the clinic's limousine arrived at Des Artistes. Heavily sedated, Bill rode beside Janice. His eyes blinked as though unused to the sunlight. Janice held his hand.

The clinic was a long, low building shaded by oak trees. Bill was taken to his room and then Dr. Geddes, the chief psychiatrist, introduced himself. He was slender, not much older than Janice, and combed his sandy brown hair sideways to cover a balding area.

Dr. Geddes explained the clinic. No drugs were used. No hypnosis. There were no guards, no hidden cameras. The only thing they requested was that Janice's visits be on a regular schedule. Janice readily agreed. After the financial arrangements were concluded, Janice went into Bill's room to say good-bye.

An impenetrable wall of silence surrounded him. Beyond his window, the shimmering meadow grass fluttered in brilliant, sun-rich waves. Janice adjusted his collar and pulled the shade to keep the sinking sun from his eyes.

She stepped to the door. Bill had made no response.

"I love you, Bill," she whispered. "Remember that always."

Dr. Geddes had business in town and drove Janice and Dr Gleicher back to New York. They kept up a casual conversation, about Bill, about the changes in the city, about the changes in the country. Dr. Geddes had a youthful, intuitive manner, rather than Dr. Gleicher's studied formality. There was a long, slow sunset, an air of tranquility, as they glided over the ramparts into the city. The purple twilight enclosed them in a misty, dreamlike atmosphere.

She thanked both doctors and stepped out at Des Artistes. For an instant, she felt the rising tide of panic, but then turned and resolutely stepped alone into the lobby.

The apartment loomed, dark and massive, around her. With Bill and Ivy gone, the living area seemed vast as a tomb.

She drank a long, cold glass of rum in limeade. Now that she was alone, the rumbles of distant plumbing, elevators, and electric appliances made a soothing symphony through the walls. The rum agreeably relaxed her. Gradually, her panic died.

There was nothing to fear, she thought. The past would die of its own momentum. What wouldn't die could not harm her. She would move, alone, into the mysterious future, and learn what she had to learn. That was how Ivy would have wanted it. And Bill, were he himself.

Janice opened the window in Ivy's room. A warm night air wafted in, redolent with the smell of the distant river, and the summer dust. In her bed, which now had one pillow, Janice, for the first time in months, slipped into an untroubled sleep.

Chapter Three

Breakfast alone, and the sunshine poured into Des Artistes. Janice drank Colombian coffee and ate muffins with jam beside an open window. It was a curious feeling, secure and quiet in the kitchen.

Time slowed to a crawl now that people stopped paying calls on account of Ivy. The mail decreased. The telephone rarely rang except for Carole Federico.

Carole and Janice walked together toward the Marina off Riverside Drive. It had been Ivy's favorite place. With bittersweet memories, they watched yelling children crawl over the jungle gym.

"It seems so long ago," Janice said quietly. "As though Ivy were here in a dream."

Carole smiled sadly, took Janice's arm, and they found an outdoor buffet where a fat man dispensed lemonade, pretzels and socialism at no extra cost. They leaned back against a picnic table, and they watched the glittering wakes of small pleasure craft on the Hudson River.

"I thought I would be crushed," Janice said thoughtfully. "Being alone, I mean. But I'm not. I feel—"

"Independent is the word," Carole said, with a suggestion of jealousy.

"Exactly," Janice agreed. "I feel like I want a place in the world now. For me. Not as Ivy's mother. Not as Bill's wife. For me. Because I feel I have something to offer, even though I'm not sure exactly what."

"You mean a job?"

"Well, yes. A job. I can't just sit around the apartment all day. Besides, our money won't last forever."

Janice knew that her friend's mind was already clicking through any leads, connections, or even wild rumors that might help. But Carole only shook her head regretfully.

"What about going back to school?" Carole asked. "Have you thought of that?"

"Lots of times. I'm too old for that. Besides, what would I do for money while I was in school?"

"You draw, don't you?" Carole said. "You used to make the most beautiful decorations. And Christmas cards. And didn't you design some theater programs for that Armenian church?"

Janice laughed again, and crooked her arm in Carole's elbow.

"You're sweet, Carole, but that was years ago. Besides, being an art major in college and being a professional artist are two different propositions."

"Nonsense. You've got a natural talent that could be parlayed into real success."

Janice smiled, then rejected the idea.

"Well, how many Armenian churches can there be?" she said.

"The trouble with you is, you have no confidence. Let me

60

ask Russ. A lot of people from the design trade come through his shop. They always hire extra staff.''

Janice was grateful for the support that Carole gave her. She began drawing again. She enrolled in an art class, was advanced to a higher level, and studied the figure with a famous designer from Italy. She worked hard. She needed to feel the pressure of schedules, pressure to execute assignments, to meet deadlines. To feel that vast, rumbling force that throbbed through the heart of the densest city in the world.

Janice felt on the edge of a teeming life, tantalizingly close, hungering for it. She began to feel, more and more, as her figure studies improved, that she really did have something to offer. An eye for color, an instinct for gesture. She knew how to work hard, to please the most exacting of tastes, and she wanted a chance.

Every Monday at 1:45, a train dropped her at Ossining. From there she took a short bus ride to the edge of the clinic grounds. Bill remained absolutely, heartbreakingly the same. She told him about looking for work, about the plays she had seen, about Shakespeare in the Park with the Federicos and their cousins from Miami.

Bill paid no attention. He seemed to be deep in thought, as though trying to figure what in the trial had gone wrong. Janice fought back the tears. He had sunk into a torpor far deeper than Dr. Geddes had at first realized.

Bill brought the past back to her, a past that she was determined to escape. She went to the heart of the city now, in earnest, with her portfolio. Everywhere she was told that her collections of sketches and pastels—which went back to her college days in Berkeley—were out-of-date, or not professional enough, or ''simply wouldn't do.'' This last was usually accompanied by a crushing smile of condescension.

After four weeks of looking, Russ Federico invited her down for a late brandy.

"I don't know why you want to work," he said. "Frankly, I'd just as soon take long walks all day on the river."

"What are you talking about, Russ?" Janice asked, suspecting she was being teased.

"You don't know when you got it good, Janice," he sighed, taking a folded note from his pocket.

"Come to the point, Russ."

"The point is that Christine Daler, Ltd.—they're fashions for women, you know—is going to expand. And it hasn't been announced. They're gonna need an army of assistant draftsmen—er, draftspeople . . ."

"Draftspersons," Carole corrected, sipping brandy from a wide snifter.

Janice plucked the note from Russ's hand and read an address on Lexington Avenue.

"Anyway," Russ laughed, "I got it from the horse's mouth. Elaine Romine. She's head designer at Christine Daler. Well, to make a long story short, I mentioned you, and one thing after the other, and—"

"And what, for God's sake, Russ?" Janice asked.

"Well, I mean if you ain't busy at 2:30 next Tuesday—"

"Oh, my God, suddenly I feel so nervous," Janice said.

"They only need assistants. You know, people with brushes at the end of their arms. You don't have to be Leonardo da Vinci."

Janice, flabbergasted, could only blurt out her gratitude. That night, Janice furiously rearranged her portfolio seven times. She rejected five still lifes as too amateurish. Then she drew new sketches with a free-flowing hand until well past midnight. She was convinced that what she had done was no good, and went to bed downhearted, thinking she was unemployable.

*   *   *

Christine Daler, Ltd.—its logo was Big Ben with a decorative swirl of cloud that formed a CD—was located in a new building on Lexington Avenue. Janice paled at the wealth of the interior, the sculptures in the foyers, the collages by Paolozzi in the corridors. It was a high-pressure world, she realized immediately, like Simmons Advertising.

She waited several moments until the receptionist indicated for her to go to Ms. Romine's office. Janice walked down a long carpeted corridor, clutching her portfolio like a lifesaver. On one side were offices with drafting tables and designers with sable brushes, bending down under brilliant fluorescent lights. On the other side, enormous windows looked out on the entire complex of midtown buildings.

She knocked hesitantly.

"Come in," said a deep voice.

Elaine Romine was exactly as she had imagined her. A tall woman with light brown hair, she had the flat bust and long legs of a former model. Gold earrings dangled brightly, and she moved with devastating, almost aggressive self-confidence.

Without looking at Janice, Elaine untied the portfolio and examined her drawings. Janice had seen this kind of woman before, the goal-oriented woman of expensive tastes.

"Your pastels are weak," Elaine said. "But your watercolors have good control."

Elaine looked carefully at several more sketches. Janice heard her heart banging against her rib cage.

"The figures are not bad. The proportions are good. But the landscapes—these pastels—are really below standard. Have you ever used dry-brush? Don't tell me you have, if you haven't."

"No," Janice answered. "That is, I tried it a few times, but it didn't work out."

Elaine dropped the last of the pages back into the portfolio, thought a moment, then handed the portfolio back to Janice.

"Have you eaten lunch?" she asked.

"Not really—a little coffee—"

"Do you have time for a salad downstairs?"

"Why—yes, of course."

Elaine's smile was perfectly controlled, yet exuded a kind of warmth. Janice could not help but admire the woman's poise, the elegance with which she dispensed people, ideas, careers.

"Downstairs" meant a prohibitively expensive luncheon bar. The clientele was dressed in a stunning array of trendy dresses, or, with the men, in pin-striped suits then coming back into fashion. A few of them saluted Elaine with nods or gestures of the hand. Janice was wearing her best business suit, one which had set her and Bill back a good deal, but now she suddenly felt shabbily dressed.

"I have five girls working under me," Elaine said, digging into a small mountain of mushrooms, bean sprouts, avocado, and sundry other delicacies, smothered in a rich and creamy yogurt sauce. "One of them is good with dry-brush but a klutz with watercolor, so I'll split the work between you two. I'll give you the roughs, you'll work them into sketches."

Elaine studied Janice, who suddenly realized that an answer was expected.

"Yes. All right. I can do that."

"Fine. How much were you expecting to earn?"

Janice choked on a long shredded bean sprout. She washed it down with water.

"I—er—"

"Come, come. We haven't got all day."

Janice panicked. She regained her composure but had to confess a most embarrassing truth.

"Miss Romine," she whispered, "I don't know."

"You don't know? What do you mean, you don't know?"

"I was so nervous about the job, I didn't think about it."

Elaine stared at her, then burst out laughing, a sweet, musical laughter. She wiped her lips with a white napkin, looked at Janice, and started to laugh again.

"I'll have to remember that," Elaine said, her eyes twinkling. "Look. I'll pay you five hundred dollars for the project. It'll give you experience in knowing how to judge time if you ever get asked again."

"All right. That sounds fair."

"You should go to Quadrangle Art Supply House down the street, and tell Ralph—he's the one with the earring—that you're working for me. He'll start you out with a few basic brushes and things. I want you to begin with clean tools."

Janice had the sinking feeling that Ralph with the earring was about to stick her with a pretty fair-sized supply of expensive tools.

Elaine studied Janice with a different kind of eye.

"Would you like to be called Janice or Mrs. Templeton?"

"Janice, please."

"Fine. I think things will work out well. You're used to a little pressure?"

"Oh, certainly. Yes, of course."

Elaine smiled. Her manner had none of the brittleness Janice had expected. There was nothing arch or aloof about Elaine Romine. She was direct and friendly, just frighteningly self-confident. She must be a genius, Janice thought.

"One more thing," Elaine said.

"Yes?"

"My female employees do not make coffee for the male employees, get their mail, or laugh at their stupid jokes. None of that garbage around here. If anybody makes an uninvited pass at you, kick him in the teeth."

Janice laughed and promised she would.

"I like men," Elaine said, "but it's a woman's world on this floor. It's that way because I prefer it. I want my staff to have boldness and integrity, and to make beautiful design."

Janice nodded.

"So respect yourself, work hard, and you'll learn a lot."

"I will. And thank you. I'm very grateful."

"Nonsense. Your work is competent. I didn't hire you out of charity."

On the way home Janice wanted to shout for joy. Instead, testing out her new station in life, she strolled down Lexington Avenue with her portfolio under her arm. She now had a place, at least for a while, in this mad whirl of New York. In a kind of daze, she wandered past the expensive shops, critically examining her wardrobe reflected in the windows, and she decided that Elaine was the most remarkable woman she had ever met.

With her first paycheck, she bought Bill an electric wrist watch, the kind that he had long admired. Dr. Geddes assured her that there were small signs—improved muscle tone, improved responses to being touched. Bill distinguished between friendly and neutral faces. To Janice, it seemed like no change at all. Bill was a man without a personality.

Janice worked long hours to make up for her lack of experience. It probably averaged out to less than the minimum wage. But on the last night of her first project, at 1:30 in the morning, with the floor littered with scraps of paper, and her fingers black with ink, she knew that she had passed the test. Elaine asked her to stay for a second project.

Now, with the first few months out of the way, there was a little time. Time to observe the energy and direction of Elaine's changing creations. She was working on midwinter designs, and the pressure on her was intense.

Elaine was not married, and her views on men were not what Janice would have called conventional. For the first time, she felt a twinge of jealousy at Elaine's free-wheeling ease with more than one male friend at a time, for her own evenings were long and lonely. She was often too tired to go out to a movie, and reading—mainly popular fiction—began to wear thin. Sometimes loneliness just mounted up. But for an occasional dinner with the Federicos, or a call from Dr. Geddes, her life was one long siege of ennui.

One particular evening, Dr. Geddes called with a bit of good news for a change.

"Bill is responding to words," he chortled over the telephone.

"Really? Why, that's marvelous."

"Some words, anyway. Even a concept or two. Of course, it's all still rudimentary. But quite frankly I'm very pleased."

Janice heard his pleasant laughter on the other end of the line.

"Should I do anything different?" she asked. "Should I bring anything?

"No, just come at the usual time," he said. "I just wanted to share the good news with you."

"I can't tell you how pleased I am to hear this, Dr. Geddes."

"We both could use some encouragement," he chuckled musically. "It's going to be a long haul, but there are signs. Damned good signs."

After she put down the receiver, Janice felt peculiarly light-headed. Could it be that things were going to return to normal? At least, as normal as Des Artistes could be without Ivy. A new reality would be formed, around the two of them. Bill would return to work—if not at Simmons, then somewhere else. Maybe in time there could even be another child. As she looked around the apartment, a bit of the old magic, that happy combination of light, space, and sheer exuberance overflowed once again, filling the walls, and the ceilings danced as they had danced years before, with secretive lovers among the flower-draped arbors.

The summer was over, and the autumn had come with changes. But changes were not to be feared. They were to be welcomed. They were to be welcomed because they meant the end of fear, and the end of that sucking darkness, and together she and Bill would start again, sad but deeper, ever deeper in love, and cognizant of its most profound responsibilities.

Chapter Four

Autumn came as an azure tribute to the fading summer, the deep blue sky warm and endless over the Eilenberg clinic. The low, cream-colored walls of the institution were dappled by the moving shadows of low-bending oak trees.

Janice was long familiar with the grounds. She nodded briefly to a nurse as she made her way to the clinic gardens. Bees still hovered around the faded flowers but there was a sensation of aridity, even sterility, and the dust rose upward, chalk white, as she walked into the garden.

Bill sat on an iron bench, a book on his lap. He had lost weight. His white shirt fluttered in the breeze. He was still very pale, and his red bedroom slippers looked like symbols of illness against the white dusty path. He looked up as he sensed her coming. As always, the direct contact of his eyes made her uneasy. He had become someone else, a broken-hearted, altered image of the man she had known and loved.

He smiled. The lips quivered.

"Hello, Bill," Janice said gently, and kissed him on the forehead.

She sat down next to him and looked at the book in his lap. The type was small and she could not make out the words. It looked like stanzas of poetry. Bill fidgeted with the pages, as though he were very nervous.

"I feel much better," he said, his voice husky. "But sometimes I get dizzy."

Janice put her hand on his and smiled. She was gratified that he did not withdraw it.

"Oh, Bill," she whispered. "It's so wonderful to hear your voice!"

Bill's hands trembled, like an old man's. Janice wondered what powerful emotions surged through the thin frame. He looked up at the oak trees beyond the pink gravel driveway.

"Birds," he said gruffly. "Like music."

"Yes, Bill, I can hear them; oh, my, but it's good to hear you speak."

Suddenly embarrassed, he stood awkwardly, grasping his book. He looked as though he did not know whether to sit down or to walk down the garden path. Janice looked at the cover.

"John Keats," she marveled. "Why, Bill, you never read poetry."

Bill smiled. He had lost so much weight that his cheekbones were unnaturally prominent.

"Dr. Geddes makes me read," he said hesitantly. "It feels good to read about some things."

"Yes. Read to me, Bill. Let me hear your voice some more."

Awkward, Bill licked his lips, and read:

> "We are such forest trees that our fair boughs
> Have bred forth, not pale solitary doves
> But eagles golden-feathered, who do tower
> Above us in their beauty. . . ."

Overcome, Bill closed the book, but kept his finger in it to mark the place.

"We did give birth to an eagle," he said slowly. "You and I. Ivy was the most beautiful, the most courageous . . ."

He stopped. She tried to brush away the moisture from his eyes, but he pushed her hand aside. They rose, walked in silence, into the bright heat of the afternoon.

Janice felt his gait grow confused, like an old man's. She led him as quickly as she could toward the entrance to the garden and signaled to a passing nurse. The nurse came quickly, put Bill's left arm over her own shoulder, and assisted him to a bench in the shade of the clinic roof.

"I don't know what happened," Janice said, suddenly frightened. "All of a sudden, his knees began buckling."

"He's still in a kind of postshock syndrome," the nurse said matter-of-factly. "Conversation actually takes a lot out of him."

They set Bill down in front of the window to the lobby. He apologized weakly, coughed once, then blew his nose into a clean handkerchief. Janice suddenly realized that he looked like an old man, too.

"It's quite normal," the nurse assured her. "Every day he gains a bit more strength."

"Right now I couldn't lift a finger," Bill whispered hoarsely. "Christ, I feel all sucked out."

Janice sat down next to him. "Don't speak, darling," she said gently. "Would you like me to read to you?"

He nodded, then closed his eyes, settling his head against the window behind him. The nurse, who had picked up the book from the driveway, handed it to her. Janice nodded her thanks, then opened up to a well-worn passage:

"Fair youth, beneath the trees, thou canst not leave
Thy song, nor ever can those trees be bare;
Bold lover, never, never canst thou kiss,
Though winning near the goal—yet do not grieve."

Janice looked up at a strange sound. Bill's lips were moving, and in a feathery whisper he completed the stanza with deep sorrow, tinged with a delicacy she had never seen in him before.

"She cannot fade," Bill whispered, "though thou hast not thy bliss; Forever wilt thou love, and she be fair!"

Bill sighed deeply. The nurse and Janice watched him, for he smiled without opening his eyes.

"Do you believe that, Janice?" he asked softly. "That Ivy will be forever loved, and forever beautiful? I do. I'll never forget the color of her eyes . . . the way she ran . . . never . . ."

"Nor I, Bill," Janice whispered, leaning closer, squeezing his heavy hand.

Bill fell into a light sleep. When he awoke later, with an embarrassed jerk, he had no memory of reading poetry in the garden. Instead, he, Janice, and Dr. Geddes discussed the terms of his leaving the clinic. Tentatively, they arrived at a figure of about six weeks.

Privately, Dr. Geddes reminded Janice not to nurture false hopes. Bill was infinitely better, but only in spurts. He still needed time to grow a solid foundation for his thoughts.

"By the way," Janice said, as she was leaving, "Bill said you encourage him to read poetry. Is that true? He asked me to bring him some."

"Yes, a very good idea," Dr. Geddes said. "Nothing explicit. Nothing violent. But the subject of death is all right. Lovely thoughts about it. Bit by bit, Bill is coming to terms with his emotions, releasing them, diffusing them."

"Anything in particular?"

"A little of everything. The more variety, the better."

Janice returned home on the 5:25 evening train. It was already twilight, though unseasonably warm. She stopped at the library, and without thinking much about what she was picking up, collected a small armful of verse that dealt in elegies, dramas of Shakespeare, and even farces translated from French. Anything that would stimulate Bill's mind, so long fallow and destitute. Exhausted, she dropped the books in a heap on the couch at home and sat staring at her watercolor layouts.

"She cannot fade," Janice quoted dreamily, remembering Bill, "though thou hast not her bliss, Forever wilt thou love, Bill, and Ivy be fair!"

She rose, suddenly remembering she had one book left from months ago, from Hoover. She found it in her desk drawer. It was the Bhagavad Gita, a slim blue volume, published in London in 1796. Opening it, Janice smiled. The poetry of Eastern resignation. Like honey, the words flowed, half insensible, often contradictory, in what must assuredly be a ludicrous translation, like Victorian English put through a meat grinder. She recognized a few suitable phrases of comfort.

Hesitating for a long while, Janice held it poised over the fallen pile of books on the couch. At long last, the room grown darker already with the onset of the dry night, the slim blue volume lay with the others, and Janice forgot about it.

On Friday evening, Bill telephoned. He sounded tired at first, then the confidence returned to his voice.

"This clinic has lousy central heating," he said. "It's cold all the time."

"Could I bring you a sweater, darling?"

"I'd appreciate that," Bill said. "And remember those slipper socks your mother sent me for my birthday? I could use those, too."

"I will. Oh, Bill, how sweet of you to call."

Bill's voice changed, almost imperceptibly. Probably Janice was the only human being on the face of the earth who could have noticed it, or understood what it really meant.

"I've been missing you," he said simply.

"I— Me, too, Bill. It's been so long."

"Not having you around is really the worst thing in the

world. Dr. Geddes tells me that maybe I could start coming home—for a night, a weekend—something like that.''

"I'd like that, Bill. I can't tell you how much I would.''

"It sure is good to hear you say that. After all we've been through, you know, I wasn't sure. I mean, it must have been terrible for you—having to put up with all my . . .'' His voice drifted.

Janice reassured him, but he began to repeat himself. His voice grew weaker, and he pulled himself together, only to wish her good-night. Then he hung up. The apartment rang with silence.

It was an apartment waiting for someone. But whether that someone would ever come, whether it could really start all over again, with even half a faith in living, remained to be seen. For the moment, Janice was content that Bill was coming home, and that Ivy had entered his thoughts once more, and that he was overcoming his guilt and fear.

The next time she saw him, he was in a large room converted by the clinic to a kind of gymnasium. He was dressed in woolen pants with a drawstring, white slippers, and a gray sweatshirt, and he was pressing weights upward in rhythmic concentration.

Slowly, he put the long barbell back into the iron slot, ducked under, ran to her and wrapped his arms around her.

"How are you, darling?'' he said, kissing her. "I bet I smell real good, don't I?''

"Just terrific, Bill.''

"Why don't you keep me company while I shower?''

"Are you sure that's allowed?''

Bill laughed infectiously, wiping the sweat from his red face.

"You're probably right about that, Janice.''

Bill disappeared inside, then poked his head out.

"Back in fifteen,'' he called.

She waved to him, then stepped slowly across the mats on

74

the floor, over two dumbbells that clanked when she accidentally hit against them. Ropes were suspended from a rafter, and there was a kind of machine to sit in and row simultaneously.

Dr. Geddes came down in his jogging shorts and a blue-striped jacket. He seemed surprised to see her.

"I guess I shouldn't be here," Janice said.

"Well, in your case, we'll bend the rules," he said, smiling broadly, coming closer. "What do you think? I mean, about Bill?"

"It's wonderful. You've done miracles. I can't believe the changes."

"Well, he's got a tremendous desire to get back together. And this physical exercise improves concentration, promotes self-confidence."

Janice stepped closer to Dr. Geddes. He caught the changed expression and listened closely.

"Bill telephoned last Friday," she said. "He wants to come home. For a night or two."

"I know. Is that all right with you?"

"I would like that," she said, flushing slightly, "but I wasn't sure it was a good idea for him to leave."

Dr. Geddes considered for a moment.

"I think it should be tried," he said. "Bill wants to leave, and I'd like to promote that. Gradually. He's still a little dislocated."

"I just wanted to hear you say that, I guess."

Bill came from the far end of the makeshift gymnasium carrying his favorite sweater, a thin gray pullover that had holes under both arms and was unraveled in five places at the bottom.

"Are you two conspiring against me?" he asked genially.

Dr. Geddes opened his mouth to answer but Janice cut him off, saying, "We were just saying that you look so fine."

Bill laughed, but it was a trifle forced, his eyes narrowed suspiciously.

"Come on," he said, taking Janice's arm. "Don't keep staring at me. I've got a whole picnic planned."

"A picnic?" Janice said, surprised and delighted.

Together, Janice and Bill went to his room, where Bill picked up a wicker basket heavy with wrapped sandwiches and a bottle of red wine, plates, and printed napkins. Bill stuffed in his blanket. Janice watched Bill working feverishly, pathetically determined to show her a good time.

He escorted her from the clinic and out to the grounds. They slipped under the wooden fence and walked up the long, hard meadow toward the crest of the hill, holding hands. A bitter wind blew into their faces; Janice wrapped her sweater around her throat, but Bill faced the dark, rolling clouds with only a white shirt, his sweater tucked into his belt, until they crested the hill.

Down below, Ossining was tucked into a series of hollows, dull gray trucks groveling up narrow roads, and a bank of century-old warehouses beyond a clump of nearly denuded trees.

Bill's hand reached for hers and squeezed slowly, sadly. He smiled—a smile of deep, bitter resignation. He pulled her down slowly onto the blanket he had spread under two intertwined oak trees, shielded from the wind. They looked back down the brittle stalks of dead grass to where the clinic occupied a flat space beyond the fences.

"I love you, Janice," Bill whispered, and kissed her gently on the lips.

"And I love you, Bill."

Janice caressed his forehead, and, to her surprise, it was beaded with perspiration despite the chill wind. Bill leaned forward suddenly and began unpacking the wicker basket.

"I'm starving," he exclaimed. "You must be famished. Hey—I forgot the silverware. No, here it is! Good old Bill—finally wired together."

"Beaujolais!" Janice exclaimed. "Where did you get this?"

"Geddes," Bill said, brightening. "He got it for me in Ossining. Great man, Geddes."

"Delicious!" she said, biting into a chicken sandwich.

Janice poured the Beaujolais into two metal cups. They drank slowly, looking into one another's eyes.

Then Bill poured another cup. He held it up to make a toast.

"I was going to say—to Ivy," he said uncertainly, "but, well, to our next Ivy—whoever she is—or he is."

"To us, Bill. To you and to me and to our being together all over again."

The second cup warmed them more than the first. Bill replenished the cups, and soon the wind blew in vain against the oak trees. The rain fell in long slants far away over the town, almost as though a hand of God had torn the underbelly of a ragged blue cloud and it dragged downward, releasing its pent-up tons of water.

"I feel a little nervous," Bill confessed. "Sometimes I know I say things a little abruptly. You have to forgive me."

"Of course I do, darling."

"Thank you, Janice. If you only knew what I've been through, where I've been down deep inside. Hey, did you bring me any books?"

"Of course," Janice said, crawling toward her bag. "I'd almost forgotten. I brought you a whole library."

Janice reached in and dumped a handful of volumes beside her plate. Bill picked up several. He examined the titles.

"Twelfth Night?" he asked.

"It's Shakespeare. It's about the varieties of love."

"Sounds good and racy. What's this? *Sonnets from the Portuguese?"*

"Elizabeth Barrett Browning."

Bill laughed.

"You always were trying to get me to like her. What about that blue one?"

"Where?"

"By the picnic basket."

Janice hesitated. Slowly she picked it up, opened a few pages. Then she closed it again.

"Maybe I shouldn't have brought this one," she said.

"Why not?"

Janice hesitated once more, then leaned closer to Bill.

"It was given to me by—" she began.

"Please," he said. "Just read."

Searching for the most comprehensible passage, Janice paged backward and forward through the thin volume. At last, and with misgivings, she began.

" 'If someone were to strike at the root of a large tree, it would bleed sap, but live. If he were to strike at its trunk, it would bleed sap, but live. If he were to strike at the topmost leaves, it would bleed sap, but live. Pervaded by the living substance, the tree would stand firm, drinking nourishment from the earth and the sun. Therefore, know this, that the body withers and yet the substance never dies.' "

Bill smiled.

"That's like old what's-his-name. John Keats. All that sentimental garbage. Read me some more."

Bill closed his eyes, folded his arms behind his neck, and listened. Warming to her role, Janice read on with more expression, a soothing, almost maternal voice.

" 'Of what is not,' " she read, " 'there is no coming to be. Nor is there destruction of what is. Know, therefore, that all is indestructible, and pervaded by the imperishable.' "

Bill laughed gleefully.

"What wonderful bilge," he chortled. "Go on, Janice. Let me dream away."

"Are you sure?" she asked.

"It all sounds like bilge to me. But it sounds good. Go on."

Paging ahead, Janice continued. " 'Bodies come to an end, Yet the eternal embodied soul of the universe, Is indestructible and unfathomable, Unborn, eternal, everlasting, that ancient soul, That is not slain when the body is slain.' ''

Janice stopped reading. Bill's silence unnerved her. She regretted having brought the book, and, having brought it, she regretted reading it now.

"You got that from those loonies in the orange robes, didn't you?" he asked.

"Yes," Janice lied.

"Well, I'm not afraid of them. Go on."

"Bill, I'm terribly sorry. It was a bad mistake—"

"I said, read on. It's only words."

"Bill, are you really sure you want me to?" she asked plaintively.

"Sure. What the hell, Janice. I've learned a lot these last few weeks. I've learned it's better to be alive than dead. It's better to look up than down. So go ahead. I'm not afraid."

Janice bit her lip, then gave in, and paged ahead to another section. She nestled in against Bill's side, feeling his warmth and the expansion of his breathing. He moved and slid his left arm over her shoulder, still looking dreamily at the sky.

" 'Just as death is certain to one that is born, So birth is certain for one that has died. Therefore, the thing being unavoidable, One should not mourn."

She stopped.

"What's wrong?" Bill asked.

"I don't feel like reading anymore."

"I thought you believed in all that stuff."

"It doesn't mean the same now," Janice said, closing the book. "It makes me feel all—I don't know, afraid inside."

Bill turned to her.

"That's all right, honey," he said. "I know what you mean. Maybe we've had too much of all this gobbledygook. Why don't we go back inside before the rain comes?"

"All right," she said, trying to smile.

He kissed his finger and put the finger on her lips. She

smiled, though she looked suddenly pale, and then the wind rushed into the trees, shaking down twirling trails of dead oak leaves.

Bill sprang to his feet.

"Here it comes!" he yelled. "Just throw it all in the blanket!"

Janice tossed the books and a fallen wine cup into the center of the blanket. Bill pulled the four corners together, and, like a hobo, slung it over his shoulder and grabbed her hand.

"Come on!" he shouted.

A dull, roaring boom echoed over the distant flatlands, and instantly the air grew even cooler, turned direction, and before they were halfway through the meadow the rain hit them like a cold wall. Laughing, hair bedraggled and matted, they dashed into the lobby, trailing water over the carpets.

Bill embraced her and the contents of the blanket spilled over the floor, knocked a potted palm against the window.

"Next Friday," he whispered hoarsely. "I'll come home next Friday."

"For a day or two, Bill," Janice cautioned. "Dr. Geddes said—"

"I know, I know. He's right, of course. Oh, Janice, buy us some of that awful orange liqueur we like. You know, from Belgium. And get some flowers."

"I will, I will."

They kissed again, and a massive roar of thunder rattled the windows.

Janice rode home on the late afternoon train. The rain had given her a slight chill. At Des Artistes she took two aspirins, a hot bath, and lay in the suds, luxuriating. She thought again and again about Bill, and his body, and his eagerness, and she thought it would drive her insane.

She removed the aquarium from Ivy's room. Outside, the rain lashed at New York, a peculiar blue rain that seemed to shed its darkness over the rooftops. If there were no children, she thought, Bill could use the room as a study. That aspect of it was still undecided in her mind. It still seemed a profanation to think of other children in Ivy's room, and she closed the door quietly behind her as she left.

The next day Elaine beckoned for Janice to follow her into the large office studded with Elaine's designs, calendars, and sketches for future projects.

"You don't have the experience a lot of designers have," Elaine said. "And maybe you're a bit rusty on a few graphic techniques. But we get along awfully well, wouldn't you agree?"

"Yes," Janice agreed, her heart beginning to race.

"Then would you consider working here full time?"

"Would I? Oh, I'd love nothing better."

"Now, I can't pay you very much, but it would be a salary. You wouldn't have to start worrying at the end of every project."

Janice drew herself up proudly.

"Elaine," she said, "there's nothing in the world I'd rather do than work with you."

Elaine laughed delightedly. "Splendid."

At lunch, Elaine and Janice worked out the details of her job. Janice listened with a kind of rapture she had not known since the days when she first met Bill.

"And your husband?" Elaine asked after a while.

"What? What about my husband?"

"Is he going to mind your working full time?"

"No. He'll be delighted."

Elaine smiled enigmatically.

"You've never talked about your husband," she said. "All I'm trying to do is to be fair about it. For some women, it becomes a problem."

"I really and truly appreciate what you're saying, Elaine, but I'm sure Bill will be very, very pleased. And the money will help."

Elaine watched Janice growing slightly uncomfortable.

"You've never mentioned what your husband does," she said.

"He worked for Simmons Advertising. He was the third vice-president. But he's not been well. He suffered a nervous breakdown, and is hospitalized."

"I'm sorry," Elaine said. "I didn't mean to pry."

"That's all right," Janice assured her. "It's been a long haul, but he's much improved now."

Janice splurged recklessly and treated herself to a new raincoat, designed by Bill Blass, with a cape that extended out over her shoulders and left the arms free. The October chill was in the air, and the driving rain everywhere glimmered in the gloom, catching stray headlights beaming like lurid eyes out of the gutters.

That night Bill telephoned.

"Honey," he said, "guess what? I've got a fever of a hundred and two degrees. Courtesy of that damned picnic."

"Oh, Bill, what a shame."

"The clinic doctor has been tapping on my chest and feeding me big yellow pills and I can't stop throwing up."

"Oh, Bill!"

Bill moved from the receiver to cough. It was a long, hacking cough that sounded painful.

"To make a long story short," he said, a bit out of breath, "I won't be there on Friday unless I can shake this."

Janice sank down in her chair, the weight of disappointment nearly a physical sensation.

"It's probably because you'd exercised that day," she said.

"Yeah, you're probably right. I loved seeing you again. And thanks for the books. I really mean that."

Janice, staring, brooding at the black windows, watched the long dribbles of gleaming water-drops, each trailing a splattered light out of the void.

"Although, if you stop to think about it," Bill continued, "it doesn't all add up."

"What? What doesn't?"

"That stuff you read to me. From the *Bhagavad Gita*, wasn't it?"

"I don't remember."

"Well, it doesn't quite add up."

Janice licked her lips. She sat up, partially out of the chair, on its edge, and held the receiver carefully.

"I don't know what you're talking about," she said.

"Look. All that twaddle about the eternal soul going on and on, and all that. Even when the body dies."

Janice closed her eyes. For a split second, a headache threatened to form, then it receded, more by an act of will than anything else. She almost wanted to hang up.

"Bill, I really don't like talking about it."

"There's nothing to talk about," he complained. "It's loony. If there's one great eternal soul, like a universal spirit, then what the hell happened to Ivy? Know what I mean? It could all have just flowed back, or whatever. Instead of that conflict—"

"Bill, please, I beg you—"

"I mean," he added in a softer voice, "she sure as hell didn't have to go through what she did. Christ, when I remember how she suffered—"

"Bill!" Janice yelled.

"What? What are you yelling for?"

"I'm sorry. I'm not yelling. I only was trying to say that—that it's still not easy for me—to remember."

There was a long silence.

"Frankly," Bill said, "I'm surprised. You had a lot of time to work it out. More than I had, that's for damn sure."

"Yes, but it's all so distant, so confused, I mean. Bill, I can't think about it anymore. I tried. I tried for the longest time and never made sense."

83

"Okay, okay," Bill conceded. "I shouldn't have said anything. This fever's baked my brain anyway. But you got to admit that the *Bhagavad Gita* is a little naive after what happened to us."

"All right, Bill. I'll admit it. But tell me about your chest. You sound absolutely dreadful."

"I always did have weak lungs. I think I'm out of commission for a while. Listen, honey, could you do me a favor?"

Janice smiled, tucked her feet up under her as she sat back into the soft folds of the chair.

"Anything, darling," she said.

"This library here is pretty puny. All they've got are some encyclopedias and the *Guinness Book of Records*. Could you make a run to the library for me?"

"Sure. I'd love to."

Holding the receiver against her collarbone with her chin, she reached into a drawer and coaxed a pencil and a note pad from it.

"What kind of books would you like?" she asked.

"Well, as I said, this Hindu stuff is pretty weak dishwater, from what I can gather. Now listen closely. There's an older religion. It's called Jainism. It goes back to even before the Hindus knew how to cross their legs and scratch themselves."

Janice put the pencil and pad down on her lap.

"Bill," she whispered. "Don't—"

"Jainism," Bill said. "You want me to spell that?"

"No, it's not necessary."

"Great. I really need this help on the outside. Right now, I feel like somebody pumped up a balloon inside my head. Are you there, Janice?"

"I'm here."

"Okay. And if I'm not up to seeing you next week, just mail the books here, will you?"

"Yes," she said without enthusiasm.

"Wonderful. Now take care of yourself. Keep warm. It's really miserable all over the East Coast tonight."

"I will," she said dully. "And Bill—"

"Yes?"

"Be careful. And get your rest. Do what Dr. Geddes says."

Bill chuckled, a familiar, warm kind of laugh that came from deep within his throat.

"I'll be a model patient, sweetheart," he said. "I love you. Now be a good girl and we'll be together soon. I promise."

She sensed he was about to hang up. There was so much more she wanted to say, to warn him in some obscure way, but none of it came to her.

"I love you, too," she said softly. "Good-bye, darling."

He hung up. Janice wrote the word *Jainism* on the pad, tore off the top sheet, and stuffed it into her purse. She threw the pad and pencil back into the drawer and slammed it shut. Outside, the night seemed to belch forth a cold, hard rain from its blackest interior.

Janice put off her trip to the library as long as possible. Finally, she went to the New York Public Library, asked for assistance, and found that the Jains occupied so small a segment of religious thought that they hardly merited a single book to themselves. With the librarian's help, Janice plucked three volumes which seemed to have the most information, and she checked them out.

The books hung together on a shelf in the kitchen, casting a small, gloomy shadow when the light was on. When the light was off, they melded into the general darkness.

When she saw him next, Bill was dressed in his robe; a tray of orange juice, several small bottles of capsules, and several discarded magazines were at his side. He looked impatient when she came into the room.

"Did you bring the books?" he asked, his eyes slightly bright, as though the fever which had wracked his body for several days had not entirely dissipated.

"Right here," Janice said, drawing them from her purse. "Aren't you even going to say hello?"

"I'm sorry," Bill said, grinning. "You look just fabulous, Janice. I just ran out of reading material, lying here like King Tut. A guy could scream from boredom."

He took the books from her, casually flipped through them, and put them on the night table next to his pillow. He pulled her down and let her kiss him.

"I'm all right," he said. "Really, I am. They thought it had blossomed into a walking pneumonia, which is why they kept me here. But it was really a kind of bronchitis. That's all."

"Are you sure?" Janice asked. "I was so worried when you called."

"Positive. Could you open the window a half inch? A little fresh air would do wonders."

Janice went to the window. She heard him stretch over, and when she turned back, he was paging through the top book, his back to her.

"Thanks a lot, honey," he murmured. "These look just fine."

"If you really have to read them now . . ."

Bill turned and smiled guiltily.

"Poor Janice," he said. "You come all this way to watch your addled husband reading in bed. Come on. Let's mosey out of here."

Bill slipped from bed, modestly turned from her, and dressed. Janice was shocked to see how much weight he had lost. His hip bones almost protruded from his flat stomach. Even his legs looked thin. When he was dressed fully, he turned and escorted her from his room. First, however, he slipped the topmost book into his jacket pocket.

"Depressing little place, isn't it?" he confessed as they walked up the corridor. "I just can't wait to get out of here. Dr. Geddes means well, but— Here, let's duck into the library. At least it's comfortable in there."

Bill opened a door and they entered a large room containing long shelves of books, globes on stands, a few antique brass lamps, some geographer's maps on the walls, and tall, clean windows with maroon curtains.

"Pretty fancy, isn't it?" Bill said. "The clinic buys this stuff from auctions. All the one-room schoolhouses that are disappearing. Well, this is where they disappear to."

Bill turned away slightly from her, looking out the window, peering into the mist that rolled inward from the rain, blotting out the hill where he had caught his fever. There was a long silence. A dark horse, more silhouette than substance, walked slowly out of the mist, like a harbinger from a mysterious landscape.

Turning back to Janice, Bill studied her curiously.

"What have you got in your handbag?"

"What do you mean?"

"Come on. I see something with ribbon on it."

Janice smiled, then reached down to her purse and pulled out a glass jar. Inside were round, milky-white balls. Janice held out the jar to him, enjoying his puzzled expression.

"Go on, coward," she insisted. "Try one."

"They look like marbles."

Frowning, Bill unscrewed the lid, reached in, and popped a candy into his mouth. Nothing happened, so he bit into it. Suddenly, his expression changed.

"Holy shit," he marveled.

"They're filled with Calvados cognac," Janice said. "Aren't they great?"

Bill helped himself to another.

"Crazy. Where'd you find them?"

"From Elaine Romine."

"Yeah? Well, thank her for me. Jesus, I haven't had strong stuff since . . . since . . . since the trial. No, in New York . . . I don't remember."

Bill bit into another candy, savoring the hot, stinging sensation of delicate apple cognac. Janice guessed now that he remembered everything that had ever happened, and it broke some barrier between them. Possibly the last barrier, she thought hopefully.

As they calmly ate, two more horses came out of the mist, rubbing shoulders, gazing quizzically into the library windows.

Janice leaned back into the extraordinary comfort of the dark red chair, watching the horses, absorbing the tranquility of the ceaselessly moving yet ever-unchanging mist out over the meadow. There was really no sense of time at all, like the rainy days on Sunday afternoons when all motion at Des Artistes stopped, and the floor was littered with the *New York Times,* and the breakfast dishes were still on the dining room table. Bill caught her looking fondly at him, wistfully.

"Do you remember how it was at home? Sunday afternoons? We'd just all sort of lounge around, listening to the rain? Sometimes Ivy would go play with Bettina. And we'd make love . . . before a crackling fire. God, how beautiful it was."

Janice nodded, startled by the coincidence of their thoughts.

"Hard to believe, isn't it?" Bill asked reflectively. "But she's gone. Our Ivy."

Janice watched him. There were no signs of agitation on his face, only a tired and bittersweet resignation. Bill reached out to the window and traced a heart with his finger. He put an arrow through the heart and then the initials *I.T.* and *B.T.* He winked at Janice.

"Remember?" he whispered. "She used to put those on the windows. Ivy Templeton loves Bill Templeton. I'll never forget."

Janice squeezed his hand warmly as they sat in the two heavy chairs, listening to the calm, steady drizzle outside. Janice felt the drowsy atmosphere taking hold of her. She sighed and closed her eyes. When she opened them again, Bill was browsing through the book on Jainism.

"It says here that a seal was found dating back to at least fifteen hundred B.C.," Bill said. "On it is a cross-legged figure wearing a horned headdress, three faces, and surrounded by jungle animals. It's a proto-Yoga figure."

"Bill," Janice said, trying to smile and keep her voice calm, "what is this sudden interest in all this?"

"No sudden interest. It just seems weird."

Janice turned away to look out the window. The heart with the initials had melted downward into a grotesque, slumped form. Janice wiped out the lines with the palm of her hand.

"Listen to this, Janice," Bill insisted. "Jainism goes back before the Hindus. To a non-Aryan antiquity, that predated the sacred writings."

"Bill, please. I'm really not interested."

"All right. Sorry. Let's just look out the window and count raindrops."

"Why are you angry? I just said—"

"Right. You did say that. Well, maybe you're right. Why should you care? All this garbage."

For an instant, Janice could only watch the strange expression on his flushed face, a mixture of determination and confusion. He put the book under his right thigh, as if to guard against anyone's taking it away.

"I don't feel too well," Bill said softly. "I think it's the fever."

"You look a bit flushed. Maybe we should get you back in bed."

Together they walked out of the library, down to Bill's room, which had been made up in their absence, and Bill undressed and slipped under the covers, clutching his book. Janice knew by the warmth of his forehead that he was running a high fever again. His cheeks were flushed.

Bill took her hand and kissed it.

"Was I sharp with you?" he asked softly. "I didn't mean to be."

"No. No, Bill, you weren't. But I think you'd better close your eyes now. You don't look at all well."

"Kiss me, Janice."

She kissed him on his closed eyes. As she left, she saw him wave weakly to her. She knew that as soon as she closed the door behind her, he would start reading again.

She found Dr. Geddes sipping coffee in the clinic dining hall. He looked up from a journal, sensing her footsteps. Immediately, he pulled aside a second red metal chair for her. As she sat down, his smile faded.

"Dr. Geddes," Janice said, "are you aware that Bill has developed a fixation about certain subjects?"

"No. Frankly, I was not aware. What kind of subjects?"

"Well, at first it was the poetry you had him read. Keats. It was innocuous enough. Then he passed on to Eastern verses—"

"What Eastern verses?"

Janice blushed.

"I brought him a stack of books, as you suggested. About consolation and endurance. One of them was a collection from the *Bhagavad Gita.*"

Dr. Geddes frowned, slid his journal away from his coffee mug, and lit a cigarette.

"The *Bhagavad Gita,*" Dr. Geddes said. "That's the sacred writings of the Hindus. What's wrong with that?"

"He keeps rereading it."

"He's probably read Keats again, too. It's just what any man would do who's coming out of an experience like Bill's."

"Then I'm not getting through to you," she protested. "He's not only memorized half of it, he told me to bring him some more."

"On Hinduism?"

"A sect called the Jains."

Dr. Geddes shrugged, then scratched his head.

"I frankly don't know what to make of it," he admitted, "only it doesn't seem like something to worry about."

"How can you say that?" Janice spluttered. "Bill never cared for that sort of thing. In fact, it made him sick!"

"I'll tell you quite frankly what I think," Dr. Geddes said thoughtfully, "but you'll have to calm down first."

"All right," Janice conceded. "I'm sorry if I—"

"The reason that Bill broke down and you didn't," Dr. Geddes said, "was that you had support. Whether you really believed in these religious ideas—"

"I don't know what I believed. I was too confused."

"Please let me finish. During the trial, and in the hospital, you gave at least partial credence to a viewpoint that allowed you to accept what in fact finally happened. Do you follow? And after, as you explained to me, you attended several services—Buddhist or whatever—which amplified that support. Bill had nothing. He just cracked open like an eggshell and fell to pieces. Now he wants some support, too."

"So that's why he's reading all this?"

"I'll bet my state license on it. You were helped over a rough spell. Now he wants the same help. It worked with you. Why shouldn't it work with Bill?"

Janice stared out of the cafeteria window.

"There's a second reason why you shouldn't worry," Dr. Geddes continued. "Bill needs to develop his thinking muscles. His memory. Actually, I'm very glad to see him develop an outside interest."

Janice said nothing.

"If Bill seems a little edgy on the subject," he said, "it's because he's trying so desperately hard to organize his thinking. You see what I mean? His mind is still fragile."

"Maybe I jumped the gun," she said. "I'm probably the edgy one."

Dr. Geddes laughed, but added seriously, "I think you've hit the nail on the head."

She smiled, embarrassed, all defenses melted away.

Chapter Five

At 9:30 the following night, Bill telephoned.

"Hello, darling," he said brightly.

"Bill?" Janice questioned worrriedly. "Are you feeling all right?"

"A bit better. They've given me some antibiotics, so I'm still woozy from it. How are you?"

"Dragging. It's so miserable being here alone. The weather is creepy. As long as you asked."

Bill laughed pleasantly. "New York has a patent on gloom sometimes, doesn't it? Listen, I have a small favor to ask of you."

"What's that?"

"Could you get some more books for me?"

Janice paused. For a while she wanted not even to answer.

"The same kind of books?" she finally asked.

"Well, not exactly," Bill conceded. "Let me explain. The Jains do not believe in God, at least not as you and I were taught. They don't even believe in a universal soul. According to them, there is a countless number of souls, all—"

"Bill, darling, I don't mean to be unresponsive, but..."

"But what?"

"It—it just gives me the creeps, somehow. Being here alone. In this apartment. Hearing about what you're talking about."

There was a pause at the other end. She heard him sigh, though whether in resignation or anger, she did not know.

"Look, Janice," he said in a voice slightly strained. "I'm trying to explain that there's nothing creepy about it. Didn't I just say they don't believe in a universal soul and all that malarky?"

"Yes. All right, Bill. You did say that."

"It's a very old sect. According to them, everything has a soul. Rocks, trees, people, animals. And the whole universe goes through these incredible long cycles—"

"Bill, please."

"And each soul in it, according to the cycle, transmigrates; that is, it moves on to another animal, or tree or person, and—"

Janice pulled the receiver away from her ear.

"Are you there, Janice?" Bill demanded.

"Yes. I'm here."

"So this doesn't hold water at all," Bill explained feverishly. "Aren't you listening at all? Have you gone deaf?"

"Bill, you're so angry. Why?"

"I'm sorry. I'm just trying to explain a few very simple facts. Now, if that girl—you know—the daughter of..."

"Audrey Rose."

"If she—I mean, if there was a problem, she could have come back as a rock. Or a television set. Or a pair of spectacles. Who the hell knows? You get what I mean? Well, we know *that's* not true."

Janice paused a long time, trying to think of a way of

luring Bill to some other topic of conversation. But he pursued his line of questioning relentlessly, almost as though he were talking to himself.

"If there *was* a question of her returning in our Ivy— I guess I'm not being clear. I'm just trying to say that, good as these Jains are, it's not right, Janice. It doesn't explain anything!"

Bill's last words were shouted in hysterical anger and frustration.

"Calm down, Bill," Janice said. "Nothing has to explain anything."

"I need to know, Janice! I can't live like this!"

It was a heartbreaking voice, vulnerable and barely articulate, conscious of its own weakness, of grappling with things it might never truly understand. Bill was clutching, and he expected Janice to pull him up out of the quicksand.

"All right, Bill," she said quietly. "Tell me what you want me to bring you."

"Well, there's an even older religion. It exists in the mountains of Tibet."

"Tibet?"

"Yeah. It's a part of Buddhism now, but it goes back to the time when human beings first learned how to talk."

"All right. If that's what you need. Just Tibetan Buddhism?"

"Yeah," Bill said, already cooling off. "I'd—I'd really appreciate that, Janice."

"Bill."

"What is it, honey?"

"Does Dr. Geddes know you're reading all this sort of thing?"

"Dr. Geddes? Why should he know? I mean, sure, he knows everything I do. That doesn't mean I have to go tell him every time I pee, does it?"

"No, I suppose not."

"Then you'll get me a few books? I wouldn't ask you,

Janice, except that I've got nobody in the whole world. Nobody else in the world out there.''

Janice softened.

''I do truly understand, darling,'' she said softly. ''And I'm glad you're feeling better. Get your rest and I'll do as you ask.''

''Thanks, darling. I knew I could depend on you.''

After hanging up, Janice stared into the apartment, listening to the cold wind throwing itself at the long windows. Jainism, Hinduism, and now what? Northern Buddhism. Mountain style. It was all so sad, Janice thought. Bill was so confused, so fanatically looking for explanations, for expedients. It did not seem right to her. It had made her calm, once, after Ivy's death, and now the same ideas were agitating Bill.

Maybe he was just having trouble getting a grip on the concepts. Maybe he was fighting it. Maybe, after roaming the world's religions for solace, he would circle right back around and find comfort in the eternal grace and benediction of Jesus Christ. Janice sat for a very long time, listening to the wind. Poor Bill, she kept thinking, over and over again. But for the first time, she felt she was an accomplice on his road. To recovery, she hoped, and not simply watching him through an invisible partition while he struggled for sanity.

She set the alarm, determined to be at the New York Public Library when it opened. If there was such a thing as Northern Buddhism, if even only one hairless old monk with one tooth was still alive and practiced it, she would find out about it and bring it to Bill. It was their way of communication now. He need never know that it ripped open seams in her memory that were unendurable.

That night, during a troubled sleep, the past came back to assail her with a vengeance.

The voice suddenly rose to a shriek, reverberating, piercing all the corridors into Janice's ears. She covered them with her hands and heard, through the screams, the rush of blood and the pounding of her own heart.

"Daddydaddydaddydaddydaddydaddyhothothothot!!"

Rebounding, filling the hall with madness and terror, lashing out at Janice with shattering impact, Ivy rushed to the stairs. Her face was hideously distended, and deep red.

"HOTHOTHOTHOTHOTHOTHOTHOT" she sobbed, the words running together into a single blast of pain.

"Oh God! No!" Janice pleaded.

But the force of the girl was uncanny. Ivy ripped from her grasp, fell headlong down the stairs, and bolted, bleeding, across the living room.

"Ivy—!" Janice wept.

"HOTHOTHOTHOTHOTHOTHOTHOT" came the scream, further away now, as Ivy threw herself at the long, dark windows, frosted, glinting with the cold. Again and again, she beat her bandaged hands at the cold glass, looking for escape, until the blood dappled the patterns of the windows.

"Daddydaddydaddydaddydaddy—" she shrieked.

But Bill was gone, escaped to Hawaii, and the screams escalated into a single, incoherent, note of hysterical terror. From far away, as in a dream, Janice was conscious of the red light blinking on the house telephone, and without sensing her own feet, found herself picking up the receiver.

"Miz Templeton," Dominick's voice said. "There's a Mr. Hoover down here in the lobby."

"Send him up!" Janice cried, dropping the phone.

When Hoover arrived, she opened the door. Immediately he sensed the situation. He walked slowly into the apartment, unsure of his steps in the darkness. His tall, athletic body seemed to bend forward as though ready for anything. His thinning, blond hair gleamed in the light from above. Janice, fascinated, saw his pale blue eyes narrow, concentrating on the image of the whirling bundle of cloth, flesh, hair, and panic across the room.

"Audrey Rose!" he called. "It's Daddy! I'm here!"

"DADDYDADDYDADDYDADDY!!"

"HERE, AUDREY ROSE! DADDY IS HERE, DARLING!"

Slowly, as he called her by that name, that name that was now as much a part of the apartment as anything else, Hoover stepped carefully toward the dark windows. Over and over he called to her, until she heard. Lips quivering, she looked blindly for the sound.

"Here, darling," he whispered, *"I'm here! It's Daddy!"*

Exhausted, looking for him, touching his coat as he came within reach, Ivy seemed unable to believe it. Then she scampered into his arms, sobbing against his chest. Hoover rocked her back and forth. Janice stepped slowly through the quiet apartment. All she heard was Ivy's gentle, rhythmic breathing.

Hoover lifted up Ivy's arm and softly redressed the burnt hand. Then he washed her forehead, caressed her cheek, and carried her up to her bedroom. Janice followed in a daze. For a long time, he stood there, looking down at Ivy. The room was dark, and quiet, and Janice suddenly felt the aftershock of the violence. She sat down abruptly on the bed.

"Don't you see what we're dealing with here?" he asked, his eyes avoiding hers. *"We're dealing with something far greater than Ivy's physical welfare. We're dealing with her soul, the selfsame soul of my daughter, Audrey Rose. That's what we must help and try to save."*

A peculiar buzz ran through Janice's head, as though she had not slept for a week. All she wanted was for him to stop talking.

"It's a soul in such pain and torment that it will push Ivy back to that moment of death, back to the fire and smoke, if we don't help . . ."

Shut it out, her brain screamed. Don't listen!

"I—I don't know what you're saying," she managed to blurt.

. . . . ked at her.

"I'm saying that Audrey Rose came back too soon," he said simply. *"Out of fear, horror, she returned too soon, and now seeks to escape this earth-life. This is the meaning of Ivy's nightmares."*

"No!" she shouted. *"You're crazy. My husband says you belong in the nuthouse and he's right!"*

Hoover's jaw clenched. Mastering himself, he swallowed and relaxed, but his eyes blinked rapidly as though humiliated that she still did not understand him.

"That's your fear talking, Mrs. Templeton," he whispered.

"No, damn it. It's me talking. Now get out of here!"

Hoover came suddenly closer, leaning over her, until his face was only inches from her, his breath warm and sweet. Janice looked into the depths of his pale blue eyes and found an intolerable gentleness there.

"Will you open your heart and try at least to understand what I've been saying?" he entreated.

"I don't know," she said, her voice weak. *"I don't know what you want of me."*

Hoover sensed contact with her. He smiled. His eyes became bright. The words poured out in a silver rush.

"We must form a bond, Mrs. Templeton, you and I, so filled with love that we can mend her, so that the soul of Audrey Rose can find its rest. We're the only ones who can help her. You and I."

Janice felt a hypnotic power in his voice, a lulling, tugging seductiveness that weakened her. Yet she felt secure with him; his presence meant Ivy was safe.

"Don't shut the door on me, Mrs. Templeton," he breathed. *"Allow me to come into your life. Allow me to serve you, and Ivy, and Audrey Rose. This is the meaning of my life. All those years of searching, hoping, doubting—"*

He drew Janice closer to him. He saw that her eyes now darted over his face, examining him for signs, clues, some symbol of what reality had become.

99

"Can you just throw me aside?" he whispered heatedly. *"Can you?"*

"No," Janice cried weakly, feeling the wet of her own tears on her face.

"Thank you," Hoover exhaled, grateful.

He stood up, and it seemed now that he possessed the bedroom, the apartment, and all that was in it, as well as the two living beings there. He looked back at Ivy, who turned comfortably in a pleasant sleep.

"We are connected," he said with finality. *"You and I, Mrs. Templeton. All three of us. We have come together by a miracle and now we are inseparable."*

He turned, a dark look suddenly flashing across his eyes.

"Say yes, Mrs. Templeton. Please!"

"Yes," Janice wept, and she felt that she was about to fall.

Early the next morning, drugged from lack of sleep, Janice trudged to the library, selected several Tibetan books, and mailed them to Bill, resolving to think no more about it.

That night Janice found herself working into the wee hours with Elaine, trying to complete two separate sets of layouts before the spring deadline.

Two Tensor lamps cast bright cones onto their adjacent work tables. The rest of the suite was lost in the night, where bits of red and yellow lights gleamed inward from the city skyscrapers.

Together they prepared the outlines and marked out instructions for the staff in the morning. Wearily, Janice stood, rubbed her eyes, and stretched, yawning with a deadly fatigue. It was 2:30 in the morning, but Janice didn't mind. She was gratified that Elaine depended on her professional collaboration in these all-night sessions.

"It is late," Elaine yawned. *"I'm sorry."*

"It's all right," she said. *"I'm in no rush to go home to an empty apartment!"*

100

They worked in silence for several minutes.

"But you do have a daughter?"

Janice licked her lips. A nightmarish, queasy sensation invaded her, as though this one moment of perfect friendship, this island of hard work and steady hopes, might also break apart.

"What makes you say that?" Janice asked.

"Do you remember when we worked on that series of sporting outfits for pre-teens? You drew those very well. In fact, I pointed that out, and you made some joke about an artist's eyes being different from a mother's. Do you remember?"

Janice said nothing. She turned away from Elaine and listened to the subterranean rumble of the city that never died, not even at 2:30 in the morning.

"Her name was Ivy," Janice said softly. "She died eight months ago. It was an accident."

There was a long space of silence. Then Elaine said softly, "I'm so very sorry to know that."

"I should have told you long ago," Janice said. "That's why Bill isn't home. It was Ivy's death that caused his breakdown."

"It's been difficult for you. I can tell."

Janice inhaled deeply.

"It was," Janice said slowly. "I've never told anybody just how horrible it really was."

In a slow, even voice, as though she had rehearsed it for months, Janice began to tell Elaine about what it was like when she first realized that a man was shadowing Ivy. What it was like watching Ivy bend and twist, scream, and suffocate with fear, not once, not twice, but many times, until there was no remembering when it all began. It was so hard to explain what it was like, seeing a presence—Hoover's— gradually insinuate itself into your apartment, your life, your child—into your own soul.

For hours she spoke, until the dawn spread its frigid, pale

glow through the slatted blinds, and Janice, hoarse from the ordeal, groped for her coffee cup.

Elaine, divining her need, pushed it across to her. "Of course. I remember it all. The papers were full of it." Then, in a small, amazed voice: "So you're *that* Templeton."

Janice's eyes lowered. "Yes, I'm *that* Templeton."

Elaine looked away, in a seeming quandary.

"All this Buddhist stuff, or Hindu," she said. "Did you actually believe it?"

"I believed one thing. My daughter was in serious trouble and Elliot Hoover was the only person who could get her out of it."

"It must have been painful testifying against your own husband, like that."

Janice smiled bitterly.

"I had no choice. I would have signed a pact with the devil."

"And now?"

"Now? Now, I try not to think about it. It's actually a lot of hard work sometimes, not thinking about it."

"That's why Bill just stopped thinking at all?"

Janice stood up. She looked out at the gray, cold dawn on the stone streets. For a long time, she just looked out.

"Elaine," she said slowly, "Bill has started to read Hindu tracts. Buddhist texts."

Elaine stared at her in surprise. Janice turned to look at her. "I don't know what to make of it. He's become so damned obsessive about it. I can't stand to be with him when he talks about it. But what can I do? Shut him up? Only a few weeks ago, he wasn't even speaking. I can't very well reject him now!"

"Maybe he needs to—to understand," Elaine offered. "Just wants to review what happened."

Janice raised her voice.

"But I don't want to hear about it!" she said. "I don't want to go through it again! It's like a madhouse, a thousand crooked mirrors screaming at you, each one of them saying Buddha, and Karma, and transmigration, making you hear it all over again, and I don't want to listen!''

Janice paused and lowered her voice.

"I can't go through it again, Elaine. To feel myself slipping into it like quicksand—astral planes and holy cycles— getting closer and closer to believing it. It's like going insane. Slowly, but surely. Just like going insane.''

Chapter Six

Janice skipped lunch that day. Instead, she lay down on the couch, closed her eyes, and sank into the oblivion of total fatigue. Just as dream images began to form, Elaine tapped her on the shoulder.

"Telephone," Elaine said. "Sounds official."

Janice rose quickly, swayed, caught herself, then walked calmly to her work desk. She picked up the receiver and pressed her exchange button.

"Hello?"

"Mrs. Templeton, Dr. Geddes here."

"Is everything all right?"

"I tried calling you at home, but there was no answer."

"What's the matter?"

"Let me say first that Bill's all right. Just a few scratches. There was a kind of altercation."

Janice sat down slowly. Elaine came in, saw the look on her face, and discreetly left again, closing the door.

"Altercation? Bill?"

"Yes, with another patient, named Borofsky. Apparently, Bill had inveigled him into doing some kind of research. Borofsky was connected to the bookstore at Gimbels, or something like that. They had a falling out, Borofsky came to his room, and Bill thought he was trying to steal his notes."

"Notes? What notes?"

Dr. Geddes started over again, more slowly.

"Bill's been studying. Studying a lot more than we'd guessed. Newspaper clippings. Old lectures he conned out of a library in Albany. Books—you name it. And I guess he was possessive about it, and when Borofsky came down, Bill hit him with an old brass lamp from the library. Borofsky seems to be all right. He's been X-rayed and there's no fracture."

"I can't believe Bill would do something like that."

"Mrs. Templeton, can you come to the clinic today?"

"Today? It would be very difficult."

"It's quite important. Bill's a bit delirious. He thinks we sent Borofsky to spy on him. You have to come and help us reestablish his trust. Before his attitude hardens."

"All right. I'll try."

When Janice explained things to Elaine, a visible disappointment surfaced on Elaine's face.

"You don't really have a choice, do you?"

"Believe me, I'd rather not, but—"

"Don't worry about it. I'll manage."

Janice caught the 12:45 northbound to Ossining. She slept the entire trip.

She stumbled wearily through the cascading rain, caught in the cone of the taxi headlights, entered the clinic, and found Bill in the infirmary. Three long red scratches trailed vividly down his face and he gazed blankly at the door where she stood.

"He's a bit sedated," Dr. Geddes whispered behind her, closing the door.

Janice walked quickly to the bed. Bill's face turned to follow her, but it was not his face. Something had taken over. His forehead was damp with perspiration and he looked warily around the room.

"Bill," she whispered, "can you hear me?"

"Of course I can hear you, Janice," he said quickly. "Do I look dead?"

"But, darling . . . I don't understand. What happened?"

Bill laughed derisively. Dr. Geddes sauntered closer to the bed. It was a small infirmary, and the other two beds were still freshly made.

Bill turned away.

"Nobody knew you were taking those notes," Dr. Geddes said, as kindly as he could, "so how could we be spying on you?"

"The old man told you, of course."

"You know there's no covert supervision here, Bill."

"That's what you say, Geddes. I saw him in my room. I didn't invite him."

"But I don't understand," Janice persisted. "Why did you hit him?"

Bill whirled around, glaring at her, his eyes a lurid deep black, pinpoints of brightness flashing in the depths of the pupils.

"Because he had no business there!" he hissed.

"But what's so important about—"

"That's for me to say! Not you! Not Geddes! Just me!"

Dr. Geddes exchanged glances with Janice. Bill saw them looking at one another and withdrew into his pillow. One of the long scratches reopened and a thin trail of crimson dripped down onto the collar of his pajamas.

"Is he all right?" Bill asked, softer.

"Just a bad headache. No fracture."

"Well, he shouldn't have done it. It's his own goddamn fault."

"Bill, I want you to listen to Janice," Dr. Geddes said.

"You know when she lies and when she tells the truth. Will you do that for me? Just listen to somebody besides yourself for two minutes."

After staring at Bill, who lowered his eyes, Dr. Geddes walked slowly out of the infirmary. A nurse tried to come in, but Dr. Geddes blocked her way with an arm and closed the door firmly behind him. Janice gently tried to touch the bleeding line down Bill's cheek but he drew her hand away.

"What's gotten into you, Bill?" she asked heatedly.

"Nothing."

"Nothing? You practically killed an old man last night! Is that normal?"

"I just tapped him."

"Bill, listen to me. You do that again and they'll—they'll start giving you medicine, drugs. They'll give you electric shock."

Bill laughed.

"There's no shock machine here."

"Then they'll ship you someplace where there is! What do you think you're playing around with?"

Worried, Bill raised himself higher against his pillows. Janice leaned closer, her face nearly white with worry.

"Bill, listen to me," she whispered. "Whatever's going through your head now, throw it out, because if they transfer you to some other place, some place where they're used to violent cases— Jesus, Bill, you'll *never* see the light of day!"

She broke down crying, leaned against his chest. Over and over she said, "Don't you understand that, Bill? Never . . . Never . . . Never . . ."

Bill swallowed hard, and his hand gently held her around her shoulder. He squeezed softly.

"Okay, Janice," he whispered hoarsely. "I got the message."

Clumsily, he moved away from under her, struggled to the other edge of the bed, and sat up. He slipped into his trousers and pulled on a green checkered shirt.

"Where are you going?" she asked.

"Give me a hand, will you, honey? They shot me full of shit."

Janice ran to his side, lifted his arm over her shoulder, and eased him to a standing position.

"It's okay," he said. "I'm okay now. I can walk."

Gradually, he shuffled his way to the door. He paused and, with a gesture of his head, beckoned for her to open it.

"Come on," he whispered, "I've got something to show you."

Stumbling, Bill led her as quickly as he could, swaying into the side walls, holding his hands out as though feeling for invisible barriers, toward his room. Inside, it looked as though the fight had broken apart the bedroom walls. The edge of the desk tilted at a crazy angle. Books, chairs, pillows, and blankets were strewn violently over the floor, and everywhere were handfuls of paper, note cards, spiral-bound notebooks.

Janice stumbled forward, her shoes stepping on the paper. She bent down, picked up several sheets and tried to discern them in the dark. Bill's tight handwriting was illegible. But at the sides of the sheets were diagrams. The human body with dotted triangles emanating from the head, thorax, and groin.

"Bill, what is all this?"

"I've discovered things, Janice," he said. "It's time I told you about them."

"What kind of things?"

"Sit down. I have to go through these things in order. So you understand."

Janice felt for the bed, sat down slowly, still watching Bill. He was moving restlessly, and outside the rain now turned to sleet, grew so violent that it smashed into splinters around his head behind the glass, like a tortured halo.

"I've been studying for a long time, Janice," he said in that chilling, moody tone that sent shivers into her back. "I played dumb. But I was studying. Now I know too much."

He rubbed his mouth nervously and jumped at the sound of a truck passing slowly over the hill.

"I have to explain these things," he said quickly, "because then I have to ask you some things, Janice. So just listen."

"All right," she said gently. "I'm listening."

Bill licked his lips, then removed himself as far from her as he could, to the broken desk near the windows. His voice trailed coldly from him.

"It's because of Ivy, you know," he said, "that I started reading. Well, I found that this idea you and Hoover had—you know what I'm talking about—well, it all started before there were any Hindus. All of Hoover's ideas about the yogis and the river Ganges and reincarantion were half-baked. I know that now. That much is plain. Hoover was right about some things. But he was confused. He didn't get it *all* right!"

Bill began pacing and turning, back and forth, in front of the window.

"Now, if you look at this analytically," he said, "if you really pore over it day and night for as long as I have, you begin to discover a few things."

Bill paused, then straightened his back, as though in pain. His hand kneaded the back of his neck.

"Before there were any writings," he said softly, his voice oddly in rhythm with the swaying plants and undulating grass outside. "Before there were any temples and all that. There was a belief, by the people of the plains, that when you died, you passed into a heaven. But if you were really good, if you were successful, you could go up to the chief of the heavens, and there you could be with the father of all the gods, who was Yama. Now listen to me, Janice. It was called going up to the world of light. Light. You got to remember that. And if you passed upward into that light, you could unite in some way with Yama, and drink with the gods under leafy trees, and there was constant singing all around, and lutes played, and your body was young and vigorous, without imperfection or weakness. If you passed into the light."

Bill paused, savoring the recollection of what he had read. He imagined the picture, the metaphors of what he now repeated. Bill waited for a response.

"All right, Bill," Janice said. "The light."

"Yes. The light. Now that doesn't help us much with Ivy, does it? So I kept reading. And the prophets, after two thousand years, went deeper into death. And they put it differently."

Bill stared dreamily out of the window.

"The departed soul," he continued softly, "rises to the moon. If it passes on, it goes to the world of fire, and wind, and sky, and the gods. And it is dressed in exquisite robes and garlands, and perfumed with soft ointments. It goes to a lake and an ageless river, and crosses, and shakes off evil deeds. And it comes to a celestial city, Janice. A kind of palace with a long hall. A shining throne. Bathed in light. You see? *The light!* And when it sees the light, the body is truly dead, and the Creator God asks—he asks: 'Who are you?' "

Bill's voice trailed away. The dripping eaves made a steady sound behind him. Janice watched as his silhouette rubbed his eyes, but whether in fatigue or for tears, she could not tell.

"And you say something like—something that translates like—'I am real,' " Bill concluded. "It's like that, Janice. Are you listening?"

"I am. Of course I am."

"Good. Because if you don't pass on to that light, that shining light, you falter. You fumble. You find yourself back on the earth. And like a caterpillar that goes from one blade of grass to the next, you live all over again, trying to become a beautiful form. So you can pass into the light. The light of oblivion."

Bill slumped wearily, sitting against the windowsill. He breathed heavily, then smoothed his hair down with his right hand. He looked at Janice, his own face reduced to the two pinpoints of his eyes, gleaming softly at her.

"Well, that could help," he said gently. "That could lead

us somewhere. I mean, if you're really trying to understand what happened. Maybe somehow Ivy—I mean the earlier child, Audrey— There was a false continuation, but it doesn't quite make sense. Does it?''

"I—I don't know, Bill.''

"I mean, you accepted all that. What do you think now?''

"I'm prepared to believe that something like that might have happened,'' Janice said sincerely, faltering. "But the details—''

"Exactly, Janice. The details. The details will never make sense to people like us, will they? I mean, we believe in reason, in analyzing, as best we can, and then— But that's what I thought until— Now listen closely, Janice. Follow what I'm saying.''

Bill began pacing again, talking to the storm, yet listening, trying to sense Janice's responses. Then he picked up a long, heavy book from the floor and began slowly paging through it, looking for something, even while he spoke.

"Two things stuck in my mind,'' he said quietly. "First, Hoover said that Audrey Rose came back and there was only one reason. Why did she come back? She came back because her death was untimely. Isn't that it? What else was going on, it all happened because she was caught in that car. Dead before her time. And of all the books I read, all the incomprehensible poems and prayers and voodoo and parables and Christ knows what, nobody ever mentioned an untimely death. All the Hindus cared about, all the Jains cared about, all anybody cared about was what happened at the end of a long quiet life.''

Bill licked his lips. Evidently he had found his place. He peered down at the book, squinted, then backed against the window to catch some light from the low floodlights outside.

"So I had to keep looking. And then I found the Clear Light of Death,'' he whispered. "I found it in the *bardo t' odro*, the Book of Death.''

"What are you talking about, Bill?"

"Those books you gave me about Tibet. Things that Borofsky got for me. Did you know that for thousands of years the Tibetans were isolated from the rest of the world? That they perfected the science of death? I've read these verses over and over again, Janice, until I can recite them by heart! And I have to explain them to you because they make sense. They make sense the way nothing else in this evil-infested world ever did!"

Bill whipped the book upward to his chest, looking feverishly for his place. Janice found herself shivering. She unconsciously pulled the blanket from the top of the bed and gathered it around her.

"You see," he whispered, "the great fear of the Tibetans was an *untimely death*! So they analyzed the death process. They found that there is a point of no return, a sinking down past recovery. There is a feeling of being unable to maintain one's human form. A person panics. He feels as though he is falling. Dissolving. His bodily strength has slipped away. His cognition grows clouded."

Bill read directly from the volume in his hands. As he moved into the light from the driveway, Janice read the title: *The Tibetan Book of the Dead*.

"All right," Bill continued. "The next step. The warmth of the body fades. The eyes turn inward. The limbs tremble."

"Bill, please! I don't want to listen!"

"It's what happened to Ivy, isn't it? Listen, Janice. There's nothing to be afraid of. Afterward, the cognition inverts, turns into miragelike flashes, and things come unreal, just the reverse of being born: the blood slows; this is called 'the black path' because the heart is dying. It's the point of the worst panic. Vision is cut off. Memory dies. Breath is cut off. Now listen. 'The mind that rides upon the winds leaves the central channel.'"

Bill looked up, triumphant.

"Do you understand that? 'The mind that rides upon the wind'—the soul, Janice—'leaves the channel of the body.' Now follow what happens next!"

Janice, in spite of herself, was hypnotized by the rhythmic voice in front of her. Bill weaved slowly back and forth, his finger picking out phrases in the light of the rain and sleet behind him.

" 'Awareness,' " he read very slowly, " 'passes into the Clear Light of Death'!"

He looked up at her, frightened, yet gaining confidence when she offered no objection. He laughed hideously, uncertainly.

" 'The Clear Light of Death'! There it is! It's mentioned everywhere, but here it *is*! Analyzed! And if the soul can pass into the light of emptiness, without fear, if it reaches a firm communion with the emptiness—that is, Nirvana—then it has embraced bliss! There is no return, no more return. It's all oblivion . . . and peace . . ."

Slowly, as he spoke, Bill calmed down. The fire left his eyes. He became aware of the cold and shivered. The mania was gone.

"But if there is panic," he said with a dull finality, glazed, "if there is no acceptance, then there must be a return, another life . . . who knows, a hundred more lives. . . ."

Bill came forward, sat at the edge of the bed, and put his arm on Janice's shoulder. He was sweating, his shirt damp, his hair moist over his brows. He looked into her face.

"In an untimely death," he said simply, "there can be no acceptance."

Janice moved slightly back, but his hand firmly held her shoulder.

"Even for somebody trained all his life like a priest, it's almost impossibly difficult. But for somebody like Ivy—"

A hand went slowly to Janice's mouth. "Or *like Audrey Rose*!" she whispered hoarsely.

He nodded slowly. "Did Ivy have a chance to prepare for

death?" he asked simply. "No! It was too sudden. You saw what I saw, Janice. She was in a state of panic!"

Bill wearily stood. He seemed not to have the strength to move anymore. Dismally he watched the lessening rain, dripping with monotonous regularity in thin silver streaks at the window.

"Ivy could not have passed through," he said gently. "She could not have passed through into the radiance...dissolving...into a circle of pure light." Then, softly: "Hoover was wrong, Janice. Our daughter's soul is *not* at peace. She's back. *Ivy's come back.*"

Just then the main room light suddenly went on, hurting their eyes, and Dr. Geddes stood at the door. He studied them both for a few seconds.

"How are you feeling, Bill?" Dr. Geddes asked.

"Oh, better. Much better. Listen, I feel pretty rotten about what happened. I promise it won't happen again."

"I hope not, Bill. It really wasn't like you."

Dr. Geddes smiled awkwardly, sensing he had broken something between Janice and Bill, but not certain just what.

"Would you like me to call down to the gate for a taxi, Janice?"

"Yes, please—"

When Geddes left, there was a momentary impasse. Bill made a few desultory efforts at cleaning the debris from the floor. Janice joined him by carefully, timidly, scraping together the sheets and note cards into neat piles.

"I'm going to need your help," he whispered.

She stopped. "What kind of help?"

"I'll call you at home. Now just keep picking up these papers. I don't want Dr. Geddes to get wind of anything."

They worked in silence until she saw the headlights of a taxi moving up the driveway.

"It's the cab," she said. "I'd better go."

"Okay. Good. I won't call you tonight. They listen to your calls around here, no matter what they tell you. I'll find a way to call you in a couple of days."

They heard Dr. Geddes's footsteps coming. Janice stood up.

"I'd like to discuss your prescriptions," Dr. Geddes said. "I mean, with your wife. So she'll understand."

"Sure, doctor," Bill said, eager to restore a working relationship with Dr. Geddes. Janice embraced Bill. "I'll call you. I'll need your help," he whispered in her ear.

Then he separated from her and smiled broadly.

"Good night, darling," he said just a trifle loudly. "And thanks a million for coming down. I don't know what happened. I just—just flipped out—"

Dr. Geddes drew Janice discreetly off toward the lobby.

"This episode with Mr. Borofsky," he said uncertainly, "it worries me a great deal. I think you'll agree that a visit home is out of the question."

Janice said nothing. She turned slowly and looked casually over her shoulder at Bill through the open door of his room. He caught her looking at him and smiled.

"I think he knows he's in trouble," Dr. Geddes continued quickly. "I really can't countenance a departure from observation at this time. Do you disagree?"

The sudden cancellation of Bill's visit seemed to push the boulder back in front of Bill's tomb. Janice felt an overpowering sense of relief.

"No," she said, trying not to sound eager. "You're right." She hurried out of the building, over the slippery gravel, and into the taxi.

The train ride back into the city flashed by like a jagged nightmare, whispering voices, hissing insinuations, and the people waiting at the stations loomed like twisted piles of flesh, already decomposing.

Chapter Seven

During the next weeks, Bill telephoned almost daily. He wanted books. He read Janice the titles of pamphlets he needed. He wanted her to write letters to several authorities in New York, and to a psychiatrist in Berlin. Impatient for her replies, he began to call her at work.

He needed copies of articles from the encyclopedias of religion at the New York Public Library. Mailed special delivery to the clinic. When she visited him, he cross-examined her ruthlessly. He tried to trip her up to see if she had really made the telephone calls, really written the letters. Exhausted, she shoved the written replies in his face and he mumbled an apology.

Finally, at work, Bill called and demanded that during her lunch break she visit the Temple where Hoover had last been seen.

"I can't go there, Bill," she whispered into the telephone,

her fingers angrily toying with her paintbrush on the drafting table.

"Why the hell not?"

"It's where I went to the service for Ivy. I—I just don't want to go back there."

"I've got to know the answers!" he said loudly.

She held the receiver away from her ear.

"I'm sorry I yelled," he said. "Look, just a few questions. I'm going crazy here. Geddes won't let me out for another month."

"All right, Bill," she said, reaching for a pencil and note pad. "Read me your questions."

Bill slowly and distinctly read several technical questions. They involved the time delay in return of the soul. Whether time functioned in a different mode between death and the new life. Whether one could rely on earth clocks and calendars in computations.

"What do you mean, computations?" Janice asked warily.

"Never mind. Just go there. Ask the high priest or whatever he's called. And call me back when you've found out."

"Well, I can't go today."

There was a suspicious silence at the other end.

"Why not?"

"Because I've already had my lunch break and this will take at least an hour—"

"Then say you're sick."

"I won't say I'm sick, Bill. I'm not going to cut out of work for this."

"But you have to, Janice. I'm depending on you!"

"I'm happy to do the favor for you," she said, trying to hold her temper. "But I'm not going to risk my job!"

"All right. Don't get sore. Call me when you can."

He hung up without saying good-bye.

The next day, Janice gulped a sandwich while riding to Greenwich Village in a taxi. She remembered the Hompa

Hongwanji Temple all too well: the murmurs and chants, the smell of incense. She remembered a white-haired priest, called, simply, the Master.

The front of the Temple had been defaced by vandals, black spray paint over the door spelling out a code for the street gangs. Inside, several thin youths sat on a bench improbably donated by a neighboring church, and seemed to stare vacantly at where the altar should have been. Only there was no altar—simply a mass of flowers in white stone basins, sticks of burning incense and, nearly buried under the bright foliage, a faded color photograph of a yogi in cross-legged position.

It all seemed familiar, yet frightening. She clutched the list of questions in her hand.

"Excuse me," she whispered, disturbing the tranquility of a short, young man with rimless glasses. "Is the Master in?"

"He's in meditation."

"Will he be through soon?"

"Not likely. Can I help you?"

She smiled. "I had some questions—"

"Yes, of course. We all do. Do you want a cup of tea? We can talk about them on the bench at the back of the room."

"All right. Thank you."

From a low table he picked up a small pot of tea, poured it into two perpetually stained cups, and offered her one. He waited patiently.

Nervously, she referred to her list of questions.

"My, er, husband," she said, "would like to know some details about time. That is, time as it exists after death."

The youth smiled.

"Your husband sent you here instead of coming himself?"

"He's not well."

"I see. I'm sorry. Please, sit down."

They sat under a poster of the Taj Mahal, donated by the India Tourist Board. It too had faded in the sunlight from the windows, and the famous white walls looked surprisingly blue green.

"Time as it exists after death is the same as time during life. Time is like an enormous field on which the game of life is played. It does not change if a person dies."

Janice briefly noted the answer with a pencil. It was a peculiar sensation, asking the questions. Once she would have needed to know the answers. Now she was asking for Bill, and she tried to remain detached. Yet something deep within her listened hard to every nuance of the disciple's words.

"But if a person dies, the soul is on its own—" She faltered and began again. "If there is a time—I mean, space—between one life and the next—"

"An interval."

"Yes. An interval. Is that experienced as an infinity of time? Or measured in weeks, months, and years? Or is there no sensation of time at all?"

"It is not measured in weeks, months, and years, because there is no ego to measure. It is experienced as infinite: neither infinitely long nor infinitely short, simply an unbounded expression of the void; only temporal, not spatial."

Absolutely lost, Janice nevertheless dutifully copied down the answer.

"But if there is a return?"

"There is always a return," he said, smiling gently. "Unless the soul has reached the final extinguishing: Nirvana. And that happens very rarely."

"Yes, *when* there is a return to life"—the words echoed weirdly in Janice's ears, a kind of thrill of blasphemy to be saying them, horrifying, yet suddenly obsessive—"can you reckon the return in weeks, months, and years?"

"I'm afraid I don't understand."

"If a person dies on December the tenth, can you predict when the soul returns?"

The boy paused. His hand patted down on his head, where

the blond hair was thinning. He frowned. He seemed upset by Janice's question.

"I don't know," he said.

Surprised, Janice did not know how to respond. For a few seconds she thought he was going to walk abruptly away, his feelings hurt.

"You'd have to ask the Master," he said brusquely.

"When will he be free?"

"It varies. Usually about midafternoon."

"I see. But I have to go back to work."

"If you leave me your name, I'll present your question to him. If you come back tomorrow, I'll try to give you his answer."

"That's very kind of you."

She wrote down the question, along with several more from Bill. She even added one of her own. It was a fantasy she'd had from her own Catholic upbringing: Do the dead perceive, or even, in some way, "watch" events on earth? Janice felt silly writing it down; a child's question, and yet she was curious what the Temple taught on the subject. She promised to come back tomorrow, midafternoon.

When she returned to the studio, there were three telephone slips. Bill had called three times.

"You didn't get much out of them, did you?" he complained when she called him back.

"The Master was in meditation."

"Listen. Go back there and speak directly with the old man. Don't mess around with these small fry."

"He seemed a perfectly sweet and reasonable young man—"

"Was he American or Indian?"

"American."

"Forget him. He's some wipe-out from too much dope. Get hold of the horse's mouth."

"All right, Bill," she sighed.

Bill hung up, barely murmuring good-bye.

*　　*　　*

The next day, Janice grabbed a lunch at her work desk, and when 3:30 came around, slipped out to the Temple. This time the Master was sitting cross-legged among the flowers at the front of the room. He was evidently not meditating, because his eyes followed her as she hesitantly walked into the room, and he smiled politely.

He stood up and slowly, gracefully, pattered in his sandals to where she stood. With his white hair glistening, his skin looked darker by comparison, making his blue gray eyes almost transparent in contrast. He wore an orange robe draped loosely over his shoulder and tucked into itself at the waist.

"You are Mrs. Templeton?" he asked in a silvery-smooth voice.

"Yes. I was here yesterday."

"So I was told. I'm sorry I was not available to answer your questions."

"It was my own fault. I did not know your schedule."

As he escorted her from the main room, she sensed the obedient eyes of the five or six disciples following them protectively, intensely. Alone with him in the cool of the garden, where, even as she watched, dead leaves fell from stunted trees by a leaning stone wall, she suddenly grew afraid of him. It was a vague similarity to the fear she had always felt in the presence of Hoover, even when Hoover was surrounded by cops and lawyers.

"It is more conducive to explanation in the garden," he said, neither eager to push his doctrine, nor yet indifferent to her need to know. "You know that many branches of one religion can differ on some points, so what I can explain to you is only our own interpretation."

"I understand that, your . . ."

"My name is Sri Parutha," he said, sensing her awkwardness. "I am called the Master. It is not that I am a master over them"—gesturing toward the disciples inside—"but rather that I have mastered myself."

Janice visibly relaxed in the face of his modesty. He reminded her of an uncle she had known as a child, an uncle who had brought her tales of far-off Paris in a smooth, inwardly vibrant voice.

"The question as to prediction of the return is a division point among a number of sects within our philosophy. I myself maintain that there is a general limitation—let us say, two generations—within which the soul returns. Others maintain that the instant of death produces an instant of life."

Janice jotted down the answer. The Master answered several more, and amplified his disciple's answers of the previous day.

"And as to whether the dead observe, in some way, life on earth, I must say I am not in sympathy with this idea. It is natural for the bereaved to feel it is so, and no harm is done by imagining it, but the condition of the soul after death is so vastly different from earthly existence that to speak of 'observation,' implying eyes and ears, and an independent mind, would be to fabricate a whole mythology."

"I see," Janice said, feeling, much to her own surprise, a sense of disappointment, as though the child within her had been deceived by the priests and nuns of her old parochial school.

The Master smiled softly, neither with mirth nor yet with an irony.

"You have come out of a sense of grief," he observed.

"Yes, how did you know?"

"One can tell after many years of observing human beings. Was it a child?"

"It was."

"And if memory does not fail me, you were here once before. Almost a year ago."

Janice blushed and said nothing. The Master himself seemed deeply moved by the memory. He was silent. For a long time the only sound was the rustle of dead leaves in the trees of the garden.

"But you have never come back since then," the Master said.

"I found it too painful."

He nodded sympathetically. "I am not offended. But I was told that now it is your husband who had become interested."

She grew silent. Bill's obsession seemed to have an unhealthy quality, nothing like the Master's calm recitation of doctrine.

"It's been very sudden," she confessed.

"Very well. We are pleased to help in any way."

"Thank you. You've been most kind."

The Master wished to chat on about the garden for a few moments. He seemed to find a delight and a tranquility in observing the small changes, day by day, as the garden prepared for the hard, cruel winter.

"One does not fear death," he observed, "if one knows that life returns."

Janice smiled and let him accompany her to the door.

"Do I—that is, can I make a contribution?" she asked awkwardly.

"Not necessary," he said, his eyes twinkling ironically. "Good-bye, Mrs. Templeton. Come whenever you like."

She left, buoyed up by the Master's gentle but irresistible optimism. She did not even mind the slips on her desk, saying that Bill had called twice. She did not even mind his displeasure at the Master's vague answer to the question of time.

But gradually, as the climate turned colder, and the leaves clustered at the base of the buildings, and the rain began to break with fury over the cold stone, Bill's attitude began to weigh down on her. He called five times, six times a day. He called at home. He needed magazines; some had to be ordered from London or Delhi, and he needed them now. And she had to disguise them as *Newsweek*s and *Time*s to keep Dr. Geddes in the dark.

Janice went to the Temple five more times, until she felt she was studying for some cosmic final examination. Like a robot, she wandered for the thousandth time into the religion sector of the public library, looking into obscure journals with unreadable print. She felt like a marionette, with Bill jerking the strings with unforgiving violence, impatient and angry.

And yet the search, at some subliminal level, was having its effect on her. She knew too much. She refused to believe, and yet she was no longer simply a go-between. The concepts traveled around with her, a perpetual resonance from another world.

She slept alone at Des Artistes, the nights a heavy weight to endure. She neither feared the night nor yet looked forward to the dawn. Sleepless, driven by Bill, she went to work only half conscious of the exhaustion that was sapping her will to resist.

Bill called, excited. He was making discoveries, he claimed. Now he needed to know the specifics of signs.

"Signs?" Janice asked.

"Yes, the signs of reincarnation!"

"Bill, I'm exhausted. I can't do this much longer."

"Just a few more questions, honey. A few more answers. Then we'll be all set."

"Set for what, Bill?"

"Never you mind. Just get to the old geezer and pop him these questions."

Janice wearily watched her hand write down more questions on the note pad. She avoided Elaine as she sneaked out for what seemed like the hundredth time at 3:30, and headed down to the Temple.

"So, Bill sends you back again," the Master said.

"Yes, it's—it's the signs he wants to know about," Janice said, entering onto the slanted wooden floor. "It seemed very urgent to him."

The master closed the door behind them.

"Signs?" he asked, his eyes twinkling as they always did; but somehow they never denoted humor, only a steady, ice-cool concentration that was almost lyrical in its purity.

He turned, ushered her into his cold office. He lit a small stove with newspapers, shoved in sticks—the table legs of cast-off furniture—and rubbed his hands, blowing on them. Setting a battered tin pot on the stove, he went to a small basin, turned the tap for water, and made preparations for tea.

"The signs of reincarnation," Janice said fearfully.

The Master nodded slowly, as though he had heard the question, urgently demanded, a hundred, a thousand times before, but did not answer at once.

Janice thought he was merely waiting for the tea water to boil. It was his custom to begin indirectly, to make oblique references to the matter at hand to induce tranquility. That was why words made perfect sense here, and didn't quite when she relayed them to Bill.

"Things have changed so much," he said softly.

"What do you mean?"

"When I came here, there were a thousand young people clamoring at our door. And such enthusiasm. Reading and chatting and real, sincere worship. And now we are down to five students."

Janice nodded awkwardly, surprised at the realistic attitude the Master displayed.

"Fashions change," she said softly.

"Yes. Fashions. But when I came from India ten years ago, it was no fashion. At least, it seemed to be real. But now we are no longer respected."

Unaccustomed to his downcast mood, Janice said nothing. She watched him walk to the stove where he fed more paper and sticks into the stove. He stood over the water, pushing back the long, orange sleeves of his robe. Now, in the soft, Vermeer light of the shabby office, he looked indeed no older than fifty, handsome in a masculine, Western way, the white hair a subtle shock over the brown skin.

"This may be the last time the Temple will be open to you," he said.

"What? Why? Have I done something wrong?"

He smiled sadly. "Of course not. But the rent here, Mrs. Templeton. Do you have any idea what it costs to be in Greenwich Village? And now, with almost nobody left, our revenues . . ."

"I'm sorry, Sri Parutha. I didn't realize it was that bad."

The water boiled. Using an aged towel, the Master cautiously lifted the pot and with deft, long-practiced motions, filled two delicate ceramic cups.

"We will be talking about it this afternoon," he said. "I think we shall disband the Temple."

"I don't know how to express my sympathy," Janice said. "I feel very badly for you."

The Master smiled again, an enigmatic expression in his eyes. He handed Janice a cup of tea. The aroma twirled upward with the steam; a jasmine scent that, like the gentle light coming in from the frosted windows, obscured all terror, soothed all doubt, and brought a subtle tranquility down to the marrow of the bones.

"There is a phrase by one of the English poets," the Master said. "The 'inconstant lover.' Let us just say that the Americans are inconstant lovers."

Janice drank slowly, waiting for the brew to cool. She knew the Master had not forgotten why she had come, but she also knew that the realities of what he called the external world had inexplicably intruded and even destroyed his beloved sanctuary.

"Well, then, your husband needs to know the signs of reincarnation?"

The Master removed several books, fat with bookmarkers in them, and several broken brass candleholders. They sat down.

"Basically, the signs can be categorized according to the physical, the psychological, or the religious. Physical signs include birthmarks, wounds—which can reappear in modified forms—or certain congenital abnormalities. A clubfoot, for example, is repeated. Or a claw hand comes back as unexplained scars on a healthy hand. These are really so common that nobody in India would be particularly astonished if you showed up with, let us say, a dead uncle's deformity of toes, or his laughter, or his manner of expression. Is all this clear, Mrs. Templeton?''

''Perfectly,'' she answered, writing quickly onto a spiral-bound notebook.

''Psychologically, if a child has peculiar memories of a place, of people, of events that he or she has never seen. If suddenly, his mood and behavior change, with no warning but in a consistent manner. Like your own daughter, Mrs. Templeton.''

''Yes.''

''Quite often a person feels a sudden desire to travel to a part of the world he has never been to before. And when he goes, he finds that he knows how to get around, he never gets lost, and he knows the names of people he meets. Quite often there is an aspect of violence involved.''

''Violence?''

''Yes. For example, a man is compelled to travel into Madras, and there, not knowing why, he is compelled to wield an axe and he murders a distantly related uncle. It is because, several generations before, he was robbed of his inheritance by the previous incarnation of that uncle. In fact, I know of several cases in which the accused were exonerated on just such grounds.''

Janice nodded quickly, trying to cram her handwriting into the narrow-ruled pages.

''I see. And is it the same in Tibet?''

The Master paused, suddenly uncomfortable. He temporized by pouring fresh hot water into their cups.

''Tibet,'' he said softly, ''is a very old form of Buddhism.

They do things very differently in the mountains. I realize that your husband is particularly interested in these forms of religion?''

"Yes."

"Well, it is much more elaborate. The Dalai Lama, for example, the highest of the priests, is the latest in a long line of reincarnated men, and often it takes many months of searching the caves and farms to find the infant with the proper markings. I find, quite frankly, that there is something too intense about this form. The divinations, for example, take weeks in the bitter cold, and the mandalas are extremely sexual and violent.''

"Are they really?" Janice asked, perturbed.

The Master waved a vague hand, as though to dismiss them, evil thoughts, back into the cold air.

"Copulating skeletons. Drifting among death. Fire that eats out the body and films the eyelids. You see, it goes back to a very, very ancient time. Long before the Indo-Europeans came down to the plains of India.''

Janice finished with her notes, and the Master sighed, rubbed his eyes, and shivered.

"Before I go," Janice said gently, "I must ask you one more thing.''

"I will answer it if I can.''

"If there is a reincarnation—I mean, *when* there is a reincarnation—is it possible to know where the soul will return?''

The Master smiled gently. "The physical location?''

Janice nodded.

"The soul seeks the locus of its growth and its greatest happiness. That normally means very close to where it left the previous body.''

"So if a person died in New York City—''

"One must assume that it will reappear in the area. You see, it is like a gravitational field. The soul drifts and, faster

129

and faster, as it approaches life again, it falls toward its previous origin.''

Janice paled, but said nothing. For a while, she thought of not writing down that answer. Then she put her pencil to paper. Then, confused, she put the pencil and paper away, discouraged.

''Perhaps I should go now,'' she said.

''As you wish.''

The Master, in the Western manner, rose from his orange crate and escorted her to the door. Feeling lonely, or disturbed about something, he accompanied her down the dark stair-well, into the white garden. The snow was falling, smaller, colder, a bitter screen of textured dots over the fat stone walls where old basins of stained wood had been brought from temples in India.

''If you could impress upon your husband,'' he said delicately, ''not to dwell too rashly in these ideas. . . .''

''Why not? Is it dangerous?''

''Not dangerous, exactly. But I have seen too many young people who also suffered mentally as does your husband. They seized upon Hinduism and Buddhism, like drowning men clutch at the air. And in the end they misunderstood everything, and were no better off than before.''

''Yes. I'll tell him. Perhaps, in time, his enthusiasm will die down.''

''Clarity of mind,'' the Master said, leading her back through the empty Temple, where only one disciple looked up from sorting a few prayer books along the wall, jealous of Janice's proximity to the Master. ''If the mind is unclear . . . like a distorting pool . . . the doctrine becomes warped.''

Janice left the Temple. As usual, the visits to Sri Parutha left her strangely energized, eager to face the rest of the day, yet with a lingering sensation of doubt. And as the day wore on, the doubt always grew stronger. Until, finally, when the tranquility of the old Brahmin had faded sufficiently, a kind of

130

bleak terror invaded her very body, and she took to mixing Scotch with soda as a more durable, if less spiritual, antidote to the conflicts within her.

Back at Des Artistes, the telephone rang. Janice tried to ignore it, handling the ink brush as quickly as she could manage. But the ringing never stopped. She conceded, and picked it up.

"Janice," Bill exclaimed. "Where the hell were you?"

"I just came in as the phone was ringing."

"Did you see the priest at the Temple?"

"Yes. We had a very nice talk."

"Good. Very good. Listen, I've got something I want you to do."

"No, Bill."

"Janice, you have to go downtown to the—"

"We agreed this was the last time."

"Janice," he pleaded. "I'm begging you!"

"No. I've got work of my own, Bill. Be reasonable."

"But we're running out of time."

"We've got plenty of time, darling. Now I have to jot down some ideas Elaine gave me, and—"

"Then I'll do it myself."

Janice decided Bill was not fooling.

"I'm telling you, Janice," he said darkly. "If I have to, I'll bust out of this place and do it myself."

"Don't talk like that, Bill. It frightens me."

"It has to be done and it doesn't matter who does it."

"What, Bill? What has to be done?"

"Somebody has to go down to the Hall of Records. And see who was born the same minute Ivy died."

"Bill, this is all nonsense. Sri Parutha said not to be rash, and here you are—"

"Screw Sri Parutha. Listen to me, God damn it, Janice! Somebody has to go down and look at those records!"

"This is crazy! I won't do it! It's one thing to bring you

books, and—and go visit the Temple, but this is impossible!''

Bill said nothing for a while, yet she heard him breathing at the other end.

"All right," he said angrily. "At least I know where you stand."

He hung up. Janice clicked the receiver button again and again, but the line was irretrievably dead. Miserable, she resumed her work at her table, where the designs lay in sketched form under the lamp by the windows. After ten minutes, an uneasy feeling grew to where she could no longer think straight.

She called the clinic back.

"Mr. William Templeton, please," she said.

After ten minutes, during which Janice was afraid they would not find him, Bill came to the telephone.

"Yes?" he said.

"All right. You win. I'll go. But please, that's got to be all. You're chasing crazy will-o'-the-wisps."

"Let me be the judge of that. You know what you're looking for?"

"I think so."

"Tell me."

"February 3, 1975. 10:53 in the morning."

"*10:43!*" Bill shrieked. "10:43 in the morning—a mistake like that could be fatal!"

"All right—10:43—I'll look it up for you."

"Okay. And bring me notes on what the priest told you today. Okay? Will you do that?"

"Bill."

"What?"

"Why New York? Why not Baltimore? Or Chicago? Or even Pittsburgh or Hong Kong? Why would she come back to New York? She could be any place at all!"

"Because the soul seeks the locus of its greatest happiness. It's like a gravitational field, Janice. Picture a meteor falling through space. Suddenly it gets caught up in a force field and

132

it starts to accelerate downward. Well, it's like that. Back to where the soul developed.''

Janice bit her lip. Bill had answered, almost word for word, as the Master had. Evidently Bill's expertise was reaching startling proportions. Janice began to be afraid of him in the way that she had once been afraid of Hoover. There was too much knowledge at the other end of the line.

Chapter Eight

The Hall of Records stood recessed from the streets, its upper reaches in the slanted sunlight, but off the ledges of the first floor icicles melted slowly in shadow. Long windows, crisscrossed with a protective wire inside, gave off no light. The steps to the main doors were unscraped, covered with sprinkles of salt and brown dirt. Around the building rose higher structures, sleek, expressive of the supernational organization of the twentieth century, while the massive Hall, like a throwback to gray stone and marble, huddled in their shadows, a monument to weight and ornamented facade.

Janice walked the long hall, past voices behind doors, electric typewriters, obscure silences, and she looked around at the blank, dirty white ceilings, the old scrollwork nearly obliterated with curls of dust.

A young woman with short blond hair looked up.

"May I help you?"

"Am I in the birth registration department?"

"Sure are, ma'am."

"Could you . . . That is, are these open to the public?"

The girl nodded. "Sign the register," she said, turning a massive book around and handing Janice a black pen attached to the book by a beaded chain.

Janice quickly scrawled her name and the date and the girl swiveled the book back, squinting at the penmanship.

"What's the name?"

"Templeton. Mrs. Janice Templeton."

"Not you. The infant."

"That's the problem. I don't know the infant's name. Just the moment of birth."

The girl raised an eyebrow, sighed, and came out from behind her tiny desk.

"That doesn't make it easy, you know," she said.

"I'm prepared to do all the work myself," Janice said quickly. "If you could just show me how—"

"What year?"

"Nineteen Seventy-five."

"You're in luck. Anything before Nineteen Seventy-three and you'd have had to go down to the crypts. That's the storage facility underground."

"You mean this whole room is just for—?"

"That's right. These are the births since January, Nineteen Seventy-three. New York is a very fertile place. Follow me. Nineteen Seventy-five is at the end of the hall."

As they passed into the far end of the corridor, a wing opened up to view, and along the entire wall were ceiling-high metal cabinets, gray and green, with stepladders available in front. Janice paused. The vista was depressing, even overwhelming. If each cabinet was full, Janice reasoned, then the accumulated total of births would have to exceed a hundred thousand.

"Well, grab yourself a bunch of patience. This is Nineteen Seventy-five. What month was the infant born?"

"February."

The girl strolled to the western bank of cabinets, where the front labels read "February."

"What day?"

"The 3rd."

"Okay, that's your drawer up there. Get yourself a ladder. What it is, is a cross-index to registration number; you can go to the main bank behind my desk and look up the infant."

Janice stared upward at the huge files, the dusty metal still showing where old tape had been affixed, torn away, and never washed. "How many numbers are in one drawer?"

"Never counted. I would imagine quite a few thousand. Like I said. New York must be a busy place at night. Good luck."

The girl walked slowly back up the corridor, leaving Janice to wonder whether she was supposed to remove the drawer or take a note pad up to it. The answer was solved for her when it became clear that the drawer was permanently attached to its runners. Janice climbed back down, retrieved a pen and note pad from her purse, and climbed back up the stepladder. Perusing through the cards to find the beginning of the February 3 entries, she discovered to her dismay that each card was coated with scores of registrations, all entered in the most miniscule type she had ever seen. Worse, the entries had been accumulated in order of registration number and not time of birth, so that she would have to go through what conservatively looked like at least four thousand different numbers.

"Jesus Christ, Bill," she moaned aloud.

After each number was the sex of the child, the exact time of delivery, family name, and two cross-reference numbers that made no sense to her.

With a deep intake of breath, Janice leaned forward, peered into the first card and began. The numbers were so small, the type so cramped, that though she squinted, it began to blur into a mass of tangled lines. It helped for her to close one eye.

After ten minutes, Janice found it easier simply to run her finger down the "Time" column, and if it read "10" on the hour, she stopped. Then she checked the AM or PM symbol behind it. If it was *AM*, she carefully examined the minute column. In this way, she rapidly dispensed with hundreds of numbers.

She rested her eyes. Shifting weight, she began again, with a new burst of enthusiasm. Half an hour went by, close to eight hundred registrations, until watery film began forming like tears in her eyelids, but the closest she came to Ivy's death instant was 10:50 in the morning.

"Big job," commented the the girl below her.

"What?"

The girl held up two mugs of steaming coffee.

"Take a break. Have some coffee. Then I'll give you a hand. My name is Cathy."

"That's awfully kind of you," Janice said.

She stepped gratefully down from the ladder and accepted a mug. Cathy smiled.

"I had no idea it would be like this," Janice confessed. "I imagined it would be like checking a book out in a library."

"It's a real labyrinth here," Cathy admitted.

Now Janice became aware of the extraordinary dimensions of the combined halls, and the fact that they were the only two people in it, dwarfed by tons of records.

"You looking for somebody you know?" Cathy asked.

"Not exactly."

"Lots of mothers, they come here, looking for the kids they've given to adoption."

"It's not my own child I'm looking for."

"You sure? Cause it's not my business and I'd be fired for saying this, but that sort of thing just gets ugly and there's no way it can succeed."

"Well, I promise you, that's not what I'm here for," Janice said.

"Lots of times we have people from NYU or Columbia doing research. You a college person?"

"No."

"Writer?"

"Not that, either."

"Well, I got to admit, you got me really curious."

Janice laughed, but she became uncomfortable under Cathy's scrutiny.

"Let's just say it's a kind of coincidence I'm looking for," Janice finally said.

Cathy shrugged. "Well, nothing else makes sense around here, either."

By a mutual signal, they began. Cathy pulled a second stepladder to the file and, referring to the time that Janice wrote on a slip of paper, began to search through the rear files of the spacious drawer. They worked quickly, flipping cards back with mechanical monotony, pausing now and then to refresh their eyes.

In ten minutes, Cathy found a 10:43 and noted down the registration number. Janice peered over at the card to verify it. Her heart began to race. Somehow the number jumped upward from the mass of numbers and letters as though it belonged to her personally.

Fifteen minutes later, Janice came across another 10:43, but a peculiar symbol followed it. Cathy stopped to look at it.

"I think that means deceased," Cathy said. "Copy the number and we'll check it in the main bank."

When they were through, fingers sore, backs twisted, they stepped down to the main floor. Cathy slammed the drawer shut, and it was like an explosion that burst over their ears.

Janice had a premonition that the other baby did, in fact, die at or before childbirth. Leaving exactly one child born at the minute Ivy's vital functions permanently ceased. It would

139

have been better, Janice thought, if there had been a thousand possibilities. Or none. Either way, there would have been no way to trace. Reluctantly, she followed the girl back up the corridor. They edged past the desk and went to a squat, black bin divided into internal ridges, labels affixed in poor handwriting to the outside.

Cathy checked one of the registration numbers, rolled through a hundred circular containers of microfilm, and finally pulled out a loose-wrapped strip of black film. While Janice watched, she fitted it into a machine, pulled the blinds shut, and turned on the machine light. Wheeling rapidly, Cathy came to the number.

Henderson, no name. Father: James McAlister Henderson. Mother: Marcia Elise Hinton Henderson. Hospital: Columbia University Medical. Time: 10:43 AM. February 3, 1975. Signature of presiding doctor, James E. Kindermann.

Where there were spaces for more information, Dr. Kindermann had scrawled in: *surgical delivery—malformed central nervous system: medulla. Time of death: February 10, 1975. See City of New York Certificate #3486-89682.*

"Poor thing," Cathy said softly.

"That leaves only one other possibility."

"I'll get it for you now."

Janice watched the microfilm blur in the bright rectangle of the machine's projection frame. Cathy whipped the microfilm into a roll, clipped it, and replaced it. In a few seconds, she returned with a second clip. Transfixed, Janice leaned forward as the birth certificates in negative tones raced by, streaks of white jumping through the viewing rectangle, and then Cathy slowed and the columns began to be discernible, moving slower and slower into the oblivion of the cutoff. At last Cathy stopped.

"There she is."

Janice bent forward even farther.

Hernandez, Juanita Flores Ynez. Father: Patrizio Gomez y

Ruiz Hernandez. Mother: Rosa Hernandez. Hospital: Bronx General. Time: 10:43 AM. February 3, 1975. Signature of presiding doctor, Herbert M. Weissberg. Weight: 5 lbs. 11 oz. Slight jaundice. Religion: Roman Catholic. 385 118th Street, New York City, New York. Stamped: Office of the clerk of the City of New York. There was more, the mother's maiden name, and so forth, but Janice only saw the infant's name. And the address. There was even a reproduction of a scroll-work over the certificate, an imitation banner with furled ends, an obsolete vestige of generations of custom that somehow the city had not exterminated.

As she scrawled the information, Janice realized that the little girl already had two connections to her. The instant of birth and her religion. Janice smiled. Apart from that, it was all part of permutations and probabilities.

"Tell me honestly," Cathy demanded, smiling, "what are you going to do with that?"

"This address? I'll tell you, Cathy, I don't know."

Puzzled, Cathy could not help but laugh.

Janice turned to go, but Cathy objected.

"You have to sign the register," she said, smiling.

"Sorry."

Janice initialed the last column after her name, where Cathy had written in the time.

"You have good security here," Janice observed.

"That's right. Nobody comes in or goes out without signing. In person. City rules."

With profuse thanks, Janice left the department and returned to Des Artistes. She entered the restaurant bar, sat down, and ordered a split of Mouton Cadet. Then, hungry, she added a sandwich. Outside, the storm threatened but never came. Dense clouds swirled over the buildings, lit up from below by floodlights or red neon, like an angry cosmic storm.

It was in this restaurant bar, she thought, that they had first met Hoover over a year ago. He had expounded his theory of

141

rebirth, and Bill had practically landed him a punch across the table. Now Bill was in an asylum and Hoover was gone into some distant countryside where the water stank and white cows with long horns were sacred.

She ordered a second wine. She thought about the birth certificate. *Juanita—Juanita Hernandez.* It evoked an image of a tiny, tan-skinned infant, with black curly hair, eyes shut with crying. The one infant in all of New York born at precisely the wrong moment. Mercifully, she began to feel the effect of the second glass.

As Janice wearily entered the apartment, the telephone was ringing.

"No, not at this hour," she pleaded to the dark rooms. "Please, Bill . . ."

Turning on a lamp, she picked up the receiver.

"Glad I caught you," Bill said. "What did you find?"

"Nothing, Bill."

"Nothing? What the hell do you mean, nothing?"

"It's a manual system, Bill. And there was nobody to help."

"God damn all hell, anyway." Bill threw something across his room that shattered. "Look," he said, barely controlling himself. "When can you go back there?"

"Not for a while, Bill. We're swamped at the studio."

"Janice, I need you to go tomorrow."

"Not tomorrow, Bill."

"Well, then by Wednesday. Okay?"

"I'll try, darling."

"Try? You've got to do more than just try! I'm sorry— please, honey, how long is this going to take?"

Janice wondered how long she could string him along.

"Perhaps a few weeks," she said. "Maybe longer."

Bill groaned.

"I'm doing what I can, Bill, but it's going to take time."

"Right. Christ, I'm glad I've got you out there. You don't

know what it's like in this chamber of horrors. By the way, I forgot to get down what the Master said. About the signs.''

Janice explained, reading from her notes, what the Master had said about the signs: Physical, Psychological, and Religious.

"Well, screw the psychological," Bill said in disgust. "Any kid born in February, 1975 would be less than a year old. What about the physical signs? I don't remember a damned thing wrong with Ivy, do you? I mean, did she have a rash or something when she was born? It was all normal, wasn't it?''

"She was a perfect little child, Bill," Janice lied, remembering a tiny scar just below the nape of Ivy's smooth, white neck.

"Think, God damn it!''

Janice held the receiver a foot from her ear.

"Sorry," he mumbled. "But there's got to be a sign. Did she have any marks at all?''

"None that I can remember.''

"All right, all right," he said angrily. "Let me work on it. Meanwhile, you get on back to the Hall of Records.''

"When I can, Bill.''

Janice stalled a week.

The next time she visited Bill, he folded his arms, listening patiently to her explanations as to why the Hall of Records took so long to yield up its secrets. He studied her eyes intensely, examining them for the slightest flicker, the smallest indication of a lie. While in her mind she heard: *Juanita Hernandez. 118th Street. Birth: normal. 10:43. February 3, 1975.*

"When you went to Westport," Bill asked, "did Ivy look any different?''

Confused, Janice said nothing.

"The night you ran away from New York," he said calmly, "you ran off to the beach with Ivy. Did she look any different?''

"No, I don't think so—I don't remember.''

143

"Was she in pain?"

"No. I'm sure she felt fine. She loved the beach."

"Were her eyes clouded?"

"Of course not."

"Were her senses unclear?"

"Bill, I don't understand what you're asking!"

Bill, flustered, referred back to *The Tibetan Book of the Dead*, which now lay permanently open on his desk, like a small altar.

"Those are the signs of deliverance to the Lord of Death," Bill said somberly. "You say you saw none of them?"

"None, Bill. I'm quite sure."

"What about fear of holy persons? That's a very strong sign."

"No. In fact, we saw some nuns and the children of the girls' school, and Ivy became very happy."

Bill looked at her carefully, a strange mixture of triumph and fear in his eyes.

"Then the death *was* untimely, Janice."

Bill looked pale. He looked exhausted. Janice realized now that there was utterly no chance that stringing out the Hall of Records ordeal would lesson his passion one iota. His finger jabbed at *The Book of the Dead*.

"If you had known in Westport," he said. "If you had had some inkling . . ."

"What *are* you talking about?"

"Janice," he said in a voice which did not sound familiar, "on the fifteenth of the month, if there had been a clear sky and no wind—"

"There was a storm blowing."

"Ivy could have stretched out her arms, cast her shadow onto the sand."

Bill spread his arms, mimicking, but his body trembled with an unusual tension, and he closed his eyes until tears formed.

"And where her heart would be, in the shadow, carve the letter A. And Ivy would stare into it, unblinking, for seven minutes. And seven times the holy benediction would be uttered...."

"Please, darling, stop it!"

Bill leaned back, arched his spine, and called upward, to the heavens, beyond the heavens, in a voice deep from his diaphragm.

"Om ayuse samharakesvare hum phat!"

Janice covered her ears with her hands.

"Om ayuse samharakesvare hum phat!"

Bill's eyes glazed triumphantly. He stood up straight again.

"And then Ivy would look up into the sky and see her after-image. If it was pale and white, she would not die. But if it was black, she was being consumed."

Bill paused. His words came now curiously dry, abstract, devoid of emotion. In a desultory way, he riffled through the pages of *The Book of the Dead*, listless.

"But you didn't know that, Janice," he said.

"And what if I had known, Bill?"

He smiled, but only shrugged.

"In that case," he said, "if it was black, there would have been counter-rituals. There are certain kinds of flasks. Reading from the texts. Crashing of the cymbals, drums, and lutes, and the sending away of the demons. You see, Janice, we could have ameliorated her fear, circumvented her untimely return."

He turned slowly back to her. His smile remained, but now it was sad and demonic.

"The cycle would have stopped," he said. "Now it only continues."

A name, a date, and an address flashed through Janice's mind. She turned away. She did not want to think what Bill would do if he ever found Juanita. She believed him capable of anything. Yet, she could not bring herself to confide in Dr.

Geddes. Bill would crumble one final time, and forever, if she betrayed him.

The next day was Saturday, and Janice took the bus up Riverside Drive. She crossed to the northeast, just past the park, until she was in Spanish Harlem. Though it was cold, it was ferociously bright, and it hurt her eyes to look down the crowded streets. Radios blared music out of the pawnshops. There was not another white person in view.

On 118th Street were a series of small grocery stores, a laundromat, and a Pentecostal church. Opposite them was an enormous block of public housing. Janice looked in vain for the numbers. If there was a 385, the house number had long ago been ripped from the door.

She crossed the street and went into the first entrance. A tattered sign read *200 – 300*. The hall stank of mildew. Overhead were harsh, rubbery sounds, as though a child were ramming a wheeled toy repeatedly over a linoleum floor. Graffiti everywhere denoted death and crude love for whites. Janice walked slowly to a door down the hall and listened. A radio played disco music inside, the announcer speaking excitedly in a liquid Spanish.

She knocked.

When the door opened, a slight man with a pencil-thin mustache stood before her in his undershirt. He retreated, embarrassed before her, and then defiantly stood his ground.

"Is Mrs. Hernandez here?" she asked hesitantly.

He shook his head and prepared to close the door.

"Upstairs?" she asked.

He glared blankly at her.

"Um, *donde es Senora Hernandez?*"

The man shrugged, smiled politely but firmly, and gently closed the door.

Just then, two boys, aged fifteen or sixteen, came up from the basement, carrying lead pipes. They stopped and stared at her.

To ease the awkwardness of being stared at, Janice asked, "Do you speak English?"

The taller of the two stepped closer, his hand fingering the rusted edges of the pipe.

"I'm looking for the Hernandez family," Janice said.

The boys continued to stare at her, as though wondering what had brought her to this block of flats. The shorter of the two looked her up and down until she felt self-conscious.

"Hernandez," Janice repeated.

"Upstairs," said the tall one.

"What?"

"Upstairs. We take you."

Janice did not like the way he said it, nor the way his friend or brother kept looking at her. The taller one pointed to the stairs and smiled.

"Come on," he said. "We go upstairs."

"Could you just tell me which floor?"

"No. You go. We go. We show you."

"Yes," seconded the other boy. "Hernandez family is upstairs."

"No," Janice said slowly. "I'll go there myself."

The taller boy stepped forward, a bit angry. "Luis. Go help the lady. Bring Mrs. Hernandez down."

"Really," she protested, "it's not necessary."

But the other boy was already climbing the stairs, two at a time. While Janice waited, curious, she noticed that the tall boy kept smiling at her.

"Luis bring Mrs. Hernandez," he confided.

"I'm very grateful."

After several minutes, two pairs of footsteps circled down the stairwell, coming down from at least the third floor. Luis appeared, casting an ambivalent glance at Janice, and behind him was a tall, black-haired woman, wiping her hands on a towel. The woman's hair was so black, it gleamed an almost blue. She studied Janice closely, then braced herself.

"Yes? What you want?" she asked in an even voice.

"Are you Mrs. Hernandez?"

"What you want with my sister?" the woman asked suspiciously.

"I'd like to see Juanita."

The woman's features softened, then immediately hardened again.

"You're from Welfare?" she said, casting anxious glances at Janice's face, hands, and clothes.

"No, I'm a friend. That is, I'd like to be a friend."

"I no understand."

Janice smiled, and a small laugh of frustration escaped her.

"If I could explain, I would," she said. Then, more slowly, "I want very much to see Juanita. It has to do with my own daughter."

Puzzled, the woman wiped her hands, though they were certainly dry. She shrugged.

"You work for the city?" she asked, once again.

"No. I'm a writer," she lied.

"Well, if you want to come up, follow me."

The four of them went into the stairwell. The plaster showed in rough oblongs along the wall, where sharp implements had gouged holes and then enlarged them. At the first floor the two boys left, running down the corridor. Janice followed the woman into a narrower, darker stairwell.

"My sister not feel so well," the woman said. "So you not stay a long time. Okay?"

"Yes, okay."

On the fourth floor, the woman walked quickly, but soundlessly, down the cluttered corridor. A far door with a cracked glass window let in a gray, dirty light over the tricycle and boxes of woolen cloth left for unknown reasons in the middle of the hall. Crayon marks left long trails where a child had run the length of the corridor with first one color and then another.

Janice followed the woman into the doorway of a small apartment. They stood in the kitchen. On the stove an enormous aluminum pot bubbled with a thick sauce. Small laundry hung from white cord that led into the tiny living room. A crucifix hung on the wall.

"Rosa!"

A short woman, gray twined neatly into her black hair, came into the kitchen, shuffling on bedroom slippers. She stopped when she saw Janice.

For a long time, Janice looked at her, as though there might be some common bond between them. Then she realized it was foolish, and she smiled, extending her hand.

Rosa Hernandez looked at her sister, who shrugged; then, she took Janice's hand and smiled back. The woman had uncommonly pretty features, Janice thought, diminutive, oval-shaped, and her eyes were brilliant and black.

"She come to see Juanita," the sister put in.

"Juanita? But why? She's fine."

"No, no, Mrs. Hernandez. It's not like that. I want to see her for myself. For my own sake."

Mrs. Hernandez smiled, confused. The sister hovered at the stove protectively, stirring the sauce.

"Juanita is sleeping," Mrs. Hernandez said. "Maybe you sit down and tell me why you come."

Janice sat at a small, wobbling table with a brown vinyl cloth cover. Mrs. Hernandez folded her hands opposite her and waited patiently.

"Why you want to see Juanita?" she asked again.

"I'm writing an article for a magazine. About growing up in this building."

Mrs. Hernandez laughed.

"It's not very interesting here. Why you don't write about other people?"

"Well, you're curious about other people, aren't you? Other people are curious about you."

"I don't believe it."

Mrs. Hernandez spoke more out of modesty than objection. Janice marveled at the simplicity of life in the broad stone building, where suspicions flourished, but trust did, too. It would never occur to Mrs. Hernandez to ask for credentials, for the name of the mythical newspaper Janice wrote for, or anything else. Janice came from the great outer world, and therefore, what she said could not be questioned.

"But it's true, Mrs. Hernandez," Janice said. "Haven't you read the articles on the Lithuanians in New York City? It's part of the same series."

Mrs. Hernandez laughed, a modest, embarrassed laughter.

"What's your name?" Mrs. Hernandez asked.

"Janice Templeton."

The name meant nothing to Mrs. Hernandez. Nevertheless, she held Janice to be a celebrity of sorts, and found it difficult to hold her own in conversation. In the next room, the sister turned the television on softly.

"Well, what you want to know about Juanita?"

"We could start from the beginning. Was she born here?"

"I was in the hospital. But yes, I was living here."

"And the birth was normal?"

"What you mean?"

"There were no problems? She was a normal baby?"

Mrs. Hernandez thought, picturing what she remembered of the delivery room. She shrugged.

"I think she was a little—yellow—in the skin."

"Jaundice?"

"Yes. The doctor said it was nothing to worry about."

"And she's not been sick since then?"

"Oh, no. Juanita is a fine girl."

In the living room, the sister turned up the volume of the television set. Mrs. Hernandez brought a plate of a flat bread, not quite a tortilla, with a sugary coating.

"And she's lived here all this time?" Janice asked.

150

"Yes."

Janice leaned forward slightly.

"Does she ever—change? Ever seem to become different—?"

"Juanita? No. Always the same."

"She never cries for no reason?"

Mrs. Hernandez laughed. "All babies cry for no reason."

There was a slight stirring sound beyond the living room. Mrs. Hernandez looked up brightly.

"She's waking up. You like to see her?"

"Yes. Yes, I would."

Smiling, Mrs. Hernandez stood up, and Janice followed her over the linoleum floor into the living room, past the sister who leaned around them to see the television screen, and into a bedroom where the shades were drawn. It was dark, dank with the smell of the baby, and the large bed beyond was still unmade.

In the crib a small girl lay. The ears were already pierced with two shining brass studs, though she could not have been old enough to more than crawl awkwardly on the floor. The tousled black hair was exactly as Janice had imagined. But the eyes were filmy, dark but not black, more a kind of deep gray that was almost brown in the gloom of the room. Janice stepped slowly to the crib and peered down.

"She's very quiet baby," Mrs. Hernandez whispered.

The infant looked upward at Janice. The tiny eyes seemed familiar, a spark of recognition leaped outward. Janice recoiled.

"Pick her up," Mrs. Hernandez said.

"What?"

"Go ahead. She no cry."

Hesitantly, Janice edged her hands and arms under Jaunita and brought the child up out of the crib. The filmy eyes closed for an instant and then opened. Janice slowly removed the white blanket from the soft, small neck.

"Is something wrong?" Mrs Hernandez asked.

"No. I was looking for something."

"She seems to know you. Look. Her hands grab for your hair."

The small hands curled and uncurled, delicately, tenderly, twining into the black hair at Janice's temple. Janice looked again at the smooth neck. There was no scar.

"She's so light," Janice said, smiling. "My own daughter was much heavier."

"I think, because she was born small," Mrs. Hernandez said, taking pleasure in watching Janice warm to the girl.

Janice gently lowered the girl and tucked the blankets back around her neck. The girl was lively, displaying a kind of quick intelligence that absorbed things instantly.

"You say she was born small?" Janice said.

"Yes. Five pounds. Just under."

"Was she premature?"

"Two weeks."

Janice turned slowly. "Two weeks?"

"Si. Suddenly, Juanita wanted to come, so I had my labor."

"She wanted to come?"

"All of a sudden. A bad day in February. I had to take the bus with my sister and the bus got stuck in the snow. It was a very easy thing to have her. I wasn't sick, I no fall down. And she come."

Janice felt perspiration forming on her forehead. She looked down again at Juanita. The child appeared to be looking back into her eyes, looking into her, into the thunderous thoughts of her own brain.

On an impulse, Janice slowly removed the blanket and gently picked her up once again, her eyes exploring the soft, perfect neck and chest.

Juanita's small hands went to her throat.

"What—what is she doing?" Janice asked, turning quickly.

"She do that all the time. Try to touch her throat."

"It's like she's choking—"

"No. I take her to the doctor. He look at her and say, 'this is one fine girl, Mrs. Hernandez.' "

Juanita twisted and turned, trying to get out of Janice's arms. Again and again, the tiny fingers clutched at her own throat, and the tiny legs kicked futilely against the blankets.

Mrs. Hernandez laughed pleasantly.

"I take her now," she said.

In Mrs. Hernandez's arms, the girl became subdued; the kicking stopped; the small hands relaxed. Janice grew dizzy.

"I—I think I should be going, Mrs. Hernandez—"

"Yes?"

"I'm very glad to have come today. I'll come back again."

"Any time. I don't go out much."

Mrs. Hernandez followed her back through the living room, into the kitchen, where they said good-bye.

Chapter Nine

Janice walked down the flight of stairs, faster down the next flight, faster, until she practically ran from the housing block. She stumbled across 118th Street and waited for the bus. It, finally came, and she took one last look at the building, and at the floor where Juanita lay in the security of her mother's arms.

Riverside Drive, its broad pavement snaking down by the river, looked more real as the bus took her down into the better parts of town. Des Artistes rose like a haven on Sixty-seventh Street, though Janice no longer believed in havens.

She went to the bar and did not stop until the fourth glass of white wine. Then she felt sick and went upstairs, slept until the late night and awoke with a start on the couch. Sounds were stirring, cruel sounds. Were they in her head? She rose. Upstairs on the landing, Ivy's door had drifted open. Inside, a soft echo of tiny feet, scampering in pain.

Was she truly hearing a mouselike voice, twittering in horror and an insatiable need to escape, calling on her mother instead of her father? Janice shook her head violently. She felt fragile as glass.

Juanita couldn't be Ivy! Surely it was all roaring delusions and guilts—a premature birth, clutching the throat— It meant nothing, *nothing!* she repeated to herself. Having gone to the Hernandez apartment was an act of madness, and it had the predictable results. Gradually, but surely, she was being drawn into the nightmare world of Bill's sickness. She resolved not to let it happen. She would fight it, maintain her balance, her sense of reason. And somehow strive to divert Bill from the final, horrible destination his research was inexorably leading him toward.

The next day, Janice called the Hall of Records, Department of Births Registrations. Cathy recognized her voice.

"Cathy, I need to know," Janice said. "Do you give information over the telephone?"

"I don't get you."

"Well, if a man should call. If he asked the same kind of question I did, would you go look it up?"

"No, Mrs. Templeton, it's against the rules."

"Are you absolutely, completely certain?"

"Of course, I am. We don't run a reference library here. Anybody who wants information has to come in person. And sign the register."

"Thank God. I mean, thank you, Cathy."

Janice hung up relieved, but the visit to the Hernandez apartment weighed on Janice. Every time she closed her eyes, she saw little Juanita kick and struggle, reach for her throat. And the dateline, *February 3, 1975—10:43 AM.*, floated like a diseased snake through the image.

That night it snowed again, huge flakes blanketing the city.

Janice entered the apartment just as the telephone was ringing.

"Yes, Bill?"

"No. It's, uh, Dr. Geddes here. I'm, uh, sorry to disturb you."

"That's quite all right, Dr. Geddes. Is everything all right?"

"You, um, haven't seen Bill, have you?"

"Bill? Not since last Friday. Why? What's wrong?"

"Well, as you know, Bill and several other patients had permission to leave the immediate grounds. Walks to Ossining, supervised, of course."

"Yes?"

"To be quick about it, Mrs. Templeton, Bill left early this morning and hasn't returned. We've notified the Highway Police and Ossining authorities."

"Oh, my God."

"But he's completely rational and dressed for the cold. I wouldn't worry about him in that sense. It's just that we thought he might simply have wanted to visit you."

Janice tried to shake free from the dread which gripped her.

"No, he hasn't been here."

"It's quite common for patients to do this sort of thing. I regret he didn't feel he could simply come to us and talk about it."

"Yes, I— Oh, God, there's more to it, Dr. Geddes."

"What do you mean?"

"He's searching! He's—he's searching for Ivy! He's not rational, doctor."

There was a long pause at the other end. She could practically hear him thinking. At length he cleared his throat and when he spoke his voice seemed changed. Once again, he was the stern, formidable figure of authority at the clinic.

"What do you mean, searching?" he asked.

"This last month he's been crazy, studying books and making contact with authorities—"

"What kind of authorities, Mrs. Templeton?"

"Authorities on reincarnation. I've spent dozens of afternoons running errands for him, gathering information from Sri Parutha at the Temple in Greenwich Village."

"What else have you been doing for Bill?"

"Sending him books, writing to people for him."

There was a long pause.

"This is a very serious matter, Mrs. Templeton," he said slowly, without friendliness.

"I know. I was afraid to tell you. I couldn't betray Bill, but now . . ."

"But now, what?"

Janice took a deep breath and tried to gain control of her voice again. Talking to Dr. Geddes was a much harder thing than she would ever have guessed. It was like talking to a judge.

"We've found a child, born on the same day that Ivy died. The same minute, in fact."

"Oh, Christ," Dr. Geddes cursed. "You've been sprinkling gasoline on a fire, Mrs. Templeton. You've encouraged his every delusion."

"I'm sorry. I didn't mean to."

"Never mind that now. Listen to me. I can't get into the city tonight. A foot of snow's expected. So stay where you are and try to keep calm. The main thing is to locate Bill. My guess is that he needs to see you. And if he does come to your apartment . . ."

"Yes?"

"Try to calm him. No more enthusiasm for his pet project."

"I'll try."

"You've got to do more than try. He's hanging on to reality by a thread."

Janice agreed to keep in touch. She slipped her heavy wool coat over her shoulders and paced outside the building. Bill never showed up. She warmed herself inside the lobby, waiting. No one came. She went upstairs, left the door to the apartment unlocked in case Bill should sneak up the rear steps and find himself without a key.

Waiting on the couch, still wrapped in her coat, she fell asleep.

By morning, there was still no sign of Bill. Nor had the snowstorm let up. The papers were proclaiming it another blizzard of '48.

During the day, Janice interrupted work seven times to telephone the desk at Des Artistes.

"No sign of him, Mrs. Templeton," Ernie said sympathetically.

"Thank you, Ernie. If he should come—"

"I'll give you a call. We have your number."

Slowly, Janice depressed the cradle, then dialed the Hall of Records, Department of Births Registrations.

"Hello?" said a strange male voice. "Room One thirty-one."

"Is Cathy there?"

"She's on vacation. Can I help you?"

Janice's hand went involuntarily to her mouth. She swiveled in her chair, but there was no hiding from the curious stare of the assistant at the next desk.

"How— How long has she been gone?" Janice stammered.

"Since today. Is this a personal call?"

"No, I— Has a man called? A man called about a birth registration?"

The voice at the other end chuckled with self-importance.

"We get a lot of inquiries," he said. "I couldn't possibly tell you—"

"February 3, 1975."

"No, we've received no inquiries for that date."

Dazed, she slowly hung up. For a long time, she stared at the wall. When she telephoned Dr. Geddes, he advised her to go home and wait for Bill. They discussed alerting the New York City Police, but in the end, decided to hold off.

*   *   *

Slogging through snowdrifts in the direction of Des Artistes, Janice kept her eyes open for taxis. None came. She stopped in a bar to escape the bitter weather. Warming in the humid entrance, she peeked over the heads of the burly men crowded around the long bar and saw the television perched high on a shelf.

"For New York, it looks like Christmas will be more than white," the announcer said somberly. "Forecasts range from fifteen to twenty inches and winds are expected to reach thirty to thirty-five miles per hour."

A chorus of ribald shouts greeted the report, all epithets of New Yorkers who knew exactly what a storm of that dimension would do to their city.

Janice left the bar. Miserably, she trudged to the next intersection. Still no taxis. Ruefully, she considered that a horse-drawn carriage from the gates of Central Park stood a better chance of making it home than a four-wheeled vehicle.

Gradually, a raw premonition made itself felt. From a corner phone booth, she called the Hall of Records just as it was closing.

"Hello?" she said, breathing hard from the cold. "I called earlier today."

"I'm sorry," said the unctuous voice. "We get *many* calls."

"February 3, 1975."

"Oh, yes. There was an inquiry. A man...let's see...Name of William Templeton. He left about an hour ago."

Janice gasped. "Did you—did you show him the birth registrations on that date?"

"Yes, of course. We're legally obligated—"

Janice slammed the receiver down, fighting tears. Urgently, she turned back into a world of swirling white.

Through the downcoming particles, she saw the gleaming windows of a city bus, like a whale from some macabre cartoon, its huge headlights on, unblinking like morbid eyes, staring into the twilight. She ran to the open door, mounted the steps.

"How far north do you go?" she asked the driver.

"Top of the park, then east."

Janice paid, then sat down. She could feel the wheels of the bus squirming for traction underneath, grinding, groaning against the road. At every stop, she held her breath, not knowing whether the enormous mass of the bus could be held by the brakes. The windshield wipers, working furiously, clotted with wet snow.

"This is the worst goddamn snowfall I ever seen," the driver said, wiping off his window with a white cloth.

"They say there's another foot on the way," a passenger chimed in.

"I tell you one thing. This city is shutting down. Ain't nobody gonna drive out in weather like this."

Ahead of them, another taxi, trying to make the light, applied its brakes without result. The wheels curved, but the taxi kept on in a straight line, digging huge tracks right through the intersection.

"Lucky bastard," commented the driver.

This time the bus refused to move. The rear wheels ground out a plainsong of high-pitched protest, until it sounded like a scream. Janice held her hands over her ears.

"That's it," the driver said. "Everybody out."

"But I—" Janice began.

"You want to sleep here? I've got instructions not to drive when there's no traction!"

Dismally, the passengers filed out, looking in vain down the deserted streets. Janice crossed the avenue, found herself at the north edge of Central Park, went quickly across to Park Avenue, cut over, and waded through the snow under bare trees hanging down with the weight of long spears of ice.

As she crossed into 110th Street, she saw clusters of blue-coated patrolmen slogging through snowdrifts, heading north, where two long shafts of light cut across the clouds.

At 115th Street, she saw two police cars edging cautiously behind a snow-sweeping machine. The orange lights bounced luridly off the dark buildings, gleamed from the windows. A few boys threw snowballs at her, taunting her.

She followed the police cars, the only secure footing on the road, until she reached 118th Street. To her horror, she knew by now where the cars were going. Dim shouts rose in the distance, a sound of far-away bullhorns, and taxi horns from congested lanes of traffic.

A fire truck blocked access to the main blocks of public housing.

"I have to go through!" Janice protested.

"Do you live here?"

"No, but—"

"Then beat it!"

The traffic cop turned away, angrily motioning a pickup truck out of the lane, backward, to where the snow was churned up by countless vehicles turning around in the grimy mud.

Janice ducked under the cross guard and ran toward the dense group of officers in front of the probing spotlights. Their silhouettes had matted together into a single obstruction; only their helmets, denoting different ranks, gleamed in the awesome blue white light.

Janice turned. From the top window, where the spotlights crossed, she heard a woman screaming. The words were run together, a litany of Spanish and English, waving her arms. Behind her, shivering on a landing, a group of neighbors stood, looking upward at the roof. But Janice could see nothing there, only the rolling clouds cut by the spotlights, and the falling snow.

"Please," she whispered to an officer who held steaming coffee in a tin mug, "I have to talk to the officer in charge."

"The officer in charge?" he said, smiling. "I don't think

so. The chief is busy right now trying to keep that guy on the roof."

"But you don't understand, I'm his—"

"Now I suggest you get back behind the barrier with the rest of the gawkers."

Drinking coffee with one hand, guiding her with the other, he steered her back to the fire truck, the turning yellow light gleaming rhythmically off his cup.

Janice struggled free from his grasp.

"Ask the woman up there!" she yelled. "Mrs. Hernandez! Ask her who I am!"

The officer glared at her angrily, yet uncertain now.

"Exactly who are you, ma'am?" he said wearily.

"I'm Mrs. Janice Templeton. And the woman knows me!"

"Now you get back across that barrier before I lose my temper."

"I'm Mrs. Janice Templeton!" she wept. "And that man up there is my husband!"

Janice buried her face in her hands. The officer paused, nonplussed and suspicious.

"I'll let you tell your story to the chief," he said tautly, "but if you're playing games, you're going to feel very bad in the morning."

She mumbled her thanks, and felt him holding her up as her feet slipped sideways on the ice. As they passed the patrol cars, she heard bursts of static and STILL UNIDENTIFIED . . . THE GIRL SEEMS ALL RIGHT . . . WRAPPED IN BLANKET . . . REPEAT, THE GIRL STILL ALIVE AND IN GOOD HEALTH . . . Soon she was among the blue patrol cars and clusters of uniformed men, many of whom held long guns in their gloved hands, waiting for orders, sipping hot drinks.

The officer left her next to a coffee urn wedged in among two patrol cars. Her hands shaking, she tried to drink when a patrolman offered her a plastic cup. But the liquid spattered steaming into the snow.

Now Janice saw, in a bright circle, so bright that steam rose from the ice of the street, a news team aiming its video cameras upward, at the roof of 385 118th Street. Directional microphones were pointed at the top window, trying to catch Mrs. Hernandez's incoherent screams.

"My God! He's got my baby! Oh, my God! He's going to kill her!"

Evidently, the police had given up trying to calm her down, since they only watched over her head, where the steam curled past the roof, past the iron guardrail and a rusted fire escape platform. Janice peered into the darkness but saw nothing, only the low cloud covers. The snow had stopped falling. A bitter, calm cold froze everything and everybody. Mrs. Hernandez fainted at the window, her last shriek grown dismal and strained. Janice saw her sister gently pull her back into the apartment.

A tall man in a yellow slicker walked up quickly behind the officer.

"The chief's got other things to do," he said. "My name is Wilkins. I'm in charge. Now, who are you?"

"I'm Janice Templeton," she said, intimidated. "And my husband is the man up there."

"You sure?"

"I know it's Bill."

"How do you know it's Bill?"

"Because I know what he's looking for."

The officer and Wilkins exchanged glances. Puzzled, angry, suspicious, they were also frustrated by the cold, the hostile crowd that had gathered around, throwing ice balls, and now this woman who had come forward acting important.

"What is he looking for?" the officer asked as patiently as he could, rubbing his gloved hands for warmth.

Janice accepted another cup of hot coffee, this time able to keep from spilling.

"He's looking for a girl he believes to be his daughter," she said.

"What's he, drunk?" Wilkins shouted. "A psycho?"

"He's been in a sanitarium. He escaped yesterday."

The officer leaned forward again, remaining polite.

"What sanitarium is that, ma'am?" he asked.

"The Eilenberg Clinic. In Ossining."

"And what is the doctor's name?"

"Dr. Geddes. Ask him to describe me. He'll know who I am."

"Check it out, Cooper," Wilkins ordered.

Snatches of radio broadcast suddenly increased in volume: MOVING TO THE UPPER PLATFORM . . . GIRL VISIBLE . . . UP ON THE HIGH ROOF . . . RIFLES MOVE INTO POSITION . . .

Wilkins reached into the patrol car and picked up the radio phone.

"Wilkins here," he said gruffly. "No rifles. Can't see your ass from your front end up there. Let's get the kid alive, all right?"

He replaced the radio phone, just as Cooper came back quickly, slipping on the ice, then grabbing hold of the patrol car bumper. He nodded to Wilkins. His words came rushing out.

"There *is* a man escaped from the Eilenberg Clinic," he said. "Name's Templeton."

"Dangerous?"

"No record of violence."

"All right, miss," Wilkins said to Janice. "You're on. Think you can talk to this husband of yours?"

"I can try."

Janice followed Wilkins through the cordon of police. Now she saw, far overhead, weirdly foreshortened by the towering perspective, a man's form, the white shirt bright against the winter clouds. The face was lost in darkness, but against the chest was a large bundle.

"Bill!" she shouted.

No answer, but the crowd sensed something, and grew silent.

Wilkins and Janice went into the main door, now brightly lit with portable lamps and flashlights as well as the main corridor lights. Swinging arcs of the news team followed her, making their shadows leap and swarm. Wilkins angrily slammed the door shut.

"Scavengers," he hissed.

Wilkins led her up the floors, at each of which was a patrolman, armed with a long rifle. Wilkins knocked at the Hernandez door and then forced it open. Two policemen looked up. Huddled against the corner were Mrs. Hernandez, her sister, and two young men Janice had never seen before.

Mrs. Hernandez turned to Janice, her face swollen and red, the tracks of tears down her cheeks and around to her lower lip, making the once pretty face grotesque.

"Mrs. Templeton?" she whispered, puzzled.

"He's my husband, Mrs. Hernandez. I've come to help. If I can—"

"But why he do this? He say he from Welfare. I open the door. He start talking funny. I try to close the door. And look—my head. He push me down and hurt my head. Then he take my Juanita."

"He's not well," Janice said. "He's sick, up here, but he won't hurt Juanita."

"He's a dead man if he does," snarled one of the young men.

"Let's try the window," Wilkins said to one of the patrolmen.

The patrolman led the way to the living room, rammed the window open as far as it would go, and stuck his head out. He drew back in.

"It's a bad angle, sir. Especially since he moved back."

Wilkins poked his head out and bellowed. "Templeton! Listen to me! That girl is not yours! You bring her back and we'll get you some proper help! Hear me?"

They listened. There was only the soft sound below of cold men stepping on new-fallen snow; that, and a derisive crowd hooting from far away. Wilkins turned to Janice.

166

"You try."

Janice leaned so far out the window that Wilkins braced himself and held on to her.

"Bill!" she yelled. "Listen to me, Bill! The girl's name is Juanita! She doesn't belong to us! Bill! Bring her back!"

Wilkins pulled her back in.

"Gorman! There's a fire escape platform that goes up to the roof. See if you can find a way to get up there."

"Yes, sir."

"Don't go up there. Just let me know what it looks like."

"Yes, sir."

Mrs. Hernandez burst into wailing, a keening sound as though already mourning the loss of Juanita.

"Is he—is he gonna jump?" one of the young men asked.

"I don't know what the hell he's going to do, kid," Wilkins said. "Listen, Mrs. Templeton. Is he religious?"

"Not exactly."

"No priest or anybody he would listen to?"

Janice thought a moment. Wilkins's face was only inches in front of her, waiting aggressively, staring at her as though he had trouble with his eyes. They were all watching her and they sensed her sudden uneasiness.

"Maybe there is somebody," she said softly.

"Well, who, God damn it?"

"His name is Sri Parutha. He's Master of the Hompa Hongwanji Buddhist Temple in Greenwich Village."

Wilkins raised a gray tuft of an eyebrow.

"I might have known," he muttered. "You, uh, wouldn't know the telephone number?"

"Yes. It's 555-2024."

"Okay, Cooper. You know how to use the telephone."

While Cooper ran down to the telephone booth, Wilkins paced around and around. They sensed when Bill was moving by the "ooohs" and "ahhhhs" of the crowd down below. Mrs. Hernandez rocked back and forth, refusing all comfort, as though she herself had passed the brink of death.

Wilkins checked his watch.

"I don't like this," he murmured. "That girl's going to get real sick out in the cold like this."

Janice touched his sleeve. Surprised, he turned.

"Let me go up to the roof," she said. "If he saw me, he'd become himself again."

"Yeah?"

"Yes. I know it. He's a good man. He's just frightened."

"All right. Let's take a look at that fire escape."

As they went outside into the corridor, Borman came up to Wilkins, who snapped:

"What about that fire escape?"

"It's solid up to the roof. The top step is missing. Pretty bad ice, sir."

"Can we get Mrs. Templeton on the roof?"

"I'm not sure, sir."

"I wasn't really asking, Borman. I want her up there."

"Yes, sir."

Borman, Wilkins, and Janice hurriedly walked to the end of the hall. A thin vertical bar gave them purchase, but the ribbed metal stairs were slippery to the touch. Below was the gaping crowd, unaware as yet of what was happening.

"Goddamn fire traps," Wilkins growled.

Borman swung out into the air, supported by his two arms, his legs then grabbing firmly against the step. Bit by bit, the noise of the crowd solidified and rose, jeering, offering encouragement. Borman extended his hand. Janice grabbed it and swung upward onto the step.

"Keep your head down until you can verify he's unarmed," Wilkins ordered.

"Will do, sir."

Borman, one step ahead of Janice, pulled her, steadied her on the treacherous steps. The frigid wind whipped through her hair. Her hands burned on the cold metal rails. Twice she thought she was falling until Borman tilted her face upward to face the clouds, and not the ground.

"I'm going to stay just below," he whispered to Janice. "It's best he not know I'm here."

"I understand."

"Say whatever you want. Just bring him down."

"I'll do what I can."

Borman paused. "Because, I have to tell you. I've been on a few of these. They're going to choose between him and the girl, Mrs. Templeton, and it's not going to be him. It's too cold for her to be out any longer. Do you know what I'm saying?"

Janice nodded, feeling the bitter wind bite into her cheeks.

"Now you go on over the top. He won't see you for a few seconds. He's facing the street below."

Janice felt a steady pressure at her elbow, then at her hip, then her foot, and she felt the roof slide under her, and the hiss of the crowd and the glare of the arc lamps swinging madly, trying to catch her, until she knelt, then stood cautiously on the hard, icy roof.

Bill turned.

He was twenty yards from her, across the roof, partially obscured by a series of small chimneys, broken bottles, icy cardboard boxes stacked against one another. His face was unnaturally white, his hair wildly disheveled.

In his arms, clutched closely to his chest, in blankets, was Juanita. She must have been tired of crying. She only whimpered. For a hideous second, Janice thought the girl had gone into convulsions, but then she saw that Juanita breathed easily enough. Bill clutched her tighter to his chest and edged away along the guardrails of the roof.

Janice watched him.

"Leave me alone!" he barked.

She stopped. Now he had hidden himself behind the main chimney. Frantically, the searchlights pawed the darkness for him, then settled on the red brick of the chimney.

"Bill. Our child is cold. Bring her inside."

Bill wrapped Juanita tightly in blankets, even draping his

own sweater over her. He was wearing only a sweater. Somehow, he must have lost his coat. He shivered, and his lips looked abnormally dark.

"She's cold, Bill darling. Let's go home where it's warm."

"Leave me alone!"

"Bill! Look at her! It's below freezing!"

Bill rocked her gently in his arms, edging ever backward. Suddenly, Janice realized there was no railing behind him. She stopped, petrified.

"Bill, if she gets sick, an untimely death. Remember? Is that what you want?"

"Go away," he repeated, but weaker.

"When does it all end?" she pleaded. "Can you do to her what Hoover did to Ivy? Let her live, Bill! In peace!"

"She's mine," he growled.

"Of course, darling, but—"

"Then go away."

Frustrated, Janice shivered as the wind picked up again. She heard whispers below, behind her, on the fire escape. She thought she heard Wilkins issuing fresh orders. She stepped forward.

"Bill, there isn't much time. Bring her inside. I'm begging you."

Bill retreated, saw the danger at the last moment, slipped, and nearly fell the other way. A bottle soared downward out of sight. Seconds later, they heard it crash. Screams rose from the street crowd.

Bill turned to Janice, a hideous grimace on his face.

"A little more time, just a little more time. That's what you said. And all the while, you were leading me on. You knew three weeks ago."

"I did it for you, Bill!"

Bill laughed, tucking the blankets closer around Juanita. He rocked her back and forth, comforting her, while his haggard eyes glared at Janice.

"You've done nothing for me!" he snarled. "Not since the day Hoover came into our lives!"

Janice paled. She had never seen him spit such venom at anyone, much less herself. It had all backfired, she knew.

He stood upright, pointed a finger at her, "You *knew* . . . and you kept it from me!"

"I had to, Bill, for your sake!"

"*Go away*!"

Janice turned. She heard the patrolman hissing to her. She backed closer to the fire escape platform where Borman and Wilkins sat, revolvers drawn.

"Listen, Mrs. Templeton," Wilkins whispered, "we've located this holy man, but in this weather, it'll be a while before we can get him here. We can't get nets around the whole building and we think he's gonna jump. Now, I want you to get his attention. Get him to lower the child."

"No," Janice said. "I won't— You can't shoot him."

"Get in position, Borman."

"No!"

Janice ran halfway across the roof, then saw Bill back away. The gasps rose, from unseen mouths, below. He glared ominously at her.

"Bill," she pleaded. "There's a priest coming. The priest of the Temple. You'll let him talk to you?"

"I got nothing to say to anybody."

"But he's a holy man, Bill. He—he'll know the signs. The real signs. Bill, you could be wrong!"

Bill stared at her, unable to say anything. He clutched Juanita closer.

"Will you let him come?" Janice asked as gently as she could. "Let him make the determination?"

Bill said nothing, yet seemed to acquiesce. He settled himself miserably in the crook formed by the chimney and two guy wires. He turned his back to her, protecting himself as best he could from the wind.

Janice inched back to the fire escape and knelt down. Cooper's red face jerked, surprised to see her. Below Cooper was Wilkins.

"He's agreed to see the priest," she whispered. "That means he'll listen to reason."

Cooper and Wilkins looked at each other. Wilkins shrugged.

"Okay. Let's wait for His Highness," Wilkins said. "Mrs. Templeton, you better stay up there. Engage his attention, keep talking, keep him calm."

Janice went back to the corner of the roof. As she circled the guardrails, Bill's eyes followed her, but not his body, so that he remained hunched under the guy wires. Juanita seemed to sleep peacefully in his arms.

Janice settled to a spot about ten yards in front of him, at a ventilator shaft. There they stared at each other, as though across a no-man's-land, Bill's face changing from grief to hostility to guilt, but never saying a word.

He relaxed enough to lower his head, a sign of exhaustion. Then he jerked awake, scrambled to his knees, and stared feverishly into the darkness. He did not seem to know exactly where he was. Snow fell on his hair, stuck to his eyelids. He kissed Juanita's cheek gently and brushed the snow from her curly hair.

Down below the fire escape, a fresh commotion broke out as Mrs. Hernandez became hysterical with the waiting and had to be restrained.

Suddenly, jeers rose from the crowd. It was like an echo of jackals, reverberating among the alleys and the bricks. The news teams poked one another and shifted their video lenses. Bill pulled himself to his feet, and looked around as the snow began to fall heavily again, obscuring his vision.

"What?" he called. "Who's there?"

Up onto the roof, wearing black boots under his orange robe, the Master emerged. The wind whipped his robe around in a violent flutter. He blinked nervously, recognized Janice in the forms of snow and shadow among the debris. Then he followed her gaze to where Bill stood, clutching the infant.

The spotlights suddenly crisscrossed over the Master's body, like an incandescent lamp. He threw himself forward, arms outstretched, his yellow scarf billowing outward in the freezing wind: *"Om ayuse samharakesvare hum phat."*

Bill visibly paled, trembled at the words.

The Master stepped closer, out of the swirling snowstorm, and pointed directly at the girl in Bill's arms: *"Om ayuse samharakesvare hum phat!!"*

Bill retreated, until snow slipped off the near edge of the roof. The Master hesitated.

"I am Master Sri Parutha," he whispered rapidly. "Give me the girl!"

"No," Bill protested, shaking his head, afraid of the Master. "I won't! She's mine!"

"Have you passed the ninth circle of initiation?"

"What?"

"Have you?"

"No, I—"

"Then you are unqualified to judge her! It is for a holy man to say!"

Janice did not know whether the Master was making it up or whether, in fact, he was genuinely quoting doctrine. Bill too seemed puzzled. The Master leaned forward but was afraid to take a step.

Bill's left foot was already slipping on the ice at the edge of the roof.

"Give her to me!" the Master shouted.

"No. Please, don't make me—"

"Hand her to me," the Master said, softer now, almost friendly, "and let me make the determination."

Reluctantly, Bill, blinking back the tears and the snow from his eyes, took a single step and gently transferred the girl to the Master's arms. In that instant, a shot rang out, red drops

173

flew upward from Bill's shirt, and he was flung backward onto the roof.

Janice screamed from where she stood at the ventilator, and Borman climbed over the ledge, revolver drawn. Wilkins rapidly followed; the Master, face white, fell to his knees, though whether to protect Juanita or out of sheer terror even he did not know.

"Bill!" Janice shouted, and ran over the snow.

Her interposed body made it impossible for Borman to aim. Bill groaned, his legs kicking out, throwing clouds of snow into the night. He gritted his teeth in pain. As she clutched him, she saw a five-inch tear in his shirt, and flesh in his shoulder mixed with welling pools of blood.

"Bitch! Bitch!" Bill groaned.

"Bill! I meant to save you!" Janice wept.

He tried to shove her away, but she clung to him, crying; the pain finally overcame him, and he moaned, his chest heaving up and down. Janice whirled around.

"He's dying!" she yelled. *"Can't you help him?"*

"He ain't dying," Wilkins said, still crouching, but his revolver lowering. "It's just his shoulder."

Wilkins furiously hand-signaled to patrolmen in the street, pointed to an ambulance waiting at the barricade, then took Juanita from the Master's arms, felt her pulse and peered into her eyes.

"She's okay," he said. "Let's get her inside."

Two more patrolmen swarmed onto the roof. One of them took the girl carefully in his arms and, with the help of yet another patrolman, eased her down the steps and into the corridor below. Cheers, mingled with hoots, rose from the audience below, and applause, some derisive, resounded over the cleared intersection.

"You bitch!" Bill yelled, kicking futilely as Borman and Wilkins eased him to a sitting position, tore open his sweater and shirt. Soon a patrolman brought some cotton cloth and

174

bandages, Bill was read his legal rights, and they pushed him to a standing position.

Janice recoiled. Around Bill's head was an aureole of drifting snow, like an oblong halo; and his face, grimacing in pain, looked like Christ's as she had always imagined it—in agony, yet proud, and humble, but in Bill, unforgiving.

"Bill," she protested, shaking, a blanket draped over her shoulder by unknown hands, "I—I love you."

"Bitch!" he snarled.

"That's enough of the dramatics, friend," Wilkins said. "Let's go."

As they led him away, he resisted, so they hoisted him partially by the belt and partly under the good shoulder. As they approached the fire escape, more hands reached out, evidently afraid that he would try to throw himself off the roof.

"You knew!" he suddenly yelled.

A rough hand pushed his head down. Then he was gone.

On the roof, dazed, Janice walked unsteadily over the snow. Her feet cut cleanly toward the Master, himself badly shaken, readjusting his orange robe, gazing down the sheer drop to the streets below.

"Dear God," Janice whispered, "what have I done?"

"You did the only thing you could," the Master said as comfortingly as he could.

As he brushed the snow from her hair and shoulders, she swayed, grabbing his arm. He bent to support her, and then she shook her head violently, as though she were about to become ill. But she only looked dismally at the roof, the scuffles and streaks all over the snow, and a small red oval where Bill had fallen.

"Would you talk to him?" Janice asked. "Help him?"

The Master looked away. Over the neighboring roofs a pink light broke through from the adjacent city, making huge swirls of strange light around them.

"I'm not sure," he said evasively.

"Why not? You helped tonight."

"Yes, but—that was before I held the girl."

Janice stared at him. For a moment, she thought her heart had stopped.

"What?" she faltered.

"One senses these things. One has training. My perceptions, after the holy utterance, were heightened."

He backed away, but she grabbed his sleeve.

"What—what in heaven's name are you trying to say?"

"I—I'm not really sure, Mrs. Templeton. As I told you, I'm not completely versed in Tibetan Buddhism, their techniques. One has to go by impressions, purified by a life of training, of course. Strong impressions in the divination process..."

"Are you trying to say—?"

"It's not for me to say," the Master said quickly. "I think we'd better go."

"But, Master—"

"Please, Mrs. Templeton. Let me go."

The Master reached the fire escape, slipped, but found his footing and climbed down and inside. Janice went in after him, but he was quickly lost in the crowd in the dark. All she saw was a group of policemen gathered near the stairwell, and all she heard was Mrs. Hernandez weeping again, and the sound of the weeping reverberated throughout the hallway until Janice thought she would go mad.

BOOK II

JANICE

"I am beyond the perishable, and even beyond the imperishable.
In this world and in the Vedas I am known as the Spirit Supreme."

The Words of Krishna

Chapter Ten

Janice stared into the transient forms of pure space. Low drones, like Tibetan mountain horns, reverberated around her while the ragged clouds flew by and disintegrated. She stretched her legs against the narrow seat in front of her and leaned down to examine the folders in her leather handbag. Belgian printed fabrics, cost analyses, and a spiral notebook of charcoal sketches. Next to that was a bulging envelope of Marseilles summer design, nearly fifty brochures from an international design conference. Janice found her third packet, a collection of leather designs from Christine Daler Ltd.'s newest outlet in Tel Aviv. It was all there, plus photocopies of several disputed pay claims. Janice leaned back, still weary from the past two weeks of travel, delegations, hotels, and indigestion. She took pleasure in watching the clouds roll by beyond the metal wing. At five hundred miles an hour, she was going east, not west.

Her traveling case looked like a portable pharmacy. Antinausea pills, digestive liquids, antibiotics, and even powders to purify water. Passport, visa and, wrapped around the visa, a white paper. For the tenth time on the flight, she made certain the paper was there. It was an address, the only known conduit to Elliot Hoover.

Sesh Mehrotra. Hindu University, Benares (Varanasi), U.P.

The sunlight slanted in through the small curtains, white and pleasant on her hands. Janice realized she was nervously twisting her fingers into a locked mass, and she straightened her hands. She leaned back against the pillowed headrest and closed her eyes.

Once again she saw the same crowds. Crowds hooting on the ice-slick, night-reflecting alleys of Spanish Harlem. Crowds leaning over the police car as Wilkins drove her away. Crowds in the Criminal Court Building. She even recognized the corridors that led to the hall where Hoover had stood trial a year before. But this was a small chamber, and held only one lawyer, Dr. Geddes, five police officials, a stenographer, and two court psychiatrists. It all moved swiftly, like the extraction of a tooth. When it was over, Dr. Geddes grimly took her by the elbow and escorted her through the crowds.

It was then that the shock began to wear off. Janice found herself in a black limousine next to Dr. Geddes. A lawyer was next to the driver. It was a slow ride, the traffic was dense and gray in the filthy slush, and the limousine fought its way to the immense slabs of the parking structure behind Bellevue Hospital.

Bellevue was so large to her, it felt like dying to walk into its catacombs and chambers. There was no sense of emergency anywhere, only a sad, hopeless atmosphere that breathed despair from every dank corner. In the inner corridors, past the security wardens, the patients and orderlies shuffled with identical slow, lead-weight steps, as though they had all been condemned to New York's sepulcher for the insane.

Dr. Geddes impatiently showed his credentials to yet another desk official. The lawyer demanded entrance, and threatened to telephone the court. Janice signed long forms, short forms, a declaration of intent, and waivers. They were led into an older wing of the complex, where a system of metal grids blocked off the corridors.

Now there were sounds. Inhuman sounds that sent chills up her neck. There were cries, half barking, half howling, as she went by rooms where the inhabitants were unseen. The floors were covered with small drains, glistening ominously.

Janice followed Dr. Geddes and the lawyer into a room with two cots, only one of which was occupied.

It was Bill. They had shaved his hair. There were two bright scars at the back of his neck and an oblong purple bruise on his jaw. His fingernails were cracked and grimy. According to the orderly, he was in isolation now because an inmate had tried to bite off his nose.

Janice stared at his eyes sunk into a strange, hard skull, unseeing, uncaring. The marks on his face were as though painted on by a sadistic artist. He did not seem like Bill. Janice reeled, then touched his cheek, and when he made no response, she burst into tears at his feet.

Dr. Geddes gently comforted her. "The important thing is that we get him out of this hellhole."

"Where is he going?" Janice stammered.

"I couldn't take him back to Ossining," Dr. Geddes confided. "We don't have the facilities. But there is an institution on Long Island—Goodland Sanitarium part of the city's authority—and I know the administration very well. It's a very good hospital, very humane and decent, low density. Bill can get good, individual care."

Dumbly, Janice listened. Out on the streets of New York, the nightmare sensation escalated. From the hospital garage a car drove up with a guard and Bill in the backseat. Bill had been changed from his gray pajamas into his own clothes, but they no longer seemed to fit. He looked shrunken in the darkness of the thick upholstery. The driver and the guard

181

were both broad-shouldered and ham-fisted, and they kept their eyes on him.

As the car glided over the long system of bridges and thruways, Dr. Geddes began telling her about the institution. He had gone to medical school with the chief psychiatrist. The institution was opposed to the use of drug therapy. It had a relatively high rate of success. The landscape of Long Island swept by—marshland and distant stately homes obscured by clusters of brown apartment complexes, and then the lonely sweep to the sandy dunes again—and Janice saw none of it. She looked searchingly at Bill, and she knew that he was more dangerously sick than he had ever been before.

She said good-bye to him in his small, private room high on the ninth floor of the institution. There were bars on the windows, the furniture had no corners, and there were no implements of any kind in the drawers—no pens, no pencils, no scissors. Even the coat hangers were rounded plastic. Janice kissed Bill on the forehead.

"I'll get help for you, Bill," she whispered, stroking his cheek.

Now the airplane banked slightly, a warm shaft of light fell over her eyes, and she woke up. Janice strolled the aisles, her body lethargic and anxious from the two weeks of conferences, arguments, and cables back to Elaine. At least that tension was gone. But it had been good for her.

Janice looked out the round window at the endless, hot sky over the ocean. A curved horizon demarcated the end of things that could be known, things that could be felt. Beyond, an obscure haze, born of heat and dry wind, desert dust and the glare of the sun, faded to a blue white.

One senses these things. One has training. My perceptions, after the holy utterance, were heightened....

Janice remembered pounding on the door of the Temple. No one was in the sanctuary. When she went to the alley and looked into the Master's room, it was empty. A pane of glass was already broken, and beyond it a few bare shelves were visible. Even the makeshift desk had been removed. At the front door black graffiti had been sprayed in large script. Two men stood there, contemplating the dimensions of the room inside through the glass panes.

"Excuse me," Janice said. "I'm looking for the Master."

"Who?"

"The Master of the Temple, Sri Parutha."

The two men looked at each other and shrugged.

"Lady, this here is a vegetarian restaurant."

They turned away, examining small diagrams and a section of blueprint.

It was true. There was not the slightest evidence that there had ever been a temple on the site. Not a flower remained inside or in the garden behind. None of the neighboring shops had cared to learn what had happened to the Master or his dwindling group of would-be ascetics.

At Des Artistes, Janice telephoned thirteen religious study centers in Manhattan. None had heard of the Temple. None had any answer for her.

One has to go by impressions—strong impressions—in the divination process.

Janice started, caught herself staring vacantly into the blue white haze, so evanescent, yet so impenetrable that it seemed the place to which all answers had fled. Reluctantly, she sat back in her seat and tried to nap.

The first days of seeing Bill had been an all-too-familiar kind of torture. He sat unresponsive, dead to her and the rest of the world. By the end of the week, however, he had begun speaking. Incoherent secrets whispered out of his mouth. He begged Janice to bring his daughter to him. He did not hear her answer that the Hernandez family had virtually boarded itself inside its dark apartment. Bill only leaned forward, finger gently tapping her forearm, insisting that his daughter was waiting, crying; she wanted him, he wanted to see her.

By the end of the second week, Bill seemed oblivious to the presence of humans. He stepped on their toes, bumped into them, as though they were fixtures of furniture. Halfway through the third week, Bill was reduced to violent gestures, moody silences, and occasional periods of gentle crying.

"He's slipping," Dr. Geddes admitted. "Slipping badly."

"Maybe if he could be disabused of his obsession," commented the chief psychiatrist. "This fantasy of reincarnation."

But Bill was not disabused of his fantasy. He clung to it with a passion that startled Janice. Unable to articulate coherent sentences, he wrestled with his emotions, his neck muscles straining, the veins in his forehead bulging. He pleaded, wept, and collapsed in misery on his bed. The hospital staff began to consider mild drug therapy if his symptoms turned self-destructive.

When April ended, Janice felt ruined. She had neither the strength nor the hope for continuing the marathon trips to Long Island. A feverish, permanent fatigue assailed her, and her work became confused. It was late twilight with the rush-hour traffic already thinning out, when Elaine pulled up a chair near Janice's drafting table.

"Janice," she said softly, "I think we'd better talk."

Janice looked up with foreboding.

"Am I slipping that badly, Elaine?"

Elaine smiled thoughtfully. "You're tired, Janice. You're exhausted. Running back and forth between Manhattan and Long Island. You've got all the symptoms of being worked to death. I've seen it happen. I want you to take a break."

Janice paled. "Elaine, please, my job is my life."

"Don't jump to conclusions. There's a couple of assignments in Europe that we need to look up. I want you to go."

"But I couldn't," Janice protested. "Bill needs me. He's helpless."

"So will you be in another week. Janice, you look like wet newspaper. You're going to disintegrate at this rate."

Janice put down her ink brush and swiveled away from Elaine. The idea was totally unexpected, yet it had the clarity of a burst of sunlight through dark clouds.

"I suppose I could tell Dr. Geddes."

Elaine smiled. "Excellent," she said. "And if I were you, I'd start packing. The first conference starts next Tuesday."

Janice nodded, but the suddenness caused a strange vertigo. Somehow, she had never thought that any kind of escape was possible, not now, and not in the future. Guiltily, she realized how she hungered for a few days' liberty. She needed it the way a drowning animal needs air.

Suddenly Des Artistes did not feel so dark, so cold. The sight of her packed luggage was a visible symbol of a new possibility: a resurgence of hope. She checked and rechecked her itinerary. Brussels, Marseilles—and now Elaine had added the Israeli market. The passport on her desk, the letters of introduction, her confirmed hotel reservations made hope not only real, but imminent. Late at night, she spoke one last time with Dr. Geddes.

"Perfectly appropriate idea," Dr. Geddes said. "I've told you that. You need a break."

"But what if something happens? Suppose he calls for me?"

"I doubt very much that Bill will be calling for anybody in the near future. Except Ivy."

It was shortly after the Brussels conference that the idea came to her. Back in her hotel room, she raced to her luggage and pulled out her battered leather address book. There was a name, a name that had known Hoover, though she could not remember it.

Halfway through the address book, she found, simply: *Mehrotra, Sesh. Hindu University. Benares (Varanasi), U.P.* She recalled very well that after Ivy died, she had written to

Hoover, to explain to him her feelings. It was to Mehrotra that the letter was sent.

As the warm spring night drifted in, she thought of Hoover. She thought of his pale, almost recessive eyes, eyes that were handsome except that they had seen too much suffering. Pale skin and a burning sincerity that swept everything away—reason, logic, normalcy—in one tidal wave of charisma. It was Hoover who had told her Ivy was in danger. It was Hoover who could have saved her child. If Juanita was, in some way—if Juanita *could be* in a god-awful but logical way—Ivy, then Hoover would know.

I'll get help for you, Bill.

Janice cabled Elaine from Tel Aviv, asking for another five days. Elaine quickly agreed. A half day at a branch of the Chase Manhattan finally produced a draft for nearly a thousand dollars.

The travel agent looked up, his tie loosened, an ashtray bulging with half-smoked cigarettes.

"I'd like to go to India, please," Janice said softly.

"Where would you like to go? India is a big place."

"I must go to Benares."

"Ah. You're one of those pilgrims," he said, smiling. "It's Varanasi now. Not Benares. Though to everyone, it is still called Benares. You will transfer in New Delhi."

That night, Janice watched the concrete runways glide by as she walked toward the gleaming steps of an Air India jet. It was all a dream, she thought. Life had become a series of disconnected dreams. The engines roared into life, there was a terrific pull at her stomach, and she seemed to wake up in some mysterious way. She was truly flying to India.

Below, a series of white lines, in immense parallel curves, came quickly to view. Beige sand. Dark green of tropical plants. Wide roads, where trucks carried clouds of white dust. Then an immense continent, so large it seemed to bend with the earth, dark and mottled, glinting with small patches of moist ground, paddy fields, and tiny rivers. It was India. It looked like an untended world, violent and crude.

Janice swallowed. It was really India. Anxiety overcame her. She drew back into her seat, away from the window. There was no escape. The idea that she should have come so far, so suddenly, to look for Elliot Hoover, seemed obscene. Nervously, she checked for the hundredth time that Sesh Mehrotra's address was still in her travel bag, though she had long ago memorized it. She tried to imagine Mehrotra. She tried to imagine Elliot Hoover. All she saw was a kind of nervous cloud, where everything was unclear, turbulent, unformed.

Chapter Eleven

"Taxi? Taxi? You like a taxi?" said six men together, running up to her.

"Yes, I—"

"Come. You come with me. Cheap."

"Please, miss. Beautiful Buick. You come with me."

"Lowest price. No detour. Come on, miss."

Distraught, Janice fumbled in her purse for the card upon which was printed the name of her hotel. In that instant, three drivers grabbed for her suitcase; one was successful and, alarmed, Janice ran after him. The lucky driver opened the trunk of a small black Ford, dropped in her suitcase, and slammed the lid. He turned to her and smiled.

"Where to?" he asked, proud of himself.

Janice had no choice but to show him the card.

"Varanasi Palace Hotel," he read slowly. "Number one in city. Get in, please."

Janice's heart was racing so fast, she felt the pulse in her throat. There was no retreat, no going back. The highway raced forward to glide under the wheels of the taxi. To the sides were patches of mud and clumps of grass, littered with white paper and broken bottles. Filthy goats stood by mud ridges and chewed, unblinking, at pieces of fabric.

By the time the taxi entered the outer reaches of Benares, Janice's face was covered in perspiration. It plastered her blouse to her skin, her hair to her scalp. Dust and grime coated her shoes and even her fingernails. Exhausted, she stared out at the city that rapidly approached.

The highway was filled with groups of old men wearing absolutely nothing but loose, skimpy loin cloths. They seemed not to be casually walking but to have a mission, a barely concealed energy behind their movements.

"They have come to Benares to die," said the driver in a gentle English. "It is blessed to die in Benares."

"Benares," Janice whispered to herself. The sound of the city conjured frightful images. The Ganges, she knew, flowed through the city, and it was holy—and it would be noisy, and somewhere deep in the outskirts perhaps, at a study center or in a small home, was Elliot Hoover. It was as if she were keeping a rendezvous. Was he waiting for her, too, in some disturbing, almost occult foreknowledge? Or would he close his door in her face?

The Varanasi Palace Hotel was small, only five floors, and it was old. It was located at the edge of the "containment," or residential compound once built for the British and still mostly Western in character. The avenues were straight, clean, but the noise of Benares submerged the elegant palm trees in a turbulence of sound: a thousand bulls lowing, ten thousand men shouting, and everywhere, clanging through the sky, the hundreds upon hundreds of temple bells, some heavy as gongs, some light as tinkling glass, making a cacophonous music that shook the city.

The taxi came to a halt in front of the doorman. Under the awning, a turbaned Punjabi slowly opened the door for Janice and waited for the driver to take the suitcase from the trunk. She paid, took a brisk look at the spare lines of the Varanasi Palace, and followed the doorman into the hotel.

"To the desk, please," the Punjabi said, pointing.

Inside, lazy black fans turned high overhead against white ceilings. Enormous red rugs covered the floor, and the couches and chairs were also red, so that the interior looked like a huge Matisse. Glass chandeliers glittered in regular sequences through the lobby. A gentleman in white cloth read a newspaper with the aid of a magnifying glass. Janice walked slowly to the desk.

"Yes, please?" inquired a short, dark-haired clerk with a red coat.

"Mrs. Templeton. Arriving from Tel Aviv."

Fingers the shade of cocoa rapidly skimmed through a rolling file. Then he looked up, smiling, and raised an eyebrow in the direction of an aged porter. The old man immediately hobbled to the desk. There was a brisk command and then the clerk smiled obsequiously to Janice.

"Room 507, please," he said.

Janice nodded, still confused by suddenly being in India, but now reassured by the Western efficiency, even impersonality, of the Varanasi Palace.

The old man, who also wore a red coat, heaved the suitcase onto a back already bent with age. Strangely, at the elevator, he only instructed the operator, then proceeded to walk the entire five floors up to her room. Puzzled, Janice waited for him. At length he arrived, breathing hard and sweating. His hands were permanently curled by a life of hard labor.

He opened the door to room 507. Janice walked in. It was cool. The walls were white. Fresh flowers bloomed from glass bowls. The bedspread was white, patterned by its weave of fresh cotton. The bathroom was clean. There was nothing that indicated she was in India except the bent porter at the door. She gave him what she thought was a fair tip. He stared at her in mixed gratitude and defiant, almost hostile pride. For a second, she thought he would refuse it. Then he nodded, blinked his rheumy yellow eyes, and departed, closing the door.

Janice sat down on the bed. It had silent springs, firm yet resilient. Strange, confused emotions swirled inside her. She felt like laughing. She felt like crying. She felt like running around the block, overflowing with nervous energy.

Janice called down to the desk, found the correct time, and adjusted her watch. It was only 12:30 in the afternoon in Benares.

She undressed, stepped under the shower, and found the water hot and delicious in its sting. She shampooed her hair twice, rinsed thoroughly, and combed her hair down. In the mirror, she looked into her own eyes and could not decipher the look she found in them. Was she courageous or insane? She dressed carefully in beige slacks, white blouse, and sandals. The afternoon was hazy, the clouds spread evenly over the serrated skyline of high-rise apartments and slums. Down at the desk she composed an express letter to Bill.

Dearest. Am searching. Will find help for both of us. Trust and believe. All my love. Janice.

She addressed it in care of Dr. Geddes, asking him to give it to Bill or withold it, as he thought best. The stationery had the hotel's address if Dr. Geddes needed to contact her.

A taxi took her quickly from the hotel, out of the residential compound, and back into the morass of animals, bauble sellers, brass workers, fortune-tellers, precariously balanced fruit stands, pilgrims of various castes—some nearly naked, many with ash smeared across their aged breasts—and up a long hill, where Janice could see the breathtaking spectacle of nearly two thousand spires, domes, minarets, and towers rising like a vast rock crystal garden, glittering in mosaic brilliance against a pure blue sky. Now she could see the great brown river, the Ganges, rolling imperturbably toward the Bay of Bengal. The shores were hidden by clusters of shops and crumbling houses, but beyond was that same muddy wasteland of the great, hot flood plain.

The taxi swerved around a corner and stopped. In front of her was an imposing white edifice, its top story on supports, creating the impression of a vast fortress. A sign read, in three languages, *Hindu University.*

The entrance to the administration hall led to a series of foyers, each of which led to complexes of reception and office space. Janice walked slowly through the vast, black-tiled area, where the light came in through tall, narrow windows high over her head, and her heart was beating so violently she thought it would echo off the stone.

A steel-framed door led to a narrow corridor. File cabinets made the corridor even more narrow. Janice walked down throught the dusty channel and emerged at a second door that opened onto a large typing pool. The typists were all women, with brightly colored saris, and they typed with manic efficiency.

Janice leaned against a marble-topped counter and looked around. The women clattered away, some at electric machines, others at older, upright models. Finally, a young girl with jet black eyes and hair, and a subtle mustache over her full red lips, sauntered to the counter. She said nothing.

"I'm looking for Sesh Mehrotra," Janice said. "Here. Let me write it down." She spelled out the name. The girl stared blankly at it.

"He is a student here?" the girl asked.

"I don't know. He might be an instructor."

The girl walked to a horizontal steel bin. Her bracelets jangled as her dark arms riffled quickly among the entries there. From time to time, she pulled out a file, checked it against the name, and slid the file back into its holder. At last she copied something down on the slip of paper, and came to the counter. On the paper she had written: *Department of Philosophy.*

* * *

It was a small office, dominated by a single desk with a middle-aged woman, her floral print sari and brass bangles glimmering like a fallen chandelier. Behind was the landscape of Benares, leading down to the warm brown Ganges. The receptionist had white hair twined into the black, and under her dense black eyebrows her eyes were soft and brown. She waited for Janice to speak.

"I'm looking for Mr. Sesh Mehrotra," Janice said softly.

With a subtle nod, the woman disappeared toward the office in the rear. Janice waited. The receptionist returned brandishing a piece of paper. She handed it to Janice.

"This street is in Benares?" Janice asked.

"Why don't you just telephone?" she offered, indicating the desk phone.

Trembling, Janice's fingers traced out the number inscribed on the paper. There was a muted storm of static, a buzz and three clicks, and then a voice answered. It sounded old, neither male nor female, and it was asking a question.

"I'm sorry," Janice said, trying to control her voice, "do you speak English?"

Quizzically, the voice responded by repeating its question.

"English," Janice repeated, louder. "Do you speak English?"

Now the voice became irritated, in the manner of nearly deaf persons, and for the third time it shouted back its question. Janice looked around helplessly. The receptionist took the receiver from her hand. A few quick words were exchanged, and the receptionist hung up.

"Mr. Mehrotra has several jobs," the receptionist explained, pulling out a small map from a drawer. "Most likely he is at his position *here*."

"Thank you—thank you."

Elated, Janice carefully folded the map and put it into her handbag. She was so happy, she almost did not know where she was going. At a small shop—more a three-sided booth than a shop—she bought a more durable blouse and a pair of the cheap wicker sandals that all the women of Benares wore.

She hailed a taxi and showed the map to the driver, who nodded and sped off.

At last the taxi found the street. It was slimy with cow dung, wet, squashed, and mingled with dropped fruit, long mashed into a single green slime on the stones. The street was ancient, the walls leaned over it, and shadows of buyers and sellers mingled into a single ever-changing black shape against the ground. Janice paid the fare, and walked slowly, as though feeling her way. The street intersection circled on the map turned out to be the junction of two alleys, dense with brassware, portraits of religious gurus, and men who stared out at her with vacant black eyes.

Janice approached a shop. A clerk labored over a huge ledger at one side of his shelves of brass. He looked angry, as though he would rather be almost anywhere else. He looked too educated, out of place. With a burst of energy, he began computing the long columns of entries.

"Mr. Mehrotra," Janice said gently.

He looked up. His face was round, and he wore black-rimmed glasses. He needed a shave. His black hair was curly, and his eyes small and nearsighted. He wore a white shirt and white pantaloons, sandals, and three gold rings. He seemed glad to be interrupted.

"Mr. Mehrotra," Janice said. "My name is Janice Templeton."

Uncomprehending, Mehrotra shook her extended hand. Then his face paled. His eyes widened until he stared at her.

"Yes," she said simply. "It's really me."

Mehrotra leaned across the shelf, staring unashamed into her face. He swallowed nervously and tried to smile.

"I gave your letter to Elliot Hoover," he said.

"Thank you. I've come to meet Mr. Hoover."

Mehrotra smiled, but it was not a pleasant smile. It was nervous, and he backed away, casting quick glances at the neighboring shops.

"Why?" he asked. "*Why* is it you have to meet him?"

"Because my husband is ill."

"What? I do not understand, Mrs. Templeton."

Janice paused. She sensed that Mehrotra was guarding Hoover, that he would have to be won over or she would never get past the clerk. At least it meant that Mehrotra and Hoover were still in close contact.

"Will you have some time free this morning?" she asked softly, "so that I can explain?"

"Time?" Mehrotra laughed. "I have nothing but time."

He threw his columned book back onto his canvas chair. Then he violently closed the shop, shoving revolving shelves of brass trays and pots inside the booth, rolling down a quick iron gate, and locking it. He tucked the key into his pocket and took Janice by the elbow.

"Please, do not slip on the blood."

Janice gasped. In the fetid quarters of the back alleys, a heap of diseased chickens had been thrown, and the dogs had charged into them, sending flickers of blood against the walls.

"Be careful of the ox cart."

A dark brown bullock rumbled by, pulling a creaking wagon in which a man appeared to be fast asleep, holding a short black whip.

They left the system of alleys, emerged into the sunlight, and the air smelled of the turbulent Ganges not far away. Mehrotra suddenly turned on Janice.

"Why have you come for Mr. Hoover?" he demanded.

Tongue-tied, Janice did not know how to begin.

"You know," she began, "you know—about Ivy?"

"Of course I do."

"Well, after she was cremated, my husband became ill. He began to study, to think that Ivy—that Ivy might come back."

Mehrotra stamped his foot with impatience.

"Of *course* she will come back! What has that to do with your husband's illness?"

"I'm— You're making it so hard to explain."

"Come! Come with me and tell me."

They walked out from the last of the cramped buildings, the last of the brilliant wood and stone temples, the last of the ox carts. It was suddenly spacious. Enormous steps led down to the Ganges, and periodically tall sculptured stones, like rounded pyramids, rose to punctuate the miles of riverbank. The activity on the huge steps was incredible, thousands of human beings crowding into the water, some under wicker umbrellas on the steps, and smoke rising from clusters of wood and cloth, trailing high into the implacable blue sky.

"Is this—is this where Ivy's ashes—" Janice stammered, reeling, holding on to Mehrotra's arm, which stiffened as it felt her weight.

Mehrotra understood and gently supported her, putting an arm lightly around her shoulder. His voice softened.

"It was not exactly here," he admitted, "but nearby."

He pointed to a stretch of the stone steps beyond a cluster of men so old and emaciated they looked as though they had already become corpses. Mehrotra paused, sensitive now, and his voice lowered.

"In the early dawn," Mehrotra said gently, "we took the canister of ashes and went down to the Ghats—these steps—and spread the ashes slowly into the middle of the Ganges. Elliot Hoover and I. And I watched him pray, and then we came to the shore and the sun dried our clothes."

"And did he say anything?" Janice asked.

"Only that he hoped Ivy's soul had found peace."

Mehrotra took Janice down the Ghats. She was afraid of the dense groups of Hindus, afraid of the smoke, which she now realized came from funeral pyres shamelessly arranged in public. It seemed as though the whole of Benares was dedicated to death, a methodical, sober business, neither morbid nor joyful, but matter-of-fact, like selling vegetables.

"It is nothing," Mehrotra reassured her. "Death is Benares's biggest business. All these temples, woodcutters, tourist vendors—this is Lord Shiva's city, and Lord Shiva, the Dancer, is the god of destruction.''

Pyres were now visible all down the Ghats, on all the levels, almost down to the lapping water itself. Children walked among the fire-tenders, barely cognizant of the consumption of human bodies all around them.

"Was that . . . Was that the last time you saw Mr. Hoover?'' Janice asked, trying to keep pace with Mehrotra as they climbed down the river.

"No, I saw him twice more. He came to my brother's wedding, and then about four months ago . . .''

Black-skinned men, absolutely naked, faces flattened and aboriginal, came in between them. Janice fought her way to Mehrotra again. Suddenly they were on the lowest step. The Ganges splashed up and soiled her beige slacks.

"Four months ago?'' Janice insisted, breathing hard. "Where is he now?''

Mehrotra turned, the sunlight brilliant on his unshaven cheeks. He smiled softly.

"Elliot Hoover has gone on a pilgrimage,'' he said quietly.

Janice, startled, found herself unable to say anything.

"To the South,'' he continued, smiling at her mysteriously.

"Will he come back?''

Mehrotra shrugged. "Normally one is gone about a year. That would mean eight months from now.''

Janice covered her ears as a white boat, its decks overloaded with passengers, sounded its horn.

"*Eight months?*'' she yelled. "That's impossible!''

Mehrotra took her slowly along the bottom step of the Ghats. He gave a coin to a beggar, but stepped over the others.

"Why is that impossible?'' Mehrotra asked placidly.

"I need to see him.''

"Tell me why.''

"My husband thinks that Ivy—feels very sure that Ivy has come back."

"You already told me that."

"And we must know for certain."

Mehrotra looked at her, surprised.

"Why?" he asked blandly.

"Because he has been institutionalized for thinking it!" she said, and then burst out, "Because he believes he's found her."

Mehrotra's eyes fastened upon hers. "And you? What do you believe?"

Janice could only return his piercing gaze as the great and overwhelming question hung between them. She shrugged in helpless dismay.

"You mustn't have doubts," he said earnestly. "Reincarnation is a fact of life. With all of us."

"Yes, here. But in New York..."

"You're not in New York now. Look, believe your heart. What does your heart tell you?"

"It's my head," she laughed ruefully. "It doesn't quite want to latch onto it."

"You Westerners," Mehrotra mocked. "You live in little cages. Would you believe me if I proved it to you?"

She looked at him, surprised at the jocularity in his voice.

"If you had faith," he said, holding up a finger, "you would not need proof. Nevertheless, I can show you something. Yes? Come with me."

Janice followed him into a dank, dark alley. It was so moist that a kind of thick, green moss grew at the base of the walls.

Then the alley grew narrow. Finally, it was no more than a passageway between leaning stone walls.

Mehrotra turned at a wooden gate, climbed rickety steps, and stepped onto a wide, surprisingly clean, stone floor. Tall windows poured rectangles of warmth onto the stone. An aged woman, a younger woman, and five black-eyed children stared shyly at her.

Mehrotra spoke rapidly, pointed to Janice. She thought she heard Elliot Hoover's name mentioned. Then he pointed them out, one by one.

"My sister, Aliya. Her mother-in-law and the children. They're Aliya's."

Aliya smiled pleasantly.

As Mehrotra chatted with his sister, deferring in his speech to the mother-in-law, Janice looked around at the children. They huddled at the door, and when they saw her looking, they ran back into the kitchen. The enormous depths of the black eyes startled her. They were like shaded pools, naive, and troubling in their purity.

Aliya gently handed Janice a cup and saucer, then set a strainer on the cup. The tea burbled musically into the small chinaware. Aliya did the same for Mehrotra and the mother-in-law, casting shy glances at Janice.

"Arun!" Mehrotra called.

Shyly, a slender boy, about ten years old, emerged from the kitchen, and nestled himself onto Mehrotra's lap.

"Now," Mehrotra said, "my sister's mother-in-law will tell you the story of her Uncle Vinoba."

Mehrotra directed the mother-in-law to begin. The lady had a slightly humped back, so she had to move the chair to face Janice.

"I will translate," Mehrotra said.

The woman began. The language did not seem even to have syllables, only melodic rambling.

"She is speaking a very old dialect," Mehrotra whispered, "about the days of her mother. It was when the British were in India. She always begins the same way." Mehrotra translated: "In those days, not far from here, the British had rubber plantations. But they always made the men elect a foreman of their own choosing to be the go-between. In this way, they controlled the workers more easily."

The aged voice continued.

"Now Uncle Vinoba wanted to be that foreman. After all, the pay was good, he could have a hut to himself and sometimes wear the company watch on a chain."

Janice leaned toward Mehrotra to hear better.

"Now, in those days, there were always rebellions in the rubber plantations. Uncle Vinoba ingratiated himself with the workers. But also with the British. To make a long story shorter, he was elected to lead a rebellion. Now this was very bad, because he was afraid of the British. But he did not want to anger the rebels. So he said yes."

Janice nodded, sensing Mehrotra waited for a reaction. The old woman rattled on.

"The rebellion was planned for the full moon. One group would attack the soldiers on the north road. One group would sneak into the company headquarters and kill the British. Naturally, as leader, Uncle Vinoba would go to the headquarters."

Janice watched the children. Now they sat quietly in the room on the floor, as though eager to hear the story over again. Some of them anticipated, their mouths moving, as though they had nearly memorized it.

"Suspecting nothing, the men watched Uncle Vinoba walk to the headquarters building. But when he got inside, he told the British everything. A messenger sneaked out the back way to alert the soldiers. Guns were brought down from upstairs. Then Uncle Vinoba went back to the rebels."

The old woman took a very deep breath and suddenly leaned forward.

"Well, Uncle Vinoba sweated like a pig. But exactly at midnight he led the men forward. They tiptoed up the red carpets—the British love red carpets—Uncle Vinoba in front. All at once, the British jumped out from the side of the stairwell, from the bottom floor, and down from the upstairs. An enormous roar of gunfire, and all the rebels were killed.

Except Uncle Vinoba. It was said that the blood was found even on the ceiling.''

There was a long pause. The old woman fanned herself with a paper and bamboo fan.

"Uncle Vinoba became the foreman. He lived alone, never married, and always carried a knife with him, even though he never cut the rubber himself. After all, most of the workers were related to the dead men.''

Mehrotra patted Arun on the stomach. Arun giggled.

"One night, about a year later, the widows broke into his hut. They grabbed him, tied him up, and dragged him screaming out into the forest. There they secured him between two rubber trees. The elephants were brought in, and for each man who had died, an elephant was made to step on him. That was twenty-one times, because there were fifteen in the fields and six killed in the headquarters. Anyway, his screams echoed all over the plantations. The soldiers were too frightened to come, because they thought it was an unnatural sound, or maybe the wild dogs from the mountains. In the morning the British found a length of rope, broken ferns all around, and tangled-up pieces of broken, red bones. Poor Uncle Vinoba.''

The story went on, but Mehrotra ignored the old woman.

"Now, Mrs. Templeton. There are fifteen dead men in the fields. Six in the headquarters. How many is that?''

"Twenty-one.''

Mehrotra lifted Arun's shirt. Spread across his back, in uneven double rows, were peculiar cherry red markings, like scallops in shape. Their shape fascinated Janice. They were almost delicate, not at all gruesome or disfiguring, and Arun smiled shyly.

"Have you ever seen an elephant's footprint?'' Mehrotra asked.

She looked at him, startled.

"Look, Mrs. Templeton. Here are the toes, the heavy weight at the back, where the marks are thicker.''

She found it difficult to believe.

"Twenty-one marks, Mrs. Templeton," Mehrotra said measuredly. "Five years ago, when we visited our cousins where the rubber plantation used to be—it's a shirt factory now—Arun became very frightened, and he did not know why. Now he will tell you what he said."

Mehrotra whispered in the boy's ear.

Arun turned to face Janice, closed his eyes, and with difficulty, formed the words, "I—hear—guns."

"See?" Mehrotra demanded. " 'I hear guns.' In English, Mrs. Templeton! And he never studied English, then or now!"

"I—hear—guns," Arun repeated, pleased at the reaction.

Arun slid off his lap, and went to join the other children.

"Every village, every town, every quarter of every large city is filled with these stories. A girl has the markings of a dead aunt. Or a man suddenly acts strangely and speaks a different dialect. Or a child must visit a certain area where he has never been. Why? Because they are the living incarnations of the dead! That's why! Believe, Mrs. Templeton!"

Janice followed Mehrotra back into the brilliant sunshine that poured upon the multitudes who pressed upon the sacred Ganges. He took her by the elbow and led her through waves of ascetics and urban faithful.

"About Elliot Hoover," Janice stammered.

"I was afraid—I must confess—you had some romantic interest," Mehrotra shouted above the prayerful cacophony. "I protect him."

"Then you can tell me where he is?"

"Elliot Hoover is at an *ashram* on the Cauvery River."

"Where is that?"

"In the State of Tamil Nadu."

"Is there a telephone there?"

Mehrotra laughed. "Not at the *ashram*. And it will take at least a week, if you are lucky, for a letter to find its way into the mountains."

Mehrotra pulled her gently toward him, just as an ox cart lumbered by, dropping loose sticks of firewood for the Ghats. He felt her trembling.

"I think you must go yourself," he said quietly. "It is the quickest."

Janice looked at the round, still-unshaven face, the owl glasses, and she saw the steadfast darkness of his eyes, the unwavering compassion. She knew now why he and Elliot Hoover were friends.

"I think I'd be afraid to," she said weakly.

"Afraid? Of India? Don't travel after dark, that's all."

The mere thought made Janice's head dizzy. The South conjured up an unpleasant image, vague but festering with gross jungle growth, animals like baboons, villages with dysentery.

"Do you have money?" he asked.

"I can change some more."

"Good. You can fly to Mysore City. I will show you what to do after that. I only wish I could go with you. Elliot and I have a firm friendship."

Mehrotra led her into his shop. He shoved several volumes of Schopenhauer, Hume, and Tagore onto the floor. Several notebooks he pushed more gently onto his chair. From a drawer he extracted an ancient atlas printed in German, and paged through the faded color areas.

"This is the Cauvery River," Mehrotra said matter-of-factly. "It is like the Ganges, a holy river."

Janice watched, fascinated as the lean brown finger traced the path southeast from Mysore City into the mountains and then to the valley of the upper Cauvery.

"You see? Not so far," he said smoothly. "From Mysore City there is a train. To Kotagiri. Then you must take a bus—I will write down its name—going east toward Erode, then it goes south. Right here"—he indicated an area where few village names were inscribed on the map—"is the *ashram*."

The empty area on the old map looked intimidating. There were German phrases in parenthesis which seemed to indicate the central mountains were poorly explored.

"How do I know when I get to the *ashram*?" she finally asked.

"It is a Hindu temple and it is dedicated to *Tejo Lingam*—the fire incarnation of God. I can write that down for you."

Mehrotra sat at his desk and in a lovely calligraphy wrote out the name of the *ashram*. On a separate sheet of paper, he wrote a brief description of the *ashram*'s location, in various languages.

"In case nobody speaks English, just show them this," he said, handing her the letter. "But pilgrims go there all the time. You will have no difficulty."

Janice gingerly took the letter. She folded it and put it carefully into her handbag. For a long time, she looked at the gleaming brassware on curved trays, many hanging from silver chains over the shop.

"Please tell Elliot that I—" Mehrotra faltered. "That I have been unable to come this year, but that I look forward to seeing him again in Benares."

Moved by the depth of his feeling, Janice agreed. She thanked him, they shook hands, then Janice stood up. Mehrotra looked very sad.

"You will have good luck. I will pray for you."

She smiled, waved good-bye as she stepped away, and it was only when she reached the empty boulevards of the residential area that the anxiety returned. She stepped resolutely into the hotel.

Chapter Twelve

"I need to fly to Mysore City," she told the desk clerk. "Can you connect me with the proper airline?"

"Mysore City?" he asked, raising an eyebrow. "Of course."

In fifteen minutes, all was set. At 9:55 in the morning, a plane would leave, stopping only once at Hyderabad. Trains for Kotagiri left only twice daily, but there seemed to be an hour for her to make the connection, provided she reserve a seat immediately. She did so, through the clerk, and he advised her to wait until they reached Kotagiri before attempting to locate the proper bus.

"Mrs. Templeton," the desk clerk asked, in a changed tone of voice.

"Yes?"

"Excuse me, but why are you going to such a place?"

"To visit an *ashram*."

"But there are plenty of *ashrams*, much more famous, much more beautiful."

Janice looked at him quizzically. The desk clerk cleared his throat.

"What I mean to suggest, Mrs. Templeton, is that this area has been under attack."

"Attack?"

"Not exactly attack. One should say, a small rebellion. Really, they are only bandits with a flag, but still, I would advise you . . ."

"Is the area unsafe?"

"Not exactly unsafe. Only there are no conveniences. The post offices are not reliable. There is no television. Even the telephones are a matter of good *karma*."

He laughed feebly at his own witticism. Janice smiled.

"Thank you," she said. "I'll be very careful."

"If I could advise you . . . ?"

"Yes. Please do."

"When you go south of Kotagiri, do not travel at night."

"Thank you," Janice said, smiling graciously. "Good night."

She slept well, considering that she felt she had just walked off a gangplank. All decisions had been made. If not tomorrow night, then the night after, she would finally see Elliot Hoover. Surely he would know the trials she had gone through to see him. Kindness was the core of his being. That alone would force him to respond, to help them. And if he didn't?

Mercifully, sleep came before an answer did.

This time the flight seemed to last days, not hours. It was late afternoon when she touched down at Mysore City. It was early evening by the time she secured her seat on the train. The night was sultry, and it smelled like stagnant water.

It was not until 10:45 that the train chugged unevenly into the dirty town of Kotagiri. Remembering what the desk clerk in Benares had recommended, and longing for a clean bath and some sleep, Janice went in search of a tourist office. It was closed. There were no taxis.

She carried her small suitcase down the street. A small "hotel" sign blinked on and off. No answer. She knocked again. A sound of muffled steps. A man in a dirty undershirt looked out at her, blinking in surprise.

"One night," Janice said, holding up a single finger, gesturing sleep.

The man nodded. Janice entered the hotel and instantly regretted it. It smelled of stale beer and urine. Outside, Kotagiri looked even worse. The man closed the door. From his desk, he pulled out a battered ledger, turned on a small amber desk lamp and pulled out a black fountain pen, carefully shaking it three times. He wrote out the cost and handed it to her on a slip of paper.

Janice paid him the rupees. He seemed surprised that she did not argue. He beckoned her to follow, and they went up a narrow staircase. Her room was barely wide enough for the bed and standing room. The bathroom was down the hall.

As she undressed, she smelled the changed atmosphere in the South. It was impregnated with rain, and yet the rain remained in the clouds. Unwilling to bathe in the dirty bathroom, she washed standing up at the cracked basin. Mrs. Templeton, she thought wryly to herself, you have stayed in fleabag hotels in your time, but this one not even a self-respecting flea would come to.

On the street below, a police car drove by, and behind it a dark convoy truck with about ten soldiers bumping along in the back, rifles pointed up.

Janice felt reluctant to climb into the sheets. The smell of rain increased, and several times Janice looked out the window. Rain would have been lovely since it would have broken up the pressure in the atmosphere. But each time she looked, it was the identical dusty, caked iron railing that she saw. Perspiring in the hot night, she fell into an uncomfortable sleep. In the morning, she needed something to drink, but she refused to touch the water from the tap. At the bus station, not far from the train station, she bought a warm bottle of Coca-Cola.

The morning was overcast and even more humid. A bright, painful haze was scattered over Kotagiri, so that nobody cast shadows. It was all subsumed in the overcast heaviness of a rain-filled sky that did not rain. Janice waited in line behind short, round-limbed men who argued excitedly among themselves. She was reminded of Mexico, the relaxed pace of life that had something lethal in it.

She showed her note to the man behind the ticket cage. He wrote out the cost with a contemptuous air, and she paid. At 11:25 there was an announcement over the loudspeaker; the ticket seller waved to get her attention, then pointed to the bus coughing smoke outside. Janice emerged into the main yard, followed the dark-coated men into the bus, and sat down in the back. As the bus pulled away, a few spires rose into view, and some leafy streets, but Janice hoped she would never again see Kotagiri for the rest of her life.

As the bus continued east, then cut to the South, Janice saw mountain ranges to both the east and west. The land was rolling, green and gray where the boulders were stacked, and there were no fences. It looked unbounded, wild, and primitive. The villages the bus rumbled through were composed of mud-encrusted wood huts, many with thatch intertwined on the roof, and rusted iron which helped support the porch pillars. Children watched in amazement, a curious passivity on their lovely faces, as though the bus belonged to a different, and superior, solar system.

The road turned pink, then red. The villages were fewer and farther in between, smaller, and now no children came to gawk. Army soldiers watched, bored, at key crossroads.

Janice felt certain that the *ashram* could not have taken this long to reach. She went to the front of the bus and showed the driver the note that Mehrotra had written. The driver became so confused, he stopped the bus in the middle of the highway and engaged the entire crowd of passengers in a heated argument concerning its location. Then he gestured for Janice to sit down, and he started the engine and serenely drove on.

A sudden spasm shook her abdomen, making her gasp. Silently, she cursed whatever it was that made. Western digestive systems vulnerable to half the world.

The driver stopped the bus and motioned for Janice to step forward. As she came near the driver's seat, he pointed to a small dirt road just off the highway.

"Ashram?" Janice asked again and again, and showed him her note.

He brushed her note aside and pointed to the dirt road. He opened the door and ushered Janice out into the blazing day. Another man gently handed her the suitcase and with a smile pointed to the dirt road. The bus coughed, ground its gears, and rumbled on, ever uphill, toward the distant southern peaks.

Janice had never felt so lost. She fought back tears. Who the hell knew how far away the *ashram* really was? Was it just a short walk up the road? Or far across the valley? Or in some no-man's-land where the soldiers forbade entrance to tourists?

Janice walked down the road raising brown dust over her trousers. From time to time she paused, catching her breath. Though she was thirsty, she would have to wait until she got to the *ashram*. Not only would they have a well, they would take pains to boil the water for her first. Janice came to the top of the slope. There was no *ashram*.

There was a gentle valley, covered in loose deciduous forest. She noticed that the road continued down the slope toward the forest. Maybe the *ashram* was tucked among the thick trees. It made sense, that feeling of being reclusive in the woods.

Janice crossed the top of the slope. The road twisted down into the darkness of the forest. As she walked, she felt certain that the *ashram* must be around the next curve. Monkeys leaped among the treetops, screeching. The trees became so dense and the clouds so dark, that it was like night. The sweat had long since ruined her blouse and her trousers, and the ubiquitous red clay soiled her sandals like a *tanduri* food dye. The suitcase pulled heavily at her arm. She looked for the orange robes among the trees, but saw only the thick, tangled roots of trees that seemed perched halfway into the air.

She became frightened that she might pass the *ashram* without seeing it. It might be disguised in the thickets, the shrine being no more than a conglomeration of vines, branches, and a tiny stone sculpture. Perhaps it had a secret entrance. Janice had heard of religious orders holed up in caves turned into temples.

The forest cover became so thick that, had the rain finally broken, she would not have noticed. She listened to the birds making a raucous din overhead. The whole of India seemed to be screeching at her, warning her not to enter. At least, if the animals of the forest set up a racket, she thought, the *ashram* would immediately know a stranger had come. Surely at least one member would have the curiosity to take a look. A Western woman in the foothills. Hoover would have to catch wind of that. If Hoover was anywhere around at all.

There was a sound of heavy wooden wheels. Janice stopped. Out of the gloom of the down-winding road came a farmer, his ragged black hair plastered down with dirt and sweat. His clothes were so dirty that there was no color under the caked earth and dung on them. He stopped dead in his tracks when he saw Janice. As she approached, she took out Mehrotra's letter and gently showed it to him. He backed away, being illiterate, frightened of the script. He picked up the support poles of his cart and began hurrying up the trail.

"*Ashram?*" Janice shouted after him, feeling like a fool.

He cast one dark glance backward over his shoulder, turned the corner and was gone. Janice listened to the silence. It was an uncanny silence. A second ago the monkeys, birds, and chattering insects had kept up a din of voices, and now it was silent. As soon as she had shown the farmer the note, like a magic talisman, everything had become still. Now when she walked, her own footsteps made the only sound.

Her sandals padded softly on the dark red clay, winding down, down toward the river. There were no clearings in the forest, only the rank, primeval growth. Gradually, as she walked, distraught, the chatter of the forest began again, until the air was filled with a shrill crescendo of screams.

Then she saw a marker: a post painted red at the top. Within the red paint was an image. She leaned closer. It was a crude carving of a tiger. A smaller path led from the post into the depths of the forest. She paused. It was obvious that something lay at the end of the path. But what? *Tejo Lingam* meant *incarnation of fire,* or *something* about fire—not tiger. Still, the path invited her. It wound gently into the darkness, through the creeping vines and the glossy plants that looked like a hothouse gone rebellious. What attracted her was that the path was neatly cut. Somebody tended it. It was the kind of activity that a religious order would do—like the Temple in Manhattan—that neatness, that manicured care which expressed internal harmony.

Janice looked down the path, walked twenty paces, and saw the path emerging from the woods into the sultry fields again. She returned to the tiger post. She glared down at the hideous face, cut so deep that the vermilion paint had filled in the carved lines, making a pure red against the grain of the wood. Janice took a deep breath and entered the narrow path.

Chapter Thirteen

No sunlight filtered down through the woods. Only a gray, leaden light that seemed to belong to the Pleistocene Era, it was so rank, so humid. Orchids burst into glorious sprays of white overhead, but they no longer looked beautiful, they looked carnivorous in some strange way. She avoided huge, glistening black beetles under her feet.

There was a second tiger post. The path continued, meandering into thickets. The birds flew low under the canopy of overhanging leaves, diving among the vines. There was a third post, a fourth. Then she smelled smoke far away, coming in low through the cool, dry odor of rotting roots and dead logs. Janice paused to catch her breath.

She knew Elliot Hoover was near. This was his landscape. Primeval. Frightening. Yet strangely beautiful. He would have the courage to live here, in prayers and ritual, afraid of nothing. There was something savage in his faith, some power that Janice never comprehended. Yet it was for that strength, for that charismatic compassion, that she had come so far, against every shouting voice in her conscience. For Bill. It seemed so strange that her destiny had led her to such a hideously lovely forest, so far from home, so alien to everything she knew. She suddenly wondered if Bill knew where she was. And was there something deep inside her that wanted to see Elliot Hoover, not for Bill, but for herself? Janice became frightened. The thoughts had a life of their own, as though the tangled wealth of forest creepers, flaming flowers, and glittering leaves had whispered their own ideas into her brain. Was she just frightening herself with false ideas? Or was a dark truth emerging, now that she was on the threshold of finding him?

She walked on. Abruptly, there was a pair of tiger posts, and then a clearing. Yellow, dry grass grew where the forest had been cleared, an island of tranquility surrounded by dense undergrowth. The yellow grass was parched, sloped upward to a small house made of forest logs tied together. Inside the hut—it had no door—was a smooth, polished floor, and it looked like burnished mahogany. There was brass, or gold, gleaming inside the hut, and a vermilion image of a deity rising from the painted flames, and next to it several ocher bowls hanging from the roof.

Next to the shrine was a second, longer house. Janice now saw men on its porch, and her heart raced violently.

They were all Hindus, their bodies short, rounded, faces down low to the ground as they conversed. They wore carmine cloth tucked up into their belts, and their hair was so greasy or pomaded that it glistened from across the empty field.

Janice desperately looked between the two buildings. There was no Hoover. A figure came from behind the long house, carrying a bucket of water. The figure was tall, his slender shoulders sloped slightly from the weight of the load. Janice gasped. As the figure turned, she saw that the face was aboriginal, flat-nosed, nearly black, and the slim limbs graceful and jet black. Two more figures came into view as Janice walked slowly toward the compound. They tended a rusted can strung over a fire by a single wire on stick supports. Neither was Elliot Hoover.

Janice took another step, left the path, and entered the compound itself, where a small gate had been erected with a small brass bell. Suddenly, one of the men tending the fire leaped to his feet and raced forward, his orange robe flying behind. He waved his arms violently at her.

"No woman!" he shouted. "No woman!"

"But I must find—"

"No! Forbidden!"

Backing away at his vehemence, Janice was appalled at the ferocity of his black pupils, the narrow slits of anger that the eyes had become. She had no doubt whatsoever that he would kill her if necessary to preserve the sanctity of the *ashram*.

"Elliot Hoover," Janice called from the path where she had retreated. "An American! Is Elliot Hoover here?"

But the man only glared at her. Janice backed away farther to the edge of the forest. Satisfied, the man walked slowly back to the fire and sat down cross-legged, poking at the coals with a sharpened stick.

Janice walked back out from the path, but this time did not approach the gate with the bell. She went past it, parallel to the field of yellow grass. The man looked up from his fire but did not move. She looked from her new perspective, but saw only a single woodcutter, hacking branches from a dead tree with a primitive instrument that looked like a hoe.

"Elliot Hoover!" she called.

There was no answer. After ten minutes of standing alone, feeling ridiculous and yet determined, Janice saw a monk walking slowly toward her. His head was down, and yet his legs seemed to move in a familiar stride, direct and yet soft, as though his whole being knew exactly where he was going and how many paces it would take, and that he had all of eternity to get there.

"Elliot?" she whispered.

The monk looked up. It was a brown face, thin, the face of an ascetic. The eyes were very dark, almost black, and they seemed to look out at her with irritation.

"Why is it you have come to disturb us?" he asked calmly.

"I beg your pardon," she stammered. "I truly am sorry...."

"What is your purpose here?" he asked in a flutelike voice that reminded her of one who took drugs, it was so otherworldly and disassociated.

"I am looking for a friend," Janice said softly.

"Who is your friend?"

"Elliot Hoover, an American, about six feet tall, blue eyes—"

"Yes. We know Elliot Hoover very well. He is not here."

"Not here?"

The monk sighed, as though regretting the complication of an explanation. Over his shoulder, Janice saw the other monks, oblivious of her presence, worshiping, some out in the field now, in the lotus position of trance.

"There was a subdivision among the order," the monk said. "You must know that we believe in performing works of charity and *ahimsa*—that is, peace and nonviolence to all living beings."

Janice pretended to know it with a nod.

"And you must, by now, know about the revolts to the south?"

"Revolts?"

"Yes. The North has repressed the facts. But it is very bad. This whole area has been evacuated."

Astounded, Janice's mouth opened. The idea of warfare was incongruous against the tranquility of the ancient forest and the sloping field of prayer.

"Then why are you still here?" she finally asked.

The monk smiled indulgently.

"The vicissitudes of material life do not concern us," he said defiantly, looking directly into her eyes, challenging her very existence.

"But Elliot Hoover . . . ?"

"He and several others decided to help the victims of the conflict. They left nearly a week ago."

Janice felt weak. If she had known where he was, if she had flown straight from Tel Aviv to Mysore City and then taken the train south . . .

"Where? Where is he now?" she asked.

"I am sure that he is where the fighting is. And that is over the mountains."

The monk gestured to the heavy black clouds to the south. Janice heard a deep rumble of thunder that echoed through unseen mountain valleys. She looked up. There was a sense of rain, but the forest, the path, the compound were all bone dry.

"Very bad," the monk added sorrowfully. "When the rains come, the villages suffer disease. Disease from the floods, you understand?"

"Yes. I see. Do you expect floods?"

"There are always floods. It is the nature of things." The monk gazed at her with compassion. "Perhaps if you go down to the village in the valley below, you can ask at the military compound. They screen everybody who goes beyond the Cauvery River. They will know where our members are."

"Thank you. Thank you very much."

"Do not fear the army. Do you have your passport?"

"Yes."

"Explain to them that you come from the *ashram*. So they will not be suspicious. But do not fear them. They are still disciplined."

"Thank you very much."

"May you find your friend."

The monk turned abruptly and walked slowly, placidly,

back to the compound. The birds screamed at his departure. Janice stood alone in the shadow of the great forest, feeling utterly alone. At length she picked up her small suitcase and followed the road down into the valley. She felt more secure when it entered the main road. As she descended the slope, the forest rapidly thinned until she looked across a steep drop of dried grass to the rapid Cauvery.

Across the river was a stone bridge, buttressed by logs. A flag flew from what appeared to be a military outpost. At least there were two convoy trucks and a jeep parked in front of it. The ground was heavily plowed by the tires of the heavy trucks, as though they had only come there recently, and it was still the scene of feverish activity. But now there was no one visible. The river made a dull music against the stones of the bridge, and the logs rose and fell, banging and grating against the wires that held them.

Janice walked out from the forest. Sheep moved slowly away from her, looking for green grass. The dried pellets of manure covered the path and were impossible to avoid. Janice looked for a sign of life, but there was still no movement in the village.

A donkey suddenly brayed, a vicious, snarling laughter. Then a soldier walked around the rear of one of the convoy trucks. He stopped as soon as he saw her and bristled. He looked illiterate, his uniform was two sizes too large, and suddenly the monk's phrase "still disciplined" came to mind. It was easy to see that military discipline was a burden barely imposed on the village mind.

Janice reached into her handbag and showed her passport. The soldier examined it, saw that the photograph matched the person, but did not know the purpose of a passport. He went to the door of the outpost, knocked deferentially, and opened it. He gestured for Janice to follow him in.

A sergeant sat at a large, scarred desk. He had a drooping mustache and black hair. His uniform was spotless and a little tight. He took special pride in his leather cross-belt with its shining medals. A black revolver hung at his belt. He was very surprised to see Janice walk in by herself. He kept looking for someone to come in after her and when no one did, he ordered that the door be closed. In the gloomy dank air, Janice finally noticed a second soldier, as unkempt as the first, who had snapped to attention when she entered.

Suddenly, the thunder rolled overhead, drowning out the sound of the river. Janice presented her passport. The sergeant took a long time to study it and her, buying time, since he clearly did not know what to do.

"American?" he finally said.

"Yes. You speak English?"

"No."

He scrutinized her entry stamp in the passport, showed it to the soldier, who spoke a few words while still at attention. The sergeant handed her the passport.

"Area is closed," he said in good English.

"I'm looking for someone."

"No."

"I've come from the *ashram.*"

The sergeant stroked his mustache and looked at her clothes.

"Tourist?"

"I'm not a tourist. I have business here. I'm looking for my husband."

"Husband?" the sergeant said suspiciously.

"Yes," Janice faltered.

Suddenly the air had taken a chill. The sergeant glanced nervously over his shoulder at the black sky.

"Rain," he said, agitated. "Soon too much rain."

He snapped his fingers, pointed at Janice's passport in her hand; she dropped it on the desk. He telephoned and waited a long time. He spoke quickly, then pronounced her name very slowly, with bad pronunciation. Janice waved to get his attention.

"His name is not Templeton," she whispered.

"But he *is* your husband?"

"Yes."

"What is he called?"

"Elliot Hoover."

"Ell-i-ot Hoo-ver," he said into the receiver, then waited.

"American," Janice whispered.

The sergeant gestured impatiently for her to be quiet. He nodded, listening, then hung up.

"Mr. Hoover is registered in a village in sector number five. He is with three members of the *ashram* that worships—*Tejo Lingam.*"

"Yes, I understand."

"The sector is stable, so it is not impossible to meet him."

"God bless you," Janice blurted.

"Excuse me?"

"I said, thank you very much. Very, very much."

The sergeant blushed, cleared his throat, and stood up. He tried to be angry, as though to restore a sense of his command.

"A truck will move to sector five tonight."

Janice nodded.

"There is a small house," he continued, "next to the river. You can rest there."

The sergeant smiled, satisfied that things were under control. He spoke to the soldiers waiting at the door. They indicated for Janice to follow them down a small path among the saplings.

The house had once been whitewashed, but now it was caked with dried mud along the bottom and large cracks showed down the walls. Inside it smelled of feces and dry dust. She saw a tattered mattress, heavily mildewed and rotted at one end. On it the soldiers had carefully placed two blankets stamped with the insignia of the Indian Army, and one soiled pillow. From her suitcase Janice selected fresh underwear and stockings. She changed beneath the privacy of her blanket and gingerly settled on the mattress. Then she put one blanket under her, the other around her, and lay her head on the clean end of the pillow. The saplings outside rustled in the wind. The river splashed, strangely irregular, as though too much water was funneling down from the heights. She wondered if the rains had started further south. Janice dropped into a heavy sleep, and the last thing she thought she heard was bells far away, perhaps from the *Tejo Lingam ashram*.

Janice awakened at eight. It was dark. Fires were lit to boil tea. Then boots quickly stamped them out. Shouts were heard. The trucks exploded into action, the engines roaring, soldiers jumping into their seats. The sergeant looked anxiously for Janice and found her on the stone steps of the headquarters.

"Come," he ordered. "You shall ride with me. First class."

Janice swallowed and climbed into the cab. She was pinched between the sergeant, who stroked his mustache and kept looking into his own sideview mirror, and the driver, a short man with a sloping forehead and thick eyebrows. The sergeant waved an arm, and the two trucks slowly pulled out of the outpost.

In the darkness, Janice saw the headlights pick out rough tracks of other trucks. Scrub brush grew in profusion along the rutted road. The trucks were climbing, at first gradually, then making hairpin curves that left the driver sweating and offering apologies to the sergeant.

"The bandits all run away," the sergeant chuckled. "Look. How many do you see?"

Janice looked straight ahead, hoping to see nothing but the livid forms of dirt that the powerful headlights threw up suddenly from the humid void. The truck plowed into the hard clay at the side of the road and stopped. The supply truck had innocently followed and was now also stuck in the dust. Cursing, the sergeant had the men dig out the supply truck, and the two vehicles then backed down the road. Shamefaced, the driver bent low over his wheel and peered into the darkness.

"You must love your husband very much," the sergeant said after a while. "To come all this way for him."

Janice smiled. "Yes, I do," she said simply.

After two hours, the supply truck honked its horn. The lead truck stopped, the sergeant jumped out, and there was a waving of arms and arguments. Janice looked into the sideview mirror. She saw the sergeant slap a soldier across the face. Then the soldiers leaped back into the cab of the supply truck. Soon they were laboring up the mountainside again.

"The problem," the sergeant said, when he had regained his composure, "is the monsoon."

"The monsoon?"

"Yes. When it does not come, the earth dies. When it comes, the earth drowns. And these stupid people, they do not understand why the government must interfere in their lives and build dams!" He laughed. "They are like children. Like baboons. They believe in magic. Their children die, but still they go to the magician, not the doctor. I tell you, we shall teach them a lesson!"

Again, he patted his revolver. What worried Janice was his need to reassure himself. The sergeant licked his lips and peered anxiously into the darkness on all sides. After half an hour, the trucks stopped, maps were brought out, and the sergeant finally decided which of two mountain roads to take. The trucks rumbled on.

Janice was just dozing off when the trucks abruptly halted.

"Sector Number Five," the sergeant said.

Eagerly, Janice jumped down from the cab. The ride had taken so long that her legs had cramped, and she had to walk slowly, unstiffening them. As the soldiers clumsily unloaded their wooden boxes, she followed the sergeant toward a dark hut.

"I will ask about your husband," he said softly.

As he went inside, the horizon glimmered. Jagged mountain peaks were suddenly visible. Then the thunder rumbled into the darkness. Soldiers ran back and forth in rain ponchos, but there was no rain. The breeze turned cold as it had the night before. The sergeant came out.

"The group from the *ashram* are in the first village. The village is in the valley. When the rain comes, the village will drown."

"But I have to go there!"

"My officer says no. It is a bad idea."

"My husband is there!"

"There is nothing I can do."

The sergeant walked away. Janice ran after him.

"What if I disobey your officer and go?" she called.

"You will drown."

"How can you be so sure?"

The sergeant looked at her, fatigued, bored with her, and eager to get some sleep.

"Every year the village drowns," he said. "I told you, they are like baboons. Like children."

As the sergeant turned, Janice shouted after him.

"What will you do to me if I go?"

He shrugged. "Bury you," he said.

Dismayed, Janice walked back to the two trucks. They were empty. Blocks had been placed around the tires. The compound looked deserted. She walked back toward the huts where the soldiers slept. She found the sergeant coming back from the latrine.

"I am going down," she told him. "Tonight."

The sergeant sighed, then shrugged. "The road continues down the mountain. Follow it."

"How far?"

"Two miles."

"All right, then. I'm going. May I leave my suitcase?"

"As you wish."

Janice shivered. Her own bravado began to sound hollow. Nevertheless, she had come too far only to find another empty village, a place where Hoover had been. By now, he might have heard from a pilgrim, stopping at the *Tejo Lingam ashram* that an American woman was looking for him. Perhaps Mehrotra had been able to reach him in some way. He might be in Benares, or back at the *ashram*, looking for her. Or he might be over the mountain. Or he might be dead.

Chapter Fourteen

The road was tricky to follow, since she had no light. She also felt like a fool. India was full of tigers, as everybody knew. India was full of poisonous snakes. India was full of rebels and scorpions and panthers. But it seemed so unreal. There was only the night, and the hard, baked road that she sensed out of the corner of her eye, leading down, going around curves through the scrub brush and dry earth. India also had monsoons. Her imagination began to conjure images of walls of water, islands of houses swimming around, sucked under in great whirlpools.

"Come on," she whispered. "Get hold of yourself."

After half an hour the vegetation at the side of the road had become dense. She was soaked through with sweat, and she knew she was grimy from head to toe. She thought she heard rain. She stopped. Nothing. The leaves of unknown bushes throbbed in a crosscurrent of chilly and warm winds.

An hour passed, and she began to wonder if the sergeant

had really know how far the village was. Clods of dark clay crumbled under her broken sandals. She felt too frightened to turn around and go back. She cursed herself for being such a fool as to end up in a strange country, on a dark road, waiting for the thunderstorm. It was like a fate that she had relentlessly pursued since the day she landed in India. Well, finally she had caught up with it.

She passed a deserted hut. Then a second. Debris littered the fields, dry and broken, where nothing seemed to grow but dead stalks. The debris meant the village was near. She peered into the darkness, but saw nothing but the road. It was so dark she had to feel her way, her foot scraping at the clay that meant the road.

Another half hour passed, and a third hut, this one with a donkey outside, and babies crying inside. Janice paused. The road branched suddenly into a fork. Standing in the middle of the road, she heard a strange, laughing yell. It sounded like an insane dog. Her heart beating almost out of control, she walked quickly down the right branch. After ten minutes a light bobbed into view, then another. Janice almost wept as the fear evaporated. She stumbled down into the main village, which was only five small buildings and two broken-down sheds. Bottles were littered all over the ground. There was no river in this valley. It was deathly silent, now that the dogs were quiet. Only the incoming wind hissed over the cracked piles of dirt in the fields.

Thunder boomed nearby. It was barely a mile away. The echoes died very slowly. Janice walked through the village, but all the lights were off. It was well past midnight. She was afraid to knock on any door that was closed.

She would have to wait until the morning before she could spot the orange robes of the monks and, hopefully, Elliot Hoover.

Janice peered into the first shack with an open door. Something slithered rapidly across the dirt floor. It occurred to her that body warmth would attract snakes. She walked to the second shack. It was evil-smelling but it looked cleaner. Heat lightning flared over the horizon, casting its soft glare onto the boxes and metal bolts and nails on the floor. She went in and lay down on a pile of empty canvas bags, neatly folded.

The night was endless. There was no possibility of sleep. Elliot Hoover was certainly in the next hut, or in the field she had passed, or sleeping with the animals at the edge of town. She thought of Bill, probably strapped in his bed. She wondered if Dr. Geddes would consider her as insane as Bill. It would not occur to him that half the world believed as Bill did, as she almost did, having come to believe stronger and stronger since seeing Benares. But what was the use? Bill was not in Benares. He was on Long Island. On Long Island they put you away for too many religious ideas. Or at least for acting on them.

She fastened upon one consoling thought: Elliot Hoover would know exactly what to do. Janice prayed the night would pass swiftly, that she would finally find him before the dew was even dry.

Janice lay on the canvas sacks and stared upward at a bare electric wire. The filaments dangled in tiny radiating circles. Lightning flashed behind her back, shot through the cracks and holes of the far wall, and made her silhouette leap out in front of her eyes. Rain was falling. It came without an interruption of sound, a steady drumroll on the roof. The air was cold and wet.

Something cold grazed her cheek. She screamed, bolted upright, and saw a dark trickle flinging itself down from the roof crossbeam. She stood up and dragged the canvas bags to the other side of the floor and lay down miserably again. Instantly the canvas bags were soaked. Janice moved to the far corner, sat down on the dusty floor, and disconsolately watched a large puddle form around the sacks. The thin trickle of water had widened to a black stream thudding into the dirt floor.

"Jesus Christ," she whispered.

Just then a chunk of mud fell from the roof beams. A column of water roared into the room, and with it the cold of the predawn. Janice stood as though afraid of the watery intruder and stared at the floor turning into mud. She backed against the wall. That wall was also wet, oozing the monsoon rain like cold sweat. When she looked up, she saw the roof beams bending down, weirdly elastic, sagging toward the floor.

Janice ran to the door. As her hand touched the doorjamb, the roof caved in. It was like being in a ship that was breaking up. Waves of water billowed down, flung by roaring black winds. The night thundered its storm, a horror of death in a steady, roaring imprecation.

"Oh God!" Janice called, her voice unheard in the roar.

The water was already ankle deep. The canvas sacks and boxes were floating, nudged back and forth by the storm. Bits of debris from the walls and corner supports bobbed at her feet. Overhead Janice saw a clear track of lightning, a perfect forked tongue of livid white against massed black sky. There was no roof anymore.

Janice stood under the doorjamb. Beyond the door was the dirt road and the village, and small palm trees driven down under the weight of the rain. The mud in the village was moving, carrying dead animals, rusted cans and vague shapes that looked like corpses.

"Elliot!" she screamed.

She could not even hear her own voice. Lightning illuminated the village. There were three structures standing and two structures with only walls. A dog was frightened and half swam, half walked uphill against the moving mud, its coat matted and slicked back until it looked like a wart hog. The darkness returned, and with it a low roar was heard under the storm: a house had collapsed, its clay and timbers were crashing together.

"Elliot!"

It was absurd. The dog was also howling. But the only thing audible now was the driving rain and the sucking, sliding mud. The mud had become more liquid, and it flowed faster downhill and around the standing houses, eddying, pushing, relentless. The support over Janice's head blew off and, soaked to the skin, she saw the mud coming her way.

She groped out into the night. An electric wire somewhere was live, flashing and spitting sparks where it flapped hideously at the violent trickles of water. Figures were moving inside, but there were no lights, and they looked as helpless as the dog. Far in the distance a piece of the hill bulged behind the outpost. Then it opened up into five holes and spouted water like a fountain. The dark earth vomited forth and shot forward into the outpost with the force of the water. A small supply truck tipped over slowly, grandiosely, like a ballet of elephants. With horror Janice saw the distant remnants of the army fighting for their lives, ignoring cries for help, grabbing and kicking for higher ground.

Janice looked around her. A raft went by—a morass of saplings, mud, a piece of religious shrine, and a screaming cat—right where her hut had been. Janice panicked, but her legs found incredible strength, and they dug against the oozing mud. Her arms paddled at the heavy liquid around her calves. The only thought in her existence now was *higher ground, higher ground*. A crimson robe floated by, oddly elegiac, like Ophelia, on the vicious waters. Janice screamed.

The water plastered her trousers to her legs, her shirt to her breasts. She felt soaked as she had never felt soaked. Her hair was a dense black mass, heavy and sodden, lumped in front of her eyes. She reached for a firm root, but the root slid upward out of the liquefied earth. Janice fell backward, rolled

231

into the rushing water, and smelled the noxious odor of the red clay in her mouth.

Tiny sharp bits—gravel or nails—stung her face. She fought to stand up, but her feet were being washed out of the mud, until there was no mud, nothing to stand on, only water. She was being pulled downstream. She swam, her arms and legs kicking in unison, swallowing the heavy water that slammed at her face. Her lungs were bursting; there was no way to breathe in the ferocious river. She felt herself trailing away, falling backward into a deep darkness, down river, down the hill, always downward into the maelstrom.

Her arms clutched something that floated. She threw her clinging hair to one side and looked behind her. Matted clumps of army boxes, blankets, and food tins bobbed up and down, catching the light of a cold gray day. The rain came down like a wall. There was no village. Only a moving river of mud, water, and bits of things that had once been huts, fences, or chairs. A piece of colored cloth rapidly floated by, and Janice remembered the crimson robe. Desperately she turned to look down the stream, and then she saw what she was clinging to: two dead goats, their forelegs locked in a death embrace.

Janice screamed, but her arms only grappled tighter against the cold, hairy forms, feeling the bones underneath. Somehow there was sufficient air in their bellies to keep them afloat. There was no sense of a river anymore, only an angry ocean of currents going in opposed directions, filling the valley, destroying everything it reached.

Far away in the darkness, form crumbled from form, and Janice knew that the hills were giving way. Huge splashes showed where boulders and entire trees on the upper slopes were rolling into the rising water. Lightning cracked in two places. Janice sensed utter physical defeat, and her arms grew weak. In horror, feebly protesting, her cramped fists beating uselessly against her fate, she saw the monsoon rip her two dead goats away, and the muddy taste knocked into her nostrils again.

Then eternity seemed to pass through her. It was loathsome and dark and vicious. She had no will, no intelligence, only a small spark of something that was afraid. It was as though she did not exist. Strange sounds, like bells, clanged far away. She felt no sensation in her legs or arms, or even her head and chest. Something dark was coming to reclaim her, to make her disintegrate once again.

Sounds of the monsoon; her head was above water; a knock from a dislodged timber; screams of iron wrenched from its beams; something steady underfoot, dislodged, whirling around; a whirlpool, falling, with timbers. The small spark inside flickered, tried to go out; lungs bursting, on fire, under water . . .

Rough hands. She knew the sensation. Rough hands, callused. With bone underneath. Along her shoulder and back. An illness, a nausea that she could not expel, shot through her. The roaring was inside, not in the storm. The rough hands dragged her upward. She sensed her own feet, far away, dragging through slimy mud. She wanted to open her eyes, but they were closed in the opiate of a leaden fatigue. Just then a sheet of pain flared along her left leg.

"Elliot!" she blurted.

Still she could not open her eyes. An undulating green roof seemed to be lifting in front of her. Something was under the stinking roof: it was herself, in some way, the remnants of what she was. She felt warmth everywhere like a fever, and she knew she was alive.

She opened her eyes. A mud plain stretched under her feet. Around her were dead bodies, most bloated, naked, their genitals scarred, their arms and faces caked with mud, their eyes squeezed sockets where the skulls had caved in. There was no river, no village, not a tree, not a blade of grass—just

233

the mud, with a thousand sloping channels where the water had receded. A cool drizzle plopped into the mud, making a million tiny holes.

Janice was being dragged up the slope. Her two feet made a trail that stretched as far as she could see. Suddenly she passed a huge bulk: a dead bull, its front legs folded peacefully underneath, its enormous horns jammed into the mud. Still she was dragged higher. Just as she wondered who was pulling her, and turned to look, the curtains seemed to come down again, and she slipped into nothingness.

Slowly her eyes opened. She was in a large room. The ceiling was mottled with decay and mildew, but it was dry. Two naked light bulbs hung from the ceiling, both on, even though the small windows showed it was day. Rain came down on the roof, but it was a smaller rain. Janice heard a chorus of moans. She turned her head. Next to her was an aged woman's face, the hands tucked under the cheek, the mouth and eyes open in silent horror, dead.

She was in a makeshift hospital. At least that was what it looked like. Two doctors in dirty white coats, pockets bulging, pants soiled by mud, pus, and streaks of dried blood, darted among twelve mattresses on a cold stone floor. The doctors were both North Indian, with the longer, more oval faces and slender noses. They were totally fatigued, their eyes glazed with weariness, and they stumbled as they walked, barking orders, irritated. Wails rose from the twelve beds; Janice realized her own mouth was giving out moans, and she grew silent.

Through the door the smaller, darker South Indians were visible. Two of them hauled a corpse up from the mud. They all wore handkerchiefs over their mouths and nostrils. A fire burned ferociously despite the rain, and Janice watched in fascinated horror as the corpse was laid, with the barest formality, on top of the flames. She turned her head to avoid the charring of flesh.

To her left Janice saw the doctors operate on a man whose arms beat wildly into the air. They had no anesthetic, and it took three villagers to hold his feet and two more to hold his other arm. Finally the doctors found a piece of rope and lashed the punctured arm to a beam in the wall, where they quickly began their incisions. Janice turned away and stared at the ceiling.

Already the dead woman next to her had been removed. Another body, this one making tiny gasps like a frightened rabbit, took her place. Janice knew where the old woman had gone. She heard the villagers throwing sticks onto the fire. Janice stared up continually at the ceiling. She had difficulty remembering who she was, or why she was among these dark people. The ceiling rose and fell as she breathed, her fever making it almost glow.

Through the day she slept, woke, watched the ceiling, and slept again. She did not turn to look when the body next to her was removed and another put its place. Vaguely she wondered why she did not die, why they did not drag her out to the huge bonfire. She turned. In the same fire that burned the bloated bodies, the doctors were sterilizing instruments in cans of boiling water.

Night came, and the steady rain kept up. The doctors did not sleep. Janice remembered how she had been pulled from the mud. She remembered the mud swirling through the village. But only gradually did she remember why she had been in the village. She craned her neck, looking for orange robes. There were only the dull, matted clothes of the villagers, many of whom slept against the walls.

This was a chamber of death, Janice thought. They had all been pulled from the mud, and those who survived at first nevertheless died later. Maybe the soldiers had shot them. Maybe they had the cholera. But they were all thrown onto the twelve mattresses until they could die and be burned.

She raised herself to an elbow, looked all around the dark

235

room. A chorus of heavy breathing, whimpers, and grunts of pain came back to her. A primeval fear of doctors overwhelmed her and she became frightened that they would come to her with their lethal scalpels. She sank back onto the mattress.

The soldiers on the porch to the long room, their arms in slings, argued loudly. The doctors remonstrated with them and stalked off. Janice wondered if the sergeant was there, or the officer who had been so unfriendly at the crest of the hill. She saw only the unkempt, wild-eyed soldiers, who bore not the slightest trace of being disciplined.

A warm hand soothed her forehead with a damp cloth.

"Elliot?" she asked, startled, looking up.

Two pale blue eyes looked down at her from a thousand miles away. A rough face, a familiar face, grizzled, drawn from lack of sleep, with a small scar on the lower lip. The hand wiped away the sweat, the mud and the confusion. Her eyes blurred in hot tears.

"My leg..." she whispered.

There was a general flow of pain through her left leg, clear to the hip, and a sensation of rough hands under her. The leg was straightened and the pain became diffuse again. The sheet, dirty and bloodied, was tucked under her shoulders. The face began to swim away from her, and she reached for the hand that had soothed her forehead.

It was not there. No one was there. Only the wall, where flies had gathered, anticipating death.

She blacked out, feeling the familiar sheet of oblivion cover her.

Days seemed to pass. Gradually voices became more distinct. In the front room the soldiers barged in, pushing the doctors aside. Janice recognized the officer from the crest of the hill. He was angrily pointing and shouting orders. The soldiers dragged a sick man from a mattress and dumped him in the rain. A wounded soldier was gently laid in his place.

All this Janice saw through a feverish haze like a movie in a hot theater.

More soldiers were brought in, more villagers dragged out. Then the soldiers shouted in surprise, discovering Janice. Grizzled faces peered into her eyes. Hands poked and prodded her in amusement. The officer shouted and Janice felt rough hands pull her up. The room jostled, she cried out in the shock of pain shooting up from her hip, and then she was outside.

The soldiers carried her like a dead log. The mud slopes were visible again: a few clots of grass, but mostly the rivulets of rainwater and mud trickling down the morass of tangled logs, boulders and dead animals far below. Janice had never seen death on such a scale. It was the earth itself that had been mortally wounded. Hills were gouged out, roads dislodged, and whole forests cracked and rubbed away.

They lowered her to the ground next to the rusted canister in which the doctors sterilized their used bandages and knives. The rain came softly, cooling her forehead. Moans rose like the sound of distant barges. A sick cow, the huge rump in the air and the forelegs buckled, lowed pitifully.

"I'm burning . . . burning up . . ." Janice heard herself say.

No one turned to look at her. An ox was brought up slowly through the rain, pulling a small cart. A tall man, head lowered, led the ox. Villagers lifted two shivering children into the cart, then Janice, and then the cart jolted, she gasped, and the landscape began to recede.

The cart brought her higher into the hills. The field hospital became smaller, and the soldiers like tiny tin figures. Smoke rose without a waver from the fire. As she watched, another small body was placed onto the fire. The villagers hardly stirred. The entire slope of the hill, the valley floor, even the higher hills where the forest had been, was mud, still slithering occasionally in sudden spurts downhill—a foul landscape, viscous with disease.

So this is death, came the thought. *It's like a fever and it looks like mud.*

The cart jolted regularly as the ox found its footing in the wet earth. As they went higher, bits of dead root and choked pools of black water went by. With each step four points of pain stabbed into Janice. The cart stopped. The man stepped down, examined the faces of the shivering children, and covered them with a thick blanket.

"Elliot—" she whispered. "Is it you?"

A voice came from the other end of the earth, gentle and kind, but almost broken by the exhaustion of suffering.

"Yes," he said distinctly.

Astounded, Janice wiped the rain from her eyes. She blinked rapidly, and her hands groped toward the hallucination. But the hallucination took hold of her hands and gently pushed her back down against the children and the blankets.

"I heard from Mehrotra," came the voice. "I went to the outpost at the river. They said I'd just missed you."

"Is it really you?"

"Lie down, Janice. We have to get away from the soldiers."

He went back to the front of the cart. The ox exhaled a steamy breath and pulled. The landscape began juggling again. A child whimpered. Janice pulled herself backward, wondering if she were dreaming. By instinct her arm went around the child; a small boy nestled against her chin, and the eyes began to close in sleep.

Janice craned her neck, staring at the driver. Now he did not look like Hoover. He was squatted down, with the posture of inexhaustible patience that all the farmers showed. Nothing moved except his chest as he breathed. He coughed, sending small puffs into the chill atmosphere.

He did not turn around. Janice sank back and huddled against the children. One of them asked her a question. She could only smile and caress the feverish cheek. It was getting dark, and the landscape was dissolving into a heavy gloom.

The cart rumbled up, up to the crest of a hill, then it wound along a path that snaked its way across a green plateau. Night came, and the cart still moved on. Janice kept waking up to different patches of black earth, to different dead trees, and finally the cart began going down the other side. The trees here were still alive. Grass glittered in the moonlight, rain-wet but alive. Water trickled everywhere, a musical, pleasant sound that made sleep easier.

A child cried out. The cart stopped. Hoover came to the rear and asked a question in Tamil. The child responded. Gently Hoover spoke again, smiled, and made a joke. The child laughed and lay down in the blanket.

"Elliot, thank God it's you."

A strong hand felt her forehead. "You're burning up. Try to sleep."

He went back to the front, slapped the ox with his stick, and the cart rumbled down. Janice watched the clouds overhead, rolling in phantasmagoric shapes in front of the round moon, obscuring it, revealing it, like the eye of a distant god—the god of destruction, satisfied with what he had wrought. The next time she looked they were in a grove of trees, miraculously still tall, still luxuriant. She slept. When she looked again, the cart was pushing its way across a swollen stream, and the moonlight glittered like a million silver fish in the leaping black water.

Then she sensed peace. The cart had stopped, she was in his arms, and he was carrying her across a wet field toward a dark house. She lay against his chest like a child, her arms around his neck. He smelled like wet canvas and like mud and like medicines. The night grew even darker, and it was deathly quiet. She was inside the house. It was dry. Quiet. She lay on a clean bed.

"You'll be all right here," he said quietly. "Back there the soldiers might have mutinied."

She nodded, not comprehending, but wanted to hear the voice go on. She stared at the face. It *was* Elliot Hoover.

"I've pulled the dirt from your wound," he said. "Cleaned it out well. But I have no antibiotics."

Janice focused her eyes on the calm face. Her hands traveled over the familiar features. There was no doubt. The pale blue eyes, the sensitive skin, now badly in need of a shave. The compassion that glowed like hot coals from deep inside. His hands covered hers.

"Don't leave me," she whispered.

He smiled. "I have no choice, Janice. I have to help others. I'll leave some food for you. Some bread and cheese that won't spoil."

"Please, don't go! I must talk to you."

"I'll be back."

Her fingers tightened around his collar, but he gently uncurled them and laid her hands across her breast. A clean blanket covered her. He stood over her, more shadow than solid form, looking down. For a long time he only breathed there, as though confused, uncertain whether to go or remain. Then he went to the two children sharing a bed next to her. They spoke quietly together. One of the children coughed badly. He showed them a white cheese. He kissed them gently on the forehead, then went outside. The ox cart began rumbling again.

The night passed slowly. Sleep was impossible. It was not the blanket but the fever that kept her warm. Janice was convinced that she would die before dawn. In the next bed two boys, aged about nine or ten, slept fitfully, their arms comically tangled. One of them kept whispering what sounded like a name—probably his mother's—but the other only wheezed steadily, frighteningly. Through the window she watched the moon go down over the jagged horizon. They were high in the mountains, and here the vegetation was still thick, even dense, like a tropical forest. Black fronds rustled near the window, whispering obscenities, and Janice finally slept.

Dawn showed white sheep foraging peacefully on green

slopes. White rocks interrupted the steady green of the slopes. Sometimes it was hard to distinguish the sheep from the rocks until there was a movement. Janice sat on the edge of the bed, shivering. She watched down the road. No sound. The emptiness was as profound as the vista of mud that had flattened the other side of the mountain.

She ate the flat bread, dry and unpleasant, and then encouraged the two boys to eat. Their small faces, round and flushed, dimly focused on her, and their mouths slowly worked at the bread. Then she had them eat some of the white cheese, though it tasted like rancid butter to her. They seemed to relish the cheese. She cooled their foreheads with a damp cloth and they fell asleep in each other's arms.

Children, she thought, helpless as newborn fawns. They were also waiting. Perhaps they had more trust than she. If she could speak their language she would ask them who was the man who had driven off in the ox cart, if he was an American, if he had really spoken English to her, or if she had hallucinated the whole thing.

Night came. Janice looked over at the boys and removed the blanket which had slipped over their faces. Once again she dampened a cloth and cooled their foreheads. She ran the cloth over their chests, down their arms, legs and necks. One pair of dark brown eyes fluttered open, gazed at her in misery, and then closed again in slumber. Wearily, Janice went to the window.

It was nearly dawn. Against a hazy purple range of mountains, tinged pink at the crest where the unseen sun hit the upper slopes, came a dot the size of a fly, soundlessly, groping its way forward. As she fed the boys the last of the white cheese and bread, Janice looked again. The dimly perceived dot had separated into an ox, a man, and a cart, silhouetted now as the earth warmed and the road showed brown against the green hills.

For nearly an hour she watched it come closer. A boy came

to the window, feebly pointed, and spoke to his brother, who smiled. Then it was no hallucination, Janice realized. Never had she doubted her own senses so completely. The illness, the dislocation from nearly drowning had thrown her system into a shock from which it had not yet recovered. Something deep inside had activated a kind of primal fear, and she felt instinctively the livid hostility of the earth.

Janice went to her bed and sank down. The chills began to emanate from her belly, until they were spasms, and she was shaking uncontrollably under the blankets. In a daze she heard the snorting of the ox. The boys tried to open the door but found the latch too heavy. Then a man came into the stone house with a wooden box on his shoulder. He put the box on the earth floor and took the boys by the hand back to bed. He spoke to them gently in a strange, flutelike language, and began preparing a mixture of powders from pills and capsules that he broke open and mixed with water. He spoon-fed the medicine into their mouths, then kissed them gently on the eyes and bade them sleep.

It was still a dream to Janice. His features, blocked up in a silhouette by the crisp sunlight of early morning, were indecipherable. At times he looked like an avenging angel, stern, the forehead well chiseled over a sensitive, an unmistakably American face. Other times he looked dark, South Indian dark, and his dirty hands were slender and bruised as though by a lifetime of manual labor.

He lifted his bag of medicines, and came to Janice's bed. Her hands instinctively groped upward at the face, like a blind person trying to read the features. Two strong, calloused hands caught hers and restrained them.

"Elliot. Everything is so strange. I don't know what's real anymore."

He bent down, made a paste of medicines, crushed them into a spoonful of water, and forced it into her mouth. She swallowed, still peering at the pale, glittering eyes of the man at the edge of the bed.

"Am I going to die?" she whispered.

His hand pushed her back onto the bed. Two pale blue eyes fixed her, speared her, frightened her with their intensity.

"Listen to me," he said, examining her face, "you swallowed a lot of contaminated water. Do you understand?"

Astounded that she understood him, astounded that some measure of reality returned with the sound of his voice, she nodded dumbly.

"You're going to live on boiled water, cheese and antibiotics," he said, "and you do what I tell you."

Her hand closed around his. She smiled, but was still confused. The room had begun to swim around her, growing elongated with every pass in front of her eyes.

"I have so much to tell you, Elliot," she whispered. "I need your help. . . ."

"Later," he said.

She tried to whisper, but her voice had evaporated. Only her thoughts appeared, and they were inchoate, more like sensations than ideas. It was impossible even to begin to speak about Bill, about Dr. Geddes, about Juanita and the Master—and just as she tried, she began to fear that he would float away. He would evaporate like a dream. She clutched at his arm, but felt strong fingers remove her grasp. Then she sank backward into a sensuous river of sleep.

Chapter Fifteen

When Janice awoke, her body was clean and fragrant, and her hair, soft and recently washed, fanned out blackly against the clean linen of the pillow. A beautiful sunlight slanted in from the mountain clouds, creating strong polygons against the rough stone wall. The two boys sat up, drinking soup out of a tin so hot their eyes winced as they greedily consumed the broth.

Hoover stepped into the house, his tall figure bending under the low-cut wooden doorjamb.

"My hair smells so pretty! I feel so clean," she said, laughing.

He cleared his throat, and dug a small, sharp knife into the edge of the door.

"You've lost a lot of weight," he said.

She blushed. She lay against the pillow, happy to be alive, breathing in the fresh odor of green grass, the cool mountain water outside the house, and to know that she had at last found Hoover.

Janice stared at him. He too looked abnormally thin, almost bony around the face, but a sense of strength radiated from him, as though the monsoon flood had burned away everything but the core of his masculinity. He was like a wolf, grown lean but sinewy from hunger.

"You must have wanted very much to see me."

"I did. I've come a long way. I have so much to tell you."

Disturbed, he walked into the room, and began boiling more soup in the corner for the boys. Their small bodies, sitting up and more animated now, blocked his face. A smell of hot water, vegetables, and fatty meats swirled around the room.

"Do you mind that I've come?" she asked hesitantly. "There's been an emergency. I needed you."

Hoover rose and rubbed his face with both hands. He deliberately ignored her.

"I went back to the *ashram*," he said, leaning against the wall. "They told me an American—a woman—had been looking for me—black hair . . ."

"Did you know then it was me?"

He nodded. For a long time neither spoke. A strong but indecipherable emotion clouded Hoover's face. He turned away, as though to examine the clouds breaking up overhead, but in reality to avoid her stare.

"I didn't want to see you," he said softly.

She watched him, sitting on the windowsill, feet on the floor, and he looked exhausted, more exhausted than it seemed possible for any man to be. His words came tonelessly.

"But when they told me you had crossed the river," he said, "I knew I had to get you out of there. The monks don't understand warfare. To them it's all a temporal part of life."

"So you followed my footsteps to the outpost. And all the time I thought I was following you."

He continued to ignore her, as though he were deaf or

trying to obliterate her, to make certain that it was he who dominated the house. He began to look worried, and his voice grew louder but less certain of itself.

"To them your death would have been accepted quite philosophically. Like an insect's."

Janice said nothing. India had changed Elliot Hoover from what he had been in Manhattan.

Something had altered him forever.

"Anyway, what does it matter?" he said. "We're both still alive."

He slumped further against the sill, looking tired enough to sleep standing up.

"I didn't want to see you," he repeated. "But I was afraid of what the soldiers might do. You don't understand this country. Down in the south, what happens during even a small war . . ."

"I can only thank you, however feeble that must sound."

"Forget it. When you feel better you'll tell me why you came to India. Now you should sleep."

She drifted into a haze of heat, a reddish cloud of slumber that was draining. Hoover slept on the floor, his soft snores rising and falling rhythmically. Janice thought she saw the two boys remove his muddy coat, push a pillow under his head, but then she fell asleep again. When she awoke, many hours later, the boys were outside, and it was late afternoon, and the ox was stamping its foot into the earth while it munched long yellow stems of grass.

"We have to go down into the valley," Hoover said quickly.

"What? Why?"

"The soldiers are moving this way. But now they're only a bunch of bandits."

Dizzily Janice saw Hoover load the cart, and the boys climb inside; then he came back into the house, took her by the arm, and led her into the warm sunshine. She walked slowly, leaning against his side. She followed his glance and saw, far off on the slope, a cluster of dark dots in a ragged movement coming down the road toward them.

"Once we get into the valley we'll be safe," he confided. His eyes shifted to her eyes and discerned the fear in them. "The *Tejo Lingam* is sacred. They won't bother us."

Janice put a foot onto the cart, but stumbled, and Hoover lifted her bodily like a sack of stones and set her onto the dirty wooden back of the wagon. He got quickly into the front, slapped the ox with a thin sapling, and the cart rumbled downhill, away from the mountain house, away from the soldiers five miles behind them.

The cart jostled down toward the south. As they descended the air grew humid again, but not as oppressive and suffocating as it had been before the monsoon had struck. This was a delicate moisture, and it brought the fragrance of crushed ferns and palm fronds.

The two boys now watched, their eyes wide, as the new landscape rolled past. They were twins. Orphans, Janice was certain. To them, life had just revealed its most brutal realities, and they were still in a daze. Instinctively they trusted Hoover. To them death was not new. It had just come closer to them this time instead of to their elders or to the animals of the field. Janice toyed with them, tickling their small bellies until laughter came, until tears came, and their happy cries rose like bird melodies over the sad, death-infested forest.

Hoover stopped the cart where two tiny streams buckled into a small rapids. A thatched hut stood in a small muddy clearing, and enormous bougainvilleas stormed upward on vines and branches around the conical roof. Crimson-robed men stopped, amazed, frozen in their tracks.

Hoover approached, put his palms together in greeting, and the men returned his bow. One of the men, overcome, suddenly embraced him. The sound of Hoover's weeping was extraordinary. A sweet, harmonious sound, like the lifting of a death curse. It seemed to release something deep inside him, unfreeze something horrible, and make him live again. He wiped his eyes, and the monks came with him to the cart.

As the monks carried the twin boys toward a series of smaller conical-roofed huts, Hoover helped Janice down to the ground. She still found it difficult to keep her balance, as she was light-headed. The brilliance of the sunlight dazzled her. The yellow butterflies among the red flowers were like a profusion of sensory impressions too strong to absorb. It was warm, and she made her way slowly toward a small hut.

"These are my friends," Hoover said.

"Yes, I know. One of the monks here told me where to find you."

Hoover looked at her, surprised. "Usually they do not speak to strangers."

"Perhaps I looked desperate."

"Probably. At any rate, they thought I was dead. We are not indifferent to one another down here."

They entered a small hut. The earthen floor was hard, swept clean, and a simple white basin and pitcher stood on a flat rock that was worn smooth by a thousand human hands.

"This *ashram* has functioned for a thousand years," Hoover said. "It's for pilgrims going to the big temples on the coast. There are several different sects that use the shrine." Hoover smiled. "You are the first woman in a long series of pilgrims," he said kindly.

Her head rolled pleasantly against a wicker mat rolled into a tube and used as a pillow. He still seemed to waver in front of her, as rays of bright sunshine outlined his shoulders and his fair hair.

"Elliot," she said, not wishing him to go, "we must talk."

"Later."

"No. It can't wait. I have to leave soon for New York."

He laughed. "Do you know how long it would take you to get to Bombay, much less New York? Do you even know where you are? Listen to me, Janice. You have illusions of health. It's going to take days before you can walk more than twenty yards without help."

Janice felt the awful fever coming again. It was the helplessness that she dreaded. At bottom, there was the fear that she would wake and Hoover would be gone.

"Elliot, I . . ."

"Go to sleep, Janice. When you wake, we'll talk."

Janice saw his face darken, the jaws lightly clench. She knew he did not want to know why she had come to India. She became afraid that he was going to ride out of the *ashram*, out of her life forever.

"You won't leave me?" she begged weakly. "Not before I've explained—oh Christ, I feel like such a helpless child. I can't lift my own arms. I can't keep my eyes open. Elliot, I need your help."

"I know," he said, confused, both angry and yet softening to her obvious desperation. "I know you do. But . . ."

"But what?"

"Things are different, Janice. They've changed."

"Don't frighten me. You sound so dead."

"Reality is not what I thought it was, Janice. I've made a terrible mistake."

"What are you talking about?"

"What do you think I'm talking about?" he said almost angrily.

He suddenly knelt down closer to her. She drew back. His eyes blazed, and his feet kicked up a small cloud of brown dust that caught the shaft of sunlight and drifted toward the door.

"I'm talking about Ivy," he said, his voice taut with the difficulty of saying the name. "Your daughter, Ivy, and Audrey, my Audrey Rose."

His voice choked and he retreated to the wall. The small earthen hut had become an arena. It was as though he were fighting her to the death, yet Janice did not understand why.

His passion took hold of him, animating his slender arms, blazing out of his steel blue eyes. He crouched in her direction for emphasis, as though he were ready to pounce on her.

"I had thought," he fumbled, "I had thought that there would be peace, that Ivy's death had ended the struggle, the struggle of a soul in torment." He rubbed at his eyes as though trying to gouge out the sight of Ivy broken by shattered glass, lying on the hard tile floor of the Darien hospital. "I should never have gone to New York," he whispered darkly, gutturally, a strange voice that must have been bottled up for nearly a year. "Never, never, never. My being near the Audrey that was in her, called up this struggle. I started it, Janice. I started it and I kept it up. I wouldn't let go of her. I pursued her until I killed her."

He stared blankly at her, blinking away tears. Furiously he wiped his eyes. He was not the man she remembered, not the man she had come ten thousand miles to get help from.

"I should have gone away once I realized that *I* was causing her nightmares. And I *did* know it. But I rationalized, temporized. I couldn't go away. Not when I was so close again."

Janice struggled to a sitting position. Though the room was undulating due to her fever, she followed the words carefully, as though a revelation were unfolding in the hot shaft of sunlight.

"Because of me," he said simply, "the soul of Audrey and Ivy was filled with fear and confusion. Therefore there was no tranquility when death claimed Ivy. There was no peace for her soul. Though I believed it at the time, I know better now."

Janice watched him pour a small stream of water into an earthen mug. He brought it to her. She drank, the water was cool, and then he dipped his hands into a basin and began to wash her hot face. The spinning stopped slowly. She focused on his sorrowful eyes.

"Her terrible death prevented a peaceful transition," he said quietly. "There must be a rebirth. No doubt it has already taken place." His voice cracked. "Somewhere, a child lives with a soul that continues to cry out in terror. . . ."

He could not continue. For a long time he stood there, drained by his own confession. He looked at her.

"Have you understood what I've said?" he asked gently.

"More than you know."

"Really?" he said, surprised. "What does that mean?"

"It's why I've come to India. It's why I've had to find you."

"I don't understand."

He looked as though her words fulfilled his worst fears.

"Bill needs your help, Elliot."

Hoover watched her, studying her face suspiciously. "I don't believe that could be possible," he said simply.

"Then I had better explain. After Ivy died—immediately after—Bill had a nervous breakdown. He began to study—to study all kinds of things. Religious things. He became fixated, fascinated, utterly absorbed in it."

"Bill Templeton? Involved in religious studies? That would have been funny once."

"And not just religion, Elliot. Eastern religion." Janice took a deep breath. "He's become convinced, just as you are, that Ivy's been reborn. *And that he's found her.*"

Hoover's face dropped. He stared at her, blinking rapidly.

"And you?" he asked in a choked voice. "What do you think?"

Janice faltered. She found herself dizzy in front of him. She gathered her courage and looked him in the eyes.

"I think it may very well be true," she said. "But I don't know. That's why I came to India. To ask for your help. To beg you to return with me."

Hoover laughed, a disdainful laugh; but underneath there was acute anxiety.

"Do not even suggest the possibility," he said, trembling.

Janice leaned forward but he visibly retreated as though she might contaminate him.

"Elliot," she whispered urgently; "Bill and I are lost without you."

"It's taken me a year to find even a small amount of peace."

His booming voice dropped into an abrupt silence. He paced the room, his face hideous in confusion. His arms waved wildly as though protecting himself from visible thoughts.

"It's punishment," he whispered. "That's why you've come."

"Elliot, if you loved Audrey Rose . . . listen to me . . ."

He stopped dead in his tracks and glared at her. "For love of Audrey Rose I ruined the soul's progress," he said quietly. "I won't do it again."

His face clouded with the memories of New York. He found it impossible to maintain his composure. He sat down on the edge of a chair.

"What do you expect me to do, Janice?" he asked desperately.

She rose and walked slowly to his side. "You admit to having made a terrible mistake with Ivy. Can you allow Bill to make the same mistake? You must come to New York, Elliot. You must speak to him. Reason with him."

Hoover laughed hideously.

"New York?" he hooted. "Why don't I just go down into hell? What are you asking of me?"

"Elliot, only you can reach him. Only you can break through to him. You must explain to him . . ."

"What? That I did the equivalent of killing his daughter? Caused her to be reborn in misery? Is that what Bill needs to hear?"

Hoover calmed himself by a violent exertion of will, like wrestling against his own body. Slowly his face and breathing returned to normal.

"Bill has to learn to live," Janice said, pleading. "He has to give up this obsession."

Hoover softened. He was wavering.

"Yes," he whispered sadly. "He must give up the obsession. I'd give my right arm if someone could have prevented me."

Outside the monks chanted, a rock-steady chorus, attuned to each change in the timbre of their voices. The sound of them restored Hoover's self-discipline.

"But I can't do it, Janice," he said, rising again. "Don't even ask."

Slowly Janice stood up to face him.

"Bill escaped from the sanitarium last February. He went searching for his daughter."

Hoover's face became even more drawn.

"I pity your husband," he mumbled. "I pray for his soul. But you must leave me alone. You don't know what your being here has done to me."

"He kidnapped a little girl, Elliot. He went to Spanish Harlem and stole her from her mother's arms."

"Dear God," he whispered.

"They shot him, Elliot, to get the girl back. I had to betray him so they could shoot him on a rooftop—"

His large rough hand sealed her lips.

"Please stop," he whispered stridently. "You're crucifying me. Isn't one soul burden enough? Am I to bear Bill's too?"

She saw the moist eyes, white and an annihilating blue. A stranger on whom her life depended.

"You're the only man in the world he will believe anymore," she said. "As long as he believes his daughter exists again . . ."

"Then what?"

"Then he lives inside his own black world. No one can reach him. He trusts no one. He just disintegrates more each day."

A baboon laughed raucously among the dense black tropical forms far away. Hoover's head turned, attuned to the signals of the forest. The branches creaked in a sudden breeze, lifting and falling. He watched them as though they communicated a secret, occult message.

"I can't go to New York, Janice," he said softly.

"Elliot, what about the belief in *ahimsa*—nonviolence to living beings?"

Suddenly he leaped forward, grabbed her arms, and hissed into her ear. *"Go home!* I need to be alone! I need to atone! I need isolation."

His breath was hot, sweet-smelling. His body was crushed up against hers, and his eyes were wild.

"I need to be where there are no women!" he blurted.

Then he stormed out of the hut and across the compound. Through the open door she watched him run toward the edge of the *ashram,* pick something from the ground—a bedroll—and disappear like a wild beast into the forest.

"Elliot!" she shouted, her voice shocking the humming of the forest into silence. "Elliot!"

But he was gone. Janice hesitated, then returned to her hut. His last words buzzed angrily through her mind. What disturbed her most was how vulnerable Hoover turned out to be. It was he who was lost, utterly, alone, fighting for his sanity as much as Bill.

Janice lay on the reed mat. She looked at the thatched roof. There were no answers for her. None.

Chapter Sixteen

Elliot Hoover did not appear in the morning or in the afternoon. The monks ignored her. They did not object when she prepared a few tomatoes and peppers for herself, or drank from the well. Neither did they help her in any way. At nightfall only the two boys, Meti and Sanjay, acknowledged her existence. Though she looked she found no paths that led from the *ashram* into the jungle.

On the third day one of the monks bowed slightly to her and beckoned for her to follow. Janice rose from the doorway of her hut and followed the flapping crimson robe into the thickets.

As the monk led her away from the compound a weird gloom enveloped them, a perpetual twilight caused by the thickness of the vines and leaves overhead. Butterflies floated twenty feet over their heads like underwater fish, brilliant scarlet, yellow, and white. The monk never looked back.

There were no posts, no notched trees, no signs that she could see, but he walked unerringly, rapidly into the depths of the forest.

They found Elliot Hoover at a small pool. A trickle of rainwater fell like a thin waterfall over a mossy ledge into the pool. Apparently pilgrims had used the site often, for one edge of the shore was worn smooth, and a tiny wooden shrine had been built, supported on posts. A painting of a many-armed deity was visible, and below it, Elliot Hoover, legs folded, aware of all things around him and within him. The monk spoke lightly to him, bowed slightly, and left. For a long time neither Janice nor Hoover moved. Then he opened his eyes and looked peacefully at the placid pool, where the jungle breeze created cross-patterns of ripples on the silvery green surface.

"This was the only peace I ever knew," he said distantly.

"There are those who have never known peace," she replied very quietly.

He closed his eyes.

Tall grasses shivered on the shore. Peculiar floating reeds moved in subtle currents just under the surface, making the water dense and green. Yellow fish darted through the reeds, gulping. Hoover seemed to be aware of them, smiling sadly in sympathy, listening to the movement of water, though his eyes remained closed.

"I have prayed to Lord Shiva," he said. "And to Lord Krishna. And I must go to New York." A gentle breeze stirred his nearly blond hair, as though caressing his sorrowful face. "One accumulates debts," he said. "Spiritual debts. And one must repay them."

"There is no way that I can thank you enough," Janice whispered, afraid to say more, afraid of disturbing his un-earthly tranquility.

For a long time he said nothing else. A branch floated like a spear, turning around slowly, end over end, as it reached the base of the waterfall. It glided like a living thing over the dense mass of submerged reeds, nosing its way toward Hoover, black and glistening.

"Whether or not your husband *has* found his daughter," he said gently, "I must insure that he not commit the same crime that I did."

He closed his eyes. His days of prayer seemed to have drained his physical strength. Once again his face looked drawn, as though he needed more than anything to sleep quietly again.

"Yes," he concluded, to himself, "such is my duty."

Hoover stood up painfully. Gently he dusted off his dark crumpled trousers. He looked defeated. He gazed at the pond in affection.

"It will take us a week to get out of the mountains," he said. "Are you well enough for the journey?"

"Yes. I can make it."

He laughed, a laugh that seemed to come from the far side of the ocean, not his at all, as though his soul had laughed and his soul was no longer in his slender body.

"Physical journeys wear out the body, but spiritual journeys are the most dangerous."

"Believe me," she said earnestly, "I do not underestimate the self-sacrifice."

"No, but you underestimate the dangers."

Hoover led her back into the forest. She had the intuition that he was frightened of her. More than that. As she followed his sure steps over the thick green vines, on the ever-damp jungle floor, she knew that his spirit found no peace in her presence. A woman knows what a man means when he holds her, even for a split second. And the passion that had pressed her against the darkness of the hut had nothing to do with religion.

That was why he avoided her eyes. Like a country pilgrim going to Benares, he shifted his glance away, afraid of himself in her presence. Afraid of her in his presence. For the body also speaks, and in the jungles of South India it speaks with authority.

The *ashram* compound was busy with new arrivals, on their way south. They had brought many orange flowers, wreaths, but were humble and silent. The *ashram* absorbed them easily. Nothing ever disturbed the compound. For a thousand years monks had modestly cleared a few square yards from the jungle, kept it beautiful, and attended to the rites. The *ashram* had survived scores of generations, and it might last until the end of history.

"Wait here," he whispered.

Hoover ducked into a small hut, spoke for a long time with three of the monks. There was a short ritual, a prayer, and a long farewell. As they left, the monks did not watch their departure. Nor did Hoover expect them to.

They walked in unison on a rutted road, and the moon, nearly full, peeked over the edge of the jungle. Silhouettes of mountains were at their side, the air was warm and pleasant, and the moonlight was so strong they could easily see miles down the clay of the road.

They slept in a small thicket of low-hanging trees. Hoover unrolled his slender bedroll for Janice, and she got into it. He slept at the base of a thick white tree that gleamed in the shafts of moonlight. She sensed him aware of her, like a gravitational force in the darkness. Finally he stirred and moved farther into the jungle until he was out of sight.

When they woke he came back out of the woods, and after a sparse breakfast they continued on their journey.

As they walked, perspiring in the heat, their steps together, it seemed that they understood one another perfectly. When to rest, when to eat from his rucksack. Questions were answered before the questions were verbally uttered. They stopped simultaneously to watch a small herd of water buffalo cross the road, the heavy tread mashing the road into mud. Then they continued, ever downhill, toward the heat, until their clothes were indistinguishable from the mud and insects that clung to them.

The second night they slept in a small ravine that cut upward into a tangle of brilliant red roots. Hoover moaned in his sleep. Janice watched him, as the fading moon made his shape barely discernible against the matted jungle floor. She knew the meaning of his restlessness. She knew the meaning of the sleep-drowned moan. She was not afraid of him, though with each hour of walking in the hot sunlight he seemed to grow more turbulent inside, more distressed, and several times he stopped, meditating on something before continuing. Now, while he slept, she watched his face in fascination. It twitched as though avoiding the horrors of his tortured dreams.

When she woke, she found him watching her.

The third day they came to a fork in the road; they took the eastern fork, and continued down the slopes. A farmer gave them a lift on his manure-ridden cart. Janice did not object to the smell or the sight of the manure. Nothing mattered to her anymore but getting back to America. As the cart jostled slowly onward it threw Hoover against her side. She felt the heat of his body through his filthy shirt, and he was trembling, his muscles knotted with the effort of keeping his balance.

Then, as the clay road receded in slow bumps, as they both watched the hills change gradually into flatlands of tall grass, scattered farms and short canals, a strange idea came to her. It was an idea that came of its own accord, floating into her brain like one of those wild scarlet butterflies, driven by its own nature. Suppose Hoover embraced her? Suppose his weight covered hers, drowned her weary body with his hunger? Suppose he entered her, found satisfaction within her? The image came to her, clear as though it had happened, and it surprised her. It was as though her body—loveless now for over a year—had begun speaking its own language.

The cart stopped. They descended, Hoover helping her

down. They took a different fork, and the cart bounced slowly away. Hoover stopped her and his hands gently pried the filth from her arms, her legs, and her soft, rounded breasts. She did not object, but only watched him work.

"Excuse me," he said, smiling. "But they do not allow shit in the finer restaurants of Pondicherry."

She laughed. But his hand hesitated at touching her more, and they caught the subtle tremble of their own bodies, and avoided looking into each other's face. The body was taking over the mind, Janice realized in fear. More than anything else in the world she wanted the comfort of his strong arms around her—and yet she was taking him home to save her husband. The confusion made her dizzy, and the dizziness had a sensuous quality, a seductive vagueness, that altered every thought until it returned to Elliot Hoover.

Then, there was a small village. After a few questions Hoover found a tiny, unused shed. They slept the night there. Hoover paced the floor, and the moon fitfully illumined him through the juggling palm fronds. Janice did not sleep. He knew she was awake. Then his hand rested on her shoulder. Gently, as though he were touching a child. Her heart seemed to pause, then raced forward.

She did not move. The slender, trembling fingers stroked her shoulder. They came around to the front and slid softly under her dirty shirt. Her breasts expanded, her breathing became harder, as the soft fingers rounded under the fabric. Instinctively she pressed his hands into her breasts, until her whole chest was tight in his grasp. His face came closer, the heat of his cheek against the back of her neck, and she felt his desire through the back of her clothes.

"Elliot," she whispered.

Something scampered across the floor of the hut—a tiny lizard—and darted toward the exterior. A child in the village cried, and its mother softly sang it back to sleep. The jungle stood only in small thickets around the tilled fields, but it still exuded the humid warmth of fetid growth.

"Elliot—please . . ."

"Janice," he breathed hotly into the back of her neck.

His hand slid gently, firmly, down the inside of her shirt, over her belly, along her hip. She stirred, rolled over, until they were pressed close against one another. Suddenly a jackal laughed hideously in the darkness, and the echoes trailed slowly through the village. Hoover released his grasp as though stung. He went to the window and peered out. Still breathing heavily, Janice slowly buttoned her shirt, her breasts rising and falling; the darkness had become a moral darkness, and she felt herself falling into a whirlpool of hell because she wanted this man—and all his hard, hot strength, and an end to the torment that had been eating at her for an eternity, though she had tried to deny it.

"Forgive me," he whispered.

"There's nothing to forgive."

"I'd better sleep outside."

"Elliot . . ."

Abruptly he went outside, leaving her inside with his bedroll, and he slept at the edge of a tilled field. She saw his form vaguely, as it slithered downward, miserably, to the mound of hard earth that had been plowed up. Once again the jackal cried.

She wanted to go to him, to beg him for love, if necessary. She found herself a slave to something so deep inside her that it altered her, made her a creature she barely recognized. Dimly she realized how strong the passions were—like a storm that easily crushes any ship foolish enough to set sail on the sea—and it took nearly an hour before she knew she would not leave the shed to join Hoover.

In the morning he bought several eggs, some milk, tomatoes, and yogurt from village families. He prepared them swiftly at the side of the road, and he also boiled some water, knowing that Janice still had no immunity against the south country microbes.

263

"We must be very strong," he said.

She blushed, turning her head. The day was different from the night. In the dark she was so different, so overmastered by her primitive instincts, but in the day she wanted to think clearly, to see clearly, to act correctly.

"The stakes are too high," he said, trying to be matter-of-fact. "For both of us. In different ways."

"I know," she replied without conviction.

He looked at her. "It should be easier now that we come closer to civilization. Still, I don't want to take any chances."

"Nor do I," she said defensively.

"Good," he said simply, embarrassed. "Very good."

By noon a passing truck stopped in the village and met them two miles out on the road. They squeezed in the cab. The driver spoke a little Hindi and a little Tamil, and soon Hoover had him chuckling loudly. The truck careened down the road. Suddenly the road became paved—a miracle of a smooth ride—and the driver agreed to drive all the way into Pondicherry.

He left them at a small hotel. There was only a single room left so Hoover slept on a lumpy couch in the fetid lobby, oblivious of the heat. Janice washed herself as best she could, soaked her clothes—her pitiful underclothes made her wince—and lay naked in the sheets. She tried to recapitulate all that she had seen in India, but it seemed to have happened to another person. As it had, she thought. Because she sensed that she *was* different. She was physically able to endure things that once would have crushed her. She had seen death—death on a vast scale. She had endured the hostility of the indifferent universe and survived.

And something else had changed. Had Hoover stepped quietly up from the lobby and knocked gently at her door, she would have let him in. It was not moral. It was indefensible. It would destroy Bill if he even suspected. But then, India had taught her about the struggle for existence. About the closs relationship between fecundity and annihilation. And she was part of it now. She did not fight it, she welcomed it. Like Hoover, she would have to relearn how to graft a veneer of civilization upon a living being that had been through far too much.

Janice pondered long into the darkness of the night. She wondered if she had become tough or had merely degenerated in some terrible way. For an hour she nearly followed her impulse to go down to Hoover, to seek comfort from his warmth. But she resisted, though she did not know why. Who would know? Who could care? Down here, on the southeast coast of the Indian subcontinent? She stared into the darkness and wondered. Mercifully, sleep drifted into the seedy hotel and she knew only the partial answer of oblivion.

Elliot Hoover had prevailed upon the hotel keeper to prepare an English breakfast: muffins, bacon, tea, and marmalade. Sitting in a small dark room, with pictures of erotic sculptures of Khajuraha, it felt more like a honeymoon than a rescue mission—the warmth of the morning, the wallpaper peeling decorously from the wall, even a painting of the Duke of Wellington, much faded, over the table. The scene was too relaxed, too humorous to speak of the emergency waiting for them in Manhattan.

Hoover cleared his throat, enjoying watching Janice consume her hearty breakfast. There was a twinkle in his eye.

"I thought we would take a boat up to Calcutta," he said. "Then a flight from Calcutta. I think it hops to Munich and then to New York."

"But what about our belongings? I've left everything in—God knows where sector five is."

"You're right. I've an account at Barclay's in Calcutta, but there must be a branch office in Pondicherry." He smiled. "I'll draw out enough money to see us back in style."

"When we return I want to pay for your trip to New York," she said soberly.

"It doesn't matter."

"Please. I'd rather."

"As you like. But don't forget that I am not exactly in want."

She studied him. He was a complex man, a gathering of contradictions. He could chant prayers all night with the utter belief of a Hindu native, and yet he was as shrewd as a stockbroker when it came to managing his fortune. He lived in two worlds, fit into them equally well, a man whose charisma seemed to flow outward from himself in an undisciplined discharge.

Hoover bought a brown jacket and trousers, some white shirts, leather shoes from Italy, and he had his hair cut at Pondicherry's best hairstylist, where the barber threw up his arms at the matted, wild locks when Hoover walked in. Janice chose two short skirts, white blouses, and a new handbag. She bought a pair of sandals. Slipping into new underwear was an almost erotic thrill. She had forgotten the soft luxuries. It was like remembering a former life. Then she had her hair shampooed, cut, and styled. When she saw Hoover on the street they burst out laughing.

"I feel very strange," she confessed, displaying her new skirt.

"It takes a few days to get used to it," he agreed. "When I first arrived in New York from India I felt weird for a week."

They booked passage on a freighter that left Pondicherry for the north. After four hours of pacing the deck in agitation, Hoover calmed down. There was a magnificent hoot overhead that resounded through the harbor, the hawsers were thrown off, and a tiny tug nudged the coffee freighter out into deep water. As they turned around, Pondicherry seemed to bank slowly, gliding into the distance, its crowded white alleys and waterfront busy with traffic the way ants swarm over a dead white log.

The eastern seacoast of India glided by: sand dunes, bits of jungle refuse thrown up into clotted tangles at the mouths of rivers, and the broad blue ocean churned into a long white trail, arching backward as far as the eye could see. Janice and Elliot Hoover leaned against the orange rail and watched the continent go by.

"It's a lovely land," Janice said softly.

"The most beautiful in all creation."

"I never suspected, never realized."

He smiled. "Most people never do. India is too big. Too profound. One must come here to be changed."

For nearly an hour they watched the herons dip low over the shore marshes, the tall egrets nesting where the tidal flats were shimmering in seawater. Boys were visible, pushing boats with long poles, nets outstretched for fish, and wooden shacks leaned precariously over the muddy concourse of the incoming tides.

"It's life itself," mused Hoover. "It is the source of all beauty. Life in all its complexity. It is the only source."

Janice watched the sunlight reflecting from his well-tanned face. In his new clothes it would be difficult for anyone else to know what spiritual depths animated his every action, his every word. He looked like a German tourist on his way back to Bremen.

"In the mountains," she confessed, "it occurred to me that you might have lost your faith. But I see I was mistaken."

"Not lost it. Just realized it was far more difficult than I had thought. One wishes to do good, and ends up doing . . . doing. . . ."

She placed her hand on his. "And ends up by doing good," Janice said quietly.

Hoover smiled gratefully. He tried to express his feelings, but found himself curiously tongue-tied. Then the crew became extraordinarily busy, and the freighter curved around a semisubmerged obstruction and plowed serenely to the north.

It was not until well into the night that they reached

Calcutta. The wharves were ablaze with lights from cranes and towers. Ship after ship was piled into the harbor, an army of sweating laborers bending low, pulling ropes, lifting coffee, rubber, bales, and auto parts up from holds. The sea was black, glistening with reflections of the world's freighters at anchor.

They stayed at a large dark hotel near the waterfront. In separate rooms. Hoover went to his bank in the morning to cash another draft, and emerged with the equivalent of a thousand dollars in cash and a small packet of checks. The balance of the day was spent at the American Embassy trying to secure a temporary visa to replace the passport Janice had lost in the flood. The difficulty was in establishing proper *bona fides*. It was a dreary wait between cables to and from New York and Washington. That finally accomplished, it then took an eternity to find a taxi. Another eternity to get to the airport. They sat on the couches of the Calcutta airport for four hours. Once Hoover's hand squeezed hers and an electric thrill went through her. Their fingers slowly relaxed and drew apart. Not looking at him, Janice went to the large plate-glass window and watched the runways. It seemed impossible that she was leaving India. Somehow it was her home now, her real home, where she had become someone else, someone a thousand times more mature, a thousand times stronger.

She cabled Elaine and Dr. Geddes. No apologies. A brief explanation. Would see them in New York. Regards. Hoover rose, took her arm, and they joined the line of passengers filing into the entrance corridor.

"Nothing seems real anymore," Janice said.

Hoover knew exactly what she meant. They had had the chance to express the beauty of themselves to one another, but had not, and the chance would most likely never come again.

"Nothing *is* real," he said. "But one learns to survive."

They went onto the plane. The flight was delayed for two hours due to a faulty tire. Then the crewman waved a yellow flag, and Air India lifted its plane into the skies. There was a brief circle of a sensuous, compact city, and Calcutta banked and drifted under the wings of the plane, and then there were only clouds. Clouds that tore apart as the plane roared through. Janice closed her eyes.

She was crying, and she did not know why.

BOOK III

ELLIOT

"And I am in the heart of all. With me come memory and wisdom.
I am the knower and the knowledge of the Vedas, the creator of their end."

The Words of Krishna

Chapter Seventeen

A large city rotated underneath like an octopus, its radiating arms busy with slow-moving metallic gleams. Around it were green marshes and reflective bits of cold water.

"New England," Hoover whispered to Janice. "Down there is Hartford . . . that must be the Interstate Thruway . . . See the sand dunes on the coast?"

He paused. They both realized that Darien, Connecticut, also lay somewhere underneath them. A nondescript town with its hopes, fears, ambitions, and its hospital. A hospital where Ivy died, surrounded by thirteen physicians and assistants, in full view of the horrified court. Where Bill broke apart like the glass around the hypnosis chamber. Unlike the chamber window, he could not be replaced, and he still pawed through life, suspicious, half dead, threatening to come apart still more.

Hoover licked his lips slowly, and Janice thought she saw his eyes grow moist. They avoided looking at one another, but they became intensely aware of each other's breathing. Then Connecticut passed slowly under the fuselage, the thruways grew dense and tangled, and the great metropolis came into view.

"It feels like a lifetime since I was here," Janice said in a distant voice.

"It is. You have become a different person."

Suddenly the great World Trade Towers, twin steel structures, light blue and gray where the clouds were reflected, rolled underneath. The warning chime sounded and the seat belts were requested. Seats were pushed upright, cigarettes extinguished, and with a sudden lurch the jet began to roar and Janice saw the flaps move downward.

"Oh, God," she whispered, suddenly frightened. "Are we doing the right thing?"

"I believe so," he said, holding her hand. "As firmly as I have ever believed anything."

The jet suddenly screamed. Janice looked out the window, saw white clouds stream past like smoke. White concrete appeared, racing by in streaks, and beyond it the familiar layout of Kennedy International. With dread and horror she saw the ground leap up, slam against the tires, and a blast of air resounded in their ears. Then they were slowing, the great engines in reverse, slower and slower, taxiing to the terminal.

"Manhattan," Hoover said to the taxi driver. "West Sixty-seventh Street."

The taxi maneuvered slowly through the traffic crowding around the various terminals. Finally it inched along a thruway ramp, out to another system of highways, and then picked up speed on the south shore of Long Island. As they passed the rippling marsh grass, the shivering gray ocean in the sound, Janice turned to look out the north window.

"Somewhere up there," she said. "That's where the institution is."

Hoover crowded closer to get a look. "May God grant him

peace," he said, peering into the dark, rising clouds to the north.

Then the taxi slowed, crawled onto the Tri-Boro bridge, and a cityscape spread before them. Brown and gray tenements, crowded streets, all slow-moving and dull, as though life had nowhere to go, no place to grow but only went round and round in dilapidated rituals.

Janice found herself staring at her homeland as though it had become a foreign country. The dizziness refused to go away. It seemed as though something were missing, either in the landscape or in her.

"It's all like a big vacuum."

He smiled. "You see? India *has* changed you."

Then the taxi drove rapidly into the canyons of the city and passed through Central Park. Against the leafy, humid summer afternoon were roller skaters, elderly people on small benches, and boats on the lake. Suddenly Janice's heart constricted in an old pain as they approached the west side. By the time they got to Sixty-seventh Street her heart was beating rapidly and the dizziness was now troubling. Des Artistes stood in front of her, implacable stone, rain-stained, gray, like a prison and a fortress, full of threats and nearly forgotten promises. Janice found it difficult to step from the taxi. She was afraid that the slow maelstrom of despair would once again suck her in. And when she saw Mario, the doorman, emerge from the lobby, she quickly turned to Hoover.

"Elliot," she whispered, "it would be better if they didn't see you. Some of them will remember your face."

"Yes, of course. I'll find a hotel. Give you a call when I have a room."

Hoover ducked his face as Mario opened the door and helped Janice out.

"Why, Mrs. Templeton!" he exclaimed. "We sure missed you. You've been gone a long time."

"Hello, Mario. Just a little vacation. I'm entitled, no?"

"Yeah, sure," Mario laughed.

He escorted her into the lobby as the taxi drove off with Elliot Hoover.

The shock of seeing the familiar white-covered tables in the restaurant, the chandeliers, and the elevator—all signs and symbols of past joys and terrors—overcame her and she felt an arm reach for her as she swayed.

"I'm all right," she murmured.

But she was sitting on the bench in the elevator. The door was closed, she was riding up, and Ernie stared at her in concern.

"Ernie," she said weakly. "How are you?"

He laughed, his teeth gleaming against his light brown face, an infectious laughter.

"How are *you*?" he exclaimed. "You stay away for two months and come back without a word and as soon as you walk in the door you start to pass out."

"Did I?" she said softly. "How embarrassing."

"You want a doctor?"

"No. Thanks, Ernie. I just haven't eaten today."

"Well, I'll bring you up a sandwich, okay?"

She smiled gratefully. When they got to her floor and the doors opened, her knees once again felt weak. Ernie assisted her to the door.

"Oh, I've lost my key," she said.

Ernie produced a ring of keys, found hers, and opened the door. The vista of stained-glass windows, familiar carpets, and the lovely painted ceiling was too much for her. It wanted to reclaim her, to drain away every bit of strength she had gained in India, to reduce her once again to an automated shell struggling for the smallest spark of life.

"Have you been sick, Mrs. Templeton?" Ernie asked. "You look like you lost twenty pounds."

"A little bit, Ernie. But I'm fine now. Has there been much mail for me?"

"I can check for you. You want me to open some windows before I go?"

"Thank you."

As he opened the kitchen window, fresh air began to circulate through the apartment. Already the familiar sensation had risen like dust in a breeze: Ivy's door that was always ajar, the wedding portrait, now a perpetual reproof, the souvenirs of happier times, all now bitter mockeries. And yet she felt that this time, for the first time, she was equipped to fight them all, even conquer them.

The telephone rang: a harsh, strident shriek that startled her. It was Elliot Hoover.

"I've gotten a room at the Windsor-Newton. It's only three blocks away. How are you feeling?"

"Very strange. It's very weird to be back."

"Have you called Dr. Geddes?"

"No. I've been afraid to."

"Well, call him. He'll have to prepare Bill to accept my presence."

Janice sat down again, unsteadily, on the couch.

"It seems so sudden. Everything seems to be rushing ahead so fast."

"You're worn out. Get some sleep. There's a restaurant on the corner of Columbus and Sixty-eighth. We can have breakfast there. Right now call Dr. Geddes and arrange a meeting for tomorrow."

He waited for Janice to respond.

"Isn't that what we want, Janice?"

"Fine. That will be fine."

After she hung up, a peculiar emptiness circulated around the apartment. Her confidence was evaporating. She began to think it might have been a terrible mistake to have brought Elliot Hoover to New York. She remembered the hostility Bill once had for him. True, Bill now was a believer, an even purer believer, in some ways, than Hoover. But did that mean he would accept the man who had disrupted his life? Whose existence stood for everything he had once hated? But then, Bill *was* different now. And she fought the doubt that threatened her.

The doorbell rang, Ernie brought a plate of sandwiches with hot tea. She thanked him. As she ate the roast beef and bread, a bit of confidence returned. After the hot tea, she felt remorseful that she had ever doubted what she had done.

But when she telephoned the Eilenberg Clinic Dr. Geddes was adamant. He would not permit Elliot Hoover to speak with Bill. Janice even had the distinct impression that Dr. Geddes was trying to shield Bill from *her*. But at last he agreed to meet Elliot Hoover for a short interview the following afternoon. That was no guarantee that he would let him speak with Bill.

That night Janice slept uncomfortably in her bed for the first time in two months. She had bathed, and then examined her naked body in the full-length mirror. Her hips now jutted out, angular, and her breasts seemed slimmer. But mostly it had been the face that shocked her. What a stranger she had become to her own eyes. Then came the silence. The silence of lying in bed in an apartment vacated for so long, doubly vacated by two others, one dead, the other emotionally dead, but both leaving residues of sorrow at every corner, every object in the place. So she lay, her body oriented halfway between India time and Western time, listening to the vague sounds of the city.

Elliot Hoover was a welcome sight in the small restaurant at the corner of Columbus Avenue. He rose politely as she came in and beamed a lovely smile.

"Did you sleep well?" he asked.

"I was a little anxious," she confessed, sitting down beside him. "It's so strange to be back. I feel I'm living someone else's life."

278

"Your previous kind of life will soon try to catch hold of you," he warned in a kindly way. "Don't let it. Now, this restaurant seems to specialize in *palachenka,* those breakfast crepes from Vienna, filled with cream and fresh jam."

"Sounds lovely."

The *palachenka* were delicate as a layer of snow and about as thick. The jam was country-fresh, homemade, and it was so peaceful to sit in the corner booth, among the sagging East European faces that hung over the nearby tables, arguing in Yiddish, Russian, or Hungarian, that neither wanted to break the spell. Outside, the sunlight bathed Columbus Avenue in a crisp, clear light, and small pools of water from night rain reflected the shops upside down.

"When will Dr. Geddes speak with us?" he finally asked, as gently as he could.

"Not until late this afternoon. He can't leave Ossining until three o'clock. He'll meet us about four o'clock at the hospital."

He touched her right hand, which had begun to crumple the white napkin into a ball.

"Don't be nervous," he said softly. "In some way, Bill must know that help is on the way."

She smiled and relaxed. "I hope you're right. So much rides on this."

"Trust me. And trust yourself."

He looked around the restaurant, enjoying the babble of European voices, the easygoing, inelegant comfort of the place, where the customers and the staff knew each other as old friends.

"Then we have the whole morning to ourselves," he said, turning slowly back to her.

"Do you want to see the little girl?" she asked simply.

He nodded, very slowly, a gesture of serious determination. "God knows I shouldn't. And yet—"

"It may be difficult, considering all that's happened. Still, we can try."

"Is the child . . . pretty?"

"Yes, Elliot. She's a lovely girl."

His eyes seemed to soften and he smiled a gentle, sad smile as he settled back in his chair and signaled the waiter for the bill.

When they arrived at the Hernandez address he stepped very slowly onto the pavement. He smoothed his hair back, adjusted his coat, and looked up and down the street.

She took him by the arm and escorted him into the dark and fetid gloom of the tenement, stumbling over broken toys strewn over the cracked floor. As they climbed, the echoes of their steps preceded them like an ominous, bass tremolo.

She felt resistance in his arm, but he resolved to go farther, climbed the next flight, and then his body tensed again. He perspired heavily. He was ashamed, but he could not hide his nervousness.

"I don't think I can go on," he whispered.

"Elliot, you'll haunt yourself for the rest of your life if you don't."

He started to answer her, then grimly closed his mouth and followed her into the darkest part of the stairwell. She thought she saw his lips move, as though he purified himself by some quiet prayer.

They emerged onto the top landing. Graffiti had been sprayed in huge black swirls since she had last been there. Parts of the tile on the floor had been badly marred, even dug up, as though by heavy boots or some sort of portable equipment. There was no other sign of the police having occupied the place. It was a scene of sadness, the dinginess relieved only by the light at the very far end, at the fire escape, where the Master had escaped from her grasp so suddenly and so terribly.

"Was it here that Bill . . . ?"

She nodded. Their footsteps now sounded heavy and dull as lead. She brought him to the fire escape and they looked downward into the brown alley at the garbage spilling out of broken cans and the cats that slinked along black rails.

"It was the dead of winter," she said softly. "Everything was covered in ice. Bill was up there, on the roof."

She pointed to where the black metal steps twisted up toward the roof.

"He was holding the girl in his arms. I remember the wind kicking the snow across like a blizzard, and waiting, and being afraid. And then the Master came to talk to him, and Bill listened and handed over the child to him. Then they shot him."

Hoover licked his lips, looking up and craning his neck to catch a glimpse of the roof, as though by so doing he could better imagine the scene.

For a long time he stood at the bright window, wondering at the sad, incomprehensible mingling of destinies that had brought him, a second time, to New York.

He looked significantly at Janice, waiting for her to make the first move. She said nothing, but walked briskly to the door by the stairwell. Quietly he followed.

"This is the apartment?" he asked gently.

She nodded. She found it difficult to speak. He reached in front of her and softly rapped against the door. There was no answer.

He rapped louder and waited. She saw the perspiration appearing a second time on his forehead, and then he made a fist and hit the door three times, squarely, so that the blows reverberated into the rooms behind it.

"Don' have to break it!" said a voice with a Spanish lilt in it.

Hoover whirled around, focusing his eyes at the darkness behind him.

"It's not locked," said the voice.

A thin, almost emaciated janitor, wearing a denim cap and overalls, stared back at them. He was barely thirty years old, but the face was slightly squashed, as though a heavy weight had pressed in the right cheek and temple, and the right eye wandered uselessly as he spoke.

He gestured at the door.

"You can go in," he said kindly. "Nobody there."

"Nobody?" Hoover asked, then turned to Janice.

She looked into his eyes, as confused as he was, then abruptly she pushed open the door.

A smell of dust, decayed food odors, and old paint billowed out. On the floor were balls and strings of dust, and specks of black that looked like dead bugs, and huge black stains covered the wall over where the stove had been. The apartment was utterly empty. Not a chair, not a shred of gauze curtain, not a piece of carpet remained. The breeze blew in from the window over dusty, scarred floors, and seemed to accentuate the desolation.

"You from welfare?" the janitor asked.

"No . . ." Janice stammered.

Hesitantly Janice took a single step onto the grimy kitchen floor. Hoover stepped past her, examining the living room where four rust spots marked the position of the absent television set. The windowsills were cracked, stained by mud and something like oil, and Janice surmised they were souvenirs of police activity at the apartment that February night.

She turned to the janitor, who had followed them, his dim mind perceiving a kind of game being played by these strange people. He lolled at the kitchen door, a simpleton's smile on his face.

"Didn't Rosa Hernandez live here?" Janice demanded.

"I don't know if her name was Rosa."

"But it *was* Hernandez?"

"Yeah, that's right."

"Where are they now?" Hoover asked.

"Home."

Hoover turned to Janice. She shook her head, uncertain

282

what "home" meant. Hoover turned back to the young janitor.

"Where is home?"

"Puerto Rico."

Hoover stared at the janitor.

"There was trouble. Bad trouble. This man come, he take the little girl. Police shoot him down. So they go home, be with friends and family."

"Oh, dear God," Janice sighed, closing her eyes.

Hoover turned to Janice.

"It doesn't matter, Janice," he said gently. "It really doesn't matter."

"It's just that I wanted so much for you to see her."

He gently touched her arm.

"It's just as well," he said quietly. "Don't you see? It's a sign to let well enough alone."

Taking one last look, studying the apartment, Hoover held open the door for Janice.

Outside, the Hispanic janitor dragged his broom across the floor as they approached.

"Police everywhere," he burbled, "screams, crying! They shoot down the man! He look dead! Yelling! Cursing God!"

Hoover took her by the elbow and led her into the dank stairwell. The janitor followed right behind, breathing in their ears.

"Blood on floor! Crazy man! Everybody go crazy!"

They stumbled over the broken toys on the ground floor, and struggled toward the door. As though afraid of the gloom, they moved faster and faster. They burst through the door and into the sunlight and the noise of the day's ordinary summer.

A taxi, looking forlorn and isolated in Spanish Harlem, got caught in a one-way street. Backing up furiously, it passed them, and Hoover signaled the driver. They were driven quickly crosstown, Janice glancing anxiously at her watch. It was already 2:39, and in bad traffic, Long Island was a long way from them.

Throughout the drive, Hoover's eyes were closed, his lips moving silently, and the passing sunlight flashed intermittently over his sensitive face. He was organizing himself for meeting Bill. She bit her lip and looked away. At last, the institution was visible, brown and gray, and suddenly the sun was completely gone. By the time they stepped from the taxi small droplets of rain fell, an invisible mist that hurtled down in a south-driving wind.

Standing in the parking lot as the taxi drove away, Hoover smiled nervously at her.

"The ten-thousand-mile journey," he said gently. "It ends here."

Chapter Eighteen

The monstrous facades of the psychiatric complex, stained by the veils of blown mist, rose over them like the craggy cliffs of Chinese paintings, obscure and vaguely menacing.

"Come," he said simply; they walked into the lobby.

As the mist turned to an uncertain rain, the lights went on throughout the lower wings. A nurse walked briskly past them, ignoring Hoover's question. Then a young man in casual clothes and a security pass stapled to his sweater pointed them toward a conference room.

Dr. Geddes was bent over a stack of folders at a long table. A damaged fluorescent light flickered fitfully on his white coat, his pale hands, and his broad, pale forehead. He seemed to have aged in the two months Janice was gone. He looked diminutive, fussy.

"Dr. Geddes," Janice said.

He looked up at them, studied the tall man, examining him carefully but nervously.

"Mrs. Templeton," he said, as graciously as possible. "You're looking very well. Please, won't you and Mr. Hoover sit down?"

Dr. Geddes closed the topmost folder, pulled a chair closer to them, and said nothing. It was his habit not to rush into an encounter, to maintain silence until he felt ready, but even so, Hoover's presence disturbed him. He stared at the pale blue eyes that did not flinch, the foreign-made brown suit so incongruous against the sunburned face and neck.

Dr. Geddes stood up, and lit a cigarette. As the smoke curled up past his balding profile, he pressed a switch at the base of a coffee-maker and the machine began to gurgle. He stood without speaking during the entire duration of the process. At length black liquid trickled into a glass beaker, steam rose, and Dr. Geddes filled three cups. He carried two cups to Janice and Hoover.

Hoover ignored his cup, studying Dr. Geddes with the same dispassionate, cool analysis with which Dr. Geddes examined him. Dr. Geddes slowly drank his coffee, and then he sat down again and turned to Janice.

"I showed Bill your cable," he said. "But there was no mention of Elliot Hoover."

Janice faltered, looking down at her own hands intertwined nervously in the straps of her handbag.

"I was afraid to tell him."

Dr. Geddes nodded, sipping his coffee slowly. An eternity of silence passed as he studied her. He no longer acknowledged Hoover in the seat next to Janice.

"Why were you afraid to tell him?" Dr. Geddes asked.

"Because . . . You know why. Because of what happened. Because Bill holds Elliot responsible."

"Sensible," Dr. Geddes agreed. "Then why do you wish for this meeting to take place now?"

Janice swallowed, found the courage to face Dr. Geddes, and leaned forward on the table until their faces were less than two feet apart.

286

"Because Bill does not listen to you. He does not listen to me. He does not listen to anybody in this hospital. But he will listen to Elliot Hoover because he's the only man who could have saved our daughter's life, and Bill knows it!"

"Did Bill tell you that?"

"He didn't have to."

"I see."

Dr. Geddes found his cigarette was out. He relit it and exhaled slowly toward the ceiling. For a long time he said nothing. Hoover leaned forward, but Janice restrained him by putting a hand on his knee. Dr. Geddes caught the gesture.

"Mr. Hoover."

"Yes, Dr. Geddes?"

"What is your purpose in seeing Bill Templeton?"

"To cure him."

Dr. Geddes raised a sardonic eyebrow.

"Are you a psychiatrist?"

"No."

"A psychologist? A medical specialist of any sort?"

Hoover licked his lips, though whether in irritation or nervousness Janice did not know. He leaned forward, resting his elbows on the long conference table, and stared directly into Dr. Geddes's eyes.

"I have been through exactly what Bill has gone through," he said. "And I know his pain."

Hoover swallowed his coffee, more to buy time, to feel the situation, than for any taste for the bitter brew.

"I too lost a daughter," he continued with difficulty. "Like Bill's, an only daughter. I searched for her—for a justification for her death. And I know the torture that Bill must feel."

"Do you? And how do you propose to help him?"

"What I have learned from my own ordeal," he said distinctly, "is the error I committed in the name of love. Bill must not make the same error. He must renounce the child. Give her up."

Dr. Geddes softened. He nodded. But then his eyes narrowed suspiciously.

"But suppose one believes in reincarnation?" he asked. "What then?"

"All the more reason to give up the child. The scriptures are clear. One does not possess a child's life. A child is only an honored and much-loved guest in one's home."

Janice seized the opportunity and leaned closer to Dr. Geddes, in front of Hoover.

"And this is what Bill must learn, and accept," she pleaded. "To let the child go."

"*Especially* if he believes she has returned," Hoover added.

Dr. Geddes examined them both, his eyes darting back and forth from Hoover's face to Janice's. Janice touched Dr. Geddes on the wrist to get his attention.

"The point is that Elliot Hoover and Bill both believe in the doctrine of reincarnation. They have that in common. They are linked by their beliefs."

Dr. Geddes backed away. He went to the coffee machine, and wiped up some spilled coffee with a paper towel.

"The sick treating the sick," Dr. Geddes muttered.

Janice rose to her feet and stepped closer to him.

"That too is the point," she said earnestly. "*You* don't accept the doctrine. I'm not sure what I believe. That's why Bill rejects us both."

"True."

Hoover came to his feet, sensing Dr. Geddes's weakening position.

"And Bill and I are intimately connected. We were together through it all."

"At least," Janice persisted strongly, "it could open an avenue, just a little. Just to make Bill feel there are human beings who believe and are ready to help him."

"Could you sit down, please? It's disquieting to have everybody jumping around the room."

After a long silence, Dr. Geddes daubed perspiration from his forehead.

"What, actually, would you *say* to Bill?" he asked. "Assuming that I let you see him?"

"Exactly what I've said to you. That he must renounce the child. He must accept his loss."

Dr. Geddes nodded.

"That is what we've been trying to tell him," he observed somewhat doubtfully.

"The difference is," Hoover said, smiling, "that Bill understands my language."

"The jargon of religion, you mean?"

"Yes. He will respond to that. He's been studying it for months now. That's all he *will* respond to."

"Will you wait here?" he asked.

Then he turned and abruptly left the room. Janice and Hoover waited in silence. The conference room was a chilling, antiseptic environment.

After ten minutes no one had come to the room. Then there was a distant, low-rolling rumble. Janice and Hoover looked up.

"Even in this hospital nature finds its voice," he murmured.

Janice stopped fidgeting. Once again the deep bass reverberated in the clouds piling over the island.

"Like the thunder before the monsoon?" she said softly.

For a moment they smiled at one another, exhausted by the long day of waiting, and remembering the subcontinent that devoured them, changed them forever, and spit them out again.

The door opened. Dr. Geddes walked in, and behind him was Dr. Boltin, the director of the hospital. Behind the director were two more physicians and a lanky staff assistant who carried the relevant files in his arms as though they were religious totems. The door closed.

"Be seated, gentlemen," Dr. Geddes said, extending a cursory hand at the chairs around the table.

As the thunder rolled Dr. Boltin reached for the pile of folders at his right hand. Looking through them, he pulled out a stapled pair of tissue-thin, typed reports.

"Templeton, William. Severe depressive and delusionary. Well, you gentlemen know the case as well as I do," the director said, turning his attention to Janice. "Mrs. Templeton, before we proceed you should be made aware of certain changes in the direction of the case. During your absence your husband attempted suicide."

Hoover's face blanched. Janice rose, stunned.

"Suicide . . . ?" she stammered.

"Attempted asphyxiation," Dr. Boltin elaborated.

Janice's hand involuntarily went to her mouth.

"The facts are," Dr. Geddes interrupted, "that Bill was able to procure some matches and oily rags from the kitchen. He barred himself in the room by pushing his bed against the door, and sealed the windows. He filled the air with fumes and smoke."

"He was unconscious when we broke the window from the ledge outside," Dr. Boltin concluded.

The director and the rest of the assembled physicians seemed to wait for a response.

"The same death as Ivy's," Hoover said. "He was trying to atone."

Dr. Boltin eyed him balefully. "For what, Mr. Hoover?"

"For feeling himself responsible. For allowing the death of his daughter. Which he might have prevented."

"We consider this was a serious act toward suicide," Dr. Boltin said, peering first at Janice and then at Hoover. "It was not a mere gesture, a cry for help, as it were."

"I understand," Janice said, barely audible.

"That is why we are willing to let you talk to him, Mr. Hoover," broke in one of the physicians.

"We're very grateful for your understanding," Hoover said.

"Yes," Dr. Boltin said ambiguously as he drummed his

fingers on the table, exchanging glances with Dr. Geddes. Neither Janice nor Hoover could decipher what the signals were, but after a long pause, Dr. Boltin raised an eyebrow and the lanky assistant went quickly from the room.

"When Bill comes in," Dr. Boltin said more kindly, "he may be disoriented. He may not know you, or feel uncertain about expressing his feelings at seeing you, Mrs. Templeton. He may break into tears. You must just accept whatever he does as natural and support him."

"Does he know I've come?" Hoover asked.

"Yes."

"And?"

"And what?"

"And what did he say?"

"I don't believe he said anything at all, Mr. Hoover."

The door opened. Janice gasped. A travesty of Bill stood blinking in the doorway. His collarbones protruded sharply and his shoulders bent inward. His trousers hung loosely at the waist. He looked as though he were recovering from an operation.

"Bill!" Janice whispered, standing up, taking a step closer.

He gazed at her blankly, and then his face made a mask with a smile on it.

"Hello."

Pathetically, he took a step closer to her, tried to mumble something, but only blinked rapidly. He looked around at the assembly of white-coated physicians and seemed terribly ashamed to be under their scrutiny.

"I'm so happy to see you," he whispered, edging still closer.

As though he had recognized one friend out of the multitude, Bill shuffled in tiny steps sideways toward her, to protect him from the onslaught of the eyes that examined him and dissected him.

"I'm—okay," he whispered confidentially. "Just—just a bit cold—and—and—it's good to see you. . . ."

He stood now next to her, his arms uncertain whether to touch her or not, until she put her hands on his shoulders and pressed him forward. Suddenly he trembled like a baby.

"So—good to—see you," he cried into her shoulder, shaking.

"Oh, Bill. Darling Bill. I've worried so much about you."

"Don't go away again. Please don't go away. . . ."

Hoover, much affected, now felt the attention of the assembly shift slowly but inexorably onto him. Bill, with Janice holding his hand, was seated next to Dr. Geddes. It took Bill a full two minutes to realize that they were not going to ask him any questions. Slowly he became aware of the tension filling the room. Overhead, the thunder cracked abruptly, viciously.

Bill turned slowly, following his instincts, following where Dr. Geddes stared, where the two physicians gazed, where Dr. Boltin had stationed the lanky staff assistant. Down at the other end of the table, perspiring in the humidity, confident, boldly immobile and staring back, was Elliot Hoover.

Bill blinked rapidly. He looked at Janice, then at Dr. Geddes. He looked back down the long table at Elliot Hoover. He smiled an awkward, pathetically inappropriate smile. Then the smile vanished. He simply stared.

"Hello, Bill," Hoover said softly.

Bill rubbed violently at his eyes, the way an infant might, as though some piece of grit had gotten lodged under the eyelids. It was an abrupt gesture, as though he tried to rub out what he was seeing.

"I've come to talk to you," Hoover said hesitantly. "Do you mind?"

Bill pressed his lips together, stared down at the table, and his fingers violently pressed into the cheap veneer and polish.

292

He looked up quickly at Hoover, opened his mouth, but said nothing.

Janice put a hand gently on Bill's shoulder. A tremulous shudder rolled through Bill, and he brushed the hair from his forehead.

"I—I knew you were here," he said in a stilted voice. "They told me."

"Things have changed, Bill. For both of us.

"They told me," Bill said, louder, fighting off the mental anarchy by raising his voice against the confusion. "They told me Elliot Hoover was here."

Hoover leaned forward, his features softened by compassion.

"Listen to me, Bill. We've suffered. Both of us. In the same way."

"What?"

Bill turned, his face in a grimace, as though he was hard of hearing. His movements were jerky, exaggerated, like an abnormal child who playacts his aggression.

"I can't *hear* you!" Bill complained.

Hoover slid into a seat closer to Bill, and kept his voice soft and distinct.

"We must help each other, Bill. We must forgive each other."

"What?"

Janice had never seen a display of willed autism before. Bill was only partially in control of himself, driven by some twisted mechanism inside, some machine perpetually breaking down, trying desperately to defend itself against one more wound.

"I've come to talk to you, Bill—in humility—about what happened—and why."

Bill nodded vigorously.

"Good, good," he said in a strange monotone. "I'm glad to hear that."

Hoover looked nervously around the conference room. Dr.

Boltin gave him an almost imperceptible nod of encouragement. Hoover licked his lips and leaned forward. Janice's grip on Bill's shoulder tightened.

"When I heard that you were searching, Bill, as I had searched," he began, "my heart was filled with . . . with sorrow. And with understanding. Because I'd gone through just that very search."

Bill stared disconsolately down at the tabletop.

"And I knew the torment of that search. The doubts, the trials, the doctrines that leap against the mind like a dark and angry sea."

Sensing contact, Hoover moved closer. His voice took on more confidence, and Janice heard the familiar charisma of his passion, the love and strength that knew no obstacles, admitted to no impediments, the iron will that penetrated any soul placed before it.

"But the *error* is not *renouncing*," Hoover explained gently. "Do you recall in the *Vedas,* in the description of the progression of the soul, that beautiful description wherein it is written that the passions must renounce ere they possess? There is that extraordinary passage of the dawn of the soul, where the verse begins—"

"How did you know about me?" Bill interrupted, suddenly whirling to look at him, his expression sly as a wolf.

"What . . . what's wrong, Bill?" Hoover said, frightened by the grinning intensity, the malevolence of the gaze.

"How did you know about me?" Bill whispered.

"Well, I—I heard . . ."

"Little birds in India? Singing in your dreams?"

Hoover shot a glance at Dr. Boltin, who was staring at Dr. Geddes. Dr. Geddes had gone pale. Janice and he began whispering feverishly. Meanwhile Bill's haggard, tortured smile grew into something worse than a smile.

"Bill, listen to me. The *Vedas* exist for the benevolence of all mankind."

"Who told you about me?" he shouted.

Hoover gazed helplessly at Dr. Boltin, who cleared his throat.

"Your wife went to India, found Mr. Hoover there, and brought him back for you."

Bill clapped his hands over his ears. "No! No!" he shouted.

"Bill," Janice said, touching his cheek. "I told you I would get help."

Bill threw off her hand. He suddenly lurched to his feet and stared into Hoover's startled face. A thousand emotions shot across Bill's lips, cheeks, and eyes, and he seemed uncertain, then enraged, and then the trembling got the better of him and he could not speak without stuttering.

"H—h—has she—?" he began.

"Has she what?" Hoover asked defensively.

Bill came closer, whispering confidentially, his eyes gleaming, bloodshot.

"H—h—has she—she—a nice—*cunt*?" he said, almost inaudible, hoarse, as though his throat had been torn out.

"Bill!" Hoover said, shocked, standing.

Bill leaped forward, tried to strike him, but found his hands too tightened up to make fists or direct a blow, and fell on Hoover, his teeth clamping onto Hoover's neck.

Janice screamed, jumped forward, chairs fell backward, Dr. Geddes threw himself at Bill, and the lanky staff assistant found his own fingers bleeding profusely where he foolishly tried to restrain Bill's jaws. But in just that second Hoover managed to free himself. Gasping in disbelief and shock, he rolled to a kneeling position.

"I—is she . . ." Bill whispered, restrained by Dr. Geddes and the assistant, oblivious of Dr. Boltin and the physicians standing in paralyzed terror over the table, "is she a *good fuck*?"

Dr. Geddes edged backward to protect Janice. Bill sensed

the change, broke free, and threw himself forward. He clubbed at Hoover with a heavy glass ashtray from the table. With sickening thuds the blows landed repeatedly at the base of Hoover's skull, smashing at the hands which tried in vain to cushion the force of the blows.

The two physicians, stumbling, launched themselves onto Bill. The door opened and two burly orderlies appeared and instantly ran across the room, knocking chairs to the wall. In the tumult Janice saw a thin, awful spray of red blood fly outward as Bill was catapulted toward the wall. As they doubled him up by bending his arms behind his back, exerting pressure at his neck, she watched in numb horror as the tiny trickle of blood, like a symbol of total disaster, oozed slowly down the pale green wall to the floor.

"Take him . . . Take him . . ." Dr. Boltin faltered.

"To the restraint room," one of the physicians ordered, his voice trembling. "And stay with him!"

"Sedation," Dr. Geddes called after them. "No physical restraint."

The other physician accompanied Bill while the orderlies and staff assistant simultaneously locked him in their arms and trundled him toward the door. Janice saw the grisly sight of Bill's mouth drooling. He had lost control of his own throat in his pathological rage, and a roar of pain shook his thin frame. He glared at Janice like a tiger from a cage, and she knew that if he were free he would certainly at that moment have killed her.

"WHORE! WHORE!"

He lost coherence. The orderlies dragged him out into the hall, his ravings echoing, growing louder in the corridor, like a demented bull elephant, screaming obscenities about Janice's body, about her lust, about her death; then it subsided and faded into the distant north wing.

Janice reeled from chair to chair, and finally sat down heavily. In her shock she gazed about vaguely, apprehending nothing, seeing horrific caricatures of the men she had trusted to heal Bill. Dr. Geddes stood, half poised to sit, paralyzed, trying to think of something, anything, to end the horror. Dr. Boltin trembled like a leaf, knocking over cups of coffee, as in a dream, trying to get to Elliot Hoover on the floor.

"It's—it's all right," Hoover said, pushing the physician away.

The sound of Hoover's voice restored a sense of reality. Janice reached out, touched Hoover on the cheek, and saw thin flecks of his blood stain her fingers.

"Dear God," he whispered, "what have we done?"

"We've killed him. Inside," she whispered. "He's broken. Completely."

"God forgive us."

Dr. Boltin cleared his throat. At the sound, Dr. Geddes stirred, lifted his head, and his eyes were red.

"I must go see Bill," Dr. Geddes said. "I—I will stay the night with him."

Compassionately, Dr. Boltin nodded. "We'll confer in the morning."

Dr. Geddes sensed his impotence, muttered a few more words, and left the conference room, heading for the north wing of the complex.

Dr. Boltin went to Hoover.

"Is your neck all right?" he asked.

"Yes, I'll be all right."

Janice stood next to him, needing his strength, his warmth, his solidity, even under the gaze of Dr. Boltin.

"I am so sorry that this happened," Dr. Boltin said. "We had no way of predicting."

"Have we destroyed him?" Hoover asked after a pause.

"It is most serious now," the doctor conceded. "I believe that we must be prepared to accept the worst."

Janice sagged against Hoover's chest. "Don't go," she said, frightened.

Hoover's eyes looked bloodshot. His face was pale.

"I came to atone," he said incredulously. "I've only compounded the sin."

"Please don't leave me. I need you."

He looked down at her.

"Let me go," he pleaded. "Let me pray. Let me understand. Perhaps then I can help you. But now it's all too confused."

He stumbled toward the open door. The corridor was filled with nurses and doctors who peeked into the room where the disturbance had rocked the hospital. Hoover stopped at the door.

"Pray for Bill," he said, adding, "and for me, Janice."

He walked quickly toward the lobby. Janice followed him into the corridor, caught a glimpse of his retreating form at the double glass doors to the parking lot.

"Elliot!"

He slowed ever so slightly, then painfully opened the door, stepped outside, and saw a taxi discharging a patient with family. He raised his arm, shouted, and ran through the night rain toward the twin shafts of headlights.

"Elliot!"

Janice ran through the double doors into the cold rain. Instantly her hair was drenched, and a foul smell of the marsh assailed her nostrils. She ran through the puddles and caught Hoover just as he opened the rear door of the taxi.

"Please," she wept. "Don't leave me now."

He touched her cheek softly. "I'm no good to you now. I can't help you. I can't help Bill. When I understand, when I know what to do, I'll contact you. And we can make right everything that we've done wrong. Trust me. For Bill's sake, trust me." With a tortured look he got into the taxi and closed the door.

Janice saw the taxi grow small, then vanish into the night. The rain blew in vicious veils around her.

"Elliot . . ." she whispered.

No one heard. She turned. The lights blazed inside the

hospital. Through the rain she saw the pattern of windows and doors, the labyrinth of dementia and rage awaiting her. The rain was so cold it seemed to have seeped into her body and begun to rot away her will to act, her will even to live. Numbly she walked slowly through the oil slicks and black puddles, back toward what remained of Bill.

Chapter Nineteen

The abrupt departure of Elliot Hoover left a horrifying vacuum. It was identical to the vista of mud-swallowed mass death that she had seen after the flood. Instead of a black bull, its forelegs broken, dead or dying in the foul waste, there was Bill. Her husband lay inert in her future, accusing, wasting away in the awful solidity of decay.

Janice did not know whether Hoover had fled to find help, or to escape her. There was no knowledge of his plans at his hotel. He had simply disappeared.

The months passed.

Elliot Hoover made no sign. The universe had swallowed him up as inexplicably as it had disgorged him. Janice stared dumbly into the future, and she found there only an endless, sterile moonscape.

Three times a week she took the long train ride to the hospital. Three times a week, Bill abused her verbally. He screamed at her, he accused her of sexual acts which she barely understood. Dr. Geddes sat calmly in his chair, observing, listening. Two orderlies discreetly stood at the door. Bill raged incoherently, and there was no limit to the explicitness of his accusations. She endured them, saying nothing. But something inside her died. Their former life, in its most intimate details, was dragged out into the mud, where it was made repulsive and loathsome.

Every visit the wound reopened. She believed—she made herself believe—in human trust, but the assaults of a demented husband crushed her. He seemed to be boundless in his vehemence. He jumped, pranced, roared, and the veins bulged apoplectically in his neck, until she longed for some dark night to cover her up.

Janice married her job. She spent days, including weekends, at Christine Daler's Ltd. Her skills had rapidly returned and continued to develop. The summer slipped through to autumn, to the cold rains of November, beating against the studio windows. She preferred not to go home. There the silence of Ivy's room mingled with the silence of the bedroom and whispered hopelessness in her ear.

Late one night, she listened to the murmur of the building, the battering of the sleet against black windows, the creaking of Ivy's door.

As a child, Janice had had a fantasy when bad times came. She had called on the white figurine of Christ perched on her mother's dresser. An absurd piece of *kitsch,* arms outspread in crass forgiveness for one and all of his forgotten lambs. But she believed then, and he came for her—outstretched arms, a painted beard and all—and served as a talisman to protect her. Now, listening to the radio turned low to keep away the permanent isolation, she did not believe. No Christ came to her through the dark skies to shield her this time.

That night, Elliot Hoover came to her in a dream. He was smiling broadly, very excited, as though he had found something. Something she would very much like to see, or to have. The dream changed. They were walking through the russet autumnal fields in upstate New York. She did not know if it was Bill or Elliot Hoover walking beside her, as their daughter gamboled among the fat, ripe pumpkins in the stalks. Then the dream changed again. There was a stinking hut in South India. Elliot Hoover cleaved against her as they lay on the ground. She felt his hard, hot breathing, and she pressed his hands closer against her own breasts, and nearly fainted with desire. Then something dark happened and he was gone, and she woke up. Outside the sleet fell. Ice covered the windows, and a cold draft billowed through the seams of the panes.

By Christmas, it was clear that, legally, Bill would never see the inside of a courtroom. He was declared *non compos mentis;* the sanitarium signed reams of documents, and the one small fear of an impending trial for kidnapping was removed. Bill did not observe the legal proceedings. When Dr. Geddes explained it to him, he closed his eyes and went to sleep.

At the end of December, Janice sent a note to Sesh Mehrotra, asking if he had seen Elliot Hoover or knew of his whereabouts. By late January, a reply came in a battered envelope, in misspelled English, that Elliot Hoover had not returned. Had he returned, he would certainly have looked up the Mehrotra family. The letter contained best wishes.

It was on the anniversary of Juanita's kidnapping that Dr. Geddes told her that Bill's condition showed signs, if not of improvement, then at least of no further deterioration. Bill could not distinguish the psychiatrists from the staff members, he did not remember names, but his memory could often be otherwise surprisingly acute.

"We've achieved a modified success. Not a full success, but a minor amelioration of symptoms, based on substituting another symbol of Ivy."

Janice looked up, surprised.

"We're trying doll therapy, verbal suggestion. If we can turn his interest, even partially, to something under our control, we can relate to him through it. You see, we must come in under his umbrella of defenses."

"I suppose the best thing would be to bring back Juanita," she suggested.

"No. Absolutely not. That would trigger off the same obsessions as before. The secret of the transfer mechanism is that the emotional charge becomes slightly weaker. That is why we must try to deal through the transfer object."

"Well, then find a doll that *looks* like Juanita!"

Dr. Geddes smiled warily. "I see you remain cynical about the whole thing. I don't blame you. Bill's case was terribly underestimated for a long time. Still, I wanted you to know that there may be a brighter future, even a partial cure."

"A partial cure? What does that mean?"

"Living at home. Minor medications for the depression. Psychotherapy to explore the guilt piecemeal. A long, slow recovery."

"How many years?"

"Difficult to say. Five. Ten, possibly."

Janice stared at Dr. Geddes. His projection seemed worse than the disease. Not for Bill. For her. She could not hide the resentment bubbling slowly from the depths of her feelings. That she should spend ten years caring for someone who barely resembled the man she had loved and married, who hurled abuse at her—pornographic abuse—and she knew she would not, could not, refuse even the smallest part of that fate.

When she arrived home, she stared at the walls for nearly an hour. With a heavy heart, she dragged herself up the stairs into the studio that once had been Ivy's room, and began sketching. Then she turned on the radio. After another hour, the antidote of work performed its magic, and she rapidly filled pages with watercolor treatments. As night fell, her thoughts turned, once again, to Elliot Hoover.

Hoover must be in the United States still. She felt it. She felt him thinking of her, aware of her. He had promised to contact her when he knew what to do. That might take another week, another month, another year. But the time would come, and knowing it would come made the night softer, less desolate. The radio sent easy melodies through the room, and she worked until 3:30, then showered and slept easily. There were no dreams, only a vague presentiment that Elliot Hoover had been there during the night.

Elliot Hoover woke in the slums of Pittsburgh with a vague presentiment that Janice had been with him during the night. It was still dark. No sun appeared over the black silhouettes of tenement roofs. Only the cold ribbons of blue and dark gray of the winter clouds. He huddled in an army blanket on the edge of a cot, shivering. He rubbed his eyes, trying to restore energy to them.

Far away came the shrill, drunken hoots of a young man. Then the crash of a bottle. Hoover reached over to a small propane stove, lit it, and then shoved a beaker of cold coffee over the flame. He was oblivious to the bits of plaster falling from the roof when a cat scampered over it.

The autumn had turned to ice. Christmas and New Year's had passed in oblivion. Elliot Hoover was still driven by the image of Bill Templeton, who, under the scrutiny of no less than four physicians, had thrown himself forward like a rabid dog, teeth bared. Hoover felt the healed scars along his neck. He filled his cup with tepid coffee and drank it.

The images came, as they always came in the predawn, rapid and confused, like a commercial for insanity. There had been the flight to Florida, the long, purposeless days along the beach, barefoot but still wearing the absurd brown suit he had bought in Calcutta. Days in Catholic churches, gazing at violently painted plaster saints. Afternoons in a dubious meditation center. And alone in cheap motels, thinking, just thinking, ignoring the television sets blaring through the walls of his room.

Hoover spit out the grounds that inevitably filtered into his coffee. Why had he stayed away from New York? It had something to do with growing forward, not regressing. One's *karma* improved with severance of ties to the earth. And besides, what could Janice possibly gain by his presence? He had as yet discovered no formula to solve Bill's problem.

Hoover showered, shaved, and went to the closet. The brown suit, badly torn and shockingly filthy, still hung on the rack among the newer garments. There were oil spots on the elbows, courtesy of the Greyhound bus ride back to the north. Was it Kansas City where he had been pushed into the mud by a drunken day laborer? Or was it in Wheeling? Hoover tried to recall when he had first realized that the drifting would have to come to an end. He remembered standing at a truck stop, picking up a ride west, not east to New York, sharing the cab with a dull, hostile driver who was red-eyed from dodging highway patrols and weigh stations. Somewhere during those confused days, the filth and grit of the country seeped into the brown suit. That was why, when he arrived in Pittsburgh, the police stopped him on sight and shoved him into the drunk tank, there being no room anywhere else.

Hoover smiled as he buttoned his shirt. Now he had other coats, other trousers. But the brown suit reminded him of Janice, of Calcutta, their nights together in the South of India. And anyway, when the Pittsburgh police checked his identity and learned he was a man of wealth and property, they quickly had the suit dry-cleaned by way of apology. Hoover chuckled out loud, and the sound was strange in the large building as it died to a melancholy, lonely echo.

306

As he had left the police station, Hoover pulled the coat closely around his throat, ducked into the fierce wind that promised sleet or snow before the day was out, and walked along the sidewalks of the city. Something had led him back to Pittsburgh. Why had he not flown to Benares from Florida? Was it some kind of habit, a yearning, even a kind of nostalgia? Hoover found himself walking along stately rows of elms, where the suburban homes were not so very new anymore, and the elms had grown from spindly, protected saplings, girdled by wire mesh, into massive, and now bare explosions of branches. Then he knew why he had returned to the city.

His home lay across a gently sloping yard, filled with dead leaves, curiously unpleasant leaves, curled and dusty. It seemed as though nothing had really changed in the eight years. A bit dirtier; the garage needed to be scrubbed; some trimming required on the hedge that curved around into the backyard; but it was still the home Hoover vividly remembered.

He remained rooted and let the chill wind blow through him. It was as though he had just been inspecting new plans for additions to the pig-iron distribution systems along the Allegheny—a late meeting with charts, wearing his gray wool three-piece suit, in his office overlooking the industrial waste-land in all its magnificence at the curve in the river—and now he had come home for the day, and Sylvia was inside cooking, or studying French, or preparing a cocktail for him.

And the door would open. Audrey Rose would come running up to him, throw her small arms around his neck, and he would lift her up off the ground and happily trundle her back inside. Audrey Rose. The small girl with the dark hair, the black eyes, the sly gamin of his heart. A secretive girl, with a secret life. She shared it with him on condition that he told no one. They were only little-girl secrets, joyful mysteries. So self-assured, life held no terror for her then.

Hoover wiped his eyes. The masters of the Ganges were right. One never truly severs one's heart from the places wherein one has learned to love. But the mind can transcend such attachments, that was the instruction. So Hoover came back to watch the house with its sloping redwood porch and its large picture windows. He walked through the parks where he and Audrey Rose had run, and along the small stream that eventually cut its way into their backyard. He willed all the memories, good and bad, to return, in order to make peace with them. He even rented a car and drove along the Pennsylvania Turnpike to the very spot where, so many years before, Sylvia's car had hurtled over the embankment and down the steep incline, carrying both her and Audrey Rose to their fiery deaths. He stood among the fat green weeds and clods of earth and forced his mind to conjure the terrible image of Audrey Rose, his darling, trapped within the burning wreckage, her tiny fists pounding and pounding against the scorched panes of glass, and screaming: "DADDYDADDYDADDYHOTHOTHOT!"

In time he did make peace with the memories. They nestled within him like warm friends, and the torment slowly dissipated.

But there was one paradox. Sometimes he imagined the life as it had been with Sylvia—the intelligent, somewhat retiring woman who had shared his deepest hopes and dreams. But now, to his own confusion, after eight years, he had difficulty recalling the features of her face.

He pictured coming into the house, listening to the Bartok string *concerti*, putting his arm around her—but no clear face was there, hardly any memory at all of her figure. It disturbed him. Instead of his wife, there was now a vague sensation of Janice Templeton.

That was even more true now, he thought as he combed his hair, examining his face in the mirror. It was Janice who accompanied him through the horrors of the slums. It was Janice who believed in him, waited for him, needed him. Without her, he would have no faith, no attempt would have been possible. But now, as he caught a glimpse of the teenagers drunk in the streets outside, the old man sleeping on an iced porch in nothing but a greasy overcoat, the smoke pouring from factories just beyond the low tenement houses, he felt a purified faith, an ability to act that knew no obstacles. And more—the true purpose behind his seemingly accidental return to Pittsburgh.

The building he purchased, and in which he was now living, was an abandoned motel, condemned by the city, but still standing after thirteen years of neglect. In three more hours, the workmen would arrive, bringing more trucks of wiring, planks, and plaster. Inevitably, the neighborhood children would cluster around the piles of sand that accumulated at the base of the motel. The noise would be, as usual, deafening. But as Elliot Hoover walked slowly through the wet, rotted debris in the hall, the moldy newspaper and bottles strewn in the corners, the icy pipes visible through dilapidated walls, there was not the slightest sense of depression. There was only the feeling of going forward. A mandate for construction. These dark corridors, he hoped, would help save the world, even if only in a small way.

Rounding a corner of unlit darkness where the walls of two adjoining rooms had given away entirely and frozen ivy twirled among the rusted nails and bits of timber, Hoover stopped short. In a sudden flash he sensed Janice by his side, smiling at him, approving all he was attempting. A warmth radiated through his body. If she was indeed here in spirit with him, he thought, then his work was bound to succeed and be the pride of them both. Eagerly, he blew into his frozen hands and paced the sodden hallways, impatiently waiting for the workmen to arrive.

Chapter Twenty

Elliot Hoover was well pleased. A smell of fresh paint greeted him. As the workmen passed him, carrying glass for the windows, he examined the pastel yellow and green walls of the corridors. A warm, sensuous light dappled through the budding branches outside.

He was well pleased, too, with the two men who had joined his staff. One was named Hirsch, a conscientious objector in the Vietnam War, who wore his sandy-colored hair in a long ponytail. The other was a Mr. Radimanath, a North Indian, father of a bookseller in Bombay. Mr. Radimanath looked like Nehru and shuffled along the newly-laid carpets in his slippers, head down, urgently, as though answering a silent summon.

And there was much to do. Hoover drew them into his office, where he issued instructions, drafted letters, negotiated long legal forms. Mr. Radimanath gently closed the red curtains behind the desk. They drank jasmine tea and rested on cushions. The sounds of the slums drifted from his consciousness.

Elliot Hoover, in his trance, felt the memories of his legal battles disintegrate. The arguments with the workmen, the vandalism of the neighborhood children, and the threatening inquiries of the county health association, all faded like a distant sunset on the horizon. The teachings of his first guru returned, not so much in words, but in the form of a spiritual harness that reestablished itself within. The trance became deeper, darker. He felt the proximity of souls he had never known, passed down for countless millennia. Abruptly, he opened his eyes.

"Excuse me, Mr. Hoover," said a workman, peering in holding two boards under his arm, "but could you show us about this here swimming pool?"

"Yes, of course."

"Didn't mean to disturb you."

"That's quite all right."

In the cellar of the former motel, the supporting floor beams had been removed, and now a gaping hole, vaguely rectangular, leered out of floodlights perched in the muddy bottom.

"The whirlpool should go here," Hoover said, pointing. "Orient the blueprints from this angle. Do you see? The swimming lanes will go across to the north."

"Right you are, sir. Now, about the heating . . ."

"Yes, yes. It must be heated to the precise degree specified."

"It'll be expensive as hell. I hope you know that."

"Any more questions?"·

The workman shook his head. He did not like Hoover. He did not like Mr. Radimanath. Above all, he did not like Hirsch, who struck him as effeminate. Nevertheless, the job was handsomely paid. Hoover was in a hurry.

* * *

312

Hoover inspected the exterior yard, piled with debris, derelict with muddy tires, newspaper, bottles, and stiff rags. Children of the neighborhood watched him. How favored they were, Hoover thought to himself. Even as they judged him crazy, they were blessed by the gift of healthy spirit and lively mind.

Huge rolls of security fence were carried to the yard and unrolled, and pipes were slammed into the earth to hold it. Hoses ran water, created mud holes everywhere. Cement covered Hoover's shoes. Some of the children threw stones, but he did not mind. For they were blessed with the light within the mind, a light he himself had doused in Bill Templeton.

Blueprints were brought for his inspection. Bizarre red and yellow shapes were carried to the yard, partially covered in brown paper, waiting for installation. Hoover's eyes crept to the children again. They found him amusing. He studied them carefully, how their animal nature mingled uneasily with the innocence of their lives.

He remembered too well the crippled children he had met daily in Calcutta, in Bombay, and even in Kotagiri. Diseases that had no name in English. Forms of malnutrition. Deliberate deformity to produce beggars for parents. And the worst, the lowest of the low, at the bottom of any caste system, were those who were insane. Those were written off—by parents, by other children, by nature itself—and they died by the scores of thousands, unable to comprehend the brief torture of their own misplaced incarnations.

Even in Pittsburgh, one saw them.

Thou art a healer of children, thou shalt make their souls to rejoice again.

He smiled and leaned against a sapling recently planted. Those had been the words of his first guru. A quiet man whose *ashram* was located on the north bank of Benares. After Hoover had confessed his search for his own daughter, the guru had told him that, with a light, pleasant lilt in the voice that comforted him.

"Where do you want the floodlights, Mr. Hoover?" yelled a gruff voice.

"Along the wall, please," he answered.

Even now the words of his guru extended a protective hand over the transformation of the derelict motel. But there was precious little time. Hoover went back inside and locked himself in his office. For the rest of the afternoon he studied textbooks, the experimental data, and newsletters printed on cheap paper. He worked until he found his eyes blurring with fatigue.

Why was he doing all this, he wondered? Was it simply a pathetic and frantic effort to atone for the spiritual murder of Bill Templeton? Or did his motivations, deeply hidden in his unconscious, rise from another, less pure wellspring? It was at this moment that the image of Janice Templeton came to him: the quick intelligence, the strange mixture of hesitation and need that drove her to India, and quite simply the perfect outline of her neck and shoulders; and instead of feeling qualms of guilt, he felt better. Strangely empty, but the comfort was there. He rose, turned on a small Tensor lamp, and studied until well past midnight.

Janice sat under a gaily colored umbrella with Elaine Romine. Lunch in the park was a novel idea, but the sunshine seemed to demand it. Children raced among them, throwing bread to the pigeons, balancing their new bicycles, falling from skateboards. Elaine basked in the sunshine, then looked lazily at Janice.

"Thank you," she said.

Janice looked up, puzzled. "For what?"

"For giving us both a break this afternoon. In case you haven't noticed, you've been driving yourself like a piston."

Janice smiled. "You should be the last person to object."

"Well I do. Your zeal is contaminating. You've got the

whole shop going at full tilt. Everybody's looking over her shoulder. Honestly, Janice, even the QEII pauses occasionally to recharge her batteries.''

Janice said nothing.

Elaine pursued. ''You don't date at all, do you?''

After a while, Janice simply said, ''No.''

''Would you like to?''

''I don't know. I don't know if that's a good idea.''

''Because I know several men.''

Janice laughed pleasantly. ''I'm sure you do.''

''Well, then? What do you say?''

It was not until they entered the studio and the familiar sight of tables, pin-up sketches, and brushes and pens surrounded them that Janice answered.

''About that invitation—if it's just company. You understand, Elaine, that has to be clear.''

Elaine smiled. ''Trust me.''

It happened very casually. One of the salesmen for a photography firm, who affected a blue pinstripe suit but had a pleasing white smile in a well-tanned face, was introduced. He shook Janice's hand carefully, and evidently found it reassuring that she and Elaine were good friends.

Two nights later, he called on Janice. That weekend, they attended a Broadway show with very expensive tickets. Afterward, they had espresso coffee in a small club on a side street. Apparently, he was heir to a small fortune, his father having invented something in the electronics business. As he talked, it became obvious that he had an obsession about his father, about competing with him. He needed someone to support him in his struggle.

They walked along the southern edge of the park, where he seemed to feel very much at home among the wealthy international set that flowed in and out of the Plaza Hotel and into Harry's Bar. He seemed preoccupied with something as they said good-night. He shook her hand outside Des Artistes, and apologized for having talked so much. Janice assured him she had loved the play, and he smiled gratefully and left in the taxi.

Janice walked alone into the elevator, rode to her apartment. The one thing about a date, for all its illicit qualities, that she had never expected, not in her wildest fantasies, was its utter sexlessness.

She sat in a melancholy mood on the couch. The television was on, but she did not bother turning up the volume. The entertainment was so vapid, it passed like a dream in front of her. A curious fatigue overcame her, and she remembered, as she did nearly every night, the first time Bill had brought her to Des Artistes. He had been filled with enthusiasm for New York, for her, for Ivy—his very steps bounced along and his nighttime passions knew no stopping. She smiled. Once she had tried to count the number of times they made love. She gave up as they approached the thousands. Even now she felt a blush in spite of herself, and she remembered how surprised she had been, not only at his ingenuity, but at his athletic prowess.

She turned off the television, felt her stomach, still flat, and wondered if other men might find her more tempting than the overgrown boy who had taken her to the Broadway show. She went slowly to the bathroom and filled the gleaming tub, adding flakes of powder that richly cascaded into luxurious foam. She undressed. She examined herself in the full-length mirror. How old did she look? She could not tell. Was it the way she dressed, which subtly but unmistakably gave signals— signals that whispered, *Stay Away*?

She lay in the steaming water. She remembered how carefully Bill had looked after his body. The gym he religiously went to, the dumbbells at home, jogging every weekend. She pictured the well-sloped shoulders, the powerful calf muscles, the slim forearms. As she lay, she recalled how the pectoral muscles were so nicely defined, how symmetrical he was, the strange, heavy way a man looks when he is naked. And suddenly, an immense vacancy was in her life, an awful emptiness; and no one to fill it, no one to ease the oblique, insistent demands of her physical self, not now, not anymore, except in some small way, like a little girl, without even happiness, herself.

That night she dreamt she performed in a Broadway play. The lights were very hot, and they burned on her face and hands. In the audience, barely visible in the darkness, she thought she saw her date, except that he looked like Dr. Geddes. She escaped by running backstage, and suddenly she was in a red bus kicking up a strange pink dust that had an almost sexual tinge in the sun as it climbed high into yellow mountains. Once again she was on a journey, an urgent journey, to meet... to meet... in the landscape of India... Elliot Hoover.

Through the skylight poured an inexhaustible light, and below, in the whirling baths, arms obscured by the churning white water among the yellow tiles, was a child. Elliot Hoover squatted on his heels, talking to his staff member, Mrs. Concepcion, who stood in the waist-high whirlpool, holding the child tightly in her arms. The child screamed, raged, his fists pummeled her thick neck and shoulders, and his face had turned an awesome shade of purple. Elliot Hoover nodded encouragement. Mrs. Concepcion merely held the boy tighter, rocked him slowly side to side through the hot bath, and sang a soft lullaby. The screams resounded through the tiled swimming area, echoed from the cheerful painted tiles, like the roars of a stunted lion.

The child, Roy, at age four, had been the first patient admitted to Hoover's recently completed clinic. Most autistic children stiffened upon being touched. Or they went dead. Or they ignored whatever human being was there. But Roy fought for his life. He bit, he went for the eyes, he clawed at exposed necks, screaming that awesome, animal roar. Not even the merry bubbling of warm water could begin to drown

317

it out. Something inside the boy, something unreachable, unknowable, was like an incessant raw nerve of distilled hatred. He was like a fish on the line. The more he struggled, the more he weakened. And he fought so terrifically because he knew instinctively that he was losing now, bit by bit, but inevitably. Mrs. Concepcion, a registered nurse, had only recently been admitted to the staff, but she had immediately understood Hoover's method. The boy was being broken—by love.

Elliot Hoover indicated, with gestures, some encouragement for Mrs. Concepcion. She nodded and held the boy tighter, pushing the head toward her voluminous breasts, letting him feel the warmth there, learning to smell her. Hoover waved, gestured to his watch, and went along the pool to the accompaniment of Roy's bellows.

A short but narrow series of stairs led up to the main clinic. Even when he closed the door, Roy was audible.

In the first floor corridors, the staff members and children filled the rooms. Screams and whimpers filled the air, and now and then the crash of plastic dishes or toys. But considering the number of children at the clinic—thirteen—the astounding thing, the frightening thing, was the long spates of pure silence.

Hoover walked slowly down the corridor. In the first room, James, aged five, rocked furiously on his cot, back and forth, so violently that he began to pass out from sheer dizziness. Mr. Radimanath entered the room, fresh from the garden, where he had been supervising the clinic vegetables, and went to the cot. Keeping his own head safely out of the way, Mr. Radimanath embraced James, not so tightly as Roy needed to be held, but firmly enough. And when the rocking started again, Mr. Radimanath rocked with him, two bodies in simultaneous motion, the one holding the other, eyes closed, in a curious embrace of both love and indifference.

James had been found as an infant, literally in the rubbish

318

heap. No one knew who his parents were. No one knew even what his race was, a handsome mixture of African, Hispanic, and possibly Indian. But he was sealed off from reality. His defenses were so impenetrable that he had been diagnosed as deaf until he had been sent to the clinic and Mr. Radimanath had tricked him into revealing that he heard. He not only heard, but there were words he understood— *ball* and *supper* and, inexplicably, *teakettle*. So it was to Mr. Radimanath that the case was given. The old Brahmin was trained in the Vedic disciplines. Of all the staff members, he had the best control over his soul's strength, its capacity for boundless but directed love.

Elliot Hoover nodded his approval. He left the room. James saddened him. But in the next room was an even worse case. Lily, the girl who ate sand, who ate bugs, who ate anything repulsive and dirty. She had an inexhaustible hunger for grit. By the time she was three, she had been on intravenous feeding at the County Hospital. But Welfare had no objection to letting Hoover's clinic have a try at Lily. So they disguised her scrambled eggs with brown food color and let her eat it off the bookshelf in her room. Lily was a case which would never improve. She was very ugly, with a shower of freckles over a pointed, misshapen nose, and her eyes squinted almost shut. Hoover detected in her a soul so withdrawn that it floated helpless and disconnected through her being.

As Lily slept, a peculiar grace settled on her face. The dappled light from the exterior garden floated over her, glinting on the touch of spittle at the corner of her mouth. Elliot Hoover loved her. He loved her for her helplessness. In her mentally retarded state, she never quite understood that other human beings cared for her. The awareness kept slipping back like a giant fish sounding. Right now, it was all they could do to teach her to walk without shuffling her feet uselessly.

He closed the curtain so the sunlight would not wake her. Then he went back into the corridor, turned the corner, and gently opened a white door.

Inside were five video screens in front of five self-enclosed cubicles. A boy named Henry stared so wide-eyed at imagery of himself that Hoover chuckled. Henry was learning that he existed. The boy's face drew near the screen, where an image of Henry sat upright on the bed in his room. It was a moment of discovery, with an almost holy awe radiating from the boy's eyes. Hoover stopped smiling. Henry slapped the green plastic button and the tape began over again. At a small booth in the corner of the room, Hirsch waved cheerfully.

A second boy sat in the next cubicle. This was Jackson, the daredevil. No one remembered how he had gotten the name, but it suited him well. The small black face, the impish manner of crawling, twisting, eluding the staff members, often exploded without warning into violence. The tiny black hands beat in uncontrolled excitement on the console. Jackson had frozen the image: a test car, piling into a wall of bricks, hurled a dummy driver through the shattering glass. The film, courtesy of the Motor Vehicle Department of Pennsylvania, elicited the identical response at the identical moment. The image of the man being crushed against the bricks fired some nerve deep in Jackson's primordial personality.

Hoover left the video room. There was Mary Ann, suspected of having sustained brain damage after being beaten by her parents in her crib. She simply gave up the use of arms and legs. Hoover tried to induce her to exercise the atrophying muscles, but without success. There was Earl, the lanky seven-year-old, nicknamed Uncle Earl because of his white hair and grave demeanor. Uncle Earl looked the most normal of the children. There was none of the dead look in the eyes, the lustreless, vapid absence of life there. But after a few moments, it was apparent to anyone that Uncle Earl was just not there. He grinned a lot. Hoover was fascinated by him. The boy carved out his own planet with its own rules and formations, and his body moved obliviously through the obstructions which the earth beings called reality. And nothing reached him. Not even the Popeye cartoons on the video.

The other children were in the playground. Red and yellow jungle gyms, slides, and a merry-go-round rose up from the packed dirt and grass. Vines covered the security fence. Within the compound, six children—Neville, Randy, a girl nicknamed Suzie-Q, an obese deaf girl named Janeen, Duncan, and a slight dark-haired girl named Jennie—played, stood, or sat without the slightest awareness of one another. As far as they were concerned, the world was barren of all life forms save their own frightened psyches. Hoover caught a glimpse of the staff members discreetly observing at the far corner of the playground.

The staff numbered seven. In addition to their professional excellence, they had been chosen for their spiritual reflexes. Hoover judged applicants ruthlessly. Only these seven had passed the test.

Before lunch, Hoover rose and left the office. He went to his bedroom, which was next to Jennie's room. He lay on the edge of the bed, and he felt comfortable looking at the few icons and carvings he had brought back from the Tamil region. They restored his confidence.

But there was no sleep. No tranquility. Strange thoughts buzzed through the back of his mind like sinister hornets. The clinic was a means. But it occurred to him that he might never know to what end. He pulled out a note pad and a pen from a table under the window. He sighed, brushed his hair back, sat up, and began to write:

Mr dear Janice,

I beg you to forgive me for this long silence. I can only tell you that I have tried to come to

terms with the confusion caused by Bill's breakdown. After I left the hospital, I went to Florida

He crumpled the note into a ball and threw it into a
wastebasket. He began again.

Dear Janice,

My long silence must not be construed as a flight
from either you or Bill. On the contrary, not a night
goes by that I have not thought of you both, or
wished that things might not have turned out as they
have

He tore the note in half. For a while, he stared at his shoes.
The urgency of writing was peculiarly blocked. With an
almost muscular trembling, he tried a third time.

Janice,

It is so strange to write to you when I feel that I
have never been absent from you. You must know
that I have undertaken a work—a great work—and
though it taxes me and troubles me, I have always
sensed that you were, somehow, here with me, and
it vitalizes me, it gives me strength that I—I should
say *we*—can carry on.

I have, by the grace of God, been able to establish a
home in Pittsburgh, a clinic where the ill of spirit
among the city's poorest children—many abandoned—
can come to be healed.

He paused, looked out the window at the trees rustling in
the warm breeze. He turned back to the note, eyes glazed in
abstract, faraway thoughts, and put his pen to paper again.

For children have always meant for me—for us—

He crossed it out, resolved to recopy the letter.

> And why now, after a year, have I written? Remember I told you that things had to be worked out, they had to be ready before I could help you and Bill?

In despair, he crumpled the note and dropped it into the wastebasket. There was nothing "ready." He was no more prepared to help Bill now than he had been when he returned from India. Maybe the clinic had taught him humility, if nothing else.

Jennie walked past the open door. Her elbows were held high, over her shoulders, as though an invisible board or pole were slung over her neck, and her arms dangled from it. She shuffled slowly, absentmindedly, on tiptoes, engrossed in the thick weave of the hall carpet.

"Jennie!" he called, smiling.

But his loneliness was not eased. The child paused slightly, but she kept shuffling away. He knew better than to follow. Soon it was silent again.

A shuffling returned to the door. A small face, elfin, with a fringe of dark hair, peered in. Hoover turned.

"Five—four—three," Jennie said in a tiny three-year-old voice.

Hoover smiled, but he bent over the wastebasket, scooped up the discarded notes to Janice, and mashed them into a single angry wad.

"Yes, my little elf," he said. "Five, four, three. What comes next? Two, one, zero?"

"Six—nine—eight."

Hoover looked at her in consternation. The girl slipped away from the door and walked, self-absorbed, down the corridor. Hoover sat for a while, depressed, then cheered himself with the idea of examining the playground to plan a small flower garden there.

*　　*　　*

It was warm, sunny, and a subtle aroma of grit hung in the air. It was a nostalgic smell—distant rubber factories, something like linseed oil hovering in the air, the kind of lazy day when he and Audrey Rose had gone looking for deer in the suburban parks.

Walking along the protective fence, he looked out at the hostile slum. Sometimes it felt less like a refuge at the clinic than a form of incarceration. In the dirt yards around the clinic, nothing grew. There was only the debris, the worn rubber tires, piles of rubbish, mattresses ripped open, cars up on jacks and wooden blocks. Hoover squinted at a smashed black Ford, its glass and upholstery littering a vacant yard. A battered license plate dangled from the rear. It read 543 698.

A weird, electric thrill ran into his nerves. 543 698. So Jennie observed the world! Now she could play it back, at least a few numbers.

He ran across the street. Under the gaze of a white-haired, elderly black man who angrily tapped his cane, Hoover ripped the license plate from the Ford and ran back to the clinic. But when he raced upstairs to Jennie's room, the child was asleep.

A small victory in hell, he said to himself, standing over Jennie's cot. He slipped the license plate into her desk drawer. Like the monsoon flood that had thrown him and Janice together, Hoover reflected, time seemed on the move again. In its dark currents, where were they being taken? Only time itself, Hoover knew, would decide when and where their mutual destinies would be unveiled.

Chapter Twenty-one

September, and Elliot Hoover found no way to assuage his isolation except by throwing himself into his work. The problem of writing to Janice followed him. In some manner the clinic was preparing him for something. But what? He meditated on the roof of the clinic, during the long, hazy sunset that scattered vermilion through the smoke over the hills, but the answer did not come. So there was nothing but the work.

A second operation enabled Jackson to work the steel pincers of his prosthetic arm. Fortunately, his aggressive instincts began to diffuse into erratic behavior, or else the other children would have been endangered. Lily remained the same, as did Uncle Earl. But the raging Roy suddenly broke down and wept in Mrs. Concepcion's arms, and his small arms clutched her neck, and from that day he made no sound, only followed her with his eyes. Mrs. Concepcion slept in the same room as Roy. The boy began to realize that she was there, she would always be there; and instead of rage he began to show signs of curiosity. He climbed into the curtains, examining the pattern of the weave, and he poked among the pots and pans in the kitchen, peering into his reflection in the stainless steel.

But the weirdest case was Jennie. She had grown still more independent, more sure of herself. Her withdrawal now seemed to mask a decisive personality that refused to reveal its complexity. She watched Hoover with soft green eyes that were as distant as Jupiter's moons.

Hoover typed a reply to the University of Ohio, which had agreed to publish a favorable report on the clinic and its "love" therapy. Far in the distance Henry was crying, a singsong, monotonous lament that had no cause and no end. The door opened in the office, and Hoover saw Jennie peer up at him. She walked coolly to his desk, pulled out three felt-tip pens and walked back to the door.

"You're welcome, Jennie," he chuckled.

"Three-two-one," she said softly.

Hoover shrugged.

"One-two-three," he answered, looking for a stamp.

He licked the stamp and patted it onto the envelope. He wearily tossed it into the "out" wire basket. He lay back in his chair. It was a quiet afternoon. It was nearing three years since he had first seen Janice and Ivy outside the School for Ethical Culture. A rainy day, in a sea of umbrellas. Janice had looked as he had imagined. Brunette, a bit chic, something decisive about her, but fragile. Upstairs, Mr. Radimanath roared with Neville. A new turn of therapy—to let the boy know that rage was not offensive so he might as well give it up.

Jennie remained at the door.

"What is it, darling?" he asked. "What are you trying to tell me?"

She thought he was going to get up, and she instinctively retreated.

"Do you want a number?" he asked. "I'll give you a number. Listen. Five-five-three-three. Five-five-three-three. Can you say that?"

"Five-five-three-three," she said shyly.

So Jennie was willing to acknowledge that she understood a spoken number! She was hungry for numbers. Hoover did not have to write them down anymore.

"One-four-two-one," he tried, smiling.

"Six-nine-five-four."

"What? Let's try again. Five-five-three-three."

"One-two-four-eight-seven."

Hoover laughed, scratching his head in amused frustration.

"That's more numbers than I gave you," he said. "What are you doing, adding them?"

His smile froze. Something cleared at the back of his mind as though he had crossed a strange threshold, into a room where he was now awake, where he breathed a different atmosphere than he had ever breathed before. Jennie waited at the door. For what?

"Jennie," he said, leaning forward, "are you adding the numbers?"

She smiled like a leprechaun, unable or unwilling to understand what he asked. Hoover licked his lips, trying to fathom what she wanted.

"Seven-three-two-six-four," he said.

"Seven-three-two-six-four."

"Okay. Let's see. I'd better write this down. Two-five-five-one-eight."

"Nine-eight-seven-eight-two."

Not a second's hesitation. Hoover added the numbers: 98782. It was correct. He could not believe it.

"Eight-eight-one-five-six-three-two-two-four-eight," he said.

She repeated the number in that soft, elusive voice, a voice that sounded like gauze curtains rustling in the autumn breeze.

"Nine-seven-three-five-one-one-four-two-nine-three," he said.

"One-eight-five-five-no-seven-four-six-five-four-one."

It took Hoover a few seconds to add his numbers. She was correct. Except that she said "no" instead of "zero." He stared at her, amazed. He stood and walked toward her, but she darted down the corridor, and when he found her again, at the edge of the grass, she showed no signs of interest in him or numbers.

Hirsch remembered studies of autistic children who fixated on numbers, but he had never read of one who could manipulate them at such extraordinary speed. What was the meaning of her ability? And what was the extent of her gift? Did it end with addition or could she perform other feats? And was she trying to say something with the numbers? Hoover and Mr. Radimanath spent the rest of the evening preparing logical and numerical tests for Jennie.

In two weeks they determined Jennie's limits. There were none. She could add any column of numbers, no matter how long, provided they were enunciated clearly. And her answer, in that quiet, whispered voice, came back faster than they could write down the numbers themselves. Suddenly she began to come up with extraordinarily long numbers. She was multiplying. Hirsch bought an electronic calculator to keep up with her. Jennie could divide. Strangely, she never subtracted. Nor did they know why she sometimes added the numbers, sometimes divided, other times multiplied. And who had taught her? She was not old enough to have been even in nursery school.

"Perhaps, in a previous incarnation, she was a mathematician," suggested Mr. Radimanath.

Hoover's head jerked around.

"Do you really think so?"

"Her gift *is* extraordinary, is it not? So fast. And never mistaken."

"Yes. Extraordinary. I've written to Penn State. Maybe they've hit on cases like this."

But the clinic at Penn State had not run across such mathematical quickness in autistic children. Only cases of memory of numbers, never manipulation of them. They suggested tests with letters and words. Memory tests, manipulation tests. The tests were performed, but Jennie stared blankly through the colored boards of objects, words, and letters, and went dead, signifying that she was through with the game.

Hoover became obsessed with Jennie. He knew that she was trying to communicate with him, but her only language was the one of pure number. What was the meaning behind her burgeoning and fixated talent? In some way she knew the mystery of the autist, the landscape of the lost, the universe of the undeveloped soul. Was that a pure soul? Did she know things that normal children forget when their personalities develop?

Behind it lay another hope. That Jennie could tell him, even in an intuitive way, what it was like to be himself. Somehow Jennie observed him in a pure and untutored way, a whole and trusting way, the way Audrey Rose had known him.

It was in the tiny girl that he detected a response—and even an answer—to his own motivations, to the meaning of his trials.

Hoover pondered long hours over the enigma of Jennie. Was she part of some grand design sent to him by divine providence to validate his work at the clinic? Was she a messenger from heaven sent to salve his troubled spirit and quiet the guilts he so keenly felt about Bill?

Hoover reread her data sheet from the Bureau of Welfare: Jennifer Dunn. No birth certificate. Admitted to Temple University Clinic, 1977. Diagnosed retarded, possible nervous disorder. Before that, three separate hospitals in Pittsburgh. Tendency to fevers, coordination markedly poor, no speech. A handwritten form was stapled to the dossier. Hoover turned his folder sideways. The girl, now called Jennifer Alice Dunn, found in the rubbish depot of a Woolworth's store in central Pittsburgh in August of 1974. The woman who found her, Mrs. Ora Dunn, kept Jennie nineteen months in foster care; then, unable to deal with the child's problem, brought her to the county relief agency.

And now he had her. In a sense he had adopted her; he took care of her, even, in a fashion, loved her as a father. She knew no other man as father. Why this need to see her as a substitute for Audrey Rose? Had he not finally purged the past from the present? According to the welfare records, Jennie was born between five and six months before Ivy Templeton died. Absurd, but it relieved his anxiety. Was it not a second sign? A sign to let the past recede into the past, a test of the soul's strength?

Mr. Radimanath and Hoover spoke late into the night. Jennie, they agreed, had a force over him, and Hoover did not like it. There was a desire to possess her, to claim her soul, that was absent in all the other children. So he turned her case over to Mr. Radimanath and contented himself with elaborating Jackson's unique fixation on car crashes.

But Jennie was never far from his sight or mind. Finally her sly, elfin, presence so tantalized him, that he took charge of her case once again and proceeded to a thoughtful series of video preparations, none of which elicited the slightest response from the girl.

The tragedy of autism was that retardation has the aspect of being willed, Hoover thought, watching Jennie squirm in the seat of the video cubicle. She refused to learn. Refused to be aware. Yet she was physically able to learn. Sometimes she tried to be deaf. It was all a deception. Why? To shut out pain. But there was no pain in the clinic. Something deep down had shut off, had left its imprint where the personality should have begun developing through language.

"You're just a deception," he whispered sadly, running his

fingers through her fine, jet black hair. "Just a lovely, quiet little deception."

Through the day he exhausted his prepared video tapes. Nothing worked. He detected a sly smile of triumph on her face. He grew angry. He wanted to break down the barriers, remove the potential locked up behind the grim walls and make a wonderful person of her. But she refused, willfully countered his every stratagem.

She was deception.

The idea lingered with him long after she went to bed. Jennie was a deception. Why did that have an odd ring? Something awesome toyed with his brain, edging into consciousness, dying away again. Jennie, the deception. Deceiving whom? Himself? Herself? Bill?

Suddenly he stopped. He had been walking along the side of the pool in the basement, so lost in thought that he barely realized where he was. The light flickered on the gently moving water. The banners and mobiles looked pitiful against the cold pipes, the dirt of the windows, the grime of Pittsburgh that seeped into everything, even floating on the surface of the water near the filter.

Bill? *Jennie deceive Bill?* What odd thoughts were coming? He sat down on the diving board at the dark end of the underground chamber. He pictured Bill with Jennie, but it made no sense. What was the connection? There was a missing equation. He walked the tiled floor, his shoes squeaking on the wet surface. He sensed the missing connection in this grand deception that he was plotting, but could not quite put his finger on it.

So he stared into the water. His own reflection was so distorted in the dark, moving hideously against the single bulb dangling from the far wall, that he appeared to be some form of monster come from the deep. So his thoughts worked into the idea of monster, and to heavy animals, and dark water; and, as always, he remembered lifting the enormous black bullocks from the dead children of the Indian villages, and the ugly masses of dirty, dead chickens that got stuck among the stinking boulders where the road had been, now all sucking mud. And the soldiers shooting diseased dogs. Rifle cracks echoing horrifically through the hills. A looter shot. Hoover scrambled through masses of brush, tangled debris, carrying his pitifully small canister of antibiotics, white cloth bandages, and water purification tablets.

The monster that was himself smoothed out as he remembered Janice as he had found her and washed the mud slowly from her legs. The small undulations of her hips and breasts, the navel so oddly smeared with grime, her unconsciousness throwing her pelvis forward in such deep sleep. So Janice was the missing equation, he thought.

He walked back to the diving board. Jennie was the deception. Bill was the object. Janice was the missing equation. Nothing else came to his fatigued mind, except that the meaning of the clinic was emerging. And the meaning of the clinic was more than the rehabilitation of thirteen vulnerable children. It was much more, and its purpose was on the verge of coming into the light of day.

Lying awake in his room, staring at the dark ceiling, listening to the sounds of the clinic—the warm-air heating ducts, the underground motor for the swimming pool, the kitchen refrigerators that hummed, and Uncle Earl moaning in his sleep—Hoover felt a presence in the darkness. And that presence took control of him. It was the way the growing root of a plant will insinuate itself into the crack of a rock, and with time, split it, the power so strong. Hoover's lean physique had become leaner with the hard work at the clinic, his legs thinner even than they had been in South India. But it made his body taut. It vibrated with an interior desire. It insinuated itself into his very purpose on earth. The muscle and flesh began to take on a life of its own, and he felt overwhelmed by it.

Was it the continent of America? Its absence of spirituality? Its hardness, its meanness, its grasping for the material world? Or was it the isolation? Where even Hirsch and Mr. Radimanath could not form a strong enough brotherhood to raise his spirit to its former level? Or was it Pittsburgh, which awakened the dormant memories of Sylvia—the slender arms, the soft smell of her perfume, the Bartok string quartets long after Audrey Rose was asleep upstairs and the late autumn dust filtered into the house from the neighboring woods, like the fragrance of nature itself, until their blood burned and they were consumed, the one within the other.

He was washing dishes late at night in the kitchen. All the staff shared the menial tasks in rotation. Steeped in the hot steam, the water sloshing to his elbows, the tiny radio full of tinny voices as inconsequential as the rest of the world had become to him, a different memory came to Hoover. As he carefully hosed the red plastic dishes under the spray, his yellow gloves like emblems of a foreign life, he recalled the vermilion and yellow cloth that swirled through the bazaars of Benares, the cloth that floated into the holy Ganges, where the dead and the dying came to be bathed one last time.

A rapid mélange of imagery flashed through him. Dusty hills, debates at the brotherhood, Sesh Mehrotra, rain in the hills and soldiers everywhere—like a speeding train crashing through time and space, a movie film gone insane—and he remembered, not the flood, but afterward. Not the safety of the mountains, or the loveliness of the Tamil *ashram,* but, again, inevitably, it was the dirty hut that he recalled, when his breathing had felt warm and difficult and Janice Templeton lay on the hard floor, her breasts rising and falling at the same rapid rate. Like some dark dream, as though following himself out of himself, unconscious of everything, as though the self tarried behind an unknown dimension of his own body, he had gotten close to her. He had pressed against her and her warmth had intoxicated him until he felt dizzy. His two hands pressed forward until the small, delicate softness of her breasts responded, and her hands pressed on his, and he had never in all his life been so awakened to any woman, so transformed without embarrassment by the strength of his need.

Remembering, almost dizzy with the remembrance, Hoover awakened to find himself standing in the brilliantly lit kitchen of the clinic. The water had filled over the sink and was cascading onto the floor, over his shoes, being sucked down into the drain. He turned off the tap. What had happened afterward? He remembered vaguely how he had trembled, gone off alone, to be safe, to sleep in the isolation at the edge of the tilled field. There he had prayed for deliverance, for strength, for even a portion of the purity once promised him by the master of his very first *ashram*. So the night had passed in prayer and in agony, in meditation and in hell, and somewhere in the blackness he had heard the sudden rumble of heavy hooves, the snorting of a bullock and a cow in the mud, locked in bestial, explosive copulation—or had that been a dream? Had it all been a transference of his own torment to the innocent night? There were sects, after all, which taught that the spirit may, in fact, infuse the spirit of an animal, to perform those acts which may not be performed by a religious pilgrim.

Depressed, Hoover mopped the floor. He turned off the radio. His mind felt as though it had gone through a shredder. Sleep was something of a luxury now. Every time he lay down, Janice Templeton came close to him in the darkness, and her spirit tortured his, not to mock him, but to challenge him, for he knew now, that like him, she had not forgotten the pressure of their bodies that distant night.

Hoover felt the need of prayer.

He needed guidance. And it had to come from outside the clinic. It was clear now that the destinies of them all—Bill, himself, Janice, even Jennie, for all he knew—were in some perplexing way intermingled, and would find fruit together.

Hoover took off his apron and toweled the perspiration from his face. He walked out of the kitchen, through the corridor, listening to Jennie mumbling incoherently in her sleep, and fat Janeen beating heavily against the protective rails of her cot. The sounds soothed him in some obscure manner. As he walked to his office, the desire of his body, aroused by the strong memory of the South Indian night, receded, relaxed, leaving only a vibrant, trembling sensation through his wracked frame.

He entered his office. The red carpet was now littered not only with cushions and a tea set, but with papers, photographs, dossiers, manuscripts, books, and correspondence. Perhaps the breeze through the window had upset the desk. Perhaps Henry had gotten into mischief during an unguarded moment. Hoover lit a small candle and brought it to the center of the room, set it on the floor, and made a clear circle in the midst of the envelopes and stationery there. There was no other light. He stuck two small sticks of incense into the quiet flame, and the ends of the incense stick sparkled, then glowed dully, and a smoke like jasmine circled lazily upward where the heated air from the candle flame issued toward the ceiling. He placed the incense sticks near him, between two fallen books, lowered his head slightly, and crossed his legs. As he sat, emptying himself of the day's thoughts, slowly purging the weariness of the physical labor, the complexities of fighting the psychic defenses of the children, his awareness seemed to simplify. He found himself staring blissfully down at his own palms, outstretched, facing upward on his own knees.

He opened his eyes. Slowly, all thoughts, all fatigue, all desires that fixated onto earthly objects began to dissolve. Specifically, he shut himself off from the open window where the curtains stirred in the fragrant, dusty breeze. Then he closed his eyes. In the dissolving, curious reddish atmosphere of the inner eye, behind closed lids, he felt the familiar, comforting atmosphere of meditation. The subtle sense of becoming less substantial and vastly more expanded, as the body withdrew from consciousness. He concentrated on the breathing, control of the diaphragm, breathing through one nostril only, one of the most difficult exercises.

In the dreamy, sensuous atmosphere where there was no floor, no wall, no sound, but only sensations that intermixed freely, he felt the wrong kind of love. It was not the vague radiance that flowed from the interior of the spinal column, and translated itself into the gentle bliss. It was not the beneficence of the accumulated teachings of yogis through the countless generations, a softness and a melodious moral regeneration. It was more like an embrace. As though a love had come to restore him, to answer the love within him and make it whole. And the sensation terrified him.

Perspiring, he opened his eyes. He was breathing hard with the effort. Calmly he rose, closed the window, lit two more sticks of incense, and then paced the room in agitation. He shuffled through a series of books on a low shelf behind the desk, and pulled out a worn volume of Vedic poems, given him by Mr. Radimanath's son, printed on his own small printing press in Calcutta.

Hoover read several poems. They seemed to exude a sweet peace, a consuming confidence that had become foreign to himself. Yet he needed them now as never before.

The verses treated of the Supreme Personality, the Godhead that inhabited and formed all moving and nonmoving entities, which passed over and through all the obstacles of growth and decay.

> *Though engaged in all kinds of activities, the pure devotee raches the spiritual kingdom.*

> *Work, therefore, always under the consciousness of the Godhead, through all the trials of conditional life.*

The supreme Lord is situated in everyone's heart O Arjuna, and directs the wandering of all living entities.

The room was so quiet that Hoover was unaware of himself, unaware of the noises of the clinic. There seemed to be only the thoughts of ancient yogis, and within that thought he now existed in pure spirit. The words burgeoned in a radiant charisma, flooding into his ego, transforming it with confidence and love. With tears in his eyes, Hoover read:

Under illusion you may decline to act according to the direction of the Godhead. But, compelled by your own nature, you will act all the same.

He reread the passage. He closed the book, mumbled the passage by heart. There was a sensation of purification, of intense potentiality to act, but now he did not know exactly where and how. The answer was in the room, in the low-hanging ribbons of incense smoke, in the mundane noises and water pipes, scratched paint, crayoned murals of the clinic. The answer lay in his memories, in his fantasies. Above all, it lay in his body, the body he had been afraid to admit to his thoughts.

Compelled by your own nature, you will act all the same, he repeated to himself.

A bit confused, feeling the warmth radiating from his own face, he sat cross-legged once again on the floor, and began to meditate. This time there was no difficulty. In seconds he slipped into a slight trance, a falling away of minute perceptions. In a few more seconds he slipped further, and was unaware of the smell of incense, or any noise, or even of his location.

A radiance spread out before him. A landscape of disintegrated form, bathed in a translucent glow. In it he recognized

337

pieces of his ego, fragments of his past, his desires, his fears, actual experiences. The shards of himself were iridescent and floated rapidly, winking out of sight as he rose above and beyond them. He was without ego. Without pain. There was no turbulence or doubt, only a rich sense of trust, as though he had entered a destiny far larger than his own. He was not afraid. Several times he had ascended to these heights, but never with such a pulsating, relentless momentum.

The elements of his religious training flew past, as though he were riding onward in an incomprehensibly rapid freight train. Faces of his first Episcopalian minister, in Harrisburg, and of the choir master at his church in Pittsburgh. And a rapid series of faces, long-haired, some bearded, some clean-shaven, the faces softened by a lifetime away from manual labor, eyes closed in the depths of inward seeking. These were the gurus, the masters of the *ashrams*, each with a subtle variant of the doctrine, each contesting for disciples, each in his own way saintly and indifferent to the life of the earth. They flew by, more pure form than individual faces, and each bore the unmistakable stamp of radiance, a light which spread out from the center of the being.

But now Elliot Hoover was in a peculiar nonspace. He recognized none of the signs. A vast array of twinkling specks inhabited his awareness like dancing diamond dust. Vague clouds appeared on the far edges—holes which led toward the pure annihilation of Non-Being Itself, and he became frightened. He felt that he needed his ego, his personality, to survive the journey toward Non-Being, but the myriad essences of his previous spiritual master accompanied him, flowing with him, without his own essence, and Elliot Hoover ceased to be, except in pure form.

The great veil—*Maya*, the iridescent and irresistible curtain of phenomena—was rendered. Behind all that which was known and seen, smelled and tasted and touched, was the oblivion of Non-Being. It was like looking into the great death of the cosmos, the overwhelming magnitude of the universe's hostility to living forms. And all that protected Elliot Hoover was the thin screen of deception. Deception of the forms of the earth. Beyond that was only a dim sense of a voice, like the deep bass voice of his first guru in Benares, still offering guidance and instruction, still speaking within the conscience of Elliot Hoover after seven years. The words were not spoken. They did not come to the ears. They rose from the most interior core of Hoover's being, and he sensed this at the far reaches of the curtain of *Maya*.

The voice said that *the deception shall not be the deception, and the frightening shall not be frightening*.

There an image formed of bright leaves, yellowed where a mystical sunlight penetrated the *ashram* roof of vines, and beyond was busy Benares, full of dusty buses, oxen pulling carts of feces and straw, and the temple bells ringing furiously in the fetid air.

The deception shall not be the deception, said the guru, looking away from Hoover. *The frightening shall not be frightening*. The guru's palms, upturned on the white-clothed knee, caught the bright sunshine, and twin auras of blinding white light shone upward through the heavens. And Hoover was more certainly in Benares, listening to his first religious teacher, than he had ever been in Pittsburgh, Pennsylvania.

It all went black, a cloudy black, and Elliot Hoover fell a thousand miles, growing fuller and heavier, until he heard his own breathing and tasted his own salt tears on his lips.

Opening his eyes, he did not move. He was surprised to find himself in a cluttered office, littered with books and strange-looking folders and papers. Was this a form of teleportation mentioned in the *Vedas*? Gradually he realized that he had been crying, and he rubbed his eyes with his sleeve. His breathing grew calmer, and his glance caught the open book of the *Bhagavad Gita*, still on his desk.

With a sigh, Hoover leaned forward, remembering everything now. He felt limp with exhaustion. That he had been elsewhere he did not doubt. He still had no sense of time. He could not focus on whether it was December or July, early evening or before dawn. He was conscious of the damp perspiration that stained his clothes, of the oppressive heat in his red office. Dimly he tried to recall the words beyond hearing, the revelation of his most difficult trance.

The deception shall not be the deception. The frightening shall not be frightening.

He did not understand. With great difficulty he uncrossed his legs. He remembered that the long meditation of the Gautama Buddha had so sapped the man's strength that Buddha had to learn to walk all over again. Hoover pulled himself up by the edge of the desk. He massaged his calves and then walked slowly around the room, breathing in deeply, exhaling regularly, to reenter the normal rhythms of life.

Before him were all the complexities of application forms, bills, letters of inquiry on the desk and on the floor, charts on the wall, play-therapy schedules, cafeteria diets, medical dosages for several of the children—all grim reminders of the work at hand.

On the wall was Mr. Radinamath's vocabulary sheet. Jennie's numbers, five of which had been associated with specific commands. Hoover smiled. The little leprechaun. *The little deception.*

He bent over a cracked burner, lit the stove, and warmed some tea. Jennie was the small deception, the personality behind a facade of deafness and retardation. The great veil of *Maya* was the large deception, the delusion that things of the earth were real. Suppose they were both, in fact, not delusions? Hoover drank his tea and stared out at the darkness of the autumn through his window.

Well, if Jennie was not a deception, what did that mean? That she was real. What did that mean? Jennie could really love him, trust him as a daughter? That she really *was* his daughter? But that was impossible. Jennie was born a good six months before Ivy Templeton died. Besides, it had never been Hoover's earnest desire that Jennie actually be his daughter.

340

That was the kind of thought that obsessed Bill Templeton.

Pursuing onward, Hoover trained his thoughts on Bill. The man hovered between lucidity and madness, Hoover realized. All his thoughts fixated on needing a cornerstone on which to assuage his guilt. Bill Templeton needed to believe his daughter was alive and well, could be embraced and spoken to. Therefore, if Jennie were Bill's daughter . . .

Of course she was not. But if Hoover could make it *appear* so . . . Then the deception would not be a deception—to Bill. Bill would find his fulcrum again. Jennie would be the therapeutic instrument of his cure, and more important to the orphaned child, the beneficiary of his love.

Hoover laughed out loud. Life had broken all the circles, and the destinies had crossed, a labyrinth of shattered illusions, destroyed hopes, and forbidden desires. It made his head swim. Nothing made sense. Everything made sense. It was all a mad whirl in which he was no longer frightened. Through Jennie they would cure Bill. It was all so fantastic that Hoover sat down abruptly, spun around in the leather chair, and stopped with his feet against the wall.

The frightening shall not be frightening.

He reached for the telephone. He called the all-night Western Union number. A telegram, he instructed. With his name, address, his telephone number. The message? One single word.

Hoover repeated. One word. That was all. He hung up. The night had grown cold. He shivered in his shirt and trousers, the damp of the perspiration grown chill. He knew he had best go upstairs, shower, and sleep. But it seemed a long way from where he sat. He, who had transcended all time and all space, who had flown inwardly ten thousand miles and ten years, found it impossible to go the fifty yards up the steps to bed.

He fell asleep in the leather chair, drifting into the more common bliss, the normal relaxation and rest, which had been denied him so long.

Chapter Twenty-two

Janice was tired. She was tired of the long journeys thrice weekly into the precincts of the hospital. She was weary of the dark, dusty halls that echoed with the voices of unseen patients, mocking reminders of deformed human discourse. It was all she could do to force herself, again and yet again, into the tiny ward where the man who was legally her husband sat with his back to the wall, hearing nothing.

Bill nestled against the corner of the room, seated on his bed. It was warm, the windows closed against the chill outside. Dr. Geddes was also tired. It was as though he had run down. He sat slumped in a chair beside the bed, smiled wearily, and put a gentle hand on Bill's shoulder.

"All right," he conceded. "Maybe that's enough for today. Have you anything to say, Mrs. Templeton?"

"No."

Dr. Geddes was not surprised.

"Very well. Let's go to my office."

But even as he closed the door, locking it from the outside, their eyes sought each other's, and a grim understanding flowed from one to the other.

"Have you given up?" she asked softly, but not without bitterness.

He shrugged. "One never gives up on a patient. Many times I've—"

"Don't give me a pep talk, Dr. Geddes. Tell me the truth."

"All right. Let's look at this objectively. My feeling, Mrs. Templeton, is that we can expect very little change for a long, long time."

She listened. In a small sense it was a relief to hear there was no hope. Hope had been the cruel illusion that kept her in agony. Now that there was none, life was suddenly simpler, reduced to cold practical problems.

"I think he should be moved," Dr. Geddes continued, reaching for cigarettes in his pocket, finding none, "to a smaller place. It would be like a long-term sanitarium. Much less expensive. Kind of a nursing home."

Janice paled. "Is that what it's come to?"

"Yes," he said, his emotions violent and mixed, all savagely repressed so his voice remained smooth and professional. "That is what it has come to."

"All right. I suppose you know of a good sanitarium?"

"I'll make inquiries."

After several minutes, several platitudes, nonsequiturs that hid accusations, apologies, and unspoken griefs, Janice said good-bye and walked to the main glass doors. She heard his footsteps coming rapidly behind her. She turned. Dr. Geddes's face was all red, as though he had been crying.

"I'm so very sorry," he blurted, "that it turned out like this."

"We did what we could, Dr. Geddes."

"But I had always thought . . . If we could only produce the key, open him up . . ."

"Nobody is blaming you. You've been extraordinarily kind and generous. Maybe it all boils down to a bit of bad luck."

Suddenly overcome by emotion, she turned on her heels and walked rapidly through the parking lot. It was a dry, windblown day, and the husks of dead plants, whiskers of vines, stems, and twigs, tumbled over the cracked asphalt. The clouds were lead gray against the bright sky. Everything had gone sterile. If there was a way to be dead while still living, Janice had found it.

The taxi spun around, lurched violently away from the Goodland Sanitarium. For once she did not think of Elliot Hoover's departure the night that Bill had shattered like a flimsy piece of glass. In fact, she barely saw any of the concrete, the dried mud along the sound, the towering gray and blue steel of the bridges. In her mind everything was abstract. Financial arrangements. A future that stretched out like a white sheet covering a corpse.

It did not help that a single telegram lay on the floor, shoved under by Mario. She opened it, eyes closed, and then stared at it. There was but one word, in Western Union's square-cut, pasty typography. So bizarre, like a ransom note from Mars. It frightened her. One single word stared back at her.

COME.

Suddenly adrenaline flowed into her heart. A warmth, like a soft heat, pumped outward through her breast and she became dizzy.

"Elliot Hoover.
3546 South Tanner Street.
Pittsburgh, Penna."

A telephone number was embedded within Western Union's code numbers. That was all. She shook her head violently as though to clear the confusion from it, then stared at the single word again. The warmth now passed along her legs, through her arms, within her entire body. So he was alive, she thought. That meant that she was also alive. She went to the telephone.

Her hands trembled so much she sat down again, braced herself on the small table by the foot of the couch. There were clicks, strange whistles, as though she were underwater and the dolphins were speaking, and suddenly there was a loud click and a woman answered.

Janice was so distraught at hearing a woman's voice that she did not hear the words.

"Is Mr. Hoover there?"

"He is with the State Board of Medical Review this afternoon. May I take a message?"

"No. . . . I . . . He wrote to me. He *is* there, isn't he?"

There was a slight pause.

"Mr. Hoover is the director of the Tanner Street Clinic," said the voice calmly.

This time there was a long pause. Patiently the voice tried again.

"Mr. Hoover will return this evening. May I take your name and number?"

"Yes. No. I'll call back. Thank you very much."

Janice hung up. She walked quickly across the living room, rubbing her hands through her hair furiously, trying to calm down. She poured herself a brandy, left it on the end table, and went upstairs to her bedroom. She threw two skirts, two blouses, and a change of underwear onto the bed. Then she went downstairs, sipped the brandy, and looked in vain for a small suitcase in the hall closet. She suddenly remembered that her suitcase was still in South India. But there was Ivy's in the closet upstairs. She ran back up the stairs into Ivy's room, stood on a chair and carefully lowered a still-new brown leather bag.

The whirlwind of thoughts accelerated. She sat down on the windowsill, Ivy's bag in her arms. Though the room had been converted to a small work studio, it was still Ivy's room. With a shudder of horror, Janice realized the grim irony of combing Ivy's closet for an overnight bag, to meet Elliot Hoover. Ivy's presence, like an obtrusive emptiness, filled the room with accusations.

Do you understand, Ivy? she thought to herself, almost hearing the words dangle on the air like dust motes. Do you understand that I am still alive and hungry for life?

She threw her clothes and cosmetics, hairbrush and a pair of Delman shoes into the overnight bag and carried it downstairs.

Hoover's telegram lay on the couch. She slipped it into her purse. The woman who answered the telephone had mentioned it was a clinic. Was Elliot Hoover also in a clinic? Was it a cry for help? Was she now between two men, both crippled and needing her? Janice thought she recalled the voice saying that he was director of the clinic. Was it some kind of religious clinic, an urban *ashram* meant to establish a small movement in Pittsburgh?

Janice finished the brandy and poured herself a second. The whirlwind had died away. Thoughts came clear, analytical, and they were troubling. Why Pittsburgh? Of all the continents, all the cities on the face of the globe, why his hometown again? Janice felt, to her own surprise, a dark jealousy. Pittsburgh was Sylvia Hoover's home. It was where he had had a life with her, and Audrey Rose, and that was why he had gone back.

She reread the telegram. One single word. Entreaty or command, she could not decipher. Nothing was decipherable anymore. She picked up the telephone, dialed information for the number of Allegheny Airlines, and booked a seat on the next flight. Next she called the Tanner Street number and told a Mr. Radimanath of her impending arrival.

Janice was jostled in the rush of the passengers exiting the airplane. She stepped down the metal stairs to the pavement, where puddles rippled in a stiff cold wind. The stewardesses behind her rolled up the bottom step and the ground crew

trucked it back to the terminal base. As she walked, the
desolation of the Pittsburgh airport magnified with each step,
until there seemed to be an unending horizon of cold, damp
cement leading in all directions, like the parking lot of
Goodland Sanitarium.

"Janice. . . ."

The voice stopped her dead in her tracks. She peered
behind her, looking for its source, the way one searches for
the source of light in a tunnel.

Elliot Hoover stood at the edge of the carpet by the
terminal doors, his dark suit crumpled, somehow much taller
than she remembered. Holding his hand was a small girl,
lithe and dark-haired, who stared at her with a peculiarly
aloof expression.

Janice's hand went to her mouth.

Hoover stepped forward. His eyes anxiously searched hers.
He seemed to bend slightly forward, as though desperate that
she be there, yet hesitant, even unnerved by the sight of her
in front of him.

"Are you all right?" he asked softly.

"Yes. I am now."

She smelled the fragrance of his soap, felt the warmth of
his hand against hers as he gently clasped it.

"Janice," he softly uttered like a prayer, and she felt
absorbed into him, his strength and his weakness, and only
when he let her hand go did she really take notice of the tiny
girl just behind them.

"Ah," he said, his voice trembling through his uneasy
smile, "this is Jennie."

Confused, but curious, Janice stepped forward and extended her hand.

"Hello, Jennie," she said softly.

The girl only stared back through Janice, a hostile glance,
cold as the green of her eyes.

"Jennie doesn't talk. Or shake hands. Do you, Jennie?"

348

Hoover said, running a single finger gently through the girl's hair.

He looked at Janice. He smiled awkwardly. Something deep inside him still seemed very sad, very lost, and the cold alienation of the airport terminal only made it worse.

"My car is outside," he said.

Chapter Twenty-three

Hoover's car was an old Ford, littered in the rear with textbooks, folders, boxes of toys, even some used clothing for children. He sat down beside her and blew into his hands for warmth. After some hesitation, the Ford kicked into life and he eased into the exit lanes. They drove nearly to the thruway, Jennie between them, and all the while Hoover looked uncomfortable, as though he had a guilty secret.

"Jennie was diagnosed as mentally retarded," he said, glancing into the oncoming traffic of the thruway. "But the truth is, she's autistic."

Unaccustomed to driving, he swerved at the last moment and endured abuse from a passing trucker. He rolled up the window.

"Autism is a condition in which the child refuses to learn. But she can. I know she can."

He said no more. Nor did she press him with questions. The rural landscape fled past, an occasional large farm, a billboard, a white truck stuck in a muddy road. It was a clean, efficient countryside, where no surprises, or ruinous poverty or abnormal mysticism could shake the tranquility. Overhead dark rain clouds gathered under the general white cover.

"Things have become...become prepared," he said. "You'll see what I mean. But it was necessary for you to see it for yourself."

"Is it true that you're connected with a kind of clinic?"

He smiled modestly.

"Yes, it's true."

"And the clinic is part of being prepared?"

"It is. And so is Jennie."

His hand ruffled the child's silky hair. Jennie arched her back in distaste, then went limp, collapsing against Janice. Hoover smiled fondly and pulled her back toward him. He stroked her cheek softly with an expression that bespoke a heartbreak no longer hidden.

As they drove, an ominous silence grew up between Janice and Hoover. The rain increased from a few droplets spattered against the windshield to a major downpour. Though it was before noon, the traffic had its lights on.

"I've come to terms with everything that's happened," he finally said, glancing at Janice.

"Why did you come back to Pittsburgh?"

"If I have work to do, I can do it here as well as anywhere."

Janice watched him. "You must have been curious to see your old home," she suggested.

"I was. I've gone several times. I've purged it from my soul."

Jennie suddenly exclaimed, "Five-nine-nine-two-two!"

Hoover laughed at Janice's startled expression.

"I'm afraid you'll have to get used to Jennie's own language. She speaks fluently in numbers."

"What did she say?"

"I don't know. We're trying to decode it. So far we've got about five phrases. Most of which translate roughly as 'Bug off!' "

Janice, perplexed, studied the little girl who so suddenly had come to life. Jennie stared in animated wonder at the passing urban scene, bounced around in the front seat, captivated by the gleaming displays in shopwindows.

"Eight-eight-seven-nine!" she yelled.

"Maybe the numbers stand for letters in the alphabet," Janice offered.

"We tried that. Nothing worked. But she's developing fast. Something will blossom soon."

The Ford choked and sputtered. Hoover started the ignition again. Ahead of them was Tanner Street, a small lane with an odd collection of broken cars and spilled garbage cans. The rain was letting up, and dirty streaks covered the front windshield.

Hoover stopped the car.

"When do you go back?" he said quietly.

"It depends—on a lot of things."

He got out of the car, scrambled through the brisk wind that stirred up dust and grit in erratic gusts, and opened her door. When she got out, Hoover reached in and pulled Jennie gently to his shoulder.

"Poor little angel is tired out," he said. "But I wanted you to meet her right away."

Puzzled, Janice accepted his hand in the crook of her elbow, and he led her up three cement steps to a green two-story building. Tall bare trees poked up over the roof from behind. A tall security fence girded the structure. Other than that, it looked vaguely like a jerry-built motel.

They ducked in out of the wind, which still threw rainwater into their faces. Hoover slammed the door. For a second it was dark. Then he switched on the light. Janice saw a boy, totally limp, on the floor, crumpled into what appeared to be a lifeless heap.

353

"That's James," Hoover whispered. "Just step over him."

Cautiously, Janice stepped past the inert form. Before she could ask a question a long, low, painful howl reverberated through the carpeted corridors.

"That's Henry," Hoover explained. "He's been doing a lot of that lately."

Astounded, Janice followed Hoover and Jennie into the recesses of the building. A tall man with brown skin held a screaming child. The man's eyes were closed in what appeared to be holy rapture. The child kicked, bit, poked at the restraining arms in terror.

"The gentleman is Mr. Radimanath. He took your message. You'll meet him later."

"That child? Is he hurt?"

"No. Like Gertrude, in Hamlet, however, he protests too much."

Hoover opened a door and they were in his office. The red carpet and red curtains gave a curious flavor to the room where the charts, typewriter, desk, and filing cabinets were located. So did the cushions on the floor in lieu of chairs. Hoover closed the door and the child's screaming subsided.

"Henry fights against love," Hoover said quietly, turning on a small lamp, "precisely because he needs it so desperately."

He turned, smiling, Jennie's hand reaching absently over his face. Janice, mystified, could only laugh in confusion.

"It will make sense," he promised. "But you must keep your mind alert, and your eyes open."

He slid Jennie to the floor, where she lay against a brightly colored cushion. Hoover watched her fondly. Then his shoe toyed with her stomach. She wriggled away.

Something seemed to trouble him again, and a look of distress crossed his face.

"I'll tell you about Jennie later," he said softly.

He reached down, found a small blanket at the foot of the desk, and tucked it around Jennie's small shoulders. Evidently the girl had made a second home for herself in Hoover's office. Janice saw a red plastic cup with Jennie's name on the windowsill.

"Who are her parents?" Janice asked.

Hoover shrugged.

"The city of Pittsburgh considers her an abandoned child. A woman named Ora Dunn found her on a bench in a bus station. With a note on her. That's all we know."

"And they never tried to find her parents?"

"The city always tries, but seldom succeeds."

Jennie sighed in her sleep and rolled off the cushion onto the floor. Hoover smiled as he watched her.

"Some day we will have her add numbers for you," he whispered. "And multiply them. She's a marvel."

The awkwardness returned. The silence surrounded them as though a large question had been asked, much too large for either to answer. They found themselves looking at one another.

Hoover reached out a hand and touched her hand softly.

"When I asked how you were, that was no casual question," he said.

"I know. I'm better than I would have thought, Elliot."

"Then something worse has happened with Bill?"

"Yes. He's been judged incurable. They don't use that word, but he's going to be transferred to a permanent sanitarium. Presumably to waste away."

The strain showed in Hoover's face by a sudden pallor. Janice instantly regretted her outburst.

"Maybe it's better this way," she added more softly. "It's easier to live without false hope."

Hoover came closer. Instead of touching her or whispering comforting words, he only waited for her to look up at him. She did, and found his eyes troubled and yet containing a spark of hope.

"Janice," he said quietly, "I may not be too late."

"What are you talking about?"

"Bill. We may find the key to open him up again."

Janice turned away.

"We owe it to him to try," he said, swallowing his guilt. "We can't give up hope."

Janice sat wearily against the desk. Her eyes fixed on Jennie, sleeping peacefully near her feet, but she barely noticed the girl, only a general impression of vulnerable sweetness.

"I don't know," she said, almost inaudibly. "I'm tired of hoping."

He seemed to know what she meant. Though they stood isolated, only inches apart, a radiant silence permeated the space between. Neither could have met the other without thinking of how to help Bill; yet a healthy Bill, Janice knew, would mean that she and Elliot Hoover could never be together.

As though to dispel any abhorrent thought, or any suggestion wrought by despair and the pain of her own misery, Janice went to Jennie and knelt down. A ribbon had been wound clumsily into the black hair—by a man's hand, she thought—and she slowly untied the ribbon and then tied it again.

"Does Jennie hope?" Janice asked.

"No. I don't think she does. I expect the world is chaos for her."

"Well, then, do you look for some key to open her up?" Janice asked.

"Yes," he said eagerly. "That's exactly how we work. We have to get into the child's defenses, make her accept us because we accept her." He knelt down by Jennie. "With Jennie, we accept her number language. With Jackson it's fire, pictures of car explosions. With Lily we let her eat food from the floor." Hoover's face took on a tinge of excitement mixed with triumph. "You see? We worm our way into the citadel. Then we storm the last defenses."

"And where is the key to Bill?" she asked, looking directly at him.

Hoover licked his lips, paused, then stood up.

"I'm hoping you'll . . . that you'll see that yourself," he confessed. "I could tell you, but it would mean so much more if you saw it for yourself."

Perplexed, Janice tucked Jennie's blanket around the small shoulders.

"There's only one thing Bill wants," she said.

"Yes. I know."

She looked up.

"Have you found Juanita?"

He turned from her. The vein along his temple throbbed, and she did not know what violent emotions caused him to retreat from her.

"No."

"Did you look for her?"

"There was no point. Whether Juanita is or she isn't, is not important. We don't need her, Janice. Not now."

She stared at him. Things were not making sense. "Why did you send for me? It wasn't just to meet Jennie and see the clinic." She was almost afraid to hear the answer.

"It *was* to meet Jennie and see the clinic," he said gently. "I'd like you to meet the children. It will make you understand better. Then we can talk."

"All right."

The day passed for Janice like a deranged cinema. By darkness, she had witnessed the full range of human suffering. James rocked furiously on the corner of his bed. Lily smiled in their direction, seeing very little, her freckled face hopelessly ignorant of where she was. Janeen rolled her obese body onto the floor. When Janice touched her, the girl made absolutely no response.

Room after room, child after child, and Janice felt drawn deeper and deeper into the labyrinth of autism. It was a peculiar, silent world in spite of the howls, moans, and abrupt hyenalike chatter that erupted from the tiny throats. It was silent because there was no communication with the outer world. None of the children knew that there was anybody else in the building but himself.

"What are you thinking?" he asked after watching Jackson mechanically slam his prosthetic arm into his pillow, a robot as lifeless as the aluminum of his artificial limb.

"I feel as though I know what it's like to be insane," she said, looking back down the corridors. "All these rooms, all these terrifying rooms, and nobody can help you."

Hoover led her on. Neville was sleeping in the next room. When Janice peered into the scrunched, anxiety-ridden face, she saw something that did not appear human. It looked like a lower order of hominid, something from the Malay jungles, an imperfect human being. In the next room Uncle Earl began his low, piercing howls that had no stop, no pause, as though he never breathed, but had all the patience in the world to slowly pour out his grief and pain to the unseeing void.

Janice peered into the room. Uncle Earl simply sat like a Hindu priest, lowing like a sick cow. With not the slightest desire to do anything else, ever, until he might die.

"What pain he must be suffering," she whispered, "to simply sit there, hour after hour."

"It's almost religious," he said. "Some primal pain that can be expressed in no other way."

Energetic breathing now displaced Earl's moaning. It was James. The boy flopped among the sheets of his bed in his pajamas, his limbs jerking, rocking mechanically, a pugilist among the bright mobiles, and Janice instantly thought of her own daughter. Ivy had been the identical focus of terror, an unreachable, self-destructive maniac in her nightmares, who saw nothing around her but sheets of psychic pain.

"What we do here," he said, as they watched Roy, "is try to reach that primordial disturbance, and try to neutralize it."

Janice began to grasp something of the spiritual force that dominated the clinic, an atmosphere of calm intensity that had slowly grown on her.

"With love," he said. "We try to cure them through intense, spiritual love."

He took her hand.

"Come with me, Janice," he whispered.

And she sensed that he led her, not to another room, a different child, a different variety of torture, but into the labyrinth of his own heart. The children were analogues of his own psychic wounds. The clinic was the exhibition of his most secret motivations, and like a slow whirlpool, the passion of it grew stronger as he approached the center.

The next room was dark. One single bed. A blue light on at the floor, and then her eyes made out a child's limp hand. It was Jennie, washed and tucked into the sheets by the staff. Hoover stepped quietly over the carpet.

"Janice," he said, half in supplication, half in demand.

She slowly approached him and looked down at the sleeping child.

"Who does she look like?" he whispered.

"I don't know what you mean."

"Yes you do, Janice."

"She—she looks like a million children."

"Janice, has your heart not been opened? Have I shown you suffering for nothing? Look!"

Jennie's small face was cast in a blue shadow. At the nostrils, a black shadow suddenly began, like the eclipse of death over the pale skin.

"She reminds me . . . of Ivy . . . I suppose."

"Exactly!"

"It's the eyes. No, it's the expression, really. Trust and fear . . . a little secretive . . ."

He smiled triumphantly.

"Janice," he whispered. "She reminded me—so forcefully— of my *own* daughter."

Janice sat down on the edge of the bed. For an instant neither spoke. Jennie's softened face glowed like the rim of a distant planet, against the annihilating darkness. Life never

359

appeared more fragile than in the face of the sleeping child.

"Listen to me, Janice. For months, I thought—believe me, I truly thought..."

"Jennie?"

"Yes. Amazing that my life should end in such a strange but certain destiny."

He knelt down to be with her. His voice trembled, and his eyes glittered in the blue light.

"Elliot, this can't be true."

"No. Of course it can't. She was born six months too early."

Jennie turned in her sleep. The small hand flopped against Janice's. Janice placed the hand on the carefully tucked sheet.

"Then what are you saying? What strange and certain destiny are you talking about?"

"Jennie is not my child. Nor could Juanita ever be your child. But we wanted them to be!"

The last words hissed out between clenched teeth. It startled her. The silence abruptly descended. He became afraid that he had frightened her. With a great will he resumed control of his voice, and he lowered it and tried to speak reasonably.

"It was the *wanting* that we perceived," he said with an almost infinite sorrow. "Not the reality."

Janice felt a pang of regret shoot into her heart. She knew all too well that he was right.

"Once life was filled with pretty things," she said softly. "Now it's all gone so dark. Was it really so much to hope for?"

Janice's head slowly lowered onto his shoulder. He was surprised, then simply cradled her face in his hand. He felt the hot tears coming into his palm, and he blinked rapidly.

"I'm so alone," she whispered.

He stroked her hair, but found himself unable to speak.

"So alone," she repeated in a tone so desperate that it frightened him. "Alone...alone..."

"Each of us . . . equally alone," he whispered.

She stirred. Something in Jennie's sleep changed. The child's eyes were open, looking at them, through them, the green irises now dark in the blue lamplight.

"She does seem like Ivy," Janice said, smiling faintly. "So mischievous, all-knowing. Why do I feel this kinship? Even when I know better?"

"I told you. It's the wanting that you perceive."

"No. It's something else. Something that makes me feel strange."

"Haven't you guessed what it is?"

She turned. He was smiling at her, the pupils of his eyes catching glints of the night lamp. His face had softened.

"Because we both wish it to be so. Don't you see why?"

"Because . . ."

"Because we share the wish to be together. And she makes it possible. Without guilt. Without sin."

Janice acknowledged what he meant by "sin" and turned away. The silence remained. The darkness remained. And Janice remained, confused, uncertain.

"She is the medium through which Bill could be cured, and through which our relationship can be made whole," he said in a dark, hypnotic voice.

She looked at him. He was more silhouette than man. He came closer but she felt only the darkness of his form, and the subtle rim of blue around his shape. Her own body seemed to have dissolved, leaving a residue of purest darkness, afraid of him, afraid of herself, as they edged together in a compact that knew neither reason nor patience.

"H-how can she do that, Elliot?" she stammered.

"If Bill were to believe that Jennie is his child, he would have reason to live again—become whole again."

"But—"

"I said *believe*, not she *is*. But that he *believe* it."

She was silent. Hoover reached for her and took her hand. "If he only thought it. *And he could be made to think so.*"

361

"Elliot, I can't be a party to this. What if he found out?"

"The whole point is to establish a bridge into his fortress," he said softly. "That's what I've learned here. You must learn how to include yourself in the interior panic, in the terror, where the fantasy begins."

She shivered in the cold. He drew her against him.

"It can't work, Elliot."

"It can't fail! We'll simply produce a suitable birth certificate. . . ."

He ignored her glance, the surprise she showed at how well his plan was worked out, even down to forgery.

"Introduce him to the child. Time will take care of the rest."

"It's you who live in fantasy, Elliot. He believes that Juanita is his child."

"Then I'll convince him otherwise."

She laughed bitterly.

"He's in no condition to be spoken to."

For a long time Hoover said nothing.

"I know that kind of deafness," he said. "These children have it. But they do hear. Unconsciously."

But she only shook her head in despair. And they both understood that behind the struggle for Bill's sanity was the secondary struggle, the most complicated of their lives: if, through Jennie, they could be together while curing Bill. But it was Janice who suddenly broke it off.

She got up and began walking slowly from the room.

"Wait!" he insisted. "You could put a *doll* in the room and Bill would think it was his!"

Janice was startled by his remark. "They tried dolls in the hospital."

"But how much better a real girl. And Jennie has that quality, hasn't she? Of awakening love?"

"Elliot, how can it possibly succeed?"

"Because I know it will."

His voice had an odd ring to it. It reminded her of his voice when he first came to New York. A disembodied, yet passionate voice, nervous because of fear of his own strength.

"How? How do you know it?"

"Because I've had proof."

"Proof?" she asked vaguely.

The dreamlike quality of the moment dominated again. The seesaw of reality to unreality switched for the thousandth time. Once again there was a different system of rules, the kind of rules that one believes in India or in *ashrams,* places where the material world grows transparent and vaporous.

"I had a visitor," he said strangely. "Let me show him to you."

Hoover creaked open a door and they went inside. He flicked on a light. It was his bedroom. Long red curtains ran down to the floor across the windows. A disarray of books, stationery, a radio, and crumpled clothes lay over the floor. Artifacts from India: sculptured goddesses, the elephant deity painted crimson, incense holders, gold-spangled saddlebags, and teakwood carvings of Krishna lined the room. It was a voluptuous, softly lit environment, completely different from the analytical, cold corridors. Even the unmade bed, the sheets clean but rumpled in the amber light, seemed to glow softly like a hazy sunrise.

Hoover went to his desk. Behind a framed painting of the blue-skinned Krishna relaxing in the courtyards of pleasure in the moonlight of the Himalayas, Hoover gently removed a faded photograph. Shyly, he brought it forward. It was a small photograph, a passport photograph of an old man with surprisingly black eyebrows under white hair, with an unkempt white beard.

"I keep the picture protected," he said softly. "It's my only real treasure here."

She stared at the unfamiliar countenance. She guessed the man was about seventy years old, stern, yet with soft eyes that showed pale, almost white in the photograph.

"My first teacher," he whispered.

"In India?"

"In Benares. I don't even remember how I got there. Somehow I ended up in an *ashram* speaking not a word of Hindi, very confused, and he knew some English. He saved my life."

She looked at him, surprised at the trembling tenderness in his voice. His face had grown suffused in the amber light of the lamp.

"He began the process toward my enlightenment, many years ago."

He took back the photograph as though it were a holy relic. Carefully he returned the photograph to its hiding place behind the painting. Hoover seemed oblivious of the disorder in the room, or its sensuous reds and ambers, the soft madras fabric crumpled on the bed, the long red curtains that illumined the walls like exotic pillars.

"He came to me, Janice. Five days ago."

"From Benares?"

He laughed. "Benares? Who knows? Maybe I went to see him. Maybe I was the visitor."

She waited, but he seemed almost too happy to continue. The flush of joy did not leave his face. Nor did he approach her, but instead remained near the wall where he had hidden the photograph.

"It was in a trance," he said gently. "I . . . ascended . . . I suppose that is the best word for it. I ascended far beyond any place I had ever been, because . . . because . . . "

"Because what, Elliot?"

His face darkened.

"Precisely because of this . . . plan . . . with Jennie . . . with Bill. I was in despair, since it involved the element of deception."

In the next room Jennie made a soft sound in her sleep.

"I suppose I disappeared in some way," he explained. "Or

should I say I reappeared in some way. In any case, I saw him again."

"He's still alive."

"No. He died six years ago. But there he was, in the Benares garden, just as I always remembered him; the same sunlight, the same smell of the flowers and the incense, and his voice . . ."

Janice waited. She felt herself caught up in the passion of his remembrance. He seemed to use it to cast a wide net over her, as though she were one of the migrant butterflies that had startled them in South India, and she nervously watched him pace the floor.

"His voice was *heard* beyond the walls of oblivion," he said ecstatically, "and it told me that there shall be no deception."

He turned, happy that she did not disbelieve him, or at least made no sign of it.

"The deception shall not be a deception! That was what I heard! Don't you see? To Bill, Jennie can be, *will* be, his child again! She will be the link, the bridge on which he can emerge again into the light of day."

Janice had no doubt of Hoover's vision. It seemed too potent to be confined to the small rooms and corridors of the clinic. It belonged in a vast landscape, like India's, which could contain such dreams. Here, it threatened to burst the bounds of normalcy and sweep everything before it.

"Can you doubt it, Janice?" Hoover pleaded. "Can there be any doubt at all?"

"If it should misfire? What would happen to Bill?"

"There's very little that can happen to him," he said in a low voice, "that hasn't already."

In dismay she closed her eyes.

"Let me think about it. It seems too dangerous."

Frustrated, he only clenched his jaw. His eyes looked lost, as though he had failed miserably, and having exposed the

365

message of his trance, having shown her the sanctity of the room where his deities found their worship, he was even more vulnerable.

"I'm sorry," she said. "But you have to give me time."

"That's all right, Janice. Perhaps I've rushed things."

In the next room there was a small thump. Janice instantly remembered the nights when Ivy had fallen from bed, only to be driven half mad by the dream from which she could not awaken, the dream of her own coming death.

"Did you just think of Ivy?" he asked suddenly.

"Yes," she said, startled. "I did."

"You see? The child calls out to you. In your own heart, you can't deny her. Go to her, Janice. Tend to her."

Janice opened the door and fumbled into the darkness. Behind her Hoover followed, and they groped toward the lamp. Jennie lay on the floor, her pajamas rumpled, and a tiny trickle of red lay over her nostril.

"Elliot, she's hurt herself!"

"It isn't like her to fall out of bed. James does that with a vengeance, but not Jennie."

Janice took a tissue from the night table and quickly dabbed at the tiny nose. Strangely, the child seemed only now to awaken to the touch of Janice's hand. There was the fragrance that a mother instantly recognizes, the soft smell of a sleeping infant, and the warm cotton of the pajamas.

"F-five— T-two—" Jennie mumbled.

"She's awake," Janice said.

Hoover bent down.

"So she is. I wonder if she knows whether or not she's dreaming?"

The green eyes of the child gazed through them. Though she took notice of their presence by virtue of being alert, even aware of everything in the room around her, she refused to look at their faces. Janice sensed the protective hostility of the child, the fear that wrapped around her like a robe.

"Jennie," she whispered. "It's me. Do you know who I am?"

"F-five— T-two—"

Janice looked at Hoover. He shrugged.

"Three-three means bathroom. Maybe this is a further refinement. Would you like to do the honors?"

Janice laughed. "I'd love to. I haven't done it in a long time."

Hoover stood in the center of the room, without moving. The light went on in the adjoining bathroom. He watched as Janice gently removed the bottom pajamas, sat Jennie on the small toilet seat. Then Janice washed Jennie's hands, then her own. Hoover watched Janice comb down the girl's hair. Time seemed to slow down and die as Jennie gazed into the mirror, held in Janice's arm.

Slowly the small hand slid down Janice's neck, down the throat, toward the curve of her breast. Jennie relaxed, and the other arm wrapped itself slowly around Janice's neck. The light went off. Janice carried the sleeping girl back into the bedroom.

"What's wrong?" Janice whispered. "Why are you staring at me like that?"

"She's never returned an embrace before," he said slowly.

As Janice lowered the child to the bed, the small arm had to be pulled from Janice's neck. Jennie turned to Janice, the sleeping body curled, the arms stretched lengthwise across the sheets. From Hoover's room the amber light mixed with the blue, and a curious glow appeared on the girl's forehead.

"She seems warm," Janice said.

Hoover went to the bathroom and in the darkness wetted a towel. He brought it back, gave it to Janice, and she daubed it lightly over Jennie's forehead. Then Janice rose, took the towel back to the sink, rinsed it, and hung it on the bar to dry. She turned and was startled to find that he had followed her, looking just as tired as she.

"Will you not be her mother?" he asked, his voice oddly husky. "She needs that kind of care. The kind of love you can provide."

"No. She's a lovely girl, but—"

In the predawn gloom they spoke in slow accents, as though the long night had sucked from them any nervousness. Janice felt she had been at the clinic for a month. She was familiar with its every sound, its every smell, and the children seemed, oddly, extensions of herself as well as Hoover. She slumped against the white basin, as the sleeplessness danced into her ears. Jennie seemed to float in the light where the sheets were visible across the room.

"And the frightening shall not be frightening," Hoover said gently.

She looked up at him. Odd glints of light swarmed in her vision where he stood.

"That's what he told me. My master, the guru," Hoover said softly. "The frightening shall not be frightening."

Suddenly he leaned down over her, his lips against the soft warmth of her neck.

Her left hand instinctively went up around his neck and drew him closer. They were both exhausted, their blood racing, and the moment seemed to undulate in a slow motion, a giddiness as though the earth had wobbled from its foundations. Nor did she object when his hand slowly rested against her breast. Her breathing pushed out against him, and one by one he unbuttoned the buttons of her blouse.

She sighed, turned against his cheek, and his fingers slid across the hollow of her throat. For a long time they found comfort in each other's proximity, a dreamlike stillness, the pressure of breathing so near each other's ear. His fingertips pressed down, soft as velvet, to her undergarment, flowed down under and found the breast very warm, and there was a soft but sudden intake of her breath against his cheek.

"Elliot," she whispered, "I'm so confused without you. I'm even more confused with you."

"I am never without you," he whispered.

She felt the warm comfort of his hand against her bare breast, and was, in her confusion, grateful for it. She leaned her head against his shoulder and watched as the tinted lamp illumined her blouse, making it look as though it belonged to someone else, and watched his fingers remove the next button, felt the soft sliding of the fingertips around and under the other breast.

Her body belonged to someone else, to a Janice long buried under time's sorrow and the fatigue of survival. From far away she seemed to sense her dulled limbs awakening, pushing heavy weights away, and yet the disembodied feeling was unnatural. It made her feel anxiety in the warmth of his friendship.

"Kiss me, Elliot," she whispered.

He moved slowly toward her face, and their lips pressed together, an almost discreet encounter, mutual signal of their desolation. She stood up from the basin counter, his hand found the nipple of her breast, and she pressed herself against his lips.

The alienation went away. Janice felt herself rising from the dead, from the corridors of the asylums, from long journeys that lead to death, from the abstraction of pretending she was no woman. She closed her eyes. When they kissed again, it was delicate, though his tongue found hers; a sudden thrill passed through her, a shudder of surprise, and his hand ran down the length of her body, resting on the small of her back.

She clung to him, standing with her weight against him, on the quiet threshold to Jennie's room. It seemed to be an eternity thus, while the child slept. Dogs barked, unseen in the neighborhood, and a heavy truck rumbled past the clinic. The street became quiet again. She felt as though she were falling asleep, that in fact there could be nothing more blessed than to sleep forever in his arms, in view of the mysterious child who, in some inscrutable way, blessed their being together and reminded them of their own lost children.

She laughed softly in his ear. He raised his head, smiled, and raised an eyebrow, questioning.

"I don't ever want to move," she whispered, her face flushed. "Not ever."

He lowered his face against her neck and pressed her close.

"Then we shall not," he said softly.

"I feel like I'm dancing," she said in a faraway voice.

She sighed and accepted his tongue softly in a second kiss, a longer thrill, and did not seem ready when he broke it off, smiling. In a sudden burst of happiness he squeezed her to him. It was unmistakable, the desire that pressed against her.

"Elliot," she murmured, and her hand slipped down from his arm, hesitated, and nervously squeezed his elbow.

She was confused when there was a movement, and abruptly he had lifted her into his arms, like a child, and carried her into the red sweep of his bedroom. It swirled past like a sensuous dream, and except for the pounding of her heart, like an animal gone wild, the whole world seemed to flow swiftly and silently like a river of mist.

"Please—"

Her voice was cut off by a playful kiss on the mouth. He put her down. The light was still on. The Indian deities, the red curtains, the rumpled bed, all stretched out in front of her, a landscape more uncertain, more inviting, more dangerous than any subcontinent.

She was transfixed with fear.

Behind her, Hoover softly closed the door. Autumn leaves blew against the window, and the blood throbbed in her temples. He did not advance, but only put his hand against the small of her back, and she suddenly whispered, as though unwilling to walk any farther, unable to move paralyzed limbs.

"Carry me, Elliot."

With a slow, simple movement, as though raising an almost holy icon, he carried her as before, in his arms, and lowered himself with her to the bulging mountains and valleys of the madras bedspread, sheets and a single pillow.

He said nothing. Quickly he removed her blouse, kissing her on the eyes, so that her eyes remained closed and she saw nothing. He carefully unhooked her undergarments and removed them, and though her eyes were closed, she gasped slightly, aware that he observed her.

He did not cover her with sheet or blanket, but left her nude. She lay like a sculpture in the soft light, the rounded forms of hip and thigh clearly modulated. She felt her face was flushed and finally opened her eyes and watched Hoover's eyes and wondered if her own burned with the same radiance.

Far, far away he seemed to be, obscure, formless, and he went through motions, removing his shirt and trousers. His uncovered chest startled her with its smoothness, a pale white skin like marble against the bloodred curtains behind.

It was as though they were fighting—the two hearts like impatient birds beating their wings—and in their fatigue there was dark, driving joy. Pleasure accelerated, until Janice grew unconscious under its demands. Shamelessly she sought the last barrier to oblivion. An abrupt pulsating filled her throughout, she became dimly aware of her leg twisted around his hip, and there was the sound of her own moaning, and his, dying away like a receding thunderstorm.

Nor did he remove his body to her side, but repeated her name over and over, almost silently, in her ear. She smiled, stroked the back of his head in a dreamy, sensuous softness that had no outer definition. She had triumphed in some way, and her every sensibility had flowed to the far corners of the earth.

She felt once again that her breath was coming short. Once again he was extended deep within her. Her leg twisted slowly, languorously at first, around his hip. Now they rolled in a deep of their own making. At the bottom of an ocean known only to themselves, in a dreaminess where she commanded him, just as he commanded her, they pursued the relentless goal through the darkness. There was a sensation of a slow, irresistible welling, as though the floor of the earth, like a bubble, had begun to expand, and then she heard his small cries. Slowly then, through her exhausted body, the bulging, demanding pressure flowered a second time, and her cries followed his like an echo.

She felt that she was already asleep. He was at her side, his arm across her breasts. There was an exhaustion surpassing anything she had known. The girl in the next room burbled softly, like a nightingale, and Janice slipped like a feather into the welcome and blessed purity of dreamless sleep.

BOOK IV
JENNIE

"He who with a clear vision sees me as the Spirit
Supreme
Knows all there is to be known, and he adores me with
his soul."

The Words of Krishna

Chapter Twenty-four

Blue grit hung in the early summer air in slow currents, wallowing in the baking haze of day. New York was bottled in a smoky, whitish presence that sucked the oxygen from the river basins. Noise muffled itself in the stone canyons like muted thunder, boiling with the horrid hostility of ten million people jammed together. Day after day the atmospheric layers burned, until a putrid smell of something decomposed laid itself on everything that moved below.

Within Goodland Sanitarium, the air conditioners failed to keep pace with the heat, though water dripped from them onto towels on the floor, and steady throbs of machinery echoed down the dank corridors. Staff and patients perspired freely, and the grit flecked each and every window.

Janice nervously twisted the straps of her handbag. She was in a small lobby, an alcove where the tiles were stained by coffee and shoes, and the ashtrays stank of old cigarettes. She listened to the sounds of approaching footsteps, disappearing conversations, the vaguely threatening murmur of activity that was so horrible because it was never defined, only whispered and hinted at in the labyrinth of corridors.

Janice reflected bitterly as she sat in the steaming lobby. Upon the guilts and maneuvers of administrators depended the lives of so many broken people. Dr. Geddes was reluctant at first to enter into their conspiracy with Jennie. Palming the sick child off to Bill as an Ivy substitute offended his professional and moral ethos. But Elliot Hoover's persuasive arguments for the ultimate good that would accrue not only to Bill, but—and especially—to the orphaned child, at last mitigated the doctor's qualms and drew him wholly into their compact. In his best eloquence before Dr. Boltin, Dr. Geddes explained his approach to transfer-therapy, how Bill responded ever so slightly to objects of transference. Why not a real girl? Indeed, a girl of the right age, attractive, and with similarities of personality to those of his own late daughter? Finally, Dr. Boltin acquiesced, but demanded safeguards for the sanitarium. Dr. Geddes executed an application to the State of Pennsylvania for permission to transfer the continuation of Jennie's treatment to the Goodland Sanitarium in the State of New York, and Pennsylvania responded by agreeing to a six-month trial period of treatment. It took all of May and June to accomplish, but it was done.

As Janice exhaled slowly, she watched Jennie. The small girl wore a red jumper, sneakers, and a red plaid shirt. The black silken hair was freshly washed, brushed into a hundred soft curls that lost their form in the sultry heat. A small area of rash threatened to break out inside her elbows. Jennie's movements were now more fluid. Passing doctors and hospital personnel took no notice that the little girl on the vinyl couch looked into the air at nothing. From a distance, Jennie looked only bored, fidgeting by the tall aluminum ashtrays, waiting for a father or brother swallowed up somewhere in the recesses of the institution.

"Mrs. Templeton—"

Janice turned, and saw Dr. Geddes.

"Have they started?" Janice asked.

"No. They're waiting for Mr. Hoover." He sat down beside her on a worn brown chair.

"I don't want you to build your hopes up too much," he said. "What we're attempting is a long-shot at best."

"I only wish it were over," Janice whispered.

Down the corridor there was a blurred motion. An orderly carried a brass canister from a storeroom and disappeared into the darkness. A slow parallelogram of light diminished as the storeroom door silently shut and locked.

That was how the light had gone out behind Bill's eyes, Janice thought. It just got locked up. It took sixty days for him to realize that they wanted him to see a child. Forty-five days before he stopped cursing them all. Depriving him of his rightful daughter, he yelled. Illegitimate fruit of their lust. A scheme to falsify his religious quest. It was not until the beginning of summer that the silence began. That was worse. A slow, cynical smile on his lips, dark hostility in his eyes, and saying nothing—nothing at all.

He tore up Jennie's photograph. Laughed at their claims. But finally, maybe out of boredom or a hideous despair, he assented to see Hoover. Just once. There were a few religious questions to pose. And they damned well better be answered, he warned.

That was when matters began to spiral in. Elliot Hoover procured a copy of a birth certificate from the Pittsburgh Hall of Records, paid an engraver to duplicate the scrolls and objects embedded in the margins. Then another man was found to forge the inks and signatures. A kind of evil began to filter into the entire enterprise.

"I'd better go," Dr. Geddes said. "See if Hoover's arrived."

Behind the locked door, vague premonitions of voices insinuated themselves into Bill's mind. He could not distinguish them from other, exterior voices. Sweat broke out along his forehead. In an agony of horror he shook himself from side to side, but the voices insisted, stung, and poked icy fingers through the nerves within his temples.

Bill's wrists chafed against leather straps connected to the bar of a hard, iron bed. He could sit up, feet on floor, but his arms were bound down beside his thighs.

Suddenly the door opened. Bill stared at the incoming figure through the dampness of sweat fallen along his eyes. Bill's slow, grinding teeth were audible. In the doorway, Dr. Boltin paused, breathing heavily, mopping his neck.

"Well, Bill," he said breezily. "How are we doing? Not too badly, I trust?"

Bill's gaze followed the portly director.

"Where is he?" Bill whispered, his forearms bulging against the restraining straps.

"Come now, Bill. I was told you were calm. Calmness is everything now. Do you understand me?"

Bill licked his lips, stared moodily at the floor, and made his body relax.

The lock on the door gave off a metallic scratching, then it clicked. Dr. Geddes stepped in. Bill slumped against the wall. Dr. Geddes avoided Bill's eyes.

Dr. Boltin checked his watch. "Are you sure he knew it was for two o'clock?"

"Absolutely," Dr. Geddes said quickly.

For a long time none of the men in the chamber moved. Their breathing was vaguely audible. Dr. Geddes stared at the discolorations on the floor. They looked like streaks left by dragging shoes. Fights, violent suppressions. He turned away.

"You don't think this is all a horrible mistake?" Dr. Boltin whispered.

Before Dr. Geddes answered, the lock clicked again. An orderly opened the door, and beside him, forehead glistening with sweat, stood Elliot Hoover in a blue suit. The light picked up his light hair, like a bruised halo, and the heat had reddened his face as though he blushed.

"Good afternoon, gentlemen," he said, catching his breath, smiling. "Sorry I'm—"

"Let's get on with it, Mr. Hoover," Dr. Boltin wheezed, pointing to the single empty chair opposite the iron bed.

Hoover hesitated. Bill's body seemed to repel him with an almost magnetic barrier. Hoover seemed unable to stand the gaze of the manacled man on the bed. He stared at Bill's shoes, at the standing orderly, back at the psychiatrists; then, he went slowly to the chair and sat down. He did not look at Bill. He licked his lips and swallowed heavily. The door closed behind them and a horrific silence drummed in their ears.

"The, uh, certificate," Dr. Geddes suggested.

Hoover reached into his interior coat pocket. He produced a long brown envelope. Carefully, controlling nervous fingers, he slit it open. An elegant, scrolled document slid into his palm.

He cleared his throat. "This is the birth certificate of Jennie Dunn."

Hoover looked up, recoiled from Bill's stare, and in a kind of psychic defense, held out the document. Bill slowly pulled himself upright, using powerful forearms, until the two men sat facing each other, less than two feet apart. Dr. Geddes now observed that Bill's feet were unstrapped.

"Look at it, Bill," Dr. Boltin said.

Bill glared at Dr. Boltin, but like a talisman the document slowly drew his eyes back.

"Jennifer Dunn," Hoover recited. "February 3, 1975. 10:43 A.M. Signed by the Registrar of Births."

Bill stared at the document for a long time.

"What do you think, Bill?" Dr. Boltin asked.

"Nice forgery."

"What makes you think it's a forgery?" Dr. Geddes asked.

Bill sneered, but he could not take his eyes from the document.

"Look," Hoover reasoned. "How could anybody duplicate the old scrollwork, the emblems, of the State of Pennsylvania? Only the Hall of Records in the City Hall has these plates."

Bill's lips pressed together. He agreed to nothing, but he looked demoralized. Sensing the shift of moral power, Hoover quickly leaned to the attack.

"Now listen to me, Bill," he said. "*Ahimsa* requires it."

"Who?" Dr. Boltin asked.

"The humility of universal love. *Ahimsa*."

"Oh."

Hoover turned slowly back to Bill. Bill had softened even more. Compulsively he twined his fingers at the restraining straps. It was pathetic, ritualistic, a bizarre muscular reaction to frustration.

"Listen to me, Bill," Hoover said softly. "Jennie Dunn is a lovely girl, Bill. She is fragile in many ways, but she is also full of tiny secrets. She moves as though afraid of disturbing the air."

Bill sighed, and let his hands fall back onto the iron rail. He sat inert under Hoover's hypnotic monotone.

"When she sleeps, she curls her left leg, as though ready to fly away into the night."

"Shut up."

"She's delicate, Bill. She walks up and down, like a figure on a music box. She dances with herself in the morning sunlight."

"So does every kid."

"She needs a soft blue night-light. No other color will do. Her dreams make her sit up, still sleeping."

"Hoover, I'm warning you."

Hoover leaned forward, smiling. Suddenly Bill's foot lashed out, the point of the shoe smashed against Hoover's right knee. Hoover gasped, turned pale. The sound had cracked like the chop of an axe.

"That's all right, orderly," Dr. Boltin barked.

The orderly retreated to his place at the wall. Hoover

grimaced in pain, drew his chair back, and tried to ignore the shock spreading outward from his knee, burgeoning into brilliant throbs of agony.

He paused, seeing the hostile stare on the iron bed.

"You're lying, Hoover!"

"Jennie is frightened by birds. Isn't that peculiar? Don't you know another child who was afraid of birds?"

Bill glared at him, the eyes sunk darkly in the sockets, head lowered.

"Janice tell you this?" he demanded. "What is this, pillow talk?"

Hoover said nothing. They watched the fingers grope at the iron rail. Sweat broke out again on Bill's face, along his neck, drenching his shirt. His back trembled with a hideous effort.

"What about it, Bill?" Dr. Boltin asked. "Is all this familiar?"

Suddenly Bill repeatedly rammed his fists against the iron rail. The leather straps exploded into tautness over and over, but Bill was helpless, impotent, in a fury of rage. His legs jerked out like a demented marionette, his head shook violently, and an inarticulate roar tore from his throat.

"Wipe his mouth," Dr. Boltin ordered.

The orderly flourished a large white tissue over Bill's mouth. Bill jerked his head away, then hung awkwardly against the straps, crying silently.

"Come now, Bill," Dr. Geddes said gently. "Isn't this truly like your own daughter?"

Bill slumped, defeated, his whole body caving in. An occasional spasm crossed his back. Trembling, he tried to control his voice.

"I *found* my daughter! I held her in my arms!"

"You were mistaken," Hoover said.

Bill shook his head, sank lower, and could not stifle the sobs.

"She was my own—my Ivy. I held her in the snowstorm."

381

"But, Bill, there were no signs. How could you think she could give you any signs? Why, she was only an infant, not even a personality yet. She could not speak, walk—nothing!"

Bill only wept, losing control altogether.

"Please," he whispered. "Go away. Please go away."

"She was an illusion, Bill," Hoover said quietly. "All right, maybe by some freak of arithmetic she was born at the right time. But she was never what you thought her to be. She was never your own."

The words pierced Bill like tiny needles, exploring his body to search out the heart. He seemed to tremble at every phrase, deflate, until he was a rag doll.

"Never your own, Bill," Hoover intoned. "Never your own."

For a long moment, nobody moved. Dr. Boltin became restless. The orderly slowly shifted his weight and stared at the ceiling.

"What *karma* did I inherit," Bill whispered, "that I should live in hell?"

Elliot Hoover sensed the fatal vulnerability and lunged forward.

"Every *karma* can—is *obligated* to—improve, Bill," he said gently.

Bill shook his head.

"The seven levels of hell—I have been there."

"No. Remember the doctrine of *brahmacharya*. Self-control. Do not despair."

Bill's eyes were nearly hidden under the hair that slanted across his forehead. The two men faced each other, eyes locked in a peculiar, savage, muted combat.

"*Brahmacharya*," Bill retorted softly. "Are you clean enough to speak to me of that?"

Hoover paled, withdrew slightly, confused. "What are you talking about?" he stammered.

"Have you reddened her breasts with saffron?" Bill asked. "Have you tasted the golden nectar?"

382

"I'm not sure what you're driving at, Bill."

Bill smiled sardonically.

"Did you not," he whispered with a manic glee, "practice the deep womb-thrust? From the calves, the thighs? Did you not light the lamp of mystic jewels?"

Hoover reddened, but maintained his ground, staring back at Bill.

"This is your imagination, Bill," Hoover exclaimed. "Your wife and I have only tried to help you."

Bill laughed. Then a strange smile fixed upon his face, and he seemed to look down on Hoover from a thousand miles away.

"You have not stood firm," Bill said, mocking. "You are corrupted. You are utterly lost, Hoover!"

Hoover swallowed, looked at Dr. Boltin, whose face was screwed up in utter incomprehension. Hoover wiped the sweat from his face. He turned back, but Bill was no longer listening.

"The body is a possession like any other," Bill said in subtle simplicity. "You should not have enslaved yourself to it. The two of you are forsaken."

Bill seemed to watch them all from far away, as though he had become bodiless. He smiled bitterly.

"You see," Bill continued calmly, "man is a transitional being. He is the secret, holy workshop of evolution. Bit by bit, he transcends his past. Like one who climbs mountains, he looks down on all he has surpassed with contempt. He evolves to a new system of values. He experiences a luminous expansion."

The orderly coughed slightly, oblivious to everything. Dr. Boltin waited, making sense of nothing. Dr. Geddes, however, was transfixed by the change in Bill. Bill's face had grown serene, and the words flowed easily, without a pause in their articulation.

"Therefore, I have forsaken my wife," Bill concluded, letting the thought evaporate slowly, like a mist in the crowded air. The silence was pregnant with a bleak density. In contrast to Bill's calmness, Hoover fidgeted uncomfortably in his chair.

"Yet, by works," Hoover said at last, "one may strive for liberation. Without the performance of works, it is as a journey into the wind."

Bill laughed. "I know all about your works," he sneered. "A clinic for overflow misfits in Pittsburgh. Since when is Pittsburgh a place for spiritual works?"

"Pittsburgh was where my daughter died."

"So?"

"Therefore, Pittsburgh being the locus of her greatest happiness, it stands to reason that she would return—at some point."

"Ivy was born in New York," Bill chuckled derisively.

"Nevertheless, the problem—the tragedy—began in Pittsburgh."

Bill considered this, and finally shrugged.

"Children often inherit the sick *karma* of their parents," he observed maliciously.

"That is precisely why we must perform our rituals, Bill. You as well as I. To cure the lame of spirit."

Bill laughed softly. "Depends which rituals you perform. Do you know about the Tibetan mysteries?"

Hoover stirred uncomfortably. "No, I've never looked too closely at them."

Bill laughed again, softly but with an edge of malice. "For starters, there's too much light here. You need darkness. The darkness, say, of a cave."

"You could pull the curtains."

"And skullbowls full of red blood. Rancid butter. Decomposing dogs, goats, and wild bears along the walls."

Hoover said nothing. Dr. Boltin looked at Dr. Geddes, who shrugged.

"The painted, vermilion gods on the black stone," Bill

continued. "Death in copulation with life. Skinless carcasses on pointed posts around the fire."

"This kind of magic," Hoover said with a superior smile, "is utterly fallible. It takes a lifetime of humility, prayer, and discipline to gain any real influence, and that only over the self."

"No! That's not true!" Bill insisted. "You can control reality."

Dr. Boltin tried in vain to light a pipe. The red, round cheeks puffed and drew, but there was only a wet gurgle. "What are you talking about, Bill?" he snapped.

"I could show you better if my hands were freed."

"That's all right, Bill. Just tell us."

Bill shook the hair from his forehead. As he spoke he grew pale, shivering as though an arctic wind roared into his soul. His eyes grew small and bright.

"You start with an effigy," Bill said. "Rag doll, wood. You concentrate on it. On the nothingness of it. You identify with the nothingness. Then you write the holy syllable and you sew it in with red thread. You recite the mantra: *Om kurulle hrih! Vasam kuru hoh! Akarsaya hrih suaha!*

The orderly jumped at the sudden wail of the mantra. Dr. Boltin stared, white with surprise.

"Jesus Christ!" he blurted.

"Of course," Bill added, smiling, "you add in the name of your victim. You put your concentration into the effigy. The concentration on your victim. That's what you sew up inside. You forget your senses, your imagination, until the vision of the victim comes. Do you understand? And then, *Jah hum bam hoh! Jah hum bam hoh!* over and over until you can't breathe, until the walls swirl like a cloud of bees, and you summon, absorb, bind yourself, into the effigy! You cast off your ego! You grasp the ego of the victim!"

Dr. Boltin stared, transfixed. Dr. Geddes slowly, absently, dabbed at the perspiration at his neck.

"You start a fire," Bill whispered. "The effigy melts! Slowly! Dripping slowly! You stamp on it, reciting! It takes hours. It seems like years. Until you have no more strength. Your hands are too tired to make the signs of revenge."

Bill did not so much finish as wind down. Like a huge clock, unable to go on, he stared disconsolately at the two psychiatrists. Hoover mopped his forehead.

"Exactly what does this get you?" Dr. Boltin asked curiously.

"Power. I summoned Elliot Hoover."

Bill smiled secretively, said nothing more. An ominous atmosphere built up in the stark chamber.

"These Tibetan rituals," Hoover ventured. "They lead the laymen astray."

"Nothing leads me astray, Hoover."

"You don't really believe all that do you, Bill?"

"You're here, aren't you?"

Dr. Boltin, short of air, walked into the corridor. He found a water fountain, drank copiously, even splashed some onto his face. Vague arguments between Hoover and Bill reached him, all incomprehensible. Dr. Boltin looked at his watch, sighed, and went back inside.

"There is *no* duality!" Hoover shouted. "No subject! No object! It's—it's ridiculous! The *Atman!* The Absolute! Why, it's *a-dvaita*, just like in the Vedas!"

"Bullshit!" Bill yelled back. "Even you have to concede that the essence of the subject—the *tat tvam asi*—never returns. Never!"

"Listen to reason, Bill," Hoover insisted, poking him in the shoulder. "A liberated self cannot appear to itself! Isn't that obvious?"

Dr. Boltin leaned over to Dr. Geddes.

"Have you been, uh, following any of this?" he asked.

"Not a word. But look at Bill. I've never seen him so articulate. He's reasoning!"

"Are you sure this is reason?"

Elliot Hoover and Bill were both shouting now, a dialectic of polemics, each trying to crush the other, oblivious to the psychiatrists.

"Your illusions of individuality," Hoover yelled, "are totally unfounded!"

"You live in a perverted dream, Hoover," Bill sneered. "Without power, without development, you can achieve nothing. Nothing! The soul, I tell you, is a creator!"

The verbal flow rose and fell, a strange current of attack and counterattack that seemed to belong on the far side of the earth.

"They seem to be slowing down," Dr. Geddes observed. "It's been almost an hour."

Elliot Hoover had removed his coat and tie, and he vigorously mopped his throat through the unbuttoned shirt. Bill, exhausted, slumped on the edge of the iron bed.

"Well?" Dr. Boltin demanded, irritated. "What's the verdict?"

Hoover looked up wearily. Slowly he rolled down his shirt sleeves and buttoned them again. His face betrayed an agony of weariness, even a kind of fear, no triumph at all, only a sensation of having survived something terrible.

"He's willing to meet the child," Hoover said quietly.

Bill groaned softly.

"If she—is—Ivy," he murmured, "her soul—will—speak—to me."

Chapter Twenty-five

The orderlies unlocked the door. Inside, Bill suddenly looked up, saw Dr. Geddes put a restraining arm in front of Hoover.

"I want Mrs. Templeton to take Jennie in. Just the two of them."

Hoover nodded. Janice quickly smoothed down Jennie's hair. Janice felt she was on the threshold of something worse than an asylum room: it was the threshold of the last chance they would ever have. She nervously straightened Jennie's red jumper and stared into the quiet, lovely, mysterious face.

"Don't be frightened, Janice," Hoover whispered. "Have faith."

Janice smiled, pressed his hand, and then cautiously led Jennie into Bill's room.

The door closed behind her. Jennie shuffled her feet. Bill looked absently at Janice. Then slowly he focused on the child. Curious, nothing more.

"This is Jennie, Bill," Janice said softly.

Bill observed the red jumper, the new sneakers. The black hair surprised him. He softened when he realized how frail she was, how slender her limbs really were. But he said nothing.

"Jennie," Janice said. "Jennie doesn't talk."

"I know. They told me."

Jennie let go of Janice's fingers. A complicity of awkwardness and silence surrounded the girl. She walked in her mincing, teetering steps, across the tile floor, away from Bill.

Jennie looked down at her sneakers. A loose shoelace obsessed her. She bent down, completely absorbed in the mystery of the string. Her tiny fingers smoothed it, her foot jerked away with it. Then she broke away from it and walked against one of the orderlies, taking no more notice of him than if he had been made of stone.

Bill's eyes followed her in growing curiosity.

As she walked to the edge of his desk something bothered her. Slowly her head turned in the direction of Bill. He was staring at her with an intensity she did not like. She ran her fingers through her hair, violently shook her head, and slumped down to play dead.

The orderlies looked at each other. One felt impelled to rescue the girl, but the other gestured for him to remain at his post. Janice watched Jennie roll over slowly, then look back to see if Bill was still watching.

For a stony eternity their eyes locked. Again Jennie shook her head as though a swarm of bees attacked her. She grew still, then rose and stood in the center of the room. Her arms moved ritualistically at her sides, pumping up and down, then froze. She stared at Bill's right arm.

Slowly Bill's right hand opened, beckoned her closer.

Jennie, startled, looked back at the man's face. An almost deranged intensity poured out of her small eyes. She was frightened, rooted to the spot.

Bill licked his lips.

"Ivy . . ." he whispered.

Jennie suddenly tilted her head, looked at the ceiling, tossed her arms over her head, and stomped noisily around the room. She marched like an insane drum majorette, over the toes of the second orderly, then stopped in front of Janice, oblivious to Bill.

"Ivy!" Bill called desperately, in vain.

A horrific chill swept through Janice, and she turned, looking for Hoover beyond the orderlies at the opened door.

Jennie shook her limbs in a mindless parody of an African dance, then paused and quietly surveyed the room as though she had never seen it.

"Ivy!" Bill whispered urgently.

A strange look appeared on Jennie's face. Her eyes locked with Bill's face, now streaming with tears.

"Ivy . . ." he said, barely audible, the final whisper of his tortured need.

Janice remained rooted to the floor as the girl's smile grew softer, a steady signal of muted love, and legs carried her without awkwardness, carried her toward Bill. Like a soft fawn she fell forward, gently onto his chest, and his cheek, glistening wet, pressed down on her hair.

"Oh, Ivy . . . Ivy . . ." he repeated, the litany of a broken man.

Gradually his arms pressed her close, and her small limbs relaxed against his neck.

"Ivy . . . Ivy . . ."

Hoover, overjoyed, pushed his way past the orderlies, but Dr. Geddes grabbed his arm.

"Leave them alone!"

Janice circled closer, unable to believe it. She whirled back to the doorway, congested with men.

"Elliot—she went to him."

"Yes," Hoover whispered. "Exactly what we prayed for."

Janice, her hand to her mouth, watched incredulously. Bill rocked Jennie back and forth, and the girl seemed to have found shelter there forever, in his embrace.

Finally Dr. Geddes led both Hoover and Janice farther out into the corridor. From where they stood, they could barely see the girl, so completely was she lost in Bill's embrace. But they heard Bill again and again call her Ivy.

"This is one of the greatest days of my life," Dr. Geddes whispered. "We've made contact!"

"H-he called her *Ivy!*" Janice stammered. "And she went to him!"

"Yes," Dr. Geddes said. "You're right. Go back in and say that Ivy has to go home now. She's tired and has to rest."

Janice stared at him in confusion.

"Do it," Hoover softly urged.

Mechanically, Janice walked back up the corridor, entered the room, and saw how completely safe and secure the girl felt in Bill's arms. She was not asleep. The small, lovely eyes were open, but dreamy and at peace for the first time since Janice had known her.

"Ivy . . . Ivy has to go now, Bill. She's tired."

Bill heard nothing. Janice stepped closer.

"Bill, darling, Ivy has to get some rest."

He closed his eyes, nodded, and with infinite sorrow released the girl. Janice took her by the hand. Jennie walked in the peculiar, mincing, teetering steps once again. When the door closed, Janice caught a last glimpse of Bill's face—still tear-wet, but serene, even luminous with expansive love and, for the first time, hope.

Elliot Hoover lifted Jennie from the taxi. For a while he was unwilling to step into Des Artistes.

"The last time I came into this building," he mused, "it was to take a daughter. Now it is to return one."

Janice looked at him distantly, wondering what it was that had resolved itself in such a peculiar circle of events.

Hoover carried the girl slowly toward the elevator. He seemed to walk on tiptoe, and he ignored Mario's incredulous gaze as they rode up. Down the hallway he carried the girl, following Janice. The noise of the door being unlocked broke the silence.

The apartment door swiveled open. The stained-glass windows displayed a buoyant light, a subdued extravagance of reds and greens in the hushed atmosphere. In some unspoken way when he crossed the threshold, a terrifying sense of responsibility wakened in him.

Jennie stirred in his arms. Her eyes remained closed.

"The ceiling," he marveled softly. "It hasn't changed."

"No. The ceiling never changes."

He turned to her, having heard a deeper meaning in her words.

"But so much else has changed."

"Yes. In all of us."

Jennie stirred again.

"Shall I put her to bed?" he asked softly.

"She can sleep upstairs."

Janice led them up the carpeted steps. She paused at what had been Ivy's room. Delicately she pushed it open. Jars of paintbrushes, ink bottles, and piles of sketchbooks lay on white shelves and a desk.

"In Ivy's room . . ." marveled Hoover.

"I have a cot in the closet."

Hoover lifted Jennie carefully to Janice's arms. He went to the closet, briskly brought out a metal cot and unfolded it. Then, as directed, he brought in sheets and two blankets from the closet in the hallway. Gently he undressed Jennie down to the underpants and covered her, tucking the sheet and blanket around the slender shoulders.

"She normally sleeps like a log," he said, stroking her chin.

"Elliot, why did she go to him?"

Hoover shrugged. "She was tired. It was a long, hard

flight, a strange environment. She heard a man's soothing voice and simply went to him."

"She's autistic; she doesn't respond to voices."

"She'll hold my hand. And yours. Maybe she does distinguish tones of voices."

Janice stared at the sleeping child. "It frightened me," she confessed, "to see her go to him like that."

"We should be happy, Janice," Hoover said. "Isn't it what we worked for? To make contact with him?"

"I don't know. I don't feel right about it."

Hoover said nothing. He walked to the window and stared down at the grimy, sultry city. He almost seemed to forget her, lost in thought. To Janice the silence was unbearable.

"Will you stay?" she asked simply.

"No."

"Why not?"

"I can't. We can't. Not for a while."

"Did Bill say something that changed your mind?"

He turned to her, confused and not hiding it. "It would spoil the—the sanctity of what we've done," he said very quietly.

"Sanctity?" Janice replied almost harshly. "We *deceived* him! That birth certificate was phony! And he'll find out! He'll call the Hall of Records! You know he will."

"He'll find the certificate, properly filed, just as I told him."

"But there *is* no certificate!"

He glared at her, and she grew silent.

"*Now* there is," he said simply. "I've arranged it. That's all you have to know."

Janice looked down at Jennie sadly. "This kind of deception can come to no good."

"Look. You saw him when we left. He was joyous, calm, a gentle soul. What the hell was he before? A maniac. A vegetable."

Something dangerous filled the air, like smoke. Hoover

394

sensed it too and softened. He looked out the window again, but this time he saw only the grit and streaks that adhered to the glass.

"We are instruments of heaven," he said. "We can only follow its dictates. Blindly."

She said nothing. The feeling of vague horror consolidated into the specific fear of being discovered. She felt a peculiar darkness everywhere, hovering over her, all over the apartment.

"Will you take care of Jennie?" he asked. "For as long as Dr. Geddes needs her?"

"Yes. Of course."

Suddenly tears burst from Janice's eyes, and she turned away. Hoover quickly turned her back, held her, and she sank against his chest.

"What's going to happen, Elliot?" she said unevenly.

"I don't know what's going to happen. All we can do now is help Dr. Geddes."

"What about us?"

He stiffened. She felt him draw away. It was as though they were saying farewell forever.

"I'll come see you, Janice. But it can't be for a while."

"Elliot—"

He smiled, stroking her cheek.

"I'll be with you, darling," he whispered. "I always am."

Something softened within her.

He smiled gently. "Let me call you from Pittsburgh."

She nodded slowly. Together they went down the stairs to the apartment door. He kissed her lightly on the cheek. They tried to convince each other that there was no leave-taking, that they would be together, that night and every night, but there was a wrench of emptiness when he drew away. She watched him walk to the elevator. With a friendly smile, sweet and bashful, yet complicitous, he waved. Then he was gone.

The impact of his absence hit her as though she had fallen into a vast and empty shaft. Now the apartment was denuded of protection—Bill was gone, Elliot Hoover was gone, and upstairs was a strange child who needed help.

Janice went to Ivy's bedroom and peered in. For an instant the bundle of blankets deceived her. Then Jennie's small face appeared. An eye lazily opened and closed. Janice stroked the girl's hair, but the room seemed alive with muted whispers. They barraged her in long enfilades of obscene, mocking jeers. She looked up. It was silent. Nothing in the room was left from the night when Ivy, in that mad whirl of pain, ran from the nightmare that finally destroyed her.

"Five."

Janice nearly gasped in shock. For an instant she did not know who spoke. Then Jennie sat up, stared blankly at her.

"Five-four-two."

Janice, trembling, went to the bathroom and brought Jennie a glass of water. The girl drank greedily and hiccupped lightly. Janice kissed her forehead.

Slowly Jennie's eyes closed, the glassy, cool stare of sleep disappeared under the soft lids. The tiny lips curled around a word, like releasing bubbles, and a tiny aspiration made a sound: "Four."

What a peculiar malady, Janice reflected. A child makes an analogue of language, but not language itself. What, if anything, did Jennie speak of now, in her unimaginable dreams?

The following morning Janice cut bananas into cereal for Jennie, poured milk into the bowl, and made a ring of strawberries on top. Then she heard faint sounds overhead. They were light, delicate sounds, unlike Ivy in her terror. Jennie peered uncertainly down from the top of the stairs. A shy smile spread over the elfin face.

"Come on down, darling," Janice called.

But Jennie recoiled into Ivy's room. Janice ran upstairs, found the girl hiding under the cot, quickly dressed her, and carried her down to breakfast. Jennie had a fabulous appetite.

Her metabolic rate must be high, Janice thought, to keep her so thin.

That morning, Janice braved the department stores with Jennie. A jumper in green, two pairs of jeans, four shirts, numerous underclothes, and a dress found their way back to Des Artistes. Then Jennie, exhausted, teetered over to Janice and fell, half asleep, against her breast.

So it was nothing freakish, Janice thought. Jennie's collapse on Bill was just a lucky piece of timing. Janice, much relieved, took her upstairs to the cot for a nap, and worked through the afternoon on an assignment she and Elaine had decided could just as well be done at home.

Jennie was popular with the hospital staff. She had a sly sense of humor. She metamorphosed paper clips, file folders, and pencils into objects of ritual, forming semicircles composed of prime numbers. Psychiatrists tried to catch her at subtraction, but she only added, multiplied and divided. No one knew why. But she never made a mistake.

By early autumn, she knew the way to Bill's room. She walked in front of Dr. Geddes, avoiding the swirls printed in the tiled floor.

Bill rose eagerly on the mornings of Jennie's visits. He shaved, wore his best clothes, and paced the floor nervously. An inner love glowed from his eyes. He ignored Janice, but found delight in every action, every sound from Jennie. He became irritated at Dr. Geddes and Janice, jealous of their time with the child.

"This awareness of the child," Dr. Geddes confided as they left. "It's a real relationship. The first step to social reintegration."

In fact, to preserve his meetings with Jennie, Bill controlled his every act. He tried never to be suspicious, never angry, amenable to any test Dr. Geddes proposed. He learned to mimic the easy pleasantries of men shaking hands and discussing the weather. He read the newspaper, forced himself to discuss things with other patients, until he was certain he could speak without hesitation.

By the end of autumn he had purchased, with Janice's help, a small library of books for Jennie.

"Do you remember, Ivy?" he whispered into Jennie's ear, seating her on his lap. "You loved this one."

He read through an entire fable of the hippopotamus that worked for a baker, and barely suppressed his anger when Jennie made no response.

"Soon, darling . . . soon . . ." Bill whispered, kissing her behind the ear.

Bill bought toys, the toys that Ivy had loved, and was mystified that Jennie went dead when brought before them. He bought a red plastic phonograph and yellow records that played tinkling chimes of folk songs, but Jennie appeared to be deaf. Bill drew pictures of the pumpkins Ivy loved more than anything in those bright autumn days upstate, but Jennie clumsily stepped on the crayons and tore the pictures into shreds.

In the evenings, Bill sat by the edge of the bed, brooding in the darkness, steeling himself for patience, ever more patience.

Autumn died suddenly. The trees were bleak. The frigid winds piled detritus of the seasons in doors, grates, and alleys.

It was not until the first snow fell that Bill truly divined the mystery of autism. In the midst of tramping a path through the hospital grounds—a field of glistening white—with Dr. Geddes and two orderlies watching, he stopped. Instead of following, instead of playing the game, Jennie collapsed in the snow. A soft white spray glittered upward in the sun. Bill knelt at her side. Gently he brushed the snow from the tiny face.

"You don't understand anything, do you?" he murmured.

398

"No one knows," Dr. Geddes said, hunching down next to the girl. "Some say the child refuses to be aware, but has the capacity."

"Well, I used to be locked up, too. You just have to find the key all by yourself."

Pleased, Dr. Geddes reported to Dr. Boltin that Bill felt compassion for the girl, and understanding of another's suffering. He added that Bill had inquired about adoption.

Dr. Boltin chuckled. "Not very likely, I should imagine."

"Perhaps not, but don't you see? He's suddenly taken a look into the future. He feels the coherence within himself. So he can plan for tomorrow."

At the beginning of December, Jennie caught a cold. The fever persisted, the symptoms lasted weeks. A physician recommended bed rest. Bottles of pills, cups of orange juice, a thermometer, and several toys collected at the side of the cot. Jennie's eyes grew dazed, her arms weak.

Bill fought against despondency. He was hooked on Jennie's visits. Pretend as he might, the desolation closed in tighter and tighter as the month dragged wearily on toward Christmas.

Bill purchased seven boxes of crepe paper, five of ornaments. He and three other patients strung them across the cafeteria and along the hall leading to Bill's room. In the room itself, Bill put up the most elaborate white angels, gold stars, and glittering balls. He persuaded the nurse to bring him branches of pine trees from the edge of the hospital grounds and these he decorated with hoops of colored paper.

Dr. Geddes walked in, amazed at the frenetic activity.

"Bill. You're putting on a Christmas pageant."

Bill turned, eyes red but dry.

"Yes," he said hoarsely. "For Ivy, even though I know she can't be here. Isn't it the strangest thing? A few months ago I'd never seen her, and now..."

Dr. Geddes stepped closer.

"This relationship is a stepping-stone, Bill. You are quite right to cherish it."

Overcome, Bill grabbed Dr. Geddes's hand. He squeezed hard.

"Thank you, Dr. Geddes," he whispered. "For everything you've done."

"Bill, I just— Well, I guess I just hope for the same things you do."

Bill nodded; then, to break the impasse, moved away. He sadly fingered the twirled crepe paper that arched along the window.

"How is she?"

"Getting better, Bill."

"Won't be here for Christmas?"

"No."

"What about New Year's?"

"Maybe. I doubt it."

"Well, there's always her birthday."

Dr. Geddes smiled quickly. "Really? When is her birthday?"

"February third. Ten forty-three in the morning."

"That's right, the birth certificate."

"I called the Hall of Records in Pittsburgh."

"And?"

"Her certificate's there, all right. Guess I was wrong."

Dr. Geddes chuckled pleasantly. "Now, when you're through in here, I'd like you to come down to my office."

"Oh? Why?"

"Some legal matter. Shouldn't be serious."

At 2:30 Bill stepped into Dr. Geddes's office. Janice sat against a small window covered in brown drapes. At her side were two men, one of whom was Harold Yates, their family lawyer. Self-consciously Bill sat down, feeling all eyes fixed on him. Harold flashed him an uncomfortable smile.

The other man, in a blue suit a size too tight, introduced himself as Charles Petty, deputy assistant to the Attorney General of the State of New York. He had enormous hands and a craggy face, a thin black tie, and a habit of chewing his tongue.

"Mr. Petty has been very kind to come down here," Dr. Geddes began, "his time being limited."

Petty cleared his throat, looking Bill up and down. Petty's casual manner was studied.

"The—uh—case which provided for your original detention—"

"What case?" Bill asked.

"The kidnapping."

"Oh."

"By order of the court you were remanded, under a psychiatric provision, to the Goodland Sanitarium. Now, the theory of such placement is not punishment, but to make the person well enough to stand trial."

"Trial?" Janice blurted.

"Or whatever action the court deems, in its wisdom, to undertake."

Harold Yates held up a beefy hand for silence. "That's the formal scenario. A trial is most unlikely."

"I don't understand."

"No previous arrests or convictions. The death of an only daughter. The peculiar nature of the trial which preceded her tragic death. Its bizarre publicity. The marital difficulties, incarceration at the Eilenberg Clinic—you see, Bill acted *in extremis*. He's not an extortionist, or sexually driven."

Bill stared back at the two men.

"So what are you saying?" he demanded. "A whole task force came down just to tell me there's nothing to worry about?"

Petty cleared his throat. "There will be some formalities, affidavits, interviews."

"But Bill won't have to appear in court?" Janice asked anxiously.

Harold Yates shrugged. "Offhand, Janice, I'd say there is a ten percent chance he'll see the inside of a courtroom. I shouldn't be at all surprised if the State quashed the whole thing."

Embarrassed, Petty squirmed in his seat. "Well, I can't speak for the District Attorney. He's funny. Blows hot and cold. But I've seen him throw out better cases. I mean, stronger cases than this one."

"There? You see?" Harold insisted. "Straight from the horse's mouth."

For half an hour the lawyer and Petty detailed the material, spelling out the probable steps. Most of it was procedural, explained slowly and carefully to Bill. Exhausted by the meeting, Bill politely shook their hands, thanked them for coming, and went to the door.

"Does the cook make birthday cakes?" he asked.

"What?" Dr. Geddes said. "Oh. Yes, of course. Tell her it's for me."

"Right. Merry Christmas, gentlemen."

Only Dr. Geddes caught the fact that Bill only nodded dutifully at Janice before he left.

Harold Yates left with Charles Petty. Dr. Geddes escorted Janice to the door. The noises of the hospital were muted, as though the snow outside absorbed sound, or sealed them from the outer world. Something made Janice pause as she saw the Christmas ornaments stretched over the lobby, leading to the cafeteria.

"What did he say about a birthday party?" Janice asked.

"Oh," Dr. Geddes said, smiling, "for Jennie. In early February. She'll certainly be well by then."

"Yes, of course," Janice said lightly, but a palpable shiver went up her spine. A birthday party? For Jennie. Who, to Bill, was Ivy.

402

Janice left, crossed through the deep snow of the parking lot, and found a taxi waiting. When she arrived at Des Artistes she saw that Christmas decorations had been strung along the lobby there too. In the apartment, Jennie slept by the small window in Ivy's room. Janice paid the baby-sitter. After ten minutes she telephoned Pittsburgh.

"Elliot, he's going to give a birthday party for Jennie!"

"What about it? What's wrong?"

"I don't know. I just sense that everything's about to explode. They're going to bring Bill into court."

"What?"

"Because of the kidnapping. They say it's a formality, but—"

"Then he really is better. They don't try sick men."

"Elliot, you don't understand. The media; they'd love to roast us a second time."

"Pay them no attention. I never did."

"They'll drag up everything. They'll find out about us."

There was a long pause. Janice heard him sigh after a while.

"I see," he said.

Janice waited, but he said nothing more. "I miss you," she said simply.

"If you knew how I miss you."

They spoke generalities, pleasant hopes for the future, but it did not stall the gnawing doubts within. They did not want to hang up. It was like being together, only more ethereal. When Janice cradled the telephone, a pleasant lassitude came over her. Talking with Elliot Hoover usually did that. She relaxed on the couch, nearly asleep, and it seemed that nothing on earth could disturb the deep pleasure of listening to the city move and breathe far away in the early evening.

But in Pittsburgh, Elliot Hoover could not sleep. He stared at the vermilion icons lost in the gloom of the bedroom, and he listened to the silence where Jennie had once slept in the adjacent room. It had been thirteen days since he had prayed. Something inside him had altered, frozen to stone.

Bill was right. He had not stood firm. He was corrupted. Utterly lost.

Hoover's fingers went cold. He was divided now and he knew it. It brought upon him a peculiar fear of spiritual death. He was chained again, in the great cycle of being, in the passions of those who love and fear to lose. It made the night cold, even horrifying. The frost sparkled against the window glass, and the pane rattled in the bitter wind.

Woman made the life energy concentrate upon the body. And the body was the cage of the soul. Yet Hoover knew, staring into the cold night, lying naked on top of the bedcovers, that he was capable of preferring the unholy prison of earthly love to anything.

There were prayers, soft and insistent, but high in the sanitarium in New York. Bill was one with the night, its cold, its inhuman stars. He cherished the winds that battered the windows, for they were harbingers of liberty. He was disciplined now, enough to wait; only he did not want to wait beyond February.

"February," he whispered.

February was the darkest month. It was the month the winter sucked children into its craw. February had been the end of the trail, he reflected. The month Ivy Templeton had stopped breathing. The month all her fibers, bone marrow, and flesh had turned to ash and smoke. But the darkness gave birth once again. He looked out the window. The frost against the darkness pleased him. The crystalline structure of universal forms, producing white perfection. Beyond, small lights glittered on the sound. Whether a bridge or ship he did not know. The vastness of night pleased him. It was another form of perfection, another harbinger of the greater liberty.

Far away the hospital staff made preparations for Christmas

and New Year's. Bill lay back on the bed, arms under his head, and smiled. The earth as it moved dragged along the accumulated *karma* of its billions of living beings. It impregnated the cosmos with sorrow. None but the very few dreamt of liberation as he did.

"February," he murmured, like a prayer.

Soon it would be February again, as it had been before, and would signal his time to reenter the world of the living . . . with Ivy.

Chapter Twenty-six

Jennie recovered on Christmas day, spoke numbers on the telephone, which Bill heard with delight. By New Year's, she and Bill tramped long circles in the snow behind the dormant rose garden. Jennie recognized him now by the scent of his after-shave lotion, and gravitated toward it.

The birthday party was scheduled for the afternoon of February third.

Janice accompanied Jennie from the elevator. The girl knew the way to Bill's room, but she always hesitated, walking in big circles, before she entered. As usual, a bored orderly sat in a chair outside the door. Janice marveled at the brilliance of the room, festooned with flowers, small wooden carvings, and bright aluminum shapes.

"Come on in, darling," Bill said, smiling, extending his arms to Jennie. "Happy Birthday!"

Janice watched Bill seat the girl on his knee. On the bed were gaily wrapped presents. Somehow it always hurt her to see Bill reduce himself to win the affection of a child who, by definition, could not love. Bill noted her pitying expression.

"You can leave," Bill whispered. "If it disgusts you."

"It doesn't disgust me, darling."

"Well, why don't you just let us get on in private for a while?"

Janice sighed, watched for a while, and then went outside. The orderly looked up, smiled, then turned the page of his magazine.

Janice walked down the hall. At a small alcove at the end of the corridor was a large window, two dilapidated chairs, and a cigarette machine. She sat down. Generations of nervous relatives had scraped the floor, and no amount of wax and polish had covered it completely.

The warmth of a radiator made her remove her coat. The winter light was steady and even, a blank absence of color. It soothed the limbs, emptied the mind. Janice found herself observing the whitish mass of clouds through the window, a symbol of peaceful oblivion that she cherished.

February third, she thought. The day Ivy had died. Janice stirred uneasily. Birth and death were the same. The deity of creation was also the deity of destruction. Janice felt herself tighten up inside. The orderly was gone. The door to Bill's room was closed. Janice stood, paced the floor, sat down, then stood up again.

Screams shook the building.

From Jennie!

Horror swept through Janice. She ran down toward Bill's room at the far end of the corridor. The door was shut. The orderly was nowhere to be seen.

"Bill!" Janice shouted as she ran.

Inside, Jennie screamed. Hysterical, as though her arms and legs were being twisted off. Glass shattered. Pieces of metal smashed against the door.

"Bill!" Janice bellowed, arriving at the door just as the orderly appeared and, twisting the knob, burst into the room.

Bill stood by a broken window, in the freezing wind sweeping from the icy marshes. Janice stared down at the debris of the room.

Broken toys, creamed cakes, and incense sticks lay mutilated over the floor. In the center of the floor, Jennie sat, red-faced in terror, head held back, mouth open in a demented scream.

Then Bill reached down, shook the child, and yelled, *"Ivy! It's Daddy!"*

But the girl's arms and legs banged up and down in a manic tantrum. The small face was unrecognizable. It was as though an electric current was being shot into her mouth. Her nostrils quivered, her eyes nearly rolled back, and she struggled for breath.

"She just went crazy, started throwing things," Bill panted. "It was her birthday party."

He turned to Jennie again. The orderly had bent down to the screaming child. Bill spun on one heel and threw the ball of his fist square into the meaty face.

"Leave her alone, bastard!" Bill roared.

The orderly, smashed against the remnants of the pine boughs, slid down onto fragments of glass.

"She's mine! Mine!"

The orderly tasted the trickle of blood from his nose, shook his head and bellowed, "Mrs. Templeton! Find Dr. Geddes!"

Janice backed away, but Bill raised the desk lamp over his head and staggered forward.

"Don't take her from me!"

The orderly walked bearlike to grapple with Bill. Bill kicked, spat, and punched, but the orderly absorbed it with stifled grunts.

"Hurry, Mrs. Templeton!"

Janice ran to the elevator, rode it down, and burst upon Dr. Geddes in the annex to Dr. Boltin's room. Together they ran back to the elevator. As the door slid open, they heard Jennie's screams.

In the room, the orderly had Bill pinned onto the bed, one wrist strapped to the rail, but the blood flowed freely from the orderly's nose and ear. Bill's shoes kicked viciously, and an inarticulate howl mingled with Jennie's.

"Give me a hand, will you?" the orderly wheezed.

Mechanically the orderly sat on Bill's legs, holding a handkerchief to his nose. Dr. Geddes, trembling, looking at Bill's face, then at Jennie, strapped the ankles down.

"Christ, this guy packs a wallop," the orderly mumbled.

Bill felt his other wrist confined by inflexible leather. His body arched, then spasmodically writhed. Slowly a high-pitched whine came from his lungs, and his back fell to the bed, as though he had died there in front of them.

Dr. Geddes stared at Bill, then picked Jennie from the floor.

"What—what the hell happened?" Dr. Geddes stammered.

"It was all going so well," Janice said. "Then Jennie started screaming."

Dr. Geddes loosened the girl's blouse. "She's burning up!" He rocked her, but she did not stop screaming. "I'm taking her to the infirmary."

He began to leave.

"*Ivy!*" Bill howled, a long, drawn-out wail that sent shivers up their backs.

Mucus ran from Bill's nose. His head thrashed back and forth. Suddenly Janice burst into tears, lowered her head, and sobbed. Bill moaned, arched his back, and the long wail began again.

Janice ran into the corridor, caught up with Dr. Geddes just as the elevator doors opened. Under the bleak light inside, Jennie was shaking uncontrollably.

"Is she epileptic?" Dr. Geddes asked.

"I—don't think so."

In the infirmary, a quick injection stopped the convulsion. The frail body lay on a white cot. A nurse daubed the limbs and forehead with rubbing alcohol. Cold water filled a small basin, and Dr. Geddes undressed and lowered Jennie into it. The brilliant lights overhead threw wrinkled shadows, like goldfish, around the girl's legs.

"Might just be a return of the fever," Dr. Geddes said, bathing her gently.

"Oh, God, Dr. Geddes! He just blew apart!"

"Forget Bill, Mrs. Templeton. We thought we had him cured, but—"

"Please don't say that. . . ."

"It's over. There's no chance. I'm sorry. Just pray to whatever gods you and Mr. Hoover believe in that he didn't harm the girl."

A nurse gently toweled Jennie dry. Jennie's cheek twitched occasionally, but the color had returned. Her eyes remained closed. Janice stared at the small, soft face, and it seemed as though the child merely slept soundly. The nurse carried Jennie off to the examining room.

Dr. Geddes slumped down in an overstuffed chair next to a cabinet of gauze bandages, steel scissors, and vials of clear liquid. His hands trembled.

He leaned back, closed his eyes so tight the lids tremored. Janice saw the tears emerge from the ravaged face.

"Why?" he whispered. "We were so close. . . . So damn, damn close . . ."

Janice leaned against the white cot. She bit her lip in anguish, but there was nothing to say. The sight of Dr. Geddes in despair removed her last support. For a long moment they waited. Dr. Geddes kept his eyes closed, his head immobile. Then he stared uselessly at the ceiling.

The nurse and a physician stepped into the infirmary annex. The physician smiled and held up thumb and forefinger in a circle.

"Are you sure?" Dr. Geddes asked.

"He never touched her," the physician said.

"Thank you."

The nurse picked up Jennie's clothes and went back to the

diagnostic chamber. The physician made a few brief entries into the infirmary logbook. Dr. Geddes stood up, and he lit a cigarette with shaking fingers, avoiding Janice's pleading eyes.

"What's going to happen to Bill now?" she asked softly.

"He won't be facing any judge, that's for damn sure. He's going to a nursing home. Same one I picked out a long time ago."

Janice turned on her heel, went through the corridors to the elevator, and returned to Bill's room.

The orderly had torn down what remained of the decorations. They were swept, along with the broken glass, into a pile in the corner. A rectangle of cardboard was jammed over the broken window. With the roll of tape held between his teeth, he secured the cardboard onto the sill.

Bill moaned softly. Janice pulled up a chair. Gently she smoothed his hair back, cleaned the flecks of dirt from his lip. The face, once again, was not his. It belonged to an animal, a caricature of the man who sought love so desperately, so unforgivingly.

"She remembered," he mumbled. "I know she did."

"I can't hear you, Bill."

She leaned over, her ear to his face. The warm breath of her husband muttered sibilant syllables.

"She remembered. . . . She remembered. . . ."

"That's all he says," the orderly ventured.

For nearly ten minutes she tried to speak to Bill. But his lips worked over and over those vague sounds as though he himself no longer knew what they meant. Janice felt the tears coming, so she rose to go.

She gave the orderly ten dollars.

"I'm sorry he hit you," she said. "Please be kind to him."

"Right, ma'am. And thanks."

Then Janice slowly left, went down to the infirmary, and took Jennie home.

* * *

Janice dressed Jennie in new pajamas and covered her with several blankets. Chills alternated with the fever. She had relapsed into the December illness.

"Five-five-five—"

Mechanically Janice brought a glass of water to the cot, helped Jennie drink, and was glad to see the small eyelids close again.

She telephoned Allegheny Airlines, reserved two seats for the early evening flight. She telephoned the clinic, but Hoover was at Temple University. Miserable, she hung up. Outside, the wind screeched up Sixty-seventh Street, banging potted plants over the sidewalks. A garbage can rolled over and over, echoing against cement.

"No-no-no-no—!"

Upstairs Jennie recited the numbers. Was it a string of zeroes, or was she refusing something? Hesitating, Janice went slowly up the stairs.

Jennie's eyes were open, but they were glazed in tormented sleep.

"No-no-no-no—"

The glassy face looked as though it were in the throes of denial. Denying something from within.

Janice took her temperature. Just under 100 degrees. She looked at the clock. They had two hours to catch the flight.

"No-no-no—" Jennie whispered plaintively.

"Nobody's going to frighten you ever again, darling."

In thirty-five minutes, the taxi deposited them at LaGuardia Airport. Through the blackness swirled the lights of departing aircraft, livid behind the falling sleet.

The flight was delayed due to the storm. When it took off, an uncomfortable shiver shook the wings, and the passengers laughed nervously. In her arms, Jennie grew warmer. Janice took her to the lavatory and kept her face cool with wet paper towels.

Sleet turned to heavy snow, flailing past the red light at the

413

wing tip. White particles out of nowhere, flashing, then disappearing to nowhere.

A bang of tires on hard cement, a second thud, a third, and then the plane decelerated and taxied carefully to the terminal.

This time Elliot Hoover stood at the bottom of the steps. He raised his hat in mute, worried greeting.

"They told me you were coming."

He took Jennie in his arms, kissed her, but it was not until they nearly reached the terminal building that he saw the flush on her face.

"She looks ill," he stammered.

"The fever. It's come back. Elliot, I had to get her out of New York! Bill's collapsed! He's become a raving maniac! Dr. Geddes wants to lock him up and throw away the key!"

"This is terrible," Hoover murmured. Jennie stirred in his arms.

"It was during the birthday party," Janice continued stridently. "They were alone together in his room. Jennie started screaming. Wouldn't stop. By the time we entered the room, the whole place was a shambles and she wouldn't stop screaming."

Hoover swallowed. A wave of despair passed over his face.

"Did he say anything?"

Janice took a deep breath. "He said, 'She remembered.' Over and over, Elliot."

Hoover sighed. The sorrow of the night was softened in the deep snow. The warehouses, coal cars, and stacks of iron pipes looked like fanciful sculptures. Only a few red lights blinked high on the water tower, and then the Ford stopped in front of the clinic.

"Let's get her to the clinic."

"Elliot. What's happening?"

He put a gloved hand on hers. "I don't know." Then gently, "Come. Let's take her home."

Inside the clinic most of the children were in bed. Roy peered suspiciously from behind a bookshelf. The carpet was littered with toys, pictures torn from magazines, and pieces of crayon. A smell of wet wool permeated the halls.

Mr. Radimanath, surprised, stood up from the desk in Hoover's office and came into the hall.

"Mr. Templeton has had a relapse," Hoover said calmly.

Mr. Radimanath's hand went to his mouth.

"Please listen. I want you to fix up Jennie's room. She has a bad fever."

With an anxious glance at Janice, then at Hoover, Mr. Radimanath shuffled rapidly to the stairs.

Hoover hung his coat on one of a small series of pegs. He took Jennie from Janice's arms and felt the girl's neck and forehead. Mrs. Concepcion peered in from the hallway leading to the kitchen.

"Rosa," Hoover whispered, "could you prepare a hot drink for Jennie?"

"Right away, Mr. Hoover."

Hoover turned Jennie's face to him, smiled, and kissed the small forehead.

"No-no-no—" she murmured sleepily.

"Yes, yes, yes," he said, smiling.

Mrs. Concepcion returned with two cups of steaming broth. Shivering, Janice accepted a cup. Then Mrs. Concepcion spooned the broth gently into Jennie's mouth and carried her upstairs to her room. The clinic's quiet was broken by a low moan upstairs.

"You see?" Hoover said after a while. "Nothing changes here."

Janice looked anxiously out the window. Fat flakes continued to fall. The sills were blocked up with snow.

"The roads will be closed by morning," Hoover said. "At least two feet. That's what the radio forecast."

Janice sipped the soup, fondling the cup. The trembling did not go, even though she was finally warm. She put her coat across a child's desk and leaned wearily against the wall. The stairwell light went off. After several minutes the upstairs lights went off. A thin outline of luminosity rimmed Hoover's forehead.

"Good night, Mr. Hoover," came Mrs. Concepcion's voice from above.

"Good night, Mrs. Concepcion. Thank you."

"Good night, Mr. Hoover," followed Mr. Radimanath's voice.

"Good night and peace to you, Mr. Radimanath."

Another light went off. Hoover slumped against the wall, head down, massaging his face.

"What next, Janice?" he whispered.

She walked to him slowly. He felt her presence, but did not move.

"I've tried everything," he said hoarsely. "I've given everything I have. Everything."

She put a hand against his neck, gently pressed on the knotted muscles, slowly eased the tension there.

"Poor Elliot," she whispered ironically, and yet afraid that she was all too correct. "I've ruined you, haven't I?"

"Saved me, Janice. You saved me. That's the miracle."

Suddenly his cold finger traced a curve against her cheek.

"Miracle," he whispered gently. "So utterly miraculous."

She hesitated, then let him come forward. It made her feel real again. The silence was an ally, not a horror. Janice waited, and, like the falling snow, was content to be moved by the night.

"An extraordinary woman," he whispered, in all-consuming awe.

She closed her eyes and rested against him. She felt his heart beat through his shirt. A fragrance of lotion filled her nostrils.

"Elliot, I've been so lonely."

She moved, and her breasts were warm under his palms. He pressed against her until her back pushed up against the wall.

"Not here. Mr. Radimanath may come."

416

But whatever he whispered back, she caught only the urgency of it. Her back was pressed hard against the wall. His breath was hot against her ear. Her fingers hesitated, then clutched at the back of his neck.

The urgency of his entry surprised her. The violence of his insatiable need. She faltered, holding him at the wall, in the darkness. But then there was a soft, slow explosion within her belly, and she gasped, and she felt limp as a rag doll. It seemed to go on forever, exhausting her, until everything stopped, and she hung on to him for dear life itself.

"Oh God," she whispered after a dizzy moment.

"Janice, darling Janice . . ."

"Oh—I feel so—Oh, God . . ."

She hung on to his neck, leaning on his chest. He rocked her gently side to side, as though they danced. Partially dressed still, their hair and faces passed in and out of the glow cast by the streetlamps and the snow. She felt soft inside, transformed, and she pressed her body closer to his, though her mind remained troubled. For the wages of sin, she knew, was death.

"Hold me, Elliot. Don't ever let me go!"

Gently he rocked her, and his large hands rested against her back and neck.

The snow stopped. Darkness gleamed from the recesses of the neighborhood. Janice leaned, breasts against his chest, so that he might love her again. The rising and falling of his breathing comforted her. Against the window, she had descended, at long last and painfully, into a different kind of night.

Chapter Twenty-seven

Bill lay on his cot. His wrists chafed against leather restraints. Turning his head, he perceived the rotund outline of the orderly by the window. A vicious storm of sleet and jagged ice pellets beat against the cardboard taped there.

"Untie me," Bill mumbled.

"Have to get two more orderlies if I do," replied the man without looking up. "And we ain't got nobody to spare."

Bill let his neck rest, the muscles strained, and his head rolled back on the mattress.

"Untie me, for God's sake," he repeated.

The orderly turned a page in his magazine.

Then the storm brought a bulge at the cardboard. Wet stains showed in long striations. The orderly shivered and drew his white shirt tight about his throat.

"You're damn lucky you didn't ruin her," the orderly said.

"What are you talking about?"

"Child molesters rot in here. Take it from me. That's the one kind of pervert never gets out of here."

"I didn't molest her."

"Sure you didn't." The orderly turned a page of the magazine. "Goddamn kook."

Bill stared at the ceiling. The room was going cold, and only a light from the hall glinted off the metal shapes inside. Bill did not know why the window was broken, why there were no lights, only assumed that he had smashed them somehow. He closed his eyes.

"I need her," he whispered. "She was all I had."

"Then you shoulda kept your fingers off her."

"I never touched her!"

"Keep your voice down!"

Bill's head arched upward, his neck throbbing.

"She remembered! That's why she started screaming! She remembered what happened in Darien!"

"Calm down!"

Bill glared at the obsequious, immovable man at the desk chair, then settled back to the mattress.

"I saw it in her eyes," Bill whispered. "It was a kind of horrible memory. . . . But it came too fast for her. Much too fast. It frightened her."

The orderly yawned, checked his watch, and rubbed his eyes. There were footsteps in the hall. Eager for company, the orderly went to the door, poked his head out, and engaged two other orderlies in a bantering conversation. One was tall and black, the other equally tall, but with a limp that made him look diminutive. A pint of whiskey made the rounds. In the darkness there was the sound of cards shuffled.

Bill shivered in the cold that seeped into the room.

For thirty minutes the orderlies played poker and drank. The dimes and quarters glinted in the dim hallway. The whiskey bottle went empty, and was carefully hidden behind a radiator. A groan energed from Bill's room.

"Excuse me, gentlemen," said the first orderly.

He rose and lurched into Bill's room. Bill smelled whiskey-laden breath just over his face in the darkness, and felt the straps being removed from his wrists and ankles.

"Now you be good," the orderly warned. "I'll leave you loose for ten minutes, so make the most of it."

Bill flexed his wrists, but the sensation of constriction remained. Slowly he rubbed his wrists and then reached down to massage his ankles. He was too tired to sit up, and lay back again on the blanket.

The orderly's large hand tapped him lightly on the chest.

"Behave yourself. We ain't in no mood to be interrupted. You hear?"

Bill nodded.

"What's that you say?"

"I hear you, I said."

"Goddamn right you do."

The orderly lurched back to his game. For a while the coins clinked onto the glazed wooden surface. Bill shivered and crawled from under the blanket. He rose to his feet unsteadily, his senses keened, and tiptoed to the door.

For fifteen minutes the orderlies played cards. Their curses became more frequent, more amiable. Their laughter was stifled with difficulty.

"Roy, did you lock the door?"

"Sure did."

"Are you sure, Roy?"

"Sure of what, fat man?"

"The goddamn door, and watch your language."

"Don't you trust me?"

"Go check it, Roy."

With annoyance, the orderly went to the door and gave a violent pull. It opened.

"Jesus Christ," he shouted. "You're sure you done something and it turns out you ain't done it."

Alarmed by his tone, his two companions quickly joined

421

him. In the density of their drunkenness they stared at the bed. The rumpled forms coalesced into a human shape, then receded into a mixture of pillow, mattress, and blankets. With a sudden lurch all three orderlies jumped toward the bed. The black orderly's hands threw the blankets high into the air, onto the floor.

"He's gone!"

"Jesus Christ! He jumped!"

They ran to the window, laboriously stripped away the cardboard and peered down in the storm. The hospital lights illuminated a small patch of white snow below, obscured in the driving sleet.

"Do you see him?"

"There's something dark on the snow—I can't tell."

The sleet drove down, almost horizontal to the ground. The lights were small bulbs of opaque light in the dizzying storm. The ground was caked in ice, and the whistling wind covered the sound of a man's feet over the frozen earth.

Bill wore a long black overcoat, stolen from a closet on the first floor. It stretched from his shoulders clear down to his knees; an expensive, severely styled black coat with thin strips of fur along the collar and down the lapel. His feet were still in slippers, and they slipped painfully over the ice.

Bill thought he saw a smaller figure emerge from the sanitarium, limping under the small globes of light. He ducked his head and ran south, cutting across the parking lot. A man's voice called out to him.

"Dr. Henderson!"

Panicked, Bill whirled, lost his balance, and nearly fell. Two enormous headlights swirled slowly toward him out of the darkness blinding him. He held his hand in front of his face. The door of a taxi opened.

"Here, Dr. Henderson, climb in."

In the distance, a limping figure made its way under the

windows of the dormitory wing of the building. His feeble arms were waving.

Bill scrambled quickly into the cab.

"Sorry," laughed the cab driver, "but I had my lights off. You couldn't see me but I spotted you."

Bill craned his neck backward through the rear window. He saw an orderly running toward them, losing ground.

"Hell, I'd recognize that black coat anywhere, Dr. Henderson," the driver chuckled.

Under the gentle noise of the radio, Bill heard the sound of the wheels spinning out of control, digging down to the asphalt beneath the ice. The taxi went slowly sideways in a great arc, then straightened and skidded slowly ahead.

"It's a lot better on the main road. Pisser of a night, isn't it?"

Bill coughed. He felt the severe chill penetrating the overcoat, through to his legs covered only with thin pajamas. He felt nothing at all in his feet. Dimly he saw them and thought they had turned blue. Ice melted very slowly from his ankles, sliding off in crinkling little cakes of light.

The taxi swerved, jolted, and finally found traction. The sanitarium very gradually glided past them. Bill ducked as far back into the seat as he could, and he kept his face averted from the driver. For several minutes they drove in silence, and the storm buffeted the car, while the driver wrestled it back to control.

Bill stared wide-eyed at the vision of the night. Headlights swarmed in his mind. It had been a lifetime since he had seen the manic jaws of civilization so close about him. From time to time he saw his own reflection in the dark panes, pale as dirty snow, the eyes deep in sockets of shadow, like two tiny animals hiding in caves.

"You're going the wrong way!" Bill shouted.

"You're not going home to Glen Cove?" the driver asked, surprised.

"Manhattan!"

The driver noted a different inflection in the voice than the one he was used to. He peered in the rearview mirror. Bill huddled in his coat and did not look up, but shrank against the door, in the shadow where the driver could barely see. The driver shrugged.

"To the city, then," the driver mumbled, changing lanes.

The taxi fought its way back around a jug-handle, then up a ramp, and bumper to bumper with traffic on a single lane. Flashing red lights everywhere revealed the touch of a thousand brakes on the slippery road. Then they were moving west again.

The taxi picked up speed, occasionally slipping on ice patches. The city was a hallucination of glimmering yellow and red lights, streaks of blinking neon in the black, and clouds livid with painfully bright reflections.

The driver set his lips hard and fought his way down into the Queens Midtown Tunnel, dipping and rising toward the main heart of Manhattan. He leaned back. Heading north on the East Side Drive, the driver glanced in the rearview mirror.

"Where exactly did you want to go?"

"Des Artistes."

The driver screwed up his face.

"Where?"

"Home!"

"Home?"

The driver turned. His eyes widened.

"Hey, you ain't Dr. Henderson!"

A violent screech of brakes, horns, and shouts snapped his head back to the slapping windshield wipers. The cab skidded to the center divider, bounced lightly off it, and regained its momentum as Forty-second Street momentarily came into view.

"I ain't got no money," breathed the driver quickly, his eyes darting back and forth. "See that sign? Driver carries no more than five bucks change—"

"Des Artistes!" Bill roared, leaning suddenly forward.

"I don't know what the hell you're talking about, mister!"

"Home!"

"You're a goddamn loony! That's what you are! I'm taking you right back to the asylum!"

The cab skidded onto the Forty-second Street off-ramp, the driver pressed on the accelerator, the tires whined, spat snow in a long arc behind them, and then Bill reached through the small opening in the glass wall that divided driver from passenger, and grabbed the driver's hair. With a murderous yank, he jerked the driver's head backward.

In incoherent rage and frustration, Bill beat the driver's head back against the glass divider, then bit the man's finger until red spurted into his mouth.

"Help! Help!" the driver yelled, arms flailing, his legs kicking wildly, smashing into the dashboard.

The taxi began to decelerate, finally crashing into the car ahead at a traffic light. Immediately there was an angry snarl of car horns. Bill looked around wildly. It seemed all of New York poured its alien, annihilating light directly at his heart. In a single, terrible lunge, he was out in the cold, white as a rabbit, stock-still in the middle of the street.

The driver came out, holding his ear, wobbling, pointing at Bill.

"Grab him! He's a maniac!"

Bill leaped across the snow that divided the road, slipped, and somersaulted in the black overcoat over the ice. His hands emerged bleeding. He picked himself up, and ran in his iced and torn slippers into the heart of the crowds and flashing, swirling lights.

He ran down Forty-second Street, away from the tangle of red flashes, shouts, and glistening roads.

The swirling storm turned to blankets descending in soft folds. Traffic was stalled. Disgusted, police stood by patrol cars.

Pedestrians walked around Bill as he ran from the reflection of his own form in dark windows. Slipping, his ragged slippers torn in half, he went sprawling into a filthy snowdrift.

"Here you go, friend. Up and easy."

Two strong hands grabbed him under the elbow.

Bill looked into the eyes of two priests. They backed away from the intensity of his stare.

"Dr. Geddes?"

"What's that? You want a doctor?"

Bill stumbled backward, frightened, tore himself away, retreating down Forty-second Street. He ran into the lights that poked holes in the darkness, glittered through the falling snow. Evil followed him everywhere, and he looked back over his shoulder.

Bill reached an enormous structure that exhaled warmth. It smelled like New York. Gritty, sweaty, oily. Something seemed to click into place. Cautiously, he walked down the stairs, went through large glass doors, and looked around at the rolling, incessant crowds under brilliant lights.

It was Grand Central Station. Bill smiled. He had been here before. In another incarnation. Bewildered, he ducked away from the vents that roared at him with hot air. A group of sailors jostled him. Businessmen pushed him out of their way. A roller skater shot past him with a radio blaring rock.

Instinct led him to a kind of bright tunnel. There was a series of urinals. Trembling, he relieved himself. Then he examined his feet. They were soaked, dirty, bleeding, and the toes tingled ominously, as though the flesh was barely alive. He tucked the black overcoat carefully over the pajamas and went to the shoeshine stand in a lobby.

A crippled black boy bent over shining black shoes on metal forms.

Bill waited until the last man left the washbasins, then he went to the stand, grabbed the shoes, and ran.

"Hey— What the hell are you doing?" the cripple yelled.

Bill escaped into the crowd.

426

He was lost in Central Park. He stopped. The snow was cold and wet on his bare feet, shivering within the black shoes. But he recognized the park. The configuration of black trees, paths, and the hillock over the rowing lake. It triggered primitive memories. Carefully he retraced his steps, then struck out over virgin fields of white.

"Ivy," he whispered happily.

Nobody heard him. The streets were deserted. New York at night was a study of black recesses in dull white. Snow filled the crevices of soot and oily asphalt. Bill sensed a maze of bizarre patterns gliding by, but he kept his head down, following his black shoes. They knew where to go.

Disoriented now, he walked very carefully. He distrusted each side street that opened up—a truncated vista of fire escapes, back doors, stone steps.

"Ivy!" he called.

But the voice died away. The city absorbed all sounds. Slowly he continued toward the north.

Silently, the soul that had been frightened peered out through the eyes of Bill Templeton. He saw Des Artistes. He stopped. That, certainly, had not changed. It haunted him, that image of a different life. It sent out unpleasant signals in the darkness and cold.

He drifted toward the entrance of the building. A man in uniform beat his arms for warmth. Bill came closer, hesitated. The doorman stopped beating his arms, peering into the blackness.

"Mr. Templeton . . ." gasped the old man.

"Yes. I've come home. It's good to be home. Very, very good."

"Yeah . . . Sure . . ."

"I want to go in now."

"Of course. Right this way. Goodness, but you gave me a fright."

Bill licked his lips, afraid. He followed the doorman into

the narrow vestibule, and then very slowly descended the steps into the lobby. The warmth and bright lights frightened him. He retreated. The doorman turned, surprised.

"Right this way, Mr. Templeton."

The doorman escorted Bill to the elevator. Bill dared to look around him. The walls, the familiar entry to the restaurant and bar had a lurid, dangerous light.

Mario, shocked, stared at Bill.

"P-please, Mr. Templeton. Step in."

Bill walked into the elevator, leaned against the wall, and saw the doors glide shut. Mario punched a button, and the elevator hummed upward through the building.

"You look great, Mr. Templeton. That is one hell of a coat."

Bill's jaw clenched, a nervous reaction to the claustrophobic space.

"We'll have you upstairs in no time."

The door glided open. Bill stared vacantly at the wall opposite. Mario waited. Bill did not move.

"You don't have a key, do you?" Mario asked quietly. "That's all right. I have a master key."

Mario walked into the hallway. Bill hesitated, then followed. With each step toward the apartment door he went slower and slower. Finally, he stopped nearly ten feet away, while Mario unlocked the door. A black abyss greeted him.

"Why is it so dark?"

"What? You want me to turn on a light?"

Mario reached an arm into the apartment, flicked a switch, and three soft lights glowed from lamps.

"Where are they?"

Mario turned, shocked at the maniacal roar. Suddenly an immense force hurled him into the apartment. Ceramics showered into fragments, and a table leg crashed upward into his shoulder.

The door slammed, and a livid Bill stood over him.

"Where did they go?" he hissed.

"I—I don't know, Mr. T-Templeton."

A rough fist seized Mario's hair, yanked him to his feet. A bright hailstorm passed before Mario's eyes, and the pain leaped down into his skull. Bill shook the head violently, side to side.

"Where are they?" Bill bellowed into his face.

"P-P-P—"

Bill slapped the trembling cheeks hard with two resounding cracks.

"Tell me!"

"P-P-Pittsburgh—"

Bill stared at him in disbelief, then gritted his teeth and threw the diminutive man back against the remains of the coffee table.

"Pittsburgh?" Bill whispered.

"Mr. Hoover's clinic, sir. The girl was sick."

Bill wiped his sweated face, then shook himself. He stared viciously at Mario. Mario tried to crawl away, but his arms were entangled in the broken table legs.

"P-please, Mr. Templeton . . ."

Bill spun him around and wedged his arms behind his back with a belt. He carried Mario, who kicked furiously, toward the main closet and threw him in. He tore the electric cord from a lamp, held it out between two hands, and advanced into the closet. Mario went white, but the cord only lashed his feet.

Bill bounded upstairs. There were violent sounds of drawers being emptied, thrown onto the floor. Objects fell from dressers, more glass smashed, and he kicked something heavy away from him. Then he did the same through every room and closet upstairs until he found what he sought.

Suddenly Bill opened the closet door and seized Mario.

"Mr. Templeton! Let me get a doctor for you!"

"I have to go to the airport!"

"Rest here. Untie me. . . ."

Bill shook Mario until the teeth rattled.

"How do I get to the airport?" Bill growled.

"G-go downstairs. Tell the doorman. He'll get you a taxi."

"A taxi? Yes, of course. Mario, I . . ."

But he lost his train of thought. Furious, he shoved Mario back in among the coats and shoes, then slammed the closet door. Mario heard the apartment door close, and footsteps pattering quickly to the stairwell.

Bill ducked against the rear seat of the taxi. It was late, but he did not want to be seen.

"Don't turn back," he muttered.

The taxi driver turned down his radio and leaned back.

"That's that?"

"I said, don't turn back."

"I wasn't going to turn back, mister."

Bill muttered to himself, looked out the window as Manhattan slid by. Most of the roads were closed. Only the main arteries were open, and they were clogged with traffic.

"Man must not turn back," he said. "Forward—always forward."

The driver turned down his radio a second time.

"Forward," Bill said louder.

"Where the hell do you think I'm going?"

"We are all voyagers on a dark sea. Voyaging beyond the barriers of death."

"Well, I ain't going *that* far."

They were on a dark road now, and only a few globes of light went by, their poles invisible. They hovered like visitors from Pluto. Bill leaned forward suddenly.

"I'm going to see my daughter," he said confidently.

"Yeah? Where's she at?"

"Pittsburgh. She's been sick."

"Nothing serious, I hope?"

"No. She just got frightened."

The driver glanced at him from the rearview mirror, studied Bill more carefully.

"Which terminal, sir?"

Startled, Bill looked in front. A complex of yellow and white lights were visible in the darkness. Signs directed the traffic to various terminals.

"I'm going to Pittsburgh."

"American?"

"I don't know."

"Probably Allegheny."

The taxi pulled up at the Allegheny terminal. The parking area was not plowed, covered high in snow. There were few passengers, and over the runway the ground crews worked furiously with snowplows.

The driver turned apprehensively.

"That'll be ten dollars and eighty cents."

Bill stared blankly at him.

"Ten dollars," the driver repeated. "Eighty cents."

Bill's forehead wrinkled with an effort. He looked troubled. The driver swallowed, tried to estimate the kind of passenger he had.

"Do you have any money, sir?"

"Yes. Yes, I found some in her stocking drawer."

"Show me."

Bill pulled a fistful of bills from his overcoat pocket. The driver's eyes widened. Gingerly he helped himself to several notes.

"See? Ten dollars." He held up the money. "Unless you want to tip me."

Bill stared at him, frightened. Quickly the driver added two dollars. Bill leaned forward. The driver recoiled, slamming against the steering wheel.

"Do you think my daughter . . . will recognize me?"

"Sure. Sure, mister. You're her father, ain't you?"

Bill nodded, gratified. He stepped from the taxi. Then he went to the front door, leaned in, and said, "God bless you."

The driver smiled sadly. He recognized the manic look of Bill's eyes, though few who had that look also had the money to ride in taxis and buy expensive black coats. A flicker of sympathy passed between them.

"God bless you, too, sir."

The taxi pulled away.

Bill walked into the Allegheny Airlines Terminal, carrying hundreds of dollars in his fist. First he went to a coffee shop, ate five doughnuts and drank two glasses of orange juice. The startled cashier picked the money from his fist. Bill walked away before she could give him change.

He bought a ticket to Pittsburgh. One way. He ran on pure instinct now, as he had since escaping from the sanitarium. Only now the instinct was running down, growing confused. He did not know what would take over when the instinct went haywire.

"If you hurry, sir, there is a three o'clock flight boarding now. Gate seventeen."

"Where is gate seventeen?"

"Follow the red carpet, sir."

Bill walked into a narrow corridor, felt the air grow thick and the lights overhead press down upon him.

Ahead of him, two stewardesses waited with clipboards. It seemed like a thousand miles into the airplane. Even when he sat down, it felt unlikely that he would escape New York. Below the window the snow fell, whirled in monstrous eddies by passing vehicles.

There were few passengers. Already some of them slept. Tiny rays of lights beamed onto their laps from the overhead luggage racks. Bill sank into his seat. All at once the exhaustion came—like a wave, it ravished his limbs, reduced them to sodden rubbery appendages, and his eyes grew instantly heavy. He thought he was blacking out.

"Not now," he prayed, mumbling aloud. "Please God, not now."

But he felt the lights going out inside the plane. The stewardess came to buckle his seat belt. She turned off the overhead beam of light, smiled and left. She did not see the panic on his whitened face.

The roar of the engines, like the demented gongs of a Himalayan temple, stirred his blood with power.

Then he laughed, but the laughter turned harsh and crude. The pain of the last three years flooded into him, a vile, black poison that spilled into his bones, and he choked on his own tears.

Fighting for control, he called on the one-eyed god of Tibet. The whisper of the jets soothed him. He closed his eyes.

Pittsburgh was iced, buried under a foot and a half of snow. Except for the turnpike and a few central roads, there was no traffic. Even from the air, it looked weird and peaceful. No taxis were available. The buses remained at garages. And there were no more flights until the work crews could clear the runways again.

Bill stared disconsolately across the terminal. It was cold, nearly deserted. Only an occasional menial worker strolled by, with brooms, dustpans, rags, and window cleaner.

Before him was a white booth with an Avis logo. There was no one behind the desk. There was no bell to ring. Bill slammed his fist on the desk.

A group of ground crew workers turned. They wore orange slickers and matching trousers, heavy black boots thick with melting snow.

"Hey, Herb! You got a customer!"

"Oh, hell."

A thin, rat-faced man with a small smile came out from the group, straightened his black knitted tie, and slid easily onto a stool behind the desk.

"Nice time of day to visit Pittsburgh," he said. "What can I do for you?"

"I need a car."

The man reached for a triplicate form.

"I'll have to see your driver's license, and I'll need a major credit card."

Bill stared at him blankly, then pulled out his roll of bills and thrust it at the man.

"No, no. Money's no good, I'll need to—"

With an animal grunt, Bill snatched back the money, wheeled brusquely, and stalked across the foyer toward the exit doors.

A blast of frigid air smashed into Bill's face as the doors opened automatically. Pressing forth into a strong wind, Bill spied a long line of cars parked beneath the Avis canopy. The area was deserted but for an attendant who was gassing a mud-encrusted white Dodge Dart. The attendant slapped his arms vigorously against his body for warmth. His back was to Bill, who watched him furtively from behind a pillar.

His chance came when the attendant cradled the hose, capped the gas tank, then hurried inside the terminal with the meter reading.

Bill approached the Dodge cautiously. With trembling fingers, he opened the door. The car smelled of fresh upholstery. He had trouble finding the key in the ignition switch. Then he had trouble finding the hand brake. Finally, he eased the car onto the main road, swerved, dipped into the snow at the side of the road, and then very carefully, very nervously, following signs, maneuvered toward the city.

There was little traffic. The car felt strange, immensely smooth, quiet, and powerful. After a few moments he began to relax. Then he found the light switch and turned on the headlights. The landscape rolled swiftly past. It was exquisitely cold, exhilarating. Bill drove with the windows wide open.

The signs diverged. A lane went up a long, curved ramp toward Harrisburg. Bill wiped the windshield, continued on toward Pittsburgh. Far away a cluster of lights gleamed over freshly fallen snow. Half a dozen trucks, massive headlights blazing, illumined an Arco station.

He skittered down the off-ramp, turned the wrong way onto a one-way street, circled, and stopped in the midst of the trucks' lights.

"Closed, mister," a trucker called. "No gas tonight."

A group of truckers looked idly in his direction from the gas station door. One of the vans had jackknifed against the wall. The men drank coffee.

"Closed," the trucker repeated. "Whole town's shut down. No gas anywhere."

Bill, blinded by the headlights, the reflection of the snow, glass, and metal, held his hand up in front of his eyes. He turned in all directions. The enormous filaments glared at him in a hideous crossfire. Then a trucker walked slowly to his window.

"You looking for something?" he asked, sipping coffee, his breath billowing into the brilliant cold.

"There's a children's clinic. On Tanner Street."

The trucker shook his head.

"This here is Fitzwilliam Street. Cross street there is Cummins Avenue."

"My daughter— Please . . ."

The trucker sighed.

"Just a minute, friend."

The trucker ambled back to the group. Then two of them went inside the station. They argued over a map taped to the rear of the door. Then a different trucker strolled to the Dodge.

"Go down Fitzwilliam," he said, "to Ninety-fifth. All the way. To Colman. Should be open. Turn right to Tanner. It's a real small street. A kind of industrial zone."

Bill eased the Dodge to Fitzwilliam Street. Snow whirled from the rear wheels, the rear end swung heavily, bumped against a hidden curb, and the car jerked into the middle of the road and stalled. Bill had trouble starting it again. Then it cruised easily along the quiet, snow-softened street.

He did not accelerate, though time was short. Probably the

police were alerted. From the sanitarium. From Mario. But he was content to watch the dark alleys drift by, the brilliant pools of light under the streetlamps, a few isolated neon signs, dead-looking trees. It was a malevolent night, soaked in an evil darkness. Yet it was soft and inviting.

"*Ekajata!*" Bill mumbled.

The one-eyed deity. One-breasted. One-toothed hag.

"*Za!*"

Serpent with one thousand eyes.

"*Damchen Doje!*"

Who rides a goat. Carries a blacksmith's anvil and bellows.

Were they really here? Or just articulations of teeth, tongue, and breath? Had they truly deserted him? Or did they wait, far at the end of the cumbersome roads, perhaps at Tanner Street?

Bill grinned. Colman Street. Down the center was a thin layer of snow. Once plowed, now devoid of traffic. Even the shops were dead. The cold wind ran its fingers through his hair.

"*Damchen Doje!*"

Odd sound. Here in Pittsburgh. Yet how else had his instincts taken him here? Over every obstacle? Out of every darkness? Jennie, through *their* agency, was Ivy. Ivy called to him through *their* dark powers.

Tanner Street was blocked with snow. Bill jammed on the brakes, the Dodge swerved sideways, slid, and bumped against a telephone pole. The door buckled. He crawled out the other door.

"Ivy?" he whispered.

All the houses were slums. Derelict shacks. Leaning structures, tucked under the walls of a dark factory. Mountains of junk loomed fantastically in backyards. Bill walked quickly up Tanner Street.

A far garage glowed feebly with a pale yellow light behind a window. His feet, still bare within the tight shoes, cramped. Dizzy, he clutched his forehead. A black branch sank under his weight. He looked up. There was a tangled mass of sawdust, broken snow, and pieces of tree trunk. Behind it was a fence. Behind that, a long green building.

Bill grinned. There were no lights. No tracks in the snow. It was the culmination of his journey. A journey three years in the making. Deftly, he climbed the fence and jumped into the yard.

He struggled to a long, dark window and peered in. Cheerful mobiles dangled from yellow strings. It was a dining room. In the farthest shadows was the kitchen. He stepped around to the other side of the clinic, where a fire escape crawled upward to the second floor.

He paused. Nothing moved. A sensation of breeze. Whispering in his ear. Like a soft, trusting voice, he thought.

Gently, he tiptoed up the iron steps, shuffling his way through thick piles of snow. Shivering at the top, he silently peered into the nearest window.

It was a dark room, oddly decorated. Vaguely red curtains. Icons from India. Hoover's room? An old-fashioned wooden wardrobe, richly carved. On the chair a pillow. Clothes. Bill licked his lips confused, yet eager to begin. He wiped an oval where his breath had condensed on the frosted glass.

Bill grinned a second time. But it was a death's-head grin. A spasm traveled through his brain. It shook him like a wire doll. Then the chill passed. An awesome vacuum opened before him. He bent forward to look again.

Janice, as she slept, was completely still. Only her breasts moved as she breathed, a soft undulation like a distant sea, silent, a pale memory of the body that he once had shared. Janice stirred. A man's hand slipped from her naked hip.

Bill ducked. The neighborhood was utterly silent. The trees were cased in ice. Ice covered the metal rails. The sky was livid pink over the city, but black over the clinic. Shivering, he turned again to the window, furiously wiping another hole in the frost.

The rounded torso, the long, slender arms, small but firm

breasts, the jutting pelvis, the black, completely black hair that flowed nearly to the shoulders, that had a fragrance of its own. In the gloomy interior her face was barely decipherable. An amalgam of shadows and deeper shadows. By her side, Hoover's hand stirred familiarly in sleep.

Bill jerked away. In agony he ground tears away with balled fists. He shook all over with a cold he had never experienced before. Long red marks covered his face where his hands dug in. Violently he spun around, found nothing but the frigid night, and pressed his eyes to the window a third time.

The edge of the bed was crumpled with sheets, soft red blankets, a side of a white bedcover. Janice's ankles were soft, ivory white in the pale glow of a distant streetlamp.

"Ekajata!" he whispered fervently. *"Za, Damchen Doje!* Help me!"

Had the deities ridden away? Was Pittsburgh the center of a curse? Weeping, Bill backed away, found a door on the landing, and slipped inside the building.

The tears fell hotly down his cheeks.

"Hare Krishna!" he murmured desperately.

But the Lord of Destruction and Creation had flown beyond all hearing. The clinic was polluted, profaned.

A small blue light nestled in the lower hall. It gave the only light, a glow that extended in an oval over the carpet. He crept to the light and looked in the room.

Jennie stirred. The soft cheek tinged with blue against the sheets. Bill nestled her in his arms, cradled her, and felt the living warmth against his cheek.

"My daughter," he whispered. "My own."

No, the deities had not ridden away. They were with him still, and their power was evident, their design clear. They had taken him beyond the crass and mundane realm of earthly deception into the heart of his true and single destiny. Love was no longer Janice. Love moved in his arms, small-limbed, smelling of sleep.

Bill covered her in blankets, listened. There were no movements in the clinic. Holding Jennie close, he edged sideways through the door, onto the fire escape. For a second, the window to Hoover's bedroom transfixed him. He smiled, then clutched his child tighter and bounded down the slippery steps.

Chapter Twenty-eight

Elliot Hoover had a dream.

He crouched in a cave on the slopes of Mount Everest. Outside, a storm battered the rocks, driving sleet into the cave. He was naked. Suddenly, from the dark interior of the cave came a deity riding a goat. Strings of human skulls bounced against his chest. The goat's eyes glowed red. Smoke issued upward from the long hair.

For several seconds Hoover did not realize the telephone rang. Then he stirred, shook his head, and went to his desk by the window.

"Yes?" he mumbled thickly. "When? No. No sign. Really? To Pittsburgh? I see. Yes, Dr. Geddes. Thank you."

He hung up. Mystified, he rubbed his chin. Janice propped herself up on her elbows and saw his nude form, outlined in the gray of the early dawn.

"What's wrong?"

"Bill's escaped."

"What?"

"He went to the apartment."

"When?"

"A few hours ago. The elevator man told him you were here. They think Bill's on his way."

Janice sat up, looked around for her clothes, grabbed them, and without shame, dressed in front of him.

"Look," Hoover said. "The roads are blocked in with snow. He'll never make it."

"He's going to kill us, Elliot."

"Now don't be such an alarmist. He just wants Jennie."

Suddenly Janice's hand went to her mouth. She looked white in the first light of day.

"Jennie!" she gasped.

Janice rushed into Jennie's room. She screamed. Hoover ran in. The bed was empty.

"He's got her!" she yelled.

Hoover ran his hands through the sheets. "Still warm. Look, there's water on the carpet."

They pulled open the door, saw the churned snow all over the fire escape landing. Hoover stared in dismay at the disturbance in front of his own bedroom window.

Janice backed slowly away from him.

"Elliot," she whispered, "He's seen us!"

Hoover blanched. "He can't be far."

Hoover dashed into his bedroom, threw on trousers and a sweater, socks and shoes, then ran into Mr. Radimanath's room. There were feverish whispers, a sleepy man's grunt. Lights went on in a corridor. Then he ran back to the landing, grabbed Janice's arm, and they went down the fire escape.

They saw a clear tangle of footprints leading away from the fire escape to the dining room window, then there was another disturbance of snow at the fence.

"He climbed the fence!" Hoover exclaimed, quickly unlocking the gate. They ran out into the snow of Tanner

Street. Hoover pointed. A long double line of tracks led back to Colman Street.

At a gritty rectangle in the ground, where the snow was shallow, tread marks of tires had ground deep ruts down to the asphalt.

"He's got a car?" Hoover said in disbelief.

At the side of the road the telephone pole leaned slightly. A streak of white had been gouged into its splintered side, about three feet off the ground.

"A white car," Janice added.

The dug-up snow was an icon of hideous violence. Bits of black rubber melded into the white, blackened by a manic attempt at escape. It was an icon of Bill, of them all, their spiritual natures mutually defiled.

"We'd better follow him," he said hesitantly. "Shouldn't be hard. There are tire tracks, and no traffic yet."

But he didn't move. He stood rooted to the spot, gazing at the tracks of the car, converging in the fresh daylight, narrowing in the distance, toward Colman Street. They hypnotized him. They taunted him, beckoned him, waited for him like a hideous destiny.

"The snow's falling again," he said at last. "The tracks are filling in."

He took Janice and hurried up Tanner Street, unlocked his Ford, and got in. Mr. Radimanath came, shivering in his robe, to the edge of the road.

"He has a car," Hoover shouted, rolling down the window. "It may be white. We're following. Tell the police when they come."

The Ford sputtered into life, the wipers cast off heavy coats of snow, and Hoover slid into Tanner Street. The tires skidded, caught, and skidded again. In the rearview mirror, he saw Mr. Radimanath put his palms together, with a small bow in his direction.

Hoover turned carefully onto Colman Street.

"He drove down this way," he said. "See? He's following his own tracks out of here."

Janice shivered. She tried to coax the heater, but it would not work.

The shops were still closed. Heavy rills of snow hung down from black roofs, half iced, glittering over brick and tarpaper. At times snow broke, falling in disintegrating clumps on the sidewalks. It was a wonderworld, like the first day of creation. But God had withheld his blessing.

"Where do you think he's going?" she asked, warming her fingers in her sweater.

"Probably just following the plowed roads."

"You don't think he's going back to New York?"

"I doubt he knows which direction that is anymore."

"Don't underestimate him, Elliot."

He looked at her sharply, surprised at the bitter tone of her voice. Grimly he cleared a circle in the fogging windshield. The car tracks led on, still fresh, tinged with black where the asphalt showed through.

The snow became softer and fatter, almost a rain.

"He'll be going back to the airport," she said, "if he's just following his old tracks."

"Depends on what happens at Ninety-fifth."

The tracks ahead wallowed uncertainly, dug up the snow into a foul mixture of brown black granite grit, then smoothed out onto Ninety-fifth.

"That's where he's going, all right," Hoover muttered.

At Fitzwilliam Street the tires swerved clear across the road. An immense arc had been scraped up over the curb. The snow now was very soft, slushy, and the tracks were melting into shallow undulations up the street. The windshield was spattered by fat drops of rain.

As they drove up Fitzwilliam Street, a barrier of police cars protected an overturned Volkswagen van. It was blue. The entire front hood was buckled in, the contents spread unevenly up the embankment of the highway. The barriers were being erected, sawhorses hung with red flashing lights, and beyond, the highway was completely clear of snow. A few cars already traveled on the glistening, rain-soaked road, headlights poking into the gloom.

"Damn!" Hoover exclaimed, trying to see through the fogged windshield.

Janice leaned forward. "Elliot, there's a white car!"

"Where?"

"Up on the highway. Getting on. It has lights on."

"Let's take a look."

But the policeman at the barrier waved his arm vigorously, directing them back down Fitzwilliam Street. Hoover backed the car, then rammed it up onto the steep slope that supported the on-ramp. A suitcase from the van crunched underneath, ground into the mud, and the Ford careened, spitting muddy water and snow over the police cars.

Suddenly they were on the highway.

"It's Bill!"

Far ahead of them a shining white Dodge, with its side slightly buckled, changed lanes erratically. It seemed to follow no lanes, gliding along rapidly through the downpour, fishtailing, and a mist of cold water flew from the rear wheels.

The Ford crept closer, now exceeding sixty miles an hour. Glistening lakes of water roared up into the fenders. Hoover peered ahead. Only a single head—Bill's—was visible at the driver's wheel.

Hoover flicked his lights on and off, then tried the high beam. The Dodge cruised serenely on. They saw the head turn to stare at them. The face was lost in the indistinct, murky shadows within the Dodge, but it looked back a long, long time. At the last minute, it turned back and the Dodge jumped away from the restraining barrier at the dividing strip.

"Where is he going?" Janice cried.

Slowly, very slowly, Hoover's hand stopped wiping the sweat from his forehead. His eyes softened, dilated, his whole face radiated an unearthly revelation.

"I know where he's going."

Hoover swallowed. The Dodge took a sudden off-ramp. The Ford missed the ramp, skidded, spun around on the edge strip; panicked drivers slammed on brakes all over the lanes.

Hoover glimpsed the Dodge as it plunged into a muddy pool, then shot into an industrial zone, weaving insanely through parking lots, loading zones, and out of cul-de-sacs.

"He's heading for the turnpike. I'm going to cut him off."

Hoover drove down a frontage road, past corrugated sheds, then up a long ramp. Down below, the white Dodge careened away from them, past factories and heavy equipment, throwing a violent spray behind.

Hoover wheeled the Ford onto an overpass, cut past a truck filled with new cars, and heard the mighty horn blast near his ear. A landscape of snow, cut by gashes of brown red mud, spread into the rural rain. Factories spewed black smoke to the clouds. The whole earth extended in a vista of crude mud, grit, and wet winds.

Entering the turnpike, the signs diverged, some to Harrisburg, some to Pittsburgh.

A cold chill invaded Janice's body.

"Elliot, isn't this where Sylvia and Audrey Rose were—"

"Yes! Here!"

Hoover peered forward, furiously wiping the windshield. He lowered the side window, a wet chill blew onto them. There was the full sound of wheels slapping against the hard, drenched cement below.

The rain came now in torrential squalls. Most of the snow was gone. Wisps of cloud rolled through the valleys, disintegrating, reforming, reaching fingers over the icy roadway.

The white Dodge ploughed through eddies of molten ice on the Pennsylvania Turnpike, and Bill smiled.

"Nobody will bother us ever again," he exclaimed.

In the front seat, Jennie shivered, chills shaking her slender shoulders. Bill tucked the blankets around her.

"Poor darling," he said. "Daddy is taking you home."

Bill glanced into the rearview mirror at a world of gray pools of dirty water, smoke above rows of factory walls, and grimy snow. He was exhausted. He had been without sleep so long that his fingers trembled.

Instinct had brought him here. But now instinct was confused. Instead, there was a horrifying buzzing in his head.

"Four-five-nine-no—"

Bill turned. The sweat poured down his face. His hand calmed Jennie.

"It's all right, darling. Daddy's here."

"No-no-no-no—"

"Yes, yes, it's Daddy."

The Dodge careened along the slick surface at ever-increasing speeds.

"No-no-no—"

Frustrated, Bill alternated between looking at the road and at Jennie. Veils of spray roared at the Dodge from traffic. Horns honked as he fought to maintain control.

"Don't be frightened, Ivy. I love you."

But Jennie squirmed. The chills were disappearing as fast as a fever began to rise. Her cheek quivered. Then the small limbs began to convulse.

"Ivy, what's wrong?"

A smothered gurgle stopped in Jennie's throat. Panicked, Bill felt her face. It burned with an unnatural heat. He desperately looked around, but heavy freight trucks hemmed him in. Rain blasted at the windshield.

"D-D-D—" Jennie gasped.

"Yes, yes, Daddy's here!"

A blast of horns, and Bill grabbed the steering wheel. He was driving much too fast, the wheels losing their grip on the curves. But his cold hands, like his feet, felt disconnected from his body.

He thought he saw the old Ford approaching behind him.

"D-D-D—"

"Yes, Daddy's here, darling! You'll be all right!"

But a sudden crimp of muscles arched Jennie's back. She shook from side to side. Her glazed eyes stared out at the rain. Her throat worked convulsively. Inarticulate syllables lodged there, and when she breathed it sounded like strange words. Bill's head was dizzy, light, and her voice mingled with the whispers from the fissures of his own fears.

"Da—Da—Da—"

"Going home, Ivy. Try to sleep."

"No-no-no—"

Jennie began to twist and turn. The embankment dropped beside the lane. Jennie's screams merged with the squeal of brakes behind him. Bill fought to keep her down, to keep the blankets around her, but the slender arms pummeled his face and chest.

"Ivy! You're burning up! Oh God, Ivy!"

A cacophony of truck horns, squealing brakes, and automobile horns blasted through the rain. The Dodge hit the center divider.

Through the windshield he saw the old Ford hard behind as the Dodge tumbled slowly, ever so slowly, it seemed, down the embankment, spitting mud in great arcs over itself, throwing off huge segments of metal and glass. As in a dream, through the mist, he saw the Ford skid to a stop above him, as his own car lifted into the air, rolling over and over, a twirling mass of white iron and steel. The blast blew glass through the upholstery of the front seat. Blackness, a hideous stench of near death, swallowed Bill, and the explosion deafened him.

Hoover crawled to the lip of the embankment and peered in horror at the smoldering wreckage below.

A figure, blackened and ragged, crawled frantically over the mud below, clawing at the wreckage.

"Bill!" Janice screamed, holding Hoover.

"He's alive!"

Furiously the silhouette beat his fists against the twisted body of the white Dodge.

"It's on fire!" Hoover cried, catapulting himself down the steep embankment. Rain plastered his hair. He peered into the flaming caldron below, and the brilliance of the reflections hurt his eyes. Slipping, sliding, his ankle collapsed and he fell. He hobbled, crawled, and rolled down over the slippery mud.

A strong hand grabbed him.

"Keep back!" said a deep voice. "She's gonna blow!"

A police officer held his arm. Now Hoover saw a trio of policemen with fire extinguishers, racing *away* from the Dodge. He shook off the hand, slipped under the officer's reaching arm, ducked under low, rolling clouds of black smoke and flung himself toward the burning car. At the rear door of the Dodge, where the metal was jammed immovable into the earth, Bill was weeping furiously, beating his hands against the window.

A muffled scream emerged from the Dodge, under the crackling of burning fabric.

Hoover stumbled closer. The black smoke seared his lungs. He kept low to the wet earth. There was a rush of hot air, and flames licked upward from the engine block. In the rear window, black hair torn into streamers, Jennie beat against the glass.

"daddydaddyhothothot!"

The scream barely came through the roar of the flames.

"Ivy!" shouted Bill.

"daddydaddyhothothot!"

Hoover knelt forward. The heat sucked at his eyes. Flames shot up over the roof. Smoke twined lazily from the upholstery inside. Jennie began to choke.

"IVY!!!" Bill bellowed.

"daddydaddyhothothot!"

"Dear God! No!" Hoover wailed in anguish. *"Not this time!"*

But Bill's hands flailed uselessly at the thick glass. Jennie was on the rear seat choking, and the black smoke rolled quickly through the car.

"'Leave her, Bill!" Hoover sobbed weakly. "It was ordained!"

But Bill reached to the ground, picked a heavy piece of cast steel from the engine block, and raised it over his head. With a roar of anger, fear, and sheer exertion, Bill heaved the cast steel into the plate glass and it blew apart, fragments shining, scattering over Jennie's crumpled form.

"GET AWAY FROM IT, MISTER!" called a bullhorn.

"IVY!!" Bill shouted.

The door would not budge. Smoke roared out through the shattered window, fumes of hot, acid smells. Bill leaned in, through the window, and gathered Jennie's body to his chest. He coughed furiously, and slowly the white Dodge, gathering momentum, began to slip back on top of him.

"Bill!" cried Hoover.

Bill turned. His face was haggard, blackened, deep gouges of blood gashed through his forehead and chin. Hoover tried to come forward, but the heat pressed his clothes against his own body.

"Bill!"

Bill's blackened eyes locked onto Hoover's. The Dodge teetered farther.

"Bill!"

Looking into Hoover's eyes, Bill threw the child into his arms. Their hands brushed, inches apart.

Then Hoover recoiled. A rush of intense heat swirled around him, dazed him, sizzled the water on his hair. He fell backward, clutching Jennie. He saw dirt spray oddly up into the shining air, black clods of death, and then the smoke billowed out, followed by a deafening roar, a thunder of all creation, and then came the twin horror—fire, leaping upward from the hideous pile of melted and destroyed metal, and the Dodge settling lower, rolling farther over Bill's flaming body.

Arms pulled Jennie from him. The last thing Hoover saw before he lost consciousness was the inexhaustible forces of destruction and creation, the white Dodge now utterly consumed in dense clouds of smoke, topped with leaping fingers of triumphant fire against the leaden sky, a paean to the divinity that worked its immutable will.

EPILOGUE

"*I have revealed the most secret doctrine. He who sees it has light, And his task in this world is done.*"

The Words of Krishna

The water was deep. Brown reflections rippled from rowboats, spread in long rings to the rocks. One by one, Jennie lifted green leaves, covered the pebbles at the shore, and touched them with a short sprig of elm. Her face was absorbed in the methodical ritual. The lake sent small sparkles of light across her eyes.

In the boathouse, Elliot Hoover sat opposite Janice, a table dividing them. It was early summer, and Janice studied the roses in a blue vase.

"I've always loved Central Park in summer," she said, smiling.

Hoover said nothing for a while, then nervously fingered the edge of the table. Around them a horde of children roller-skated down a walkway. The leaves shivered lightly in the breeze, and the tall stone buildings undulated in the lake, breaking apart among the green reeds.

"Jennie loves it here," he said.

Jennie playfully threw stones into the water.

"I've waited a long time to see you, Elliot. I tried to reach you."

"I know. Forgive me, but . . . There was so much to think about." He gazed at her through eyes grown haunted. "About Bill . . . and about us."

Janice's eyes lowered. "I know," she softly agreed.

A silence was suspended between them. Music blared from a small fairground over a grassy hill. Lovers sunned themselves on the rocks. A smell of stale beer and thick charcoal smoke hovered through the boathouse. Janice looked up toward Jennie squatting by the lakeside, hypnotized by the stately progress of a swan across the water. Jennie had grown since the accident, and was prettier than ever. A small mark over her ear, covered now by longer black hair, was the sole souvenir of the tragedy.

"I had a police check made on Mrs. Ora Dunn," Hoover said suddenly. "The woman who found Jennie. She's been booked on eight counts of welfare fraud."

"What?" Janice looked at him in amazement.

"She ran some kind of scheme with illegitimate children. Picking up welfare checks on more dependents than she actually had. It seems Jennie's fortuitous arrival filled in one of the blank spaces. I spoke to her. She confessed to having found Jennie six months later than she had originally claimed."

Janice could only shake her head.

"Our forged birth certificate was more accurate than we thought." He turned to Janice calmly and with reverence. "I have known the grace and power of the Almighty, yet I am still amazed at his works."

In the honeyed afternoon, the calls of children were muted, absorbed in the thick willows by the waterfront. Slants of golden light poured over them. A thick-set waiter brought two tiny espressos to their table.

Hoover looked at Janice. "You really do look fine," he said softly.

Janice blushed, and dropped a sugar cube into the black, steaming coffee. "Are you determined to go back to India?"

The question did not catch him by surprise. Nevertheless, a shadow passed over his face.

"I don't know."

"What about the clinic?"

"The clinic is finished for me. Mr. Radimanath will take over. He loves his work there and is ready to devote his life to it."

Two birds flew down onto the table. Pecking at crumbs, they hopped at will to the coffee cups, onto Hoover's arm, then flew away. Hoover swallowed heavily.

"And you?" he asked. "What will you do?"

"Me? What else can I do? I'll stay here and work."

For what seemed like an eternity they remained at the white table, unwilling to depart. Janice sensed his torment.

"Would you like to take a walk?" she asked.

"I'd love to, Janice."

They rose, and Jennie observed them from a pile of plucked grass. She came running, the legs pumping whitely through the dandelions. Hoover held out his right hand and she took it firmly.

As they walked, Hoover limped, using a slender cane lightly. Jennie held on to him with both hands.

"But what's in India for you, Elliot?" Janice asked as they rounded the path, and a vista of swans under the willows opened up beyond the boathouse.

"I truly don't know."

They walked along the asphalt, savoring the warmth that dappled them through the tall elms. Ducks arrogantly walked past, taking over the path. When they were gone, Hoover smiled in confusion.

"Maybe I never really knew," he admitted.

Janice slipped her arm into the crook of his elbow lightly, so as not to interfere with the use he made of the cane. Hoover looked troubled, unable to articulate his thoughts.

"Everything we did," he stammered. "When you came to India to find me . . . when I set up the clinic . . . our trying to reach Bill . . . It was all . . . all destined, Janice. It was all to rescue a single tormented soul. Bill's."

Jennie suddenly broke from them, ran across a patch of wild violets, chasing butterflies.

Hoover stopped, his clenched hand gesturing his difficulty.

"Janice," he said quickly, "there is one thing I must tell you."

"What is it?"

He swallowed, but was encouraged by the frank acceptance in her eyes.

"When Bill . . . when the car toppled over on him, and he threw Jennie into my arms . . ."

"Yes?"

"Well, for an instant, just before the explosion, I detected in his eyes a look of true serenity, of fulfillment. The kind of fulfillment I've seen in the faces of holy men on the banks of the Ganges. As though his soul had succeeded in completing its *Karmic* mission in this lifetime."

Janice said nothing, only held his arm. Jennie rolled down a small incline, arms flopping about in the sun. The sound of ducks echoed into the stand of trees, where the sun alternated with tall shadows alive with clouds of gnats in brilliant patches.

"I would give everything to attain peace such as that. I truly envy him, Janice."

"No matter how Bill may have appeared to you, no matter what he may have said or done in your presence, it was *you* that he truly believed in. Your example."

Hoover smiled gently. "I'd like to believe that," he said softly. "I will pray that you are right."

Jennie ran back to them, gave a handful of broken daisies to Hoover.

"Thank you, darling. They're lovely. Illegal, but lovely."

Suddenly, a circus troupe invaded the asphalt path. Balloons, clowns, wooden wagons in riots of red and yellow rolled by. A cage with a man ringed in horns, covered in gunny sacks, who rattled his chains and rolled his eyes. A sign read *The Abominable Snowman of the Himalayas*. Clarinets and snare drums echoed and blared through the park, followed by long files of yelling, taunting, shrieking children.

"Would you like some lunch?" Hoover asked.

"I'd love it, Elliot." Janice smiled, then added hesitantly, "At Des Artistes?"

Hot grass shimmered in brilliance. Janice looked uncertain, yet Hoover was sure that a dark, fatal search had come to an end. Jennie sensed it, and she ran ahead, chasing the circus.

"Yes," he said softly. "At Des Artistes."

The asphalt softened under the hot sunlight. Des Artistes seemed to be a thousand miles beyond the dust and turbulence of the city. Janice and Elliot Hoover walked slowly through the willows. Nothing else mattered. Far away, the clarinet began a long, drooping solo, like sorrow soothed in the amber of delicate honey.

FROM OTHER WORLDS!

SURPRISE YOURSELF

__**THE IMAGE**
by Charlotte Paul   *(F95-145, $2.75)*
The gift of sight came to Karen Thorndyke as the bequest of an unknown man. His camera, willed to the Eye Bank, enabled the beautiful young artist to see and paint again. But with that bit of transparent tissue came an insight into horror. With her new view of life came a vision of death.

__**CRY FOR THE DEMONS**
by Julia Grice   *(F95-497, $2.75)*
Where the lava flows and sharks hunt, Ann Southold has found a retreat on the island of Maui. Here the painful memory of her husband dims, her guilts and fears are assuaged, and she meets a dark man who calls to her—a man who wants her more than any man has ever wanted her before. Out of the deep, a terror no woman can resist...
CRY FOR THE DEMONS.

__**VISIONS OF TERROR**
by William Katz   *(F91-347, $2.50)*
Broken glass, a car crash, an explosion...these are part of Annie McKay's dream world. Ever since the illness that almost blinded her, the seven-year-old has had nightmares —and they all come true. So when Annie dreams of her own murder, her mother is forced to take action—alone, because not only does she know who the murderer is—but she is beginning to understand the truth of her daughter's VISIONS OF TERROR.

TO THRILL YOU TO THE BONE!

__**POLTERGEIST**

a novel by James Kahn, based on a story by Steven Spielberg   (B30-222, $2.95)

This is a horrific drama of suburban man beset by supernatural menace. Like "Close Encounters of the Third Kind," it begins in awe and wonder. Like "Jaws," it develops with a mounting sense of dread. And like "Raiders of the Lost Ark," it climaxes in one of the most electrifying scenes ever recorded on film. A horror story that could happen to you!

__**PSYCHO**

by Robert Bloch   (B90-803, $2.95)
      (September 1982 publication)

The book that inspired the Hitchcock movie your nightmares won't let you forget. She stepped into the shower stall. The roar of the water gushing over her was deafening. That's why she didn't hear the door opening...or the footsteps. And when the shower curtains parted, the steam at first obscured the face...the butcher's knife...And YOU will not forget!

__**PSYCHO II**

by Robert Bloch   (B90-804, $3.50)
      (September 1982 publication)

Just when you thought it was safe to go back in the shower ...You remember Norman Bates, the shy young motel manager with the fatal mother fixation. Now, years after his bout of butchery that horrified the world, Norman is at large again, cutting a shocking swath of blood all the way from the psycho ward to the lots of the Hollywood movie makers.

SHOCKINGLY FRIGHTENING!

__AUDREY ROSE
by Frank DeFelitta   *(B36-380, $3.75)*
The Templetons have a near-perfect life and a lovely daughter, until a stranger enters their lives and claims that their daughter, Ivy, possesses the soul of his own daughter, Audrey Rose, who had been killed at the exact moment that Ivy was born. And suddenly their lives are shattered by event after terrifying event.

__THE AMITYVILLE HORROR II
by John G. Jones   *(B30-029, $3.50)*
The terror continues... When the Lutz family left the house in Amityville, New York, the terror did not end. Through the next four years wherever they went, the inescapable Evil followed them. Now the victims of the most publicized house-haunting of the century have agreed to reveal the harrowing details of their continuing ordeal.

__THE KEEPSAKE
by Paul Huson   *(B90-790, $2.95)*
It was only a souvenir of Ireland—a small stone that bore, if you looked very closely, the suggestion of a human face. She couldn't know that only the power of St. Patrick had kept its evil in check through the centuries... that in her own home, when the lights were out, it could become a gateway for an unimaginable malevolence with a thirst for blood and for her unborn child.

THE BEST OF SUSPENSE FROM WARNER BOOKS

__CAUTIONARY TALES
by Chelsea Quin Yarbro   (E90-162, $1.95)

A charming teen-age ghoul solves the problem of hunger in the town morgue. The frozen steerage passengers on a floundering space ship share a gruesome fate. Malevolent forces on the other side of death are held at bay by a huge black swan. Here's an anthology of bizarre and haunting tales by one of America's finest new writing talents.

__THE WOODS ARE DARK
by Richard Laymon   (F90-518, $2.75)

It was business as usual in Barlow until Johnny Robbins broke the rules and returned to the scene of The Trees to save the girl he couldn't resist. The Devil had his number now and wouldn't let him escape. But he ran anyway, taking the victims and pursued by the terror that stalked the woods.